GUARDED LOVE

THE CRESTWOOD UNIVERSITY SERIES
BOOK 4

EMERY PAIGE

EMERY PAIGE PUBLISHING

Cover Illustrator and Designer: Andra Murarasu

Editor: Chrisandra's Corrections

Proofreader: EAL Editing Services

 Formatted with Vellum

For those who spoke the truth and were ignored, this story is for you.

I don't start drama, but I will always write the last word.

AUTHOR'S NOTE

Thank you so much for taking the time to pick up
Guarded Love. This story is so close to my heart because
it's something that I've been experiencing and dealing
with over the last couple of years and to this day, isn't
completely resolved.

Details of the story have been changed to protect those
that were harmed and because several people involved do
have very public profiles. Protecting your brand or
protecting the person you work/volunteer for shouldn't
never come before serving justice to those who were hurt.
That includes just deciding to ignore it when things get
rough.

My goal is to raise awareness that this could happen to
anyone. And I'm giving Willow the proper ending that I
should have received.

With all of that being said, this is still a work of fiction.

I did want to take the time to also give you a list of content warnings. This book isn't dark, but your mental health is important and I want you to make the best choice for you.

Content Warnings:

Sexual Harrassment

Gaslighting

Mental health representation (Anxiety and ADHD)

PLAYLIST

Touch It - Ariana Grande
ALL UP IN YOUR MIND - Beyoncé
Video Games - Lana Del Ray
past life - Ariana Grande
Who's Afraid of Little Old Me - Taylor Swift
ALIEN SUPERSTAR - Beyoncé
Your Song - Rita Ora
Shallow - Lady Gaga, Bradley Cooper
human - Christina Perri
Everybody's Fool - Evanescence
IDGAF - Dua Lipa
Vigilante Shit - Taylor Swift
Titanium - David Guetta, Sia
Vanish Into You - Lady Gaga
You can check out the playlist on Spotify

1

WILLOW

TWO YEARS AGO

S hit.

Double shit.

Triple shit with whipped cream and a cherry on top.

There's no way this could be happening to me.

Of all the parties that are going on around campus on this Saturday night, he just had to show up here?

Blaise Dalton.

I feel like the universe is playing some kind of cruel joke at my expense. Just when I need a stress-relieving break from school, he appears, looking like the very definition of awkward and yet somehow still pulling it off as cool. His blond hair is messy, like he's ran his hands through it one too many times. He's still in his red Crestwood Red Wolves hoodie. I would bet money he was dragged here straight from the rink by one of his teammates. Hell, my older brother would have been one of the people bringing him here if he was on campus this weekend. That's what best friends and roommates do, after all.

This is what I get for accepting my best friend Ari's dare to go out by myself tonight. I take another sip of the drink I have no intention of finishing, all the while telling myself to ignore him. I need to pretend his sudden appearance doesn't make my stomach drop through the floor. But before I can think of an escape plan, he spots me.

Our eyes lock across the room, and for a second, I see surprise flash in his. He looks just as shocked as I feel, like he's a deer caught in headlights and I'm sure I resemble the same. It's probably the very last place he'd expect to find me. But then he grins, a half-smile I know is meant to be casual. And I swear my stomach tumbles into hell.

There's no way I can avoid him now.

He starts working his way through the crowd, dodging the people and cups of beer with grace that, in my mind, a man his size shouldn't have. I consider slipping out the back door before he gets any closer, sparing us both this awkward greeting, but something makes me stay. Maybe it's because I'm curious about what he's doing here...yeah, that's what I'm going to keep telling myself.

"Willow," is all he says, when he finally reaches me.

He towers over me, even more than usual because I'm in flats. I slowly move my head up to meet his beautiful blue eyes.

Not that I would ever tell him that.

"Blaise," I say as I raise my brow. "Surprised to see you here alone."

He shrugs. "The same could be said for you."

Even I have to admit he's not wrong. "Touché. So what's your excuse?"

"Wilder dragged me away from my gaming session. Said I needed 'human interaction' or something equally ridiculous." He makes air quotes with his fingers, and I can't help but smile. "Said he'd meet me here or something, but who knows if *he* has even made it here."

"Sounds about right." At least that's based on what I knew about him from my brother Knox. I did my best to not hang around the hockey team, but got enough information about them from him.

"So where's your entourage?" Blaise asks, glancing around like he expects Ari or some of my other friends to materialize out of thin air.

"Flying solo tonight." I take another sip of my drink, grateful for something to do with my hands. "Ari dared me to have a night out by myself. Said I needed to 'expand my social circle' or whatever."

His eyebrows shoot up. "And you actually took the dare? I'm impressed, Sanchez."

"What can I say? I'm full of surprises."

"That you are." His eyes linger on mine a beat too long.

The music shifts to something with a heavier bass that I swear is vibrating through the floor. Someone bumps into me from behind, pushing me slightly forward. Blaise's hand shoots out to steady me, and in a split second, I'm wishing for the floor to swallow me whole. I'm grateful for his quick reflexes, but I'm not sure how I feel about having the warmth from his fingers against my bare arm.

"Sorry," I mutter, stepping back to put some distance between us. "Anyway, attending a party alone does allow for some excellent people watching experiences."

"People watching, huh?" Blaise shifts his weight before sticking his hands in his pockets. "Any interesting subjects tonight?"

I gesture subtly with my head toward a guy in the corner wearing a cowboy hat and swim trunks. "That one's been doing handstands against the wall for the last twenty minutes. No one knows why."

Blaise laughs, and my stomach raises back up from the floor and does a flip in my body. "Amateur. Check out the girl by the speakers who's collecting every red solo cup she can find. She's got a stack of at least fifteen or twenty."

I follow his gaze to spot a girl with jet-black hair with bright blue streaks swiping abandoned cups like she's on a mission. "Wow. That's some serious dedication. I wonder what her end game is."

"Frat house art installation? Recycling vigilante? The possibilities are endless."

I snort. "I'm betting on a social experiment for her psych class."

"Could be."

"Or maybe she's planning to build a solo cup throne," I toss out lightly.

"A throne fit for the queen of questionable party decisions." Blaise nods. "We should probably keep an eye on her. Witness the coronation."

"Definitely." I take another small sip of my drink, the jungle juice burning slightly on the way down. It's so strange standing here going bar for bar with him like this. Easy. Comfortable even. Which is the opposite of how I usually feel around him because I'm usually hyperaware of the 'Knox's Sister' label that hangs between us.

"So," he says, breaking the brief silence, his voice a little lower now, "aside from taking dares and analyzing people, what else brings Willow Sanchez out on a Saturday night?"

I shrug. "Just needed a break. School's been kicking my ass, and trying to balance writing articles on top of that? It's been hell."

"Tell me about it." He sighs, running a hand through his already messy hair. "Midterms are coming up, practice is brutal, and sometimes I think Coach lives purely to invent new ways to torture us."

"At least you get to hit people legally," I point out, swirling the ice in my cup. "Journalism can involve character assassination at times, but it is less physically satisfying."

He chuckles and I try to pretend I'm not affected by it.

"True. Though sometimes, after a particularly bad check, I wish I could just write a scathing article about...." he paused for a moment, "the other team's questionable hygiene."

I side-eye him before returning my gaze to the dancing unfolding in front of us. "You're ridiculous."

"Maybe," he agrees, his blue eyes sparkling with amusement. "But you laughed."

"Barely," I retort, though the corner of my mouth betrays me when I can't fight my smirk. "It was more of a pity chuckle."

"I'll take it." He leans against the wall beside me, mirroring my posture.

I look around for a second before turning to look at the man next to me. "I thought you were supposed to be meeting up with Wilder?"

"Trying to get rid of me?"

"Maybe," I repeat his earlier comment. "Or maybe I'm just wondering how long you plan on ditching the guy who supposedly rescued you from a night of playing video games by yourself."

"That's assuming video games need rescuing from," Blaise counters, crossing his arms over his chest. The movement pulls his hoodie tighter across his shoulders, and I force my eyes not to linger although every fiber of my being wants me to.

"Let me guess—you were in the middle of some epic

raid? About to level up your wizard or whatever to fight the warden of Hollow Eclipse?"

His eyebrows shoot up. "First of all, it's a warlock, not a wizard. Completely different class specifications. And second—" He stops abruptly, studying my face. "Wait. How did you know I was playing Realm of the Unknown?"

I bite my lip, cursing myself for revealing too much. "Lucky guess?"

"No way." He's fully turned toward me now and I swear his eyes are sparkling. "You play?"

"I might have reached level sixty-three with the witch last weekend," I admit. It feels weird admitting this out loud, but here we are. "But if you tell anyone, I'll deny it and then kill you."

"Your secret's safe with me. Level sixty-three? That's impressive. I can't believe Knox never mentioned you play."

"Because Knox doesn't know," I say, lowering my voice. "It's a stress reliever, not something I broadcast."

Blaise's grin widens slowly. "Okay, okay. Your secret gaming life is safe. But seriously, a level sixty-three witch? I'm impressed."

"It's not that impressive," I mumble before I take a larger gulp of my drink this time. The alcohol burns a little less, or maybe I'm just getting used to it. "It's mostly just mindless clicking after a certain point."

"Don't sell yourself short," Blaise says. "It takes dedication. Strategy."

As I feel my cheeks grow warm, I quickly realize that those words coming from him feel like the highest praise I've ever received. I finish the last of my drink in one go, and although I know I'm going to regret it in the morning, I can't careless right now.

"Whoa there," Blaise says, his eyes widening as I set the empty cup down on a nearby table a little too forcefully. "Pacing yourself isn't really your thing tonight, huh?"

"Relax." I wave a hand dismissively, already scanning the room for where I can find another drink. "My tolerance is very high." That is a total lie, but the alcohol is starting to fuzz the edges of my anxiety, making me feel bolder.

"Highest of tolerances, secret gaming skills... what other hidden talents are you hiding?" He pushes off the wall and his gaze lands on the doorway to the kitchen. "Need a refill?"

"Lead the way," I say. I immediately regret saying the words a little too eagerly, but I do my best to shake it off. After all, I can't take them back now.

We make our way into the kitchen, and I have to admit the journey there was entertaining. At least three people try to hand us shot glasses, and I have to pull Blaise past a girl in a crop top who attempts to drag him into an impromptu game of beer pong. I am surprised to find it surprisingly less crowded given this is where the alcohol is. Someone has attempted to make jungle juice in a plastic storage bin, and the surrounding counter looks like a sticky, brightly colored warzone.

Blaise surveys the scene and then says, "Looks like someone lost a fight with a packet of Kool-Aid and a bottle of alcohol."

"Or maybe it was a science experiment gone wrong," I add, wrinkling my nose at the suspicious red concoction. "Test subject: Partygoers. Hypothesis: How quickly can jungle juice lead to poor life choices?"

"Observation: Rate appears exponentially high," Blaise counters as he stares at the bin. "Conclusion: Further research required, but perhaps not personally." He scans the counter and moves past the jungle juice. He grabs two unopened cans of beer from a cooler in the corner. "Safer bet?"

"Much safer," I agree as I accept the cold can. I pop the tab and look up as he does the same.

"So, back to your earlier observation...." He takes a sip from his own can. "When you were people watching, did you find anything interesting?"

I pause, awkwardly I will admit, as I process what he said. The first thought that flies through my mind is why are we still talking to one another? This is probably the most time we've ever spent willingly speaking to each other. Usually, it's a head nod if we pass each other on campus or a quick hello if we see each other when I stop by his and Knox's room.

"Actually, the most interesting thing I found tonight

was you showing up," I say, the alcohol making me braver than usual. "Never thought I'd see you in a place like this without being physically dragged in by my brother or Wilder...speaking of which, where is he?"

I know my words make it seem as if I want Blaise to get away from me as quickly as possible, but that isn't the case.

Blaise looks around like he's just remembered he was supposed to meet someone. "Honestly? No idea. He texted that he was 'on his way' about forty minutes ago, but knowing Wilder, he was probably coming from another party and got distracted or something."

I laugh despite myself. "That tracks."

"I should probably be annoyed, but..." He shrugs, his eyes finding mine again. "Can't say I mind how things turned out."

The statement hangs between us because I can't figure out what to say in response to *that*. I take another long swig of my beer to avoid responding for a moment. I need time to think.

"So," I say, desperate to change the subject, "what's your major again? I know Knox mentioned it, but..."

"Political Science," Blaise replies, seemingly grateful for the shift in conversation.

"Seriously?" I can't hide my surprise. "I would've thought you would choose CompSci or Engineering with all the gaming."

He laughs. "Everyone does. But I've always been fascinated by political theory and politics in general. The gaming is just a hobby."

"Huh." I take another swig of my beer, processing this new information. "So you're what...planning to save the world through policy reform?"

"If only it was that simple. I'd settle for making at least a small difference," he says with a small smile.

"A *small* difference? I would say that's not something a politician would say. They'd promise to give you the world."

He laughs. "I'm a realist."

I take another sip of my beer. That's a lie. It is more like a gulp. "Realists are boring."

He gives me a look. "Didn't you just say I was the most interesting thing you found tonight?"

I point my can at him. "Yeah, and that was before you admitted your big life plan is 'mild policy tweaks.'"

He chuckles, shaking his head. "Brutal."

"Hey, don't take it personally," I say, tipping the can toward my lips again. "You're still... not the worst person to talk to tonight."

His eyes crinkle at the corners. "That sounds like a compliment. I'll take it."

"You should." I nod solemnly, though the room sways slightly with the movement. Whoa. When did the alcohol kick in? "I don't give compliments often. Especially not to hockey players."

"I've noticed," he says dryly, but there's no heat behind it. "Is that a journalism thing or just a you thing?"

"Both." I lean against the counter because I need the support. Not that I'd actually admit it out loud. "Journalists should be naturally skeptical. And I'm naturally... selective."

"Selective." Blaise raises an eyebrow. "That's a diplomatic way of putting it."

"I'm not being diplomatic, I'm being accurate." It's then I realize the booze I've consumed is definitely hitting me now. Two drinks isn't usually enough to make me tipsy, but I skipped dinner in my rush to get ready for tonight, and who knows how much alcohol was in that jungle juice. Bad decision.

"So what makes someone worthy of your attention?" Blaise asks, leaning in slightly. Is he flirting with me? Knox would lose his shit if he found out. Well, that's if he's actually flirting with me.

I narrow my gaze at him as I try to focus. "Good question. I'll let you know when I figure it out."

He laughs. "Fair enough."

The room tilts slightly as I shift my weight and Blaise's hand shoots out to steady me again. "Whoa there. You okay?"

"I'm fine," I say automatically, but I don't pull away from his touch. "Just... the floor is being uncooperative."

"You're definitely not okay."

"I'm perfectly fine," I insist, but even I can hear the slight slur in my words. "Just a little... tipsy."

Blaise's hand remains on my arm. "Right. And I'm secretly a professional figure skater."

"You'd look terrible in sequins," I say, then giggle at my own joke. It also temporarily distracts me from hating the way his touch is making me feel. However, I can blame that on the alcohol.

"Well that hit like a stab to the heart," he says. His eyes scan my face with concern. "How much have you had to drink?"

I wave my hand dismissively, nearly spilling what's left of my beer. "Two drinks? Three? Whatever."

"Two or three is pretty different from 'whatever,'" Blaise says, gently taking the beer can from my hand and setting it on the counter. "When was the last time you ate?”

I look up at the ceiling as I try to remember. "Um, lunch? Maybe?" The kitchen tilts slightly, and I grab the counter edge. "But it was just a protein bar, so technically not even a meal."

"What the hell, Willow? No wonder you're swaying. You need food."

"I'm not swaying," I protest, then immediately contradict myself by stumbling slightly. "The house is swaying. Big difference."

"Right. The house. Got it." His hand moves to my lower back. “We're going to get out of here and get you some food.”

"I don't need your help," I mutter, even as I lean into him. Fighting him is useless, but I can't help but toss the comment at him.

"Clearly," he says dryly. "Come on, we'll head back to campus and grab something."

"But the party—"

"Will continue without us," Blaise finishes, guiding me toward the door. "Trust me, no one will notice we're gone."

I want to argue, but the room spins again and suddenly fresh air sounds like the best idea anyone's ever had. "Fine," I concede. "But I'm walking on my own."

"Of course," he says, but his hand doesn't leave my back.

We make our way through the crowded living room, pass the solo cup collector (who's now up to at least thirty cups), and finally reach the front door. The cool night air hits my face, and I couldn't be more grateful to be out of that house.

"I needed this," I say just before taking a deep breath of the cool air. The cold helps clear my head, but the world still feels like it's gently rocking beneath my feet.

"Better?" Blaise asks, his hand still resting lightly on my back.

"Much." I step away from his touch, determined to prove I can stand on my own. The sidewalk tilts a bit, but I manage to stay upright. "See? Perfectly fine."

Blaise gives me a skeptical look. "Right. You're the picture of sobriety."

"I didn't say I was sober. I said I was fine." I toss my dark hair over my shoulder, a move that nearly throws me off balance again. "There's a difference."

"Semantics," he mutters, but stays close as we begin walking. He pulls out his phone and begins typing away.

When it seems like he's taking an unusually long time, I finally ask the question that has been sitting on the tip of my tongue. "Are you telling my brother about this?!"

"No," Blaise says quickly, putting his phone back in his pocket. "Just texting Wilder to let him know I left, and I ordered some food. Though maybe I should tell Knox his sister is drunk and stumbling around campus at night..."

"Don't you dare," I warn, jabbing a finger at his chest. I'm proud of myself for not tripping over my own two feet and proving his point.

"I'm kidding," Blaise says, holding up his hands in surrender. "Your drunken adventures are safe with me. Besides, Knox would kill me for letting you get like this in the first place."

"You didn't 'let' me do anything," I mutter, crossing my arms over my chest. "I'm a grown woman."

"A grown woman who can't walk in a straight line right now."

This time I roll my eyes, but I refrain from saying what I actually want to say because it would turn into us arguing until we get to wherever we are going. Speaking of which.... "Where are we going?"

"Back to my place."

Shit.

2

WILLOW

Blaise unlocks the dorm room door, and I follow him inside, trying not to feel weird about how quiet it is without Knox here. Or how weird it is to be here period without my brother around.

"I'll grab us some water," Blaise says.

I swear his voice nearly echoes in this small room, and I follow him with my eyes as he walks over to the mini-fridge. I stand awkwardly in the center, taking in the familiar-yet-unfamiliar space. I've been here dozens of times, but always with Knox as a buffer. Without him, everything feels different and I can't quite describe how. The space is divided neatly in half and you can clearly see where the division lies. Knox's side is much messier, including the way he's hung his hockey posters on the way. Blaise's side is meticulously organized with his bed made and his hockey gear put away.

Even his desk is organized to perfection with his color-coded notebooks stacked perfectly, laptop closed and centered, not a stray pen in sight. It's actually quite comical how different he is from Knox in this area, let alone me. I would argue that both Knox and I rebelled a bit when we went to college in terms of how neat we needed to be because of the rules we followed at home. While my room could be a little messy, it wasn't like I didn't know where everything was. Unless I just forgot, which happened more often than I would care to admit.

I sway slightly, still feeling the alcohol, and decide sitting is probably wise. I perch on the edge of Knox's unmade bed, thinking it's safer territory.

"Here," Blaise says, returning with two bottles of water. He hands me one and sits on his own bed, facing me. "Drink this. All of it."

I accept the bottle with a mock salute. "Yes, sir."

He watches me take a long sip, his eyes never leaving my face. The intensity makes me fidget, but I can't look away. Having him study my every move has me freaking out on the inside, but the alcohol running through my veins helps me to mask it.

"What?" I finally ask, lowering the bottle.

"Nothing," he says, then seems to reconsider before he speaks again. "Just making sure you're okay."

"I'm fine," I say automatically, then add more honestly, "Just... dizzy. And hungry."

"Food's on the way. Pizza. I ordered plain cheese. Hope that works."

"Pizza works," I confirm, taking another sip of water. "Thanks for... you know."

"No problem," he says simply, like helping drunk girls get home safely is something he does every weekend. Speaking of, why didn't he just help me back to my room and leave me be?

"Why didn't you just take me back to my dorm?" I ask, voicing the thought before I can stop myself.

"Because you mentioned being out alone. Didn't think it made sense for you to be alone depending on how drunk you are."

"Oh," I say, feeling oddly touched by his concern. "That's... thoughtful."

He shrugs, looking almost embarrassed. "Just common sense."

The room falls quiet except for the sound of us sipping water. I study him from across the small space between the beds, trying to reconcile this version of Blaise with the one I thought I knew. The one who barely acknowledges me except when Knox is around. The one who's always seemed very indifferent to whether I was in the room or not.

"You're staring," he points out, the corner of his mouth lifting.

"Sorry," I mumble, looking down at my water bottle. "Just thinking."

"About?"

"How weird this is," I admit, the alcohol making me slightly more honest than I'd normally be. "Us. Hanging out. Voluntarily."

He raises an eyebrow. "Is it that weird?"

"Kind of." I twist the cap on my water bottle. "We don't exactly... talk. Ever."

"We talk," he counters.

"No, we say hey in passing. That's different." I take another sip of water, feeling more clear-headed now but not sure how drunk I still am. It could be just a fluke.

"Maybe we should change that," Blaise says.

My eyes snap up to meet his. "Change what?"

"The not talking thing." He leans forward slightly and the move only draws more attention to his shoulders beneath his hoodie. "Maybe we should actually talk. Like real people."

I laugh, but it comes out sounding more nervous than I intended. "What would we even talk about?"

"I don't know. Normal stuff." He shrugs. "Like the fact that you're apparently a level sixty-three witch who hides her gaming habit from her brother."

"Oh fuck," I groan, covering my face with my hands. "I can't believe I told you that."

"It's not exactly a criminal confession," he says. "Though you did threaten to kill me if I told anyone, so..."

"And I stand by that," I say, pointing my water bottle at him. "Knox would never let me live it down."

"Your secret's safe with me." There's something in his expression that makes me believe him.

Also, I should have known when I admitted to being a gamer I'd drank too much. Rookie mistake.

"Thanks," I say, and mean it. "So what other deep, dark secrets should we share since we're suddenly talking like real people?"

"I don't know if I have any deep, dark secrets."

"Everyone has secrets," I counter. "Even Mr. Perfect Political Science Major with the color-coded notebooks."

Something flickers across his face before he masks it. "My notebooks aren't color-coded because I'm perfect. They're color-coded because they have to be."

"Have to be?" I tilt my head, genuinely curious now.

He hesitates, like he's weighing how much to say. "I have anxiety. The organization helps. If things are in their right place, my brain... works better."

"Oh." I wasn't expecting that level of honesty. "That makes sense."

"Yeah." He shrugs, looking slightly uncomfortable. "It's not a big deal. Just how I manage things and the systems I create to get things done."

"I get that. I mean, not anxiety specifically, but... coping mechanisms." I chew my lip, wondering if I should say more. The alcohol has loosened my tongue already, but this doesn't make me feel as uncomfortable as admitting I like to play video games.

"I have ADHD," I finally admit. "Diagnosed when I was

in middle school. It was a struggle having the people in my life constantly tell me they think I should just try harder and that would solve all of my problems." I roll my eyes. "Like I haven't been trying my whole life."

I study Blaise's facial expression and find no pity, just understanding. "That explains the gaming. Hyperfocus?"

"Yeah," I say, surprised he knows the term. "It's like everything else falls away. I can sit there for hours and not even realize time is passing."

"Must be nice sometimes," he says. "To shut everything else out."

"It is. Until I realize I've forgotten to eat or sleep or... you know, basic human functions." I laugh softly. "But it beats the alternative of bouncing between fifteen different thoughts in thirty seconds."

He smiles, and it reaches his eyes in a way that makes my stomach do that weird flippy thing again. "Sounds like we're opposite sides of the same neurospicy coin," he says. "My brain gets stuck on one thought and loops it endlessly. Your brain hops from thought to thought."

"Yeah, exactly. It's like my brain is a browser with fifty tabs open at once, and I can't close any of them."

"Mine's more like one tab that keeps refreshing with the same error message."

I laugh at that. "Wow, that's perfect. We're like the world's most dysfunctional web browser."

"Firefox and Chrome's neglected cousin nobody downloads."

"The one that crashes your computer if you try to stream video," I add.

We're both laughing now, and it feels... good. Easy. Like we've been friends forever instead of two people who barely acknowledge each other's existence outside of Knox's orbit.

A chime from Blaise's phone interrupts us, and he stands up. "That's probably the pizza."

While he handles the delivery, I take another long drink of water and walk over to his desk. The room still tilts somewhat when I move too quickly, but the sharp edges of drunkenness have softened, thankfully. I should shoot Ari a text to let her know I'm fine, but I get distracted when Blaise reenters the room.

"Pizza delivery," he announces, holding up a medium-sized box that smells like heaven. My stomach growls audibly in response, reminding me just how long it's been since I've eaten.

"Oh my gosh, that smells amazing," I say.

I watch as he walks over to his desk. He uses his free hand to move his notebooks and laptop out of the way to put the pizza down on the surface. When he opens the box, I swear I could sink down onto the floor and cry. The pizza looks as good as it smells and it needs to get into my belly pronto.

"Grab a slice before I inhale the whole thing," I say, reaching for a piece before he can even offer. The cheese stretches in perfect strands as I lift it, and my stomach does another growl of anticipation.

"Whoa, slow down there." Blaise laughs as I fold the slice in half and take an enormous bite. "The pizza's not going anywhere."

I can't respond because my mouth is full of the most delicious thing I've ever tasted, or at least that's how it feels right now. The combination of warm cheese, sauce, and crispy crust is exactly what my alcohol-addled body needs. I make an embarrassing moan of pleasure that I immediately regret.

"That good, huh?" Blaise asks, a smirk playing on his lips as he takes his own slice.

I swallow before answering. "When you're drunk and haven't eaten since noon, cardboard would taste amazing. But this is definitely better than cardboard."

"Excellent." He sits cross-legged on the floor, his back against his bed, and gestures for me to join him.

I hesitate for only a second before sliding down to sit across from him. "So," I say after devouring half my slice, "tell me something else I don't know about you."

Blaise chews thoughtfully, a strand of cheese hanging from his mouth before he catches it with his finger. "Like what?"

"Anything. Something that would surprise me."

He considers this while reaching for a second slice. "I hate hockey."

I nearly choke on my pizza. "What? But you're—"

"Just kidding," he grins. "Had to see if you were paying attention."

"Jerk," I mutter, but I'm smiling too. "Seriously though."

He leans back against his bed, pizza in hand. "Okay, real confession: I'm terrified of failing. Not just grades, but... everything. Everyone thinks I have it all figured out, but half the time I'm just pretending. I wake up some mornings and wonder if I'm on the right path at all."

I take another bite of pizza to give myself time to process his words. Once I'm done chewing, I say, "I think everyone feels that way sometimes. I know I do."

"Maybe." He shrugs. "But most people don't organize their entire existence around preventing it."

I study him for a moment once more before I respond. "Is that why you're always so..."

"So what?"

"I don't know. Serious? Reserved? Like you're constantly calculating every word before you say it."

He looks down at his pizza. "Probably. It's easier to keep things in control when you don't fuck up by saying the wrong thing."

"That sounds exhausting," I say, reaching for my second slice.

"It is," he admits. "But it's better than the alternative."

"Which is?"

"Chaos. Disappointment. People realizing I'm not who they think I am." He takes another bite.

"But isn't that part of what college is all about?

Figuring out, at least on some level, who we are? I know it's easier said than done, especially for someone with anxiety, but maybe chaos is a part of the journey?"

Blaise's eyes meet mine, and there's something vulnerable in them that I can't quite place. "Maybe. But it's not that simple when you've spent your whole life being the responsible one. The one who has it together."

"Who says you have to be that person all the time?" I ask. "And that includes around me." Why the hell did I specifically insert myself into this equation?

"What do you mean?"

"I mean, I've already seen you at a party you didn't want to be at. I know about your anxiety. And your color-coded notebooks. Your cover is pretty much blown with me."

He laughs softly. "I guess that's true."

"So maybe..." I take another bite of my pizza slice. "Maybe you can just be yourself around people. Not Knox's responsible roommate. Not the smart and ambitious hockey player. Just...you."

"Just me," he repeats slowly. "I'm not even sure I know who that is anymore."

I finish the pizza slice in my hand and then grab a napkin for my hands and face just before I give in to a thought that popped into my head. I crawl over to him. "Well, from what I've seen tonight, 'just you' seems pretty decent. Funny. Smart. Kind enough to babysit a drunk girl and feed her pizza."

"Thanks," he says softly.

When our gazes clash once more, I'm suddenly aware of how close I've gotten to him. I'm practically in his space now. The alcohol still buzzing through my system has me lingering there instead of retreating back to my side of the invisible line between us. His shoulder brushes against mine as he shifts his body and it sends a spark through me.

"I mean it," I continue, my voice lower now. "You don't have to be perfect all the time. Not with me."

Something changes in his expression, a softening around the edges that makes him look younger somehow. Vulnerable. The carefully maintained wall he keeps up seems to lower just enough for me to see through it.

"And who are you being right now?" he asks, his voice barely above a whisper. "Just Willow? Or drunk Willow?"

I think about his words for a second before I reply. "Just Willow," I decide. "But with fewer filters."

"I like fewer-filter Willow."

"Yeah?" I lean in slightly, testing the waters. "What else do you like?"

The air between us feels charged suddenly, and I watch as his gaze drops to my lips for just a second before returning to my eyes, and that's all the confirmation I need. I close the distance between us, pressing my lips against his.

For a heartbeat, he freezes, and I think I've made a terrible mistake. But then his hand comes up to cup my cheek and he's kissing me back. His lips are soft and warm against mine. At first he's hesitant, but then he gains his footing and our kiss becomes deeper. It ignites something in me, something I can't quite explain because I'm not even sure what's happening outside of my lips meeting his. His hand slides to the back of my neck, and I feel myself melting against him. For a moment, everything is perfect.

Then suddenly, he pulls away.

"Wait," he says, his voice rough. He puts distance between us, running a hand through his hair. "We shouldn't. You're—you're drunk."

I blink at him, trying to process the abrupt change. "I'm not that drunk anymore."

"Still," he insists, not meeting my eyes. "And you're Knox's sister."

The words hit me like a bucket of ice water. Of course. That's what this all comes down to, isn't it? I'm not just Willow. I'm Knox's little sister.

"Seriously?" I stand up too quickly, the room spinning slightly. "That's what you're worried about?"

"It's not just that," Blaise says, standing too. "You know this is... complicated."

"It didn't feel complicated thirty seconds ago." I grab my water bottle, needing something to do with my hands before I do something stupid.

"Willow, please. I just think we should—"

"Forget it," I cut him off, moving toward the door. "This was clearly a mistake."

"Wait," he says, reaching for my arm. "Where are you going?"

"Back to my dorm." I try to pull away, but he holds firm.

"You're still drunk. It's late. Just stay here."

I laugh, but there's no humor in it. "Are you kidding me right now?" I try to pull my arm away again, and while his grip is gentle, he doesn't let go. "You just rejected me, and now you want me to stay?"

"I'm not rejecting you," Blaise says. "I'm being responsible."

"Oh, right. Responsible Blaise to the rescue. Always doing the right thing." The words come out bitter and sharp, but I can't stop them. The humiliation of being pushed away burns through whatever alcohol remains in my system.

"That's not fair," he says, finally releasing my arm. "You know it's not that simple."

"It seemed pretty simple to me." I cross my arms over my chest defensively. "You don't want to kiss me because I'm Knox's sister. Message received."

"That's not—" He runs his hand through his hair again, a gesture I'm starting to recognize as his stress response. "Look, you've been drinking. I've been drinking. This isn't the right time to—"

"You know what? Fine," I finally say. "I'll stay. But only because it's late and I'm tired."

Relief flashes across his face. "Thank you."

An awkward silence falls between us as I glance around the room, suddenly unsure where to put myself.

"You can take Knox's bed," Blaise offers, gesturing to my brother's side of the room.

I nod, not trusting myself to speak. I spy the pizza box that still sits open on the desk with half of the slices gone. My stomach has tied itself into knots that have nothing to do with hunger.

"I can lend you something to sleep in," he says, moving toward his dresser. "If you want."

"Sure."

He pulls out a Red Wolves hockey jersey and holds it out to me. I would laugh because I've been avoiding athletes and everything about them since I broke up with my ex, and now here I am about to wrap myself in the very thing I've tried to distance myself from.

"Thanks," I say, accepting the garment. Our fingers brush, and I pull away quickly as if I'd gotten bit.

"Bathroom's down the hall," he tosses out there.

I nod again, although I only half heard him, and slip out of the room with the jersey clutched to my chest. Once I make it to the bathroom, I'm thankful no one else is in there. I walk up to one of the mirrors and stare at my reflection. I look a whole hot mess with flushed cheeks, slightly smudged mascara and slightly red eyes. I look exactly like what I am: a girl who's had too much to drink and made a move she shouldn't have.

I splash cold water on my face and change into Blaise's jersey, which falls to mid-thigh. I make the quick decision to keep my leggings on because I don't want him to think I'm trying to make another move. I hate that I even have to think that.

When I return to the room, Blaise is sitting on his bed in red pajama pants and a t-shirt and I'm not surprised to find a controller in his hands. He looks up when I enter. His eyes linger for a moment on the jersey, and something flashes across his face that I can't quite read. Embarrassment? Regret? Whatever it is, it's gone as quickly as it came, and he's back to staring at his game.

"Feel better?" he asks, his voice neutral and I know it's on purpose.

"Yep," I say with more bite than necessary. It's then I notice the pizza box and water bottles are gone as if they were never here. Everything neat and tidy, just like Blaise himself.

I make my way to Knox's bed and toss the top I'd had on onto the bed. I dig into my bag and grab my phone before getting underneath the covers. I quickly shoot Ari a text to let her know I'm fine and make a mental note to myself that I'll need to remake Knox's bed before I leave in the morning.

Blaise's fingers tap against the controller, and it's the only noise in the room. I try to settle into Knox's bed and pull the covers up to my chin. A million thoughts race through my mind as I stare at the ceiling, the events of the night replaying like a broken record. It's all too much to process and I'm still angry about it.

I steal a glance at Blaise, his profile illuminated by the light coming from the TV screen. He seems lost in the game, but part of me thinks it's an act to ignore the awkwardness between us. Well, if that's what he wants, then so be it.

"Night," I toss over my shoulder as I turn my body so that I'm lying on my side, facing the wall.

"Good night," he responds in kind. "Let me know if you need anything."

And that's the last thing I hear before I pass out.

3

WILLOW
PRESENT DAY

The last place I want to be is here.

But what would it look like if I bailed?

Not that Mom or Abue would let me anyway, so even going down that rabbit hole is pointless. And then Dad would get that tight, disappointed look— not mad, just quiet and heavy—and suddenly I'd be the problem instead of the girl simply trying not to combust.

Still, I really, truly, desperately don't want to be here, even though it's senior night and my big brother is being honored.

Which is another reason I can't leave. I won't walk away from this moment, no matter how much it's physically and emotionally choking me out. I'd regret it. And Knox would never say anything, but he'd feel it.

So I force myself to smile, even as my boots stick to dried soda and the guy behind us screams, "LET'S GO

RED WOLVES!" directly into my ear for what has to be the eighth time.

He could at least back up half an inch, but no—he's clearly on a personal mission to rupture every eardrum in section 106. The mix of his hot breath and the cold air makes my face want to freeze and melt at the same time.

This sucks.

"Everything okay?"

I turn my head to Selene Davis, my brother's girl-friend, and offer her a strained half-smile. "As okay as it's going to be until I get out of here."

Selene laughs, tucking a strand of red hair behind her ear. "Your game face is brutal tonight."

"I'm not built for this," I say, just as the man behind us belts another, "RED WOLVES, BABY!" into the void. "I'm not getting paid enough to be here."

"That's a lie," Hailey Reed says, sliding in beside us with her usual deadpan precision. It's about time she and Jade got here. "You couldn't pay me to freeze my ass off surrounded by boys who smell like body spray and bruised ego."

"You're dating one of them," I remind her.

She shrugs. "Levi's the exception. He showers."

Jade Samuels, Hailey and Wilder's best friend, appears next to Hailey with her hands wrapped around a cup of what I assume is coffee or hot chocolate. "I think it's kind of sweet. They're all so hyped. Feels big."

"Yeah, but I still would rather be anywhere else but here. And that includes the dentist," I mutter.

Selene nudges me with her elbow. "You love Knox. You'll survive."

I pretend to weigh it out. "Barely."

Then out of nowhere, I hear, "Knox Sanchez!"

Hearing my brother's name brings my attention back to the rink and I nearly jump out of my seat as the arena erupts. Knox skates out to center ice with the same calm confidence he's had since the first time he put on skates. Mom is on her feet clapping wildly. Dad stands beside her, a quiet, proud grin on his face. And Abue? Abue is waving a giant homemade sign with Knox's number painted in glitter and tiny red wolves circling it like stars.

"Your grandma wins," Jade says, visibly impressed. "That's real commitment."

Knox raises his stick in acknowledgment, smirking like the little punk he is. I clap too. Despite everything, I really am proud of him. He's worked hard. He deserves this.

"And now," the announcer's voice booms again, "number thirty-three, Blaise Dalton!"

My hands freeze mid-clap. My stomach drops like I've just taken a plunge on a rollercoaster. Two years. Two whole years I've managed to avoid being in the same room with him for more than five minutes outside of my brother's birthday party a couple of weeks ago, and now here he is. The crowd goes wild, almost as loud as they were for Knox. Blaise raises his stick in a subdued salute, and I can practically feel his blue eyes scanning the crowd. I shrink back instinctively, as if he could possibly pick me out among thousands of screaming fans.

My heart starts sprinting like it knows something I don't.

"He's having a great season," Selene says beside me, completely unaware she's pouring salt on an unhealed wound.

"Mmm," I manage.

Hailey makes a face. "He's too smooth with...everything in life. Like he actually has his shit together."

Jade leans in. "I think he's just quiet."

"Same thing," Hailey replies.

"You okay?" Selene asks, glancing over at me.

"I'm fine," I lie. "Just cold."

Abue looks over at me. I can tell she doesn't buy it for a second. "Your face is red. Are you feeling feverish?"

"I'm fine, Abue," I say, pulling my scarf higher like it'll hide the heat crawling up my cheeks. "I swear. Completely fine."

She makes a noise that says she doesn't believe me but thankfully lets it go as the announcer moves on. I stare at the ice, trying to focus on literally anything other than Blaise standing just feet away from my brother.

"Wow, he really does pretend like the crowd doesn't exist," Jade murmurs.

"Of course he does," I mutter, but I tune everything else out.

The rest of the introductions blur together as I desperately try to remember how to breathe normally. This is ridiculous. I'm a junior that is doing well in my classes, one of the best journalists on campus, and looking forward to a prestigious internship this summer, and I'm letting a two-year-old memory throw me completely off my game.

And yet my pulse won't settle.

It's pathetic.

I'm pathetic.

I've dated other people since then. Okay, fine, "dated" is generous. I've gone on a few first dates that didn't go anywhere. But still. I'm over it. Over him.

So why does it feel like my heart is trying to slam its way out of my chest?

"Look! They're starting!" Abue grabs my arm, drawing my attention back to what's happening on the ice.

The ref skates to center ice, puck in hand. Levi crouches low, while Knox and Asher flank him. Blaise moves into position behind them, and I can tell he's locked in.

The puck drops with a sharp smack.

Levi wins it and snaps it back to Blaise, who barely adjusts as he absorbs the pass and glides backward. His head lifts, just once, and then he threads a pass to Knox so smooth it looks scripted.

The crowd surges as Knox bolts down the left side, flying across the ice. Asher matches his pace on the opposite wing, creating a perfect channel for attack. Although I've avoided Knox's games in recent years, I've seen him do something like this a thousand times and it still makes me nervous.

The defender on the other team lunges at Knox, but he's already sending the puck sliding right to Asher, who zeroes in on the net. The goalie makes a desperate lunge, but comes up empty handed.

The arena erupts, and I'm almost forced to put my hands over my ears.

"GOAL!" Dad shouts, pumping his fist in the air.

Mom jumps up beside him, and Abue waves her glitter sign so vigorously I worry she might accidentally take out the guy behind us. Which wouldn't be the worst thing in the world, honestly.

Asher's teammates mob him and start howling like the wolves they're named for. They're thirty seconds into the game and already up one-nothing.

"That was sick!" Selene yells over the noise, high-fiving Jade.

I clap along, trying to look like a normal person who isn't having an internal meltdown. Because this is fine. Totally fine. Just watching hockey with my family and friends, like any other college student might do on a Friday night.

The celebration dies down, and the players reset for

the next faceoff. I catch myself watching Blaise as he glides back into position, his movements so fluid it's like he's barely touching the ice.

"Why are you looking at him like that?" Abue whispers, leaning close enough that her soft floral perfume wraps around me.

I snap my gaze away from Blaise. "I'm not looking at anyone," I reply quickly. I'm not looking at anyone.

Abue's knowing smile makes my cheeks burn hotter. "If you say so."

I try to focus on Knox, on his plays, on anything but the defenseman wearing number thirty-three. But my eyes keep finding him anyway. Damnit. I do my best to make sure Abue can't call me out again.

The first period flies by and I've almost convinced myself I'm fine when the buzzer sounds. 3-1, Red Wolves. Knox has an assist, Levi scored, and Blaise...well, Blaise has been everywhere at once, stopping shots, clearing pucks, and making passes.

"Your brother is on fire tonight," Jade says, nudging me with her elbow.

"He knows we are in the audience," I reply, grateful for the chance to talk about Knox instead. "Plus, let's be real. He's motivated by food."

"Smart man." Selene laughs, her eyes following Knox as he skates toward the tunnel.

"I need something hot to drink before I freeze to

death," Hailey announces, standing up. "Anyone want anything?"

"Hot chocolate," Jade and Selene say in unison.

"I'll come with you," I offer, desperate for a few minutes away from the ice and away from him. "Mom? Dad? Abue? Want anything?"

"Coffee for your father," Mom says. "And tea for me if they have it."

Abue waves us off. "Nothing for me, sweetheart. I have everything I need right here."

She pats her oversized purse, which I know contains everything anyone could think of, including enough snacks to feed half the arena. Abue believes in being prepared and there have been many times I've been grateful for how prepared she was is.

Hailey and I squeeze past the others in our row and make our way up the concrete steps. Once we are out of the seating area, I take a deep breath of the slightly less freezing air in the concourse. The break from watching the game and from watching him is exactly what I needed.

"You good?" Hailey asks. "You seem...tense."

"I swear, I'm fine." Was there a neon sign attached to my forehead flashing "emotionally compromised" for everyone to see? "Just not a sports fan." That's a lie too, but I hope she doesn't catch on.

"You know, it wouldn't kill you to admit when something's bothering you," Hailey says, her voice matter-of-fact and telling me she means business. "It's not like I'm going to run and tell Knox or something."

Dammit. I fidget with the end of my scarf. Hailey isn't one for small talk or beating around the bush, which is usually refreshing. Right now, it feels like being cornered.

"Nothing's bothering me except the cold and that guy screaming in my ear," I insist.

Hailey gives me a look that says she's not buying it but mercifully drops the subject as we inch forward in line. The concession stand is packed with people seeking over-priced food and drinks.

"So how are things with the newspaper?" she asks instead.

"Good. I'm almost done with my latest article. Just need to interview a few more students about the proposed campus housing changes."

"Let me guess, the administration is claiming it's for student benefit while actually just finding new ways to charge more money."

"Pretty much." I nod. "Classic Crestwood move."

"You'd think they'd at least try to be subtle about it," Hailey says, shaking her head. "But nope. It's the same story everywhere all over the country."

"At least it gives me something to write about." I shuffle forward as the line moves. "My editor loves when I go after the administration. Says it gets the most engagement online."

Hailey smirks. "The Willow Sanchez takedown special. Always a crowd pleaser."

"I prefer to think of it as holding people accountable," I say, although I can't help but grin. My articles have developed quite a reputation on campus, especially among the student body. Even some of the professors quietly encourage my investigative pieces, though they'd never admit it publicly.

We finally reach the front of the line, and I order the drinks while Hailey digs in her wallet for cash. As we wait for our order, I scan the area, a habit I've developed to avoid awkward run-ins with people I've written about. Instead, my eyes land on something worse.

My stomach plummets as I spot my ex-boyfriend, Leo Kent, standing near the merchandise booth with a small crowd around him.

The high school football-player-turned-streamer is commanding attention like he always does and the first thing I notice is his signature backward cap and perfectly styled hair visible even from here. I duck behind Hailey without even thinking about it.

"What are you doing?" Hailey asks, frowning as I try to make myself smaller.

"Leo's here," I whisper, peering around her shoulder.

"Who is Leo?"

"My ex. Just...make sure he doesn't see me. I don't want to deal with him right now." Not on top of everything else, but I leave that part unsaid.

Hailey jerks her head to look at me over her shoulder. It's then I see that she finally connects the dots. "Wait, you dated Leo Kent? The YouTube guy?"

"Streamer," I correct automatically, then grimace. "And yes. It was a mistake. One I'd rather not revisit tonight or ever."

Hailey casually shifts her position to better shield me while pretending to check her phone. "I didn't know he went here."

"He doesn't," I mutter, peeking around her shoulder again. "He graduated from Westlake U last year. Which begs the question of why he's at a Crestwood hockey game."

I peer over Hailey's shoulder and Leo is still standing there. He's using the smile that he practiced over and over again in the mirror. The one that used to make my heart race. Now it just makes me feel slightly nauseated. He's wearing a fitted black jacket that probably cost more than my tuition, designer jeans, and those ridiculous limited-edition sneakers he was always posting about. A couple of girls are taking selfies with him while he flashes his trademark peace sign.

"Orders for Hailey and Willow!" the barista calls out.

"I'll get it," Hailey says. "Stay here."

As Hailey collects our drinks, I walk away and lean against a wall that is out of the way of the crowd. I feel ridiculous, but since I'm desperate to avoid a confrontation, I have no choice. I pull out my phone and pretend to be deeply engrossed in something important. Maybe if I look busy enough, even if he spots me, he'll keep his distance.

No such luck.

"Willow? Is that you?"

I freeze at the sound of his voice. Slowly, I look up to find Leo standing right in front of me, his perfect white teeth on full display in that camera-ready smile.

"Leo," I say, keeping my voice deliberately neutral. "What a surprise."

"I thought that was you! What are the odds?" He moves in for a hug before I can stop him. I stand stiffly as his arms wrap around me, the scent of his expensive cologne bringing back memories I've tried hard to forget.

"What are you doing here?" I ask when he finally releases me, taking a step back to create some distance.

"Supporting the team, of course," he says, gesturing vaguely toward the arena. "I'm doing a collab with some of the players for my channel. Sports content and gaming is really popping off right now."

Of course he is. Everything is content to Leo.

"That's...great," I manage, searching desperately for Hailey. I spot her making her way back through the crowd, a tray of drinks in her hands and a concerned expression on her face.

"We should catch up," Leo continues, either oblivious to or ignoring my discomfort. "It's been what, almost two years? You look good."

Is he trying to gaslight me? That's cute. He can save his little performance for his fanbase and get a sponsorship out of it. Heavy emphasis on little. That is when I notice his eyes traveling down my body in the way that used to make me feel special but now just makes my skin crawl.

"I'm actually here with family," I say, relief washing over me as Hailey finally reaches us. "And friends. We should get back to our seats."

Leo's gaze shifts to Hailey and back to me. "Of course. Family and friends first, right?" His tone makes it sound like an inside joke, but there's nothing funny about it. "But seriously, we should talk sometime. I've been thinking about you."

"Have you?" I ask, unable to keep the edge from my voice. "That's interesting, considering how things ended."

His smile falters just slightly. "Water under the bridge, babe. People grow up, you know?"

"I'm not your babe," I say, taking the drinks Hailey offers me. "And some bridges stay burned."

Leo laughs like I've said something charming instead of telling him off. "Still feisty. I always liked that about you."

Hailey clears her throat. "We really need to get back."

"Right, right," Leo says, holding up his hands in mock surrender. "I won't keep you ladies. But, Willow," he pulls his phone from his pocket, waving it with that same practiced smile, "I'll message you. For old time's sake."

"Don't bother," I say, but he's already backing away, throwing me a wink as he disappears into the crowd.

"So that's Leo," Hailey says, her voice flat as she watches him go. "He seems..."

"Like a complete tool?" I add in as I help Hailey with the drinks.

"I was going to say exhausting, but tool works too." She studies my face. "You okay?"

"Fine," I say automatically, then catch myself. "Actually, no. Not fine. He's the last person I expected to see or talk to tonight."

And if he has any intention of reaching out to me, I knew it wouldn't be the last time either.

4

BLAISE

L iving with three other guys means our house never truly falls silent and tonight is no exception. I slip into my room and close the door with a soft click. I swear this is the first real breath I've taken all day. Through the walls, I can still hear Wilder's music and banging from Knox attempting to cook something for Selene. But here, in my space, there's order and calmness.

Just how I like it.

I drop my backpack next to my desk and scan my room, making sure everything is where it should be. My books stand in perfect rows on the shelves. Political science to the left while some of my fantasy novels are to the right. The small collection of gaming figurines I've allowed myself to have here are sitting dust-free on the top shelf. All in their proper place.

Some people think it's weird, my need to keep neat and organized. But they don't understand how a messy room translates to a messy mind. And I can't afford that, not with hockey and keeping up with my courseload.

I settle into my desk chair as my gaming PC hums to life with a press of a button. My fingers hover over the keyboard for a moment before I pull my glasses from their case and slide them onto my nose. I tell myself I'm only going to play for a couple of hours before working on a term paper that's due in a couple of weeks, but knowing me, I'll probably end up playing for at least three.

I queue up Realm of the Unknown, a game I've been playing since high school. I slide my headphones on and the menu music feels like a warm hug. My shoulders drop an inch. Tonight isn't about competition or achievements. It's about familiar patterns and predictable outcomes. I know every quest, every hidden chest, every dialogue option, and that brings a sense of comfort. I don't have to think too hard or worry if I'm doing things right.

While there can be pressure when I'm gaming, it's not nearly the same as what I feel when I'm trying to keep up with school and hockey. Each practice is like a test of my limits, pushing me, challenging me, and making sure I'm clocked in constantly. Then there's the tightrope of keeping my 4.0 GPA. Paper after paper, reading after reading. Some days, it's as if the work just keeps piling up faster than I can check things off my list. It feels like I'm living assignment to assignment with deadlines closing in faster than I can blink. But here, in my games, the stakes are lower. I can fail a quest or miss a target, and nobody cares. There's a freedom in not having to be perfect, in not having to prove my worth constantly.

I shift my gaze to my second monitor and throw up a couple of streams that I've been meaning to catch up on. One stream's a guy trying to shave seconds off a dungeon boss run. The other's *CozyCraft4Eva*, a girl quietly building a cottage garden in some blocky survival game while talking about what kind of soup she made for dinner. I mute them both. I don't need the noise. Just something in the background while I'm gaming.

And with that, my mind begins to quiet.

I've been managing pretty well lately. No skipped meals this week. All assignments submitted on time. Coach even nodded approvingly during yesterday's drill. Small victories, but they count.

I run through my mental checklist: Practice: done. Readings for Political Theory: done. Social media: limited to fifteen minutes this morning. Now playing something calming. Start my paper: TBD. Bed by midnight.

Time slips by without me noticing. The room stays dim except for the glow of my monitor and the soft flicker of muted streams on my second screen. I should probably turn on the ceiling light, but that would require me stopping what I'm doing and moving from my desk. Instead, I let out a long, slow breath.

I lean back in my chair and let my hands rest on the

keyboard as I think about my next move. My eyelids are starting to droop a little, but I still have the energy to continue on.

Out of the corner of my eye, a notification lights up my phone. I reach for it and find a text from Knox.

> Knox: Made extra nachos. In the kitchen if you want some.

> Me: Thanks. Maybe in a bit.

My stomach growls at the thought of nachos. I should go grab those nachos before they disappear. In our house, leftovers don't stay left for long and I'm not in the mood to cook dinner, so this is the best option outside of ordering delivery.

I save my game and stretch as my stomach makes a rumbling noise again. The nachos are calling my name and I would be silly not to answer. Plus, if Selene is here, there's an excellent chance the food will be edible. I pause the streams on my second monitor but leave my game running. One more quest and I'll be done for the night. Maybe.

The floorboards creak under my feet as I leave my room and head downstairs. The house is old but is one of the few homes near campus that hasn't been bought by the school and converted into student housing. It shows its age, but the rent is reasonable, and it's close enough to campus that we can walk to class when the weather's decent.

"Look who emerged from his cave," Knox says as I enter the kitchen. He's leaning against the counter, one arm draped around Selene's shoulders. She gives me a small wave before tucking a piece of her red hair behind her ear.

"The nachos summoned me," I reply, making a beeline for the plate piled high with chips, melted cheese, jalapeños, and what looks like actual homemade guacamole. "This looks suspiciously edible."

Selene laughs. "I supervised."

"Thank goodness," I say, grabbing a plate from the cabinet.

"I'd say I'm offended, but we all know my culinary skills are limited to protein shakes and cereal," Knox says, watching as I load my plate with a generous portion of nachos.

"And yet you keep trying," Selene teases, poking him in the side. "And that's one of the things I love about you. Remember the pasta incident?"

I snort. "You mean when he set off every smoke detector in the house and Wilder thought we were being attacked?"

"It wasn't that bad," Knox protests.

"The noodles were black," I remind him, grabbing a bottle of water from the fridge. "Actually black. Like charcoal."

Selene covers her mouth to hide her laughter. "He was so proud he'd made dinner."

"Until he tasted it," I add. "Which I'm not even sure why he did given how it looked."

Knox rolls his eyes. "At least I'm trying. When's the last time either of you cooked?"

It's silly of him to ask that given how often Selene does cook and how often she is over here trying new recipes. Most of which the whole house benefits from.

"Yesterday," Selene says.

"Two days ago," I counter. "Chicken and rice. I even used seasoning."

"Impressive," Selene nods approvingly.

"Salt doesn't count as seasoning," Knox says, grabbing another chip.

"I used actual spices," I defend myself. "Paprika. Garlic powder. That Italian blend thing Selene bought."

"Wow," Selene's eyes widen in mock surprise. "You're practically a chef now."

I take a bite of the nachos and have to stop myself from groaning in appreciation. The combination of melted cheese, perfectly seasoned meat, and fresh guacamole is exactly what I needed. "These are really good," I admit between bites.

"See?" Knox raises an eyebrow. "I'm learning."

"Under close supervision," Selene adds, bumping her hip against his. I agree he should give credit where credit's due.

"He's a work in progress," I say, grabbing another nacho. "But a fast learner when motivated by cheese."

"Pretty much," Knox agrees, his arm tightening around Selene. They share a look that's private, and for a second, I feel like an intruder. It's not an uncomfortable feeling, just somewhat weird, but not in a bad way. Like watching a scene from a movie where you know the characters but you're not part of the plot.

Knox has changed so much since Selene entered the picture. While he still can be an asshole, he's one that seems happier and more comfortable. He was unable to commit to anything outside of hockey. He always had a convenient excuse to keep things casual. His sports schedule was too demanding. No time for distractions if he wanted to go pro. Nothing could tie him down because he wouldn't let it.

But now? He's gone from avoiding connections to being completely wrapped up in Selene. He's committed to her like he's committed to hockey. Just a year ago, I'd be the one stuck as Knox's wingman, and now I'm watching him be all in with her. All the time.

"So, what are you up to tonight?" Knox asks, grabbing another chip and expertly scooping up a dollop of guacamole.

"Just gaming," I reply, taking another bite. "Realm of the Unknown. Trying to finish a quest line before I tackle a PoliSci paper."

"Ah, a battle we face often," Knox says. "One where we usually get our asses handed to us."

Selene leans her head on Knox's shoulder. "Don't listen to him. You're smart. You'll ace it."

"The paper's not the problem. It's starting it that is," I admit. "Procrastination is my actual major right now, which, oddly enough, is usually not a problem I have."

"Tell me about it," Knox groans. "I've got a presentation I haven't even thought about, and it's due Wednesday."

"You'll both be fine," Selene says.

I know she's right, but that doesn't mean the pressure isn't still there, quietly building.

"You make it sound so simple," I think, but manage a small nod. The truth is, 'fine' is a state we're constantly striving for, not one we comfortably live in. The path to 'fine' is paved with more assignments than one should realistically be able to handle and the looming threat of academic probation if your GPA slips. Not that mine is in any danger, but the fear is a constant, at least for me.

"So, Realm of the Unknown," Knox says, wiping guacamole from his chin with the back of his hand. "You actually enjoy the grind?"

"There's a certain satisfaction in completing something," I say, choosing my words carefully. "Even if it's virtual. Clear objectives, measurable progress. It's...straightforward." Unlike the rest of life, but that doesn't need to be said.

Selene smiles as she takes a few chips. "I get that.

Sometimes I just want to cook something simple because then I know exactly how it's going to turn out."

Knox looks from her to me, then back to the nachos. "You two and your predictable hobbies. Where's the thrill in knowing the outcome?"

"The thrill is in avoiding a mental breakdown, bro," I say, reaching for another chip. I'm only half kidding.

The bass from upstairs, which had been a dull throb, suddenly intensifies, rattling the cheap light fixture above us. A muffled shout follows, something about "leveling up" or "losing cups," it's hard to tell with Wilder.

Selene glances at the ceiling. "Wilder's really feeling it tonight, huh?"

"He's probably celebrating finishing a sentence of his English paper," Knox grunts. "Or finding a matching pair of socks. Either is a monumental achievement for him."

"Hey now," I say, though I can't entirely disagree. Wilder's organizational skills, or lack thereof, are legendary. "He's got...other strengths." Like an uncanny ability to find the best late-night food deals or talk his way out of almost any situation. Not to mention he's funnier than all of us on his worst day.

As if summoned by the mention of his name, Wilder stands framed in the doorway, hair sticking up in several directions, wearing a faded Red Wolves hockey t-shirt, sweatpants, and mismatched socks, confirming that Knox was wrong. One headphone dangles around his neck, which makes me wonder how the hell we were hearing his music.

"Did someone say my name, or are the nacho gods finally answering my prayers?" Wilder asks, his eyes zeroing in on the plate I'm still working my way through.

"Both," Knox says, gesturing with a chip. "And you're late. Blaise almost ate them all."

"A likely story," Wilder replies, already moving toward the counter. He grabs a spare plate and continues. "Dalton here has the self-control of a monk. Me, on the other hand..." He piles his plate high, cheese and jalapeños tumbling over the sides.

"We know," Selene says, smiling. "You have no self-control when it comes to food."

"Or anything else, really," I add, taking another bite.

Wilder pauses mid-scoop. "I'll have you know I exhibited immense self-control tonight. I didn't stay out too late and showered before deciding to grace you all with my presence." He shoves a loaded chip into his mouth. "Mmmph. Worth it."

"What profound sacrifice," Knox deadpans.

"Truly," Wilder agrees, his mouth full. He swallows. "Speaking of sacrifices, you guys missed a hell of a party earlier. Some frat house off campus. They had, like, a bouncy castle. Indoors."

My hand stills on its way to my mouth and I stare at him. Thankfully Selene fills in the blank because my brain died.

"A bouncy castle and alcohol?" Selene raises an eyebrow. "Sounds...sticky."

"And potentially a lawsuit," Knox adds. "Coach would have your ass if you got injured."

"Whatever, doesn't matter," Wilder says just before he sticks another nacho in his mouth. "Point is, it was epic. You all should've come."

"We prefer our parties without a side of potential ER visits," Knox says, snagging a chip from Wilder's overflowing plate and Wilder sends a glare his way.

Selene shakes her head. "A bouncy castle, Wilder? Really?"

"Hey, don't knock it 'til you've tried it after three beers," Wilder defends, mouth full. "It's...an experience." He winks, grabbing another handful of chips. "Almost as good as these nachos. Almost."

"An experience I'm happy to live vicariously through your questionable life choices, thanks," Knox replies.

Selene pats Knox's arm. "Be nice. At least he came back in one piece."

"And we wouldn't have these stories where he continues to live up to his name," I chime in.

Wilder grins, a smear of guacamole at the corner of his mouth. "Exactly. Someone's gotta be the chaos coordinator. It's a vital role." He shovels another chip into his mouth. "Besides, who wants boring stories? 'And then we all sat quietly and did our homework.' Riveting."

I manage a small smile. Wilder's energy is a force of

nature, one I've learned to observe from a safe distance. It's exhausting to even think about living at his frequency, but in small doses, it's...tolerable. Amusing if you will.

"Some of us appreciate boring," I say, more to myself than anyone else, but Knox catches it.

"Yeah, Blaise here is aiming for a Nobel Prize in Predictability," Knox says. "His idea of a wild night is reorganizing his bookshelf by publication date instead of author."

"Chronological by series is superior for continuity," I state. It's true. There's a logic to it that alphabetical order just can't replicate.

Selene chuckles. "See, Knox? He has his reasons. Don't knock the system."

"Thanks, Selene. I knew I could count on you to be the voice of reason when it comes to these dumb asses. And with that, I should probably head back upstairs and actually start on the paper," I say as I walk over to the sink to wash my dish.

"Don't let us stop you," Wilder says, mouth still half full. "I'm sure the paper is actually due in, like, two months knowing you, but you gotta do what you gotta do."

"It's due in two weeks, actually," I correct, washing and rinsing my plate. "Which, according to my watch, is practically tomorrow."

"Dude, relax," Knox says, reaching for the last of the guacamole. "You'll bang it out. You always do."

"Easy for you to say, your brain doesn't short-circuit if the paper isn't done at least a week early," I mutter, drying my hands. "I like to be prepared cause you never know what could happen. Something you might consider trying sometime." My comment is aimed at Wilder and he knows it.

"Hey, I'm prepared!" Wilder protests, crumbs flying. "I'm prepared for a good time, all the time. It's a different kind of preparedness, but equally valid."

Selene laughs. "You boys. Always competing."

"It's just our way," Knox says, pulling Selene closer. "Everything's a competition. Who can eat the most nachos, who can procrastinate the longest, who can come up with the lamest excuse for not cleaning the bathroom."

"I think Wilder wins that last one consistently and I end up picking up his slack," I say, moving toward the kitchen doorway. "And on that note, I really am going upstairs. Thanks for the nachos."

"Anytime, man," Knox says. "Don't stay up too late stressing over that paper. It's not worth losing sleep over."

Easy for him to say. "Sleep is part of the schedule," I reply, which is true. Eight hours. Non-negotiable if I want to function at practice.

"See? Even his sleep is scheduled," Wilder calls after me, his voice muffled by another mouthful of chips. "The man's a machine!"

I don't bother responding, instead choosing to take the stairs two at a time to get back to my room faster. Once I've shut myself in my room once more, I glance at my dual monitors. Realm of the Unknown still idles on one, its landscape peaceful. The muted streams are still paused. For the paper, I'll need silence. Or, at most, the instrumental lo-fi playlist I usually reserve for deep thinking and work.

I queue up the lo-fi playlist, click into the blank document, and stare.

Nothing comes. I do manage to write my name and today's date, but that's it.

The game flickers in my peripheral vision, but after I've written my heading, it's the only thing still moving besides my cursor. I should start the paper. I *need* to start the paper.

Instead, I sit back and exhale slowly before I turn my attention back to my game.

I'll try again in five minutes.

Maybe ten.

5

WILLOW

"Your organizational system stresses me out just looking at it."

I look up to find my friend Ari Lennon standing inches away from me, surveying the mess I've surrounded myself with. I like to call it organized chaos, if you will. I shrug, grab a peach ring candy, and toss it into my mouth.

"It's a *system*," I throw back at her, nudging some books I took out from the library for research purposes with my elbow. Of course it only makes them wobble more. "A very specific, highly personal system."

Ari snorts. "Right. Personal. Like how your coffee order is personally designed to give the baristas at Brewed Beginnings an aneurysm." She plucks a stray sticky note off my monitor, squinting at my scrawl. "Is this a reminder to breathe or bleed?"

"Depends on the day," I mutter, snatching it back and sticking it where it belongs.

She shakes her head before she pulls out a granola bar. "Here." She presses it into my palm. "Figured you'd forget breakfast. Again."

"You're a lifesaver," I say, already ripping into the wrapper. It's one of those fancy ones with flax seeds and goji berries, the kind my mom would approve of. Ari knows my fuel preferences lean more toward vending machine chic, but she tries. "And for the record, my coffee order is an art form."

"It's a cry for help, Wills." She settles into the chair beside mine and pulls out her things neatly. She usually keeps her area clean and now is no different. When she's done setting up, the only things in front of her are a sleek laptop, a notebook, and her pen. Speaking of, even her pen sits at a precise ninety-degree angle. Sometimes I think we were paired as friends by the universe because it has a wicked sense of humor.

"Yeah, yeah, yeah," I say, waving her off before rolling my eyes. I take another bite of the granola bar and realize it's actually not that bad.

"What's on the docket for you today?" Ari asks, logging into her laptop. "Besides drowning in sticky notes and pretending those library books aren't three days overdue."

"They're not—" I start, then glance at the date stamp. "Shit."

"Told you." She doesn't even look up, but I can hear the smirk in her voice.

"I'm finishing that piece on the student housing scandal. The administration thinks they can just quietly increase rates by fifteen percent for next year and nobody will notice."

"Until Willow Sanchez noticed and put a spotlight on it. Housing Director Phillips is probably having nightmares about you by now."

I grin at that, savoring both the compliment and another bite of granola. "Good. Maybe he'll think twice before trying to sneak that clause about infrastructure improvements into page seventeen of the budget."

I jump slightly when Kate Alonso's, our editor-in-chief, voice rings out before Ari can respond. "Alright, everyone, gather 'round for assignments!"

I quickly brush granola crumbs from my shirt and swivel my chair toward the center of the room where Kate stands with her phone at the ready. She's wearing her signature blazer-over-graphic-tee combo, hair pulled back in a tight ponytail that somehow manages to look both professional and like she didn't try too hard to be just that damn cool.

"Housing scandal article update, Sanchez?" she asks, eyes already moving down her list.

"Final draft by tonight," I confirm. "Got a quote from the student government president that's basically political dynamite."

Kate nods approvingly. "Perfect. That'll be our lead for Monday." She continues down her list, assigning stories about the food health inspection results and the upcoming poetry slam.

I zone out slightly, my mind already racing ahead to the edits I need to make. I'm startled back to attention when I hear my name again.

"Sanchez, I need you on something new," Kate says. "Senior Night for the hockey team was last week. I want a feature on the team's impact on campus culture, with a focus on our graduating seniors. Reactions from students, staff, that sort of thing."

My stomach drops. "Hockey?" I force out, trying to keep my voice casual.

"Yes, Willow. The sport with the sticks and the ice," Kate says drily. "I need quotes from the seniors. Plus, isn't your brother on the team? Should be pretty easy."

I can't help the audible groan that escapes my lips. Ari shoots me a quick side-eye because she knows I should have kept my mouth shut.

"Problem?" Kate asks, one eyebrow arched high.

"No, no problem," I say quickly, though every cell in my body is screaming otherwise. "Just, you know, sports. Not exactly my beat."

"It's time you branch out," Kate says, checking something off on her phone.

"But—"

"Besides," Kate continues, steamrolling over my

protest, "I need someone who won't just fawn over them. Your critical eye is perfect for this."

I slump in my chair, defeat settling heavy on my shoulders. "Fine. When's the deadline?"

"Thursday. And I want interviews with Levi Jamison, Asher Bennett, Knox Sanchez, Blaise Dalton, and Wilder Blake specifically. They're the big senior stars everyone's talking about. I'm sure the interview with your brother will be special."

Yeah that's not what makes me panic. My heart stutters at Blaise's name. Of course Kate would single him out. The universe really is determined to torture me today.

"Got it," I mutter, scribbling the assignment on a fresh sticky note while my brain screams in protest.

Kate moves on to the next person, and I turn to find Ari giving me a look that's equal parts sympathy and amusement.

"Don't," I warn, pointing my pen at her.

"I didn't say anything," she whispers, raising her hands in mock surrender.

"You were thinking it very loudly."

Ari leans closer. "Just saying, karma's finally catching up with you for avoiding every hockey game since you got here."

"I went to one last week FYI. Besides, I've been busy," I hiss back. "Actual journalism takes time."

"So busy you couldn't watch your brother play?" Ari

whispers, her voice gentle but pointed. "Or is this about something else entirely?"

I glare at her, but there's no real heat behind it. Ari knows me too well. It's both the best and most annoying thing about our friendship.

"It's about professional boundaries and you know how I feel about sports after Leo," I mutter, scribbling Blaise's name on my sticky note with more force than necessary. The pen tears through the paper. Perfect.

"You can't avoid all athletes forever," Ari whispers as Kate continues down her list of assignments. "The campus is crawling with them, and they're not all like Leo."

I crumple the torn sticky note and grab a fresh one, refusing to meet her gaze. "I'm not avoiding all athletes. Just football and hockey players." I pause, then add more quietly, "And one in particular."

Ari leans back in her chair, studying me with those observant eyes that never miss a thing. "It's been, like, three years, Willow."

"Two years," I correct automatically, then wince at how pathetic that sounds. "Not that I'm counting."

"Clearly." Ari's voice is dry, but her expression softens. "Look, you can't let one awkward night—"

"Can we not?" I interrupt, glancing around to make sure no one's listening. "Not here."

The memory of that night flashes in my mind. The taste of cheap beer and jungle juice, Blaise's jersey brushing against my skin, the warmth of his lips on mine, and then the rejection that followed. My face grows hot just thinking about it.

"Fine," Ari relents. "But this assignment might be good for you. Closure and all that."

I snort. "I don't need closure. I need a time machine so I can go back and tell Past Willow not to make an absolute fool of herself."

"Past Willow was drunk and honest. Current Willow is just in denial."

"Current Willow is trying to maintain her professional dignity," I counter, scribbling down the rest of the hockey players' names. "And survive this assignment without dying from embarrassment."

"Hey, I'm just saying, this could be good for you," Ari whispers, leaning closer so no one else can hear. "Confronting the awkward thing head-on instead of diving behind potted plants every time you see him on campus."

"That was one time," I protest, "and it was a large decorative bench, not a plant."

"And the time you pretended to be fascinated by the fire evacuation map when he walked into Brewed Beginnings?"

"I was...concerned about safety protocols."

"For seven minutes?"

I glare at her, but there's no heat behind it. "You're supposed to be on my side."

"I am on your side. That's why I'm telling you to face this thing instead of letting it haunt you for the rest of your college career." She reaches over and taps the sticky note where Blaise's name stands out like a neon sign. "Besides, it's just an interview. You ask questions, he answers, you write it up, everyone moves on with their lives."

"I mean he's graduating this year, so it would only be for the rest of *his* college career."

"Wills—"

"Right." I nod, trying to convince myself as much as her. "Professional. Detached. I interview people I don't like all the time."

"You don't dislike Blaise," Ari counters my statement. "That's the whole problem."

I open my mouth to argue, but the truth in her words stings too much. Damn Ari for knowing me better than I know myself sometimes.

"Whatever," I mumble, focusing intently on rewriting my notes. "The point is, I can handle this. It's just another assignment."

"Of course you can," Ari says, her tone softening. "And I'll help you prepare questions if you want."

Kate claps her hands, bringing our whispered conversation to an abrupt halt. "That's it for assignments. Remember your deadlines and let me know if you need anything."

As the group disperses, I stare at the names on my sticky note. Five hockey players. Five interviews. One massive headache waiting to happen.

"You know what?" I say, straightening my shoulders and walking back over to my desk. "I'm going to tackle this head-on. Knox first, obviously. Easy win. Then maybe Levi or Asher. Work my way up to..."

"The awkward one?" Ari supplies helpfully.

"I was going to say the more challenging interviews, but yes."

My phone vibrates, and I dig it out from under a stack of papers. It's a text from my brother.

"Speak of the devil," I mutter, showing Ari the notification. I wait a split second before tapping to open Knox's message.

> Knox: Selene has some questions about
> the creative writing class you're taking.
> Isla said some things and she wants to
> compare.

"Wow, perfect timing," Ari says, reading over my shoulder. "The universe works in mysterious ways."

"The universe can mind its own business," I mutter, typing a quick response to Knox. *I didn't really mean that. Forgive me, universe.*

> Me: Sure, I can talk to her. When?

"I'm going to use this as an excuse to set up the interviews," I tell Ari, already formulating my plan. "Two birds, one stone."

"Look at you, being all efficient and proactive," Ari says, nudging my shoulder. "And they say avoidance isn't a productive coping mechanism."

"It's not avoidance if I'm literally seeking them out for interviews," I counter, though my stomach flips at the thought of facing Blaise. My phone buzzes again.

> Knox: Tomorrow? Our place around 7? I can get some of the guys together after practice if you need to talk to them for that article you're probably going to write about Senior Night.

I stare at my phone. How does he know about the article already? Either the hockey team grapevine is working overtime, or my brother has developed psychic abilities. Neither option is comforting.

"Is he psychic now?" I ask Ari, showing her the message.

She shrugs. "Kate probably mentioned it to someone who mentioned it to someone else who told the team. You know how this campus works. They also probably needed to clear it with their coach and the administration."

"Great. So they're all expecting me. That makes this so much better."

> Me: How did you know about the article?

Three dots appear immediately.

> Knox: Kate emailed Coach this morning asking for access. Coach told us to "be cooperative and don't say anything stupid." Direct quote.

> Me: Fine. Tomorrow at 7 works. I'll be there.

I add a thumbs-up emoji to seem casual, then immediately regret it. Nothing says "I'm totally fine with interviewing my brother's best friend who I drunkenly kissed two years ago and have been avoiding ever since" like a forced thumbs-up.

> Knox: Bringing pizza. Don't be late or Wilder will eat your share.

"Well, that's settled," I say, tossing my phone onto my desk where it lands and knocks into my pen. "Tomorrow night I get to start interviewing hockey players. Yay. Go me."

"You know how many people would kill to be in your position?"

"And they're welcome to swap places with me."

"At least there'll be pizza," Ari offers. "And other people around. Safety in numbers."

"I'd rather eat glass than sit through an hour of hockey talk surrounded by sweaty dudes who think they're gods on ice," I say and let out a big sigh. "But you're right. Pizza is a silver lining."

"And you'll have Selene there," Ari reminds me, pulling her laptop closer.

I smile despite myself. Selene is pretty great. After getting to know her more since she's been with my brother and when we traveled to Abue's birthday party, I've realized she's smart, down-to-earth, and somehow manages to keep my brother in check. A minor miracle, if you ask me.

"True. And she actually wanted my advice about something, which is a nice change." I start organizing my scattered notes into something resembling order. "Maybe I'll just focus on her and pretend the rest of them are potted plants."

"Decorative benches," Ari corrects with a smirk.

"I hate you."

"No, you don't." She takes a sip from her water bottle. "So what's your angle for the article? Please tell me you're not going in guns blazing with the 'toxic masculinity in sports culture' approach."

I gasp in mock offense. "I would never be so predictable." Then I pause, reconsidering. "Okay, maybe I had a few thoughts along those lines."

"Willow."

"What? It's a valid perspective!"

Ari gives me her patented "I'm not buying your bull-shit" look. "Kate wants a feature on their impact on campus, not your personal vendetta against jocks."

"It's not a vendetta," I argue, though my voice lacks conviction. "It's critical journalism."

"Uh-huh. And I'm sure your ex and a certain awkward kiss have nothing to do with your objectivity."

My cheeks heat up again. "Low blow, Lennon. Low fucking blow. Plus if I was really on one, I would talk about toxic masculinity in the gaming world. Starring Leo Kent."

Ari winces. "Sorry. That was unfair."

I shrug, trying to appear unbothered even though everything within me wishes we could avoid this topic. "Whatever. It's fine."

"No, it's not." She reaches across the desk and squeezes my hand. "I shouldn't have brought him up."

"Leo Kent is old news. Ancient history."

And that's where he is going to fucking stay if it's the last thing I do.

6

BLAISE

I plan my days down to the half-hour because it keeps everything from unraveling. Well, more so it keeps me from having a small meltdown if I'm being honest. At least right now I've got a full schedule keeping me steady. Steady is a strong word. More like helping me not to spiral.

Monday through Saturday mapped out on my calendar with color-coordinated blocks. Blue is for classes, green for practice, yellow for study sessions, purple for team meetings, and red and gray for games depending on if they are home or away. Even showers and meals get their designated slots. Sunday's the only day that stays relatively blank.

I'm surprised I haven't put in a block for playing video games. Maybe that isn't such a bad idea.

My eyes land back on the blocked-out days in January

marked with "Puerto Rico Trip," in yellow. Bright enough to stand out, but not loud enough to bother me. I've already triple-checked the flight info, made a packing list, and added the emergency contact form to a folder on my laptop. The trip isn't for a few more weeks, but it doesn't hurt to be prepared early. All I needed to do was get through these last three weeks of school and the holidays and I'd be all set to enjoy weather that is much nicer than what Virginia is currently giving us.

Well coursework would be getting done too because this is a short study abroad trip for a credit, but nonetheless it should be a good time.

In theory.

And by that I mean where everything goes according to plan, no one throws up on the flight, and the Wi-Fi holds steady for the entire trip.

I scroll past the trip block and glance at tomorrow's schedule. Group project meeting at 7:15. Practice ends at 6:30, which gives me just enough time to eat, shower, and triple-check the slides for said group's presentation.

Not too bad of a day.

Professor Wallace's voice cuts through my thoughts. "Also, if anyone knows someone who might be interested in joining the trip, we've got a few open spots. A few people dropped out last minute."

I don't react, just nod like everyone else in the room, because I'm not sure I know anyone who could make this trip last minute. Some of the other students drop names of people who might be interested, but I'm drawing a blank on my end.

Three open spots.

I write it down in the margin of the itinerary printout like I might need to remember later. I won't. But sometimes writing things down keeps my thoughts from looping.

Professor Wallace taps her keyboard once, and the projector screen flickers to the next slide: *Packing Guidelines and Safety Protocols.* She adjusts her reading glasses, then glances around the room.

"No more than one checked bag," she says, pointing to the slide behind her, "and keep in mind the humidity. Lightweight, breathable clothing. And if you burn easily, pack accordingly. The sun doesn't care if you didn't *mean* to fall asleep on the beach."

A few people chuckle. I underline the line about driver's licenses and/or passport copies in my notes.

She clicks again. "Room assignments will be emailed out next week once we finalize housing. You'll be paired with someone in the group unless you've submitted a roommate request."

A hand shoots up near the back.

"What if we're not sure yet?" asks a guy I vaguely recognize. "Like...can we switch roommates if something's not working out?"

Professor Wallace sighs. "If there's a problem, come to me. I'm not going to make anyone suffer through a week of passive-aggressive silence, but I'd prefer if you all *attempt* to coexist. Like adults."

More laughter. I make a mental note to check who else from my department signed up just in case they couldn't make it tonight.

Professor Wallace switches gears and flips the slide. "Quick reminders while I've got your attention. If you're taking medication, make sure you bring enough for the full duration. I'm hoping to avoid tracking down a pharmacy if possible."

She writes out **HEALTH FORMS DUE: Dec 12** in all caps.

I already turned mine in two days ago.

Behind me, someone flips a water bottle open too aggressively and gets a splash across the desk. They whisper a curse. Professor Wallace keeps going.

"There will be one free day at the end of the trip. That means no assigned activities, but I expect you to stay near the resort, check in with faculty, and do *not* book an illegal jet ski excursion off a TikTok you found the night before. It's happened. We're not doing that again."

My pen hovers. I look around the room. I don't know anyone here well enough to guess who that TikTok jet ski person, but I'm also not surprised to find out this has happened before.

Then she clicks to the final slide: return flights and debrief.

"We'll be flying out of San Juan early that Sunday,"

Professor Wallace says, tapping her finger against the projected slide. "The group shuttle leaves the hotel at 8:15 a.m. sharp. No exceptions."

A few groans ripple through the room. Someone mutters, *"brutal,"* under their breath.

Wallace just smiles. "You can survive this, I promise."

I underline the flight time in my calendar, even though I've already done it once before. Double-checking details calms my brain and I have no plans on ever stopping that.

The meeting wraps a few minutes later.

I grab my things and shove them into my backpack before standing up. People are making their way toward the exit, all the while chatting about packing lists and how excited they are to be going on this trip. I sling my bag over one shoulder and walk toward the door as I mentally plan the quickest route back to the house.

The Political Science Department is usually quieter this time of day, because there may be only one or two evening classes happening right now. Thankfully, it also means not many people are walking the halls outside of the meeting I just got out of, making it easier for me to get out of here quicker.

Which is exactly how I like it.

My brain's already moving through what the rest of the evening will entail. What I'll eat, how long I can work before someone bugs me about something completely unrelated to whatever I'm doing. Hell, how much time I'll be able to game tonight.

I take the back hallway near the vending machines and as I turn the corner, I collide with someone. Not shoulder to shoulder. Not just a graze.

A full-on collision.

Papers hit the ground. My backpack jerks to the side. I see a phone skid across the floor out of the corner of my eye.

"Shit—" I mutter, already reaching down instinctively. "Sorry, I didn't—"

Then I see who it is.

Willow Sanchez.

Her eyes widen as they fly up to meet mine. For a split second, the usual glare she has for me is gone, replaced by pure surprise. Then it slams back into place as if she just realized who she was looking at.

"Seriously, Dalton?" she snaps, already bending to scoop up her phone. It looks undamaged, screen thankfully intact. A few loose papers flutter around her feet.

"Didn't see you," I manage, my voice rougher than intended. I crouch down, gathering the papers and avoiding her gaze. My knuckles brush against the worn denim of her jeans as we both reach for the same page. A jolt, quick and unwelcome, snakes up my arm, and I pull back as if I've been burned.

She snatches the papers from my hand without a word, stuffing them haphazardly back into a folder she must have dropped. Standing up, she smooths down her sweater, adjusts the strap of her bag.

"Right," she says, her tone showcasing just how pissed off she is that we have to share the same air. "Because looking where you're going is optional."

"Wasn't expecting obstacles," I counter, my voice flat. I straighten up, shoving my hands into my pockets to stop myself from reaching out again, from doing something stupid like brushing a stray piece of lint off her dark sweater. She smells faintly of vanilla and something else... coffee, maybe? I can't pinpoint the scent nor will she give me an opportunity to.

And I understand why, even though it's the way things need to be.

She narrows her eyes. "Funny. I could say the same thing." She tucks her phone into her back pocket. "Anyway, I should get going. I don't have time to waste."

"Neither do I," I reply quickly because I know the longer I stay in her vicinity, the more my thoughts will circle the drain about what could have been if circumstances were different. "What are you doing over here anyway?"

She adjusts the folder under her arm, avoiding my eyes. "I needed a quote for an article from Professor Simpson. Satisfied?"

Not even close. But I just shrug, leaning back on my heels slightly. "Just curious. Don't usually see campus reporters around these parts."

A ghost of a smile touches her lips, gone as quickly as it appears. "Wouldn't want to miss any potential scandals, Dalton. You guys are full of 'em."

"We keep things interesting," I say, the corner of my own mouth twitching despite myself. Why were we engaging in this conversation anyway?

"Right," she says as she looks around for a moment before her gaze returns to my face. "Are you going to be around tomorrow evening? I'm sure Knox told you I need to interview the senior hockey players for a special in the newspaper. Everyone is meeting up at your house."

"Can't. Group project meeting." It's true, but the excuse feels flimsy even to my own ears.

Willow raises a single, perfectly shaped eyebrow. A small, almost imperceptible smirk plays on her lips. "Surprise, surprise. I guess I'll follow up with you another time then."

"Sounds like it."

"Well. See you around."

"Yeah," I manage, watching as she turns and walks away, her dark hair swaying slightly with each step. The scent of vanilla and coffee lingers for a second longer before it, too, is gone.

I don't make a move as I watch her walk away until she disappears around the corner. All I can do is replay in my mind the way the sweater hugged her curves and how she'd probably want to rip my face off if she knew I was thinking that.

Fuck.

I drag a hand down my face, exhaling slowly. This is exactly what I don't need right now. I've spent years building walls between us, carefully maintaining distance after that night. And all it takes is one accidental collision in a hallway to bring it all rushing back.

That and running into her at Knox's birthday party. And seeing her when she stopped by our house sometime before that.

My feet finally start moving again, but my mind is somewhere else entirely. Somewhere dangerous. Somewhere I promised myself I wouldn't go.

I can still feel the warmth where her body briefly pressed against mine. The way her green eyes flashed with the fire I'm used to seeing directed at me. How her lips parted slightly when she first saw me.

Those lips.

I swallow hard and pick up my pace, as if I can outrun these thoughts. It doesn't work. Because why would it?

By the time I get back to the apartment, my jaw aches from clenching it so tight. I slam the door harder than necessary, tossing my backpack onto the couch.

"Someone's in a mood," Knox calls out from the kitchen. The microwave hums in the background.

"I'm fine," I mutter, heading straight for the fridge. I grab a water bottle, downing half of it in one go. Who knew thinking such dirty thoughts about someone's sister would cause me to feel dehydrated. Then again, I'm thirsty as hell for her so it all tracks.

Knox leans against the counter, arms crossed. "You're not fine."

He's right, but I can't tell him I'm thinking about how much I would love to bend his sister over and fuck the hatred she has for me out of her. I polish off the water in the bottle in two gulps.

"Just school stuff," I lie, avoiding his gaze as I crush the empty water bottle in my hand. I toss it toward the recycling bin, missing by a good foot.

Knox tilts his head, giving me a look that says he knows I'm full of shit but won't push it. "Right. Well, whatever it is, maybe punch a pillow instead of slamming a door next time."

I grunt instead of coming up with a proper response, grab the water bottle, and put it in its proper place before leaving the kitchen. I need to get away from Knox as quickly as possible. He's one of my best friends, practically a brother, but there are some thoughts I can't share with him especially when they involve fantasies about his sister.

The moment my bedroom door clicks shut, I drop onto the edge of my bed, head in my hands. I'm going to need a cold shower.

Stat.

7

WILLOW

Why am I nervous to knock on my brother's door?

It's not like I haven't been here before. Yes, I've tried to avoid coming over here for various reasons, but that's beside the point. Tonight feels different. It's probably because I'm not coming here in my capacity as Knox's little sister, but I'm stepping across this threshold as Willow Sanchez, reporter for the Crestwood Chronicle.

My knuckles hover an inch from the door and I still can't make myself do it. With the track I'm on, I'm going to end up being late for the interview.

"Just knock, Willow," I mutter to myself. "You're here for work. It's an interview. Something you've done a million times before."

I tap my knuckles against the door three times before I can change my mind.

The door swings open almost immediately, and I quickly wonder if the person on the other side had been waiting for me to knock. I plant a small smile on my face as I come face-to-face with Asher Bennett.

"Hey, Willow," Asher says with a warm smile, holding the door open wider. "You're right on time."

Yes, but only because I finally got up enough nerve to knock. Not that he needs to know that. "Thanks," I manage, stepping inside. "Didn't want to keep you guys waiting."

"You didn't. Pizza just got here so that kept us distracted for a bit. Outside of watching the game, of course."

"Of course," I repeat because I don't expect anything less. I assume the game he's talking about is hockey because what else would they have on? This is an interview, not a hangout, I remind myself as I follow Asher into the living room. But my nerves are still dancing, annoyingly, as I spot Knox and Selene walking in from the kitchen. Selene is holding cups while my older brother has two big bottles of soda in hand. Levi and Wilder are sitting on the couch.

"Hey, Wills," Knox smirks at me as he slides the bottles onto the coffee table before turning toward Selene. "You made it."

"Amazing, right?" I say, hoping my voice doesn't give

me away. "I'm here. With no last-minute excuses or trying to find a way to get out of this shit."

Knox chuckles and the noise sounds foreign to my ears. Since when does my brother chuckle? Ah. Since he got with Selene. He finally says, "That's a first, especially since sports are involved."

"Don't let it go to your head," I shoot back, shrugging off my coat. Selene takes it from me and drapes it over the back of the couch. I give her a small smile before I turn my attention to the men in the room.

"I never do," Knox says in response.

He and I can go back and forth and get into a whole sibling argument, but that would be a waste of everyone's time. So instead, I clear my throat and say, "Alright, let's get this show on the road," I announce. I pull my phone and notebook out of my bag. "Everyone good if I record this?"

Nods and murmurs flow through the room, letting me know everyone is okay with me doing so. Levi moves a stack of textbooks to make more space for me, while Asher brings up a chair for me to sit down on. Wilder at first looks around to see how he can make himself useful before deciding to grab a slice of pepperoni, folding it in half, and preparing to shove it in his mouth.

"Okay," I say, pressing the record button in my app and setting the device down. "Senior Night feature. Big deal. Let's start easy. Levi, captain duties aside, what's been the most memorable moment for you this season?"

Levi leans forward as he taps his chin with his index finger. "Most memorable? That's tough. I mean, every game out there with these guys is pretty damn good." He glances around at Knox, Asher, and Wilder, a genuine warmth in his eyes. "But if I had to pick one...probably the comeback win against Brickwood. Down by two in the third, and we just...clicked. Everyone firing on all cylinders. That feeling in the locker room after that win? There's nothing like it, especially cause it was a hard fought win."

I nod, jotting down *Brickwood comeback* even though my phone is capturing every word. It helps me remember things, which sometimes I struggle to do. And it keeps me from focusing on the empty space where a sixth person should arguably be sitting if this were a full senior lineup.

"Yeah, that Brickwood game was nuts." Wilder gestures with the pizza slice. At what, I have no idea. "Mostly memorable for me because I think I sweat out my entire body weight in the third period. And Levi owed me twenty bucks 'cause he bet I couldn't stop that breakaway."

Levi rolls his eyes but doesn't deny it. "Best twenty bucks I ever lost."

"Okay, epic saves and gambling debts noted," I say, scribbling *Wilder - sweat, $20*. Willow, focus. "Asher," I pivot slightly in the chair he provided. "As a right wing, you're often setting up plays or taking shots under pressure. What's the biggest lesson you've learned about handling that pressure over your four years here?"

Asher leans back, running a hand through his brown hair. "Honestly? Learning to trust the guys next to me. Freshman year, I felt like I had to do everything myself, prove I belonged. But hockey's not a solo sport. Knowing Knox is gonna be crashing the net, or that Levi can read the play before it even happens... it takes the weight off. You just focus on your piece of the puzzle." He waits a beat before glancing at Knox. "Most of the time, anyway. Sometimes I still gotta bail him out."

Knox scoffs as he grabs a slice of pizza. "Bail me out? Please. Who scored the game-winner against State last month after you whiffed it at the blue line?"

"Hey! It was a bad bounce," Asher protests, but he's grinning. "And you only scored 'cause I drew both defenders."

"Whatever." Knox waves his hand with the pizza in it, narrowly avoiding flicking grease onto Levi.

"Okay, settle down," I chime in as I try to steer them back to the task at hand. And I'm the one with ADHD. "Knox, same question, different position. Left wing. Pressure. Lessons learned."

Knox takes a bite of pizza, chewing slowly for dramatic effect, I'm sure. "Biggest lesson?" He swallows. "Learning when to shut up and listen to the guys who actually know defense. Don't tell the fucker that's not here I said that." His eyes grow wide for a second before he continues. "Clean that quote up because Coach will never let me hear the end of it."

"Say please," I reply as I jot some more notes down.

Knox grins and I already know his reply is going to be a mess. "Please, Wills. Wouldn't want to tarnish my pristine reputation."

"Pristine is a strong word," I toss out. I make a note to myself: Knox, defense, edit quote. The casual mention of Blaise, currently known as "the fucker that's not here" hits me harder than I expected. Does anyone else notice how hard I'm clenching this pen? Probably not. They're all too busy dissecting Knox's defensive prowess, or lack thereof.

I force my attention back to the interview. "Wilder, as the goalie, you see the whole ice. What's one thing people misunderstand about your position?"

Wilder, mid-chew, pauses with his pizza halfway to his mouth. He swallows and that's when I notice a small amount of tomato sauce clinging to the corner of his lip. "That it's just about stopping pucks," he says finally, wiping his mouth with the back of his hand. "It's ninety percent mental. You're the last line of defense, yeah, but you're also reading the play, communicating with your D-men, trying to anticipate what the other team's gonna do before they even know. It's like...high-speed chess, but if you lose, someone scores and thousands of people in the arena and elsewhere groan at you." He shrugs. "No pressure."

"High-speed chess," I echo, scribbling it down. It's a good line.

"Hailey would appreciate that reference," Levi adds.

It's then that I remember that Hailey is the president of Crestwood's Chess Club.

"Dude, not everything has to be about Hailey," Wilder mumbles something else under his breath as he shakes his head.

"Hey, a good reference is a good reference," Levi says, as he spares a glance at Wilder. "And she *would* appreciate the high-speed chess analogy. You gotta admit, it's pretty accurate for what you do."

"Or you just like bringing her up at every opportunity," Wilder replies.

"That's true and it's because I love her." Levi shrugs as if he didn't just drop a truth bomb. "You'll understand that soon, I'm sure."

Wilder goes quiet, which is weird for him.

A collective "aww" flows through the room. Knox throws his arm around Selene, bringing her closer to his body and gives her a big grin. It's sweet, sickeningly so, but sweet, nonetheless.

I glance at Wilder and see that he's not looking at anyone in particular. But the parts of his ears I can see that aren't covered by his longish brown hair are red.

Interesting.

"Okay, Romeo," I say, trying to regain control of the interview and definitely not thinking about how no one's ever declared their love for me in a room full of people. Well, once, but it only was for the benefit of his fanbase so that doesn't count. "Back to hockey. Knox, you mentioned listening to guys who know defense. Let's talk team dynamics. How has the leadership evolved this year, especially with a mix of seniors and newer players?"

"It's been...smoother than I expected. Levi's always been a natural leader, even before he got the 'C'. Asher steps up when he needs to, usually by example. Wilder keeps everyone loose with the jokes." Knox pauses, and for a split second, I think he's going to say *his* name but he just adds, "And the younger guys, they listen. They want to win. Makes things a whole lot easier."

"Okay, speaking of the younger guys, let's talk legacy. Senior Night was about looking back but also looking forward. What do you each hope the underclassmen take away from your time here, from watching you guys play?"

A comfortable silence follows my question and I know it's because everyone is trying to think of an answer. It's Levi who breaks speaks up first. "Work ethic. That's something I learned from my brother. Oh, and that nothing is handed to you. You gotta earn your ice time, earn the respect of your teammates, earn those wins. We've busted our asses for four years, and I hope they see that. That it's not just about talent."

Levi bringing up his deceased older brother is something I don't expect. Knox has told me that Levi doesn't talk about him much, so for him to bring him up is a big deal.

We just look at him, a little stunned, before Asher

responds. "We're going to earn the big one for him this year," he says quietly.

I don't want to pry too much but I assume Levi's been chasing a championship not just for himself but to honor his brother as well. I can only imagine the pressure he feels to live up to the talent of his older brother, the brother he lost too soon.

Asher clears his throat and speaks again. "And that it's okay to make mistakes, as long as you learn from 'em. We've all had shit games, bad plays. But you can't let it define you. You get back up, you work harder."

Wilder nods. "Yeah, what Ash said. And also, that it's supposed to be fun, you know? We put in the work, yeah, but at the end of the day, we're playing a game we love. Don't lose that. Don't let the pressure suck the joy out of it. Even when you're sweating out your body weight."

I make another note: *Wilder: fun, joy.* It's a good sentiment, surprisingly insightful coming from the team's resident jokester.

Then it's Knox's turn. "Legacy, huh?" He glances at Levi, then Asher and finally Wilder. "I guess...I hope they learn that loyalty matters. To the team, to each other. We haven't always agreed and sometimes the arguments and fights have been brutal." He shoots a quick, unreadable look in my direction before his gaze sweeps back to his teammates. "But we always had each other's backs. On and off the ice. That's what makes a team, not just a bunch of guys wearing the same jersey."

Loyalty.

Him mentioning that hits harder than I expect and maybe it's something I can work the article around. A theme if you will. "Good stuff, guys. Really." I tap my pen against my notebook. "So, final question for the group, then I'll let you get back to your pizza and...whatever game you're pretending to watch."

A few chuckles. Wilder shoves the last of his crust into his mouth.

"Looking ahead, beyond graduation, beyond Crestwood," I say. "What's one thing you'll take with you from being a Red Wolf, something that isn't about wins or losses, but about the experience itself?"

The room goes quiet again. This time, it's Asher who speaks first. "The discipline, I think. Juggling classes, practice, games...it forces you to manage your time, to be accountable. That's not just a hockey skill, that's a life skill."

Levi nods. "For me, it's the brotherhood. Cheesy, I know." He grins. "But these guys...they're family. That bond, you don't just leave that behind when you graduate."

My pen pauses. A second ago, I was planning how to work loyalty into this feature, but now I'm thinking about brotherhood and how that could work better. Family. Found family at that. I like it a lot.

"Okay," I say as I press the record button once more on my phone to stop it. I close my notebook and look up at the guys and Selene. "I think that's everything I need for the group stuff. Thanks, guys. You actually gave me some decent material."

"Decent?" Knox snorts and rolls his eyes. "We poured our hearts out, Wills. That was pure gold."

"I'll be the judge of that," I say, tucking my phone and notebook into my bag. "But seriously, thanks. This helps."

Wilder gives me a thumbs up. He then stands up and begins trying to balance a stack of pizza boxes on his head, much to Asher's amusement and Levi's exasperated sigh. Levi starts gathering discarded napkins and paper plates, a small frown creasing his brow as he surveys the living room.

"Anytime," Levi says, offering me a small, genuine smile as he passes by with a handful of trash.

As the guys clean up, Selene walks over to me and says, "Hey, Isla mentioned that you were in the creative writing class that she's also taking this semester. I was thinking of taking it next fall and wanted to know what you thought of it. Especially since writing is your thing."

"Oh, yeah," I say, my mind still half on hockey loyalty and brotherhood, half on the empty space Blaise hadn't occupied. "Professor Martinez's class? It's...intense. Good, but intense. Lots of reading, even more writing. She doesn't pull punches with feedback. If you're serious about creative writing, it's worth it. But don't expect an easy A."

"That's what Isla said. She loves it, but she also said she's never worked harder for a B-plus."

"Yeah, Martinez definitely makes you earn it, but it's rewarding either way. I'm very happy with how my writing has improved."

"Well, thanks for the intel," Selene says, her voice light. "Might stick to my current plan of easy electives then." She pauses, for a moment before her gaze lands back on me. "So, everyone made it tonight except for one."

My stomach clenches because I know she noticed how awkward I was at the Senior Night game. With a heavy sigh, I brace for it. Because here it comes.

"Yeah, well," I start and then pause. I'm failing at being unaffected by what she's implying. "Blaise had a group project thing. You know how it is, end of semester."

"That makes sense. Knox has talked about how rigid Blaise's schedule can be." Selene's words are casual, but the tone of her voice is anything but.

I know what she's getting at, but I refuse to take the bait. "Mhmm," I mumble, suddenly very interested in adjusting the strap of my bag instead of looking at her. "He's probably got a color-coded calendar along with his color-coded notebooks to keep up with everything."

Selene studies me for a moment longer than is comfortable. "Probably. Though it's a shame he couldn't make it. The article would feel more complete with all the seniors, don't you think?"

I shrug. "I'll catch him another time. No big deal." That

had been my plan anyway, although the thought of it annoys the shit out of me.

"Right," Selene says, but her eyes tell me she's not convinced. "No big deal at all."

Before she can press further, I glance at my phone to check the time. "I should get going. Got to start transcribing all this while it's fresh."

"Of course." Selene smiles. "I'll walk you out."

As we head toward the door, Knox calls from the kitchen, "You heading out, Wills?"

"Yeah," I call back. "Got everything I needed."

My brother appears in the doorway, dish towel in hand. When did he become so domestic? "Let me know when the article's coming out. I want to make sure you quoted my brilliance accurately."

"I'll be sure to include your modesty as well." I slip my arms into my coat that Selene hands me.

Knox grins. "That's my favorite quality."

I roll my eyes but can't help smiling. "Later, loser."

The door closes behind me, and I exhale slowly, as if I'd been holding my breath the entire time. The relief that I feel from having that part of the interview over is quickly cut short when I realize I still have to reach out to Blaise and figure out when and where we can meet up so I can have quotes from him in this article.

And we will more than likely have to do it alone.

8

WILLOW

With a heavy sigh, I rub my hands across my face because I'm annoyed. Even with my headphones on, I'm drowning in noise at Brewed Beginnings. The espresso machine is steamrolling my brain and cups are clinking loud enough to cause a headache. Slamming my head down on my keyboard might be a better alternative. Plus, it would put me out of my misery.

But I need to do this. I need to focus and finish this article on the student housing issues at Crestwood. I stare at the cursor flashing on my laptop screen next to an unfinished quote but my mind is on the interview I held with my brother and his hockey teammates last night.

The interview that's missing one crucial voice.

I take a sip of my now-lukewarm coffee and make a stank face. The caffeine isn't helping my focus. If anything, it's making the thoughts in my head race faster, which makes working even harder.

Someone drops something on the ground, causing me to flinch so hard my knee bangs against the underside of the table. Great. Now I have physical pain to match the mental.

"Damn it," I mutter, yanking my headphones off. The music wasn't helping anyway.

I check my phone. No new messages. Not that I was expecting any from him. Not that I even texted him in the first place. Which I should have done already if I was being professional about this whole thing.

"You look like you're contemplating murder," a voice says above me.

I look up to find Ari sliding into the seat across from me and placing a cranberry muffin that she purchased and utensils in front of her. Her eyebrows are raised in that way that tells me she's about to psychoanalyze my entire existence.

Groovy.

"Maybe I am," I reply, closing my laptop with more force than necessary. "The housing article is kicking my ass."

Ari tilts her head. "Uh-huh. And I'm sure that's the only thing on your mind right now."

"What's that supposed to mean?"

She shrugs off her coat. "I watched you stare at that document as I was walking up and your face has cycled through approximately seventeen different emotions, none of which scream 'I'm focused on student housing.'"

I hate how well she knows me.

"I'm just..." I start, then stop. What am I, exactly? Annoyed? Distracted? Unreasonably fixated on someone who clearly went out of his way to avoid me for years and now I need to contact him in order to write an article for the school newspaper.

"Waiting for inspiration to strike?" Ari offers, cutting the muffin in half and sliding half across the table to me like a peace offering.

"Something like that," I mumble before I stuff a piece of food in my mouth. The sweetness might help my brain function again. Maybe.

Ari narrows her eyes at me, her dark gaze missing nothing. "This wouldn't have anything to do with a certain hockey player missing from your interview last night, would it?"

I nearly choke on the muffin. "We don't have to bring *him* up."

"But I will because you're sitting here looking like someone deleted your thesis the night before it was due, and as I already said, it's not about student housing."

I swallow hard, forcing the muffin down my suddenly dry throat. "It's unprofessional. That's all."

"What is? The fact that he didn't show up or the fact that you care?"

"I don't care," I snap, then immediately regret it when

Ari raises a single eyebrow. "Fine. I care about the article. I need quotes from all the seniors for this feature, and he's making it difficult. Not that it's actually his fault because he did have prior plans. Why do I feel a crash out brewing over something so silly?"

"Because you care more than you want to admit."

"I don't care about Blaise Dalton," I insist, tearing off another piece of muffin. "I care about completing my assignment properly. As I just said."

"Mmhmm."

"Stop mmhmm-ing me. It's irritating."

"And you're deflecting." She dusts crumbs from her fingers. "But fine, let's talk solutions instead of feelings. Have you texted him to set up a one-on-one?"

I fiddle with my coffee cup. "Not yet."

"Why not?"

"Because..." The words stick in my throat. How do I explain that texting Blaise feels like opening a door I've kept firmly shut for years? That the thought of sitting across from him, just the two of us, makes me want to lose my shit?

"Because you're avoiding it," Ari finishes for me.

"I'm not avoiding anything. I'm just..." I gesture vaguely at my laptop. "Prioritizing."

"Right. Prioritizing staring at your screen and having a mental breakdown in public."

I glare at her. "You're not helping."

"Actually, I am." She reaches across the table and flips

my laptop open. "Text him now. Set it up. Rip the band-aid off."

"I don't have his number."

The look on Ari's face tells me she knows I'm purposely being obtuse. "Email him. Text your brother for it."

"But—"

"No buts. You need this for your article. He's just another source. Treat it like any other interview."

Just another source. If only it were that simple. If only Blaise Dalton were just another hockey player and not the guy who kissed me senseless in his room years ago, then pretended I didn't exist and just so happens to be my brother's teammate, best friend, and one of his roommates.

I sigh and pull my laptop closer to me. "Fine."

Emailing seems to be the most professional way to do this, plus it meant not having to go through my brother to get his number. I open my email, fingers hovering over the keyboard. What's the most professional way to ask someone you've been actively avoiding for years to sit down for an interview?

"Don't overthink it," Ari says, reading my mind as usual. "Just be direct."

"I'm being direct," I mutter, typing out "Interview Request" in the subject line. Professional. Detached. Perfect.

To: blaise.dalton@crestwood.edu

Subject: Interview Request - Senior Hockey Feature

Blaise,

As you know, I'm writing a feature on the senior hockey players for the Crestwood Chronicle. I interviewed the rest of the seniors last night but understand you couldn't make it due to a prior commitment.

I'd like to schedule a brief interview to include your perspective in the piece. Please let me know your availability this week.

Thanks,

Willow Sanchez

Reporter, Crestwood Chronicle

I read it over three times, removing any hint of personality or emotion. It's the most sterile email I've ever written, which is exactly what I need right now.

"There," I say, hitting send before I can change my mind. "Done. Happy now?"

Ari gives me a small smile. "Ecstatic. Was that so hard?"

"Yes. Excruciating. I might need medical attention."

"Drama queen." She takes another bite of the muffin. "Now you can focus on your housing article while you wait for him to respond."

Right. The housing article. The one with the blinking cursor that's been mocking me for the past hour. I stare at the screen, willing the words to come, but my brain keeps circling back to that email sitting in Blaise's inbox.

Will he respond right away? Will he ignore it? Will he make up another excuse?

"You're not focusing," Ari points out.

"I'm trying."

"Try harder."

My phone buzzes, and I nearly knock over my coffee reaching for it. It's just a notification from social media. Not him.

Of course it's not him. I literally just sent the email.

"This is ridiculous," I mutter, shoving my phone into my bag. "I can't work here. It's too loud."

Ari gives me a knowing look. "The noise wasn't bothering you ten minutes ago."

"Yes it was. And it's bothering me now."

"Mmhmm."

"Stop that."

"Stop what?" She blinks innocently.

"The mmhmm thing. With the eyebrow. And the knowing look." I wave my hand in front of her face. "All of...this."

"I have no idea what you're talking about." She finishes her half of the muffin. "But if you really can't work here, why don't you try the library? Or your room?"

My room is the last place I want to be. And the library means potentially running into him, which is absolutely not happening until I'm mentally prepared.

Ari speaks again and distracts me from coming up with potential places I can go to. "Actually, I was going to mention something that might interest you."

I narrow my eyes. "What?"

"Remember that study abroad program to Puerto Rico I was telling you about a few weeks ago?"

"Maybe?" I vaguely remember her mentioning it, but it wasn't something I paid much attention to. Traveling is something I wanted to do more of, but I'm focused on the internship I'll be doing in New York City this summer.

"Well, they've reopened applications. A few students dropped out, so they're looking to fill spots. It's open to non-poli-sci majors now."

I blink at her. "And you're telling me this because...?"

"Because it's a week in Puerto Rico during winter break. And you mentioned wanting to get away...sounds like a great opportunity to do so." She pulls a folded flyer from her bag and slides it across the table.

I pick up the flyer. "When's the deadline?"

"Two days from now. It's tight, but doable."

I scan the details. The program focuses on the political history and culture of Puerto Rico. It includes cultural immersion activities, visits to historical sites, and credit for a short intensive course.

"A week in Puerto Rico," I say as I think about whether I could make this happen. "The timing is..."

"Perfect," Ari finishes. "It's right after finals, the holi-days, and before the spring semester starts."

She's right. The timing is perfect. Too perfect, almost, like the universe is handing me an escape route from this Virginia weather on a silver platter.

"I'd have to talk to my parents about the cost," I say, but I'm already calculating whether I could cover it myself. It's not like I have Knox's NIL money to throw around, although he would more than likely lend me the money to go. "This isn't exactly cheap."

"There's financial aid available," Ari points out, tapping a section of the flyer I hadn't read yet. "And it's all-inclusive. Flights, accommodations, most meals."

I fold the flyer carefully and tuck it into my bag. "I'll think about it."

"That's Willow-speak for I'm definitely doing this but don't want to admit it yet."

I roll my eyes, but don't contradict her. "I said I'll think about it."

My phone buzzes again, and this time I resist the urge to lunge for it. Instead, I take a deliberate sip of my now-cold coffee and make another face at the taste.

"You should get a fresh cup," Ari suggests.

"I've had enough caffeine," I say as I push the cup away. "Any more and I'll vibrate through the floor."

My phone buzzes a third time. With a sigh, I fish it out of my bag.

Three new emails.

None from Blaise.

Of course.

I shove the phone back into my bag with more force than necessary. "I need to go."

Ari raises an eyebrow. "Where?"

"Anywhere that isn't here." I start packing up my laptop. "I need to clear my head if I'm going to finish this housing article."

"And think about Puerto Rico?"

"And think about Puerto Rico," I repeat, zipping my laptop case and sticking it in my bookbag. I put my coat on and then look back at my friend. "Are you going to stay here?"

"I'll stick around for a bit," Ari says, pulling out her own laptop. "Got a sociology paper to finish."

"Good luck with that." I swing my bag over my shoulder, almost hitting a guy walking past our table. "Sorry."

Ari's eyes shift from the guy back to me. "Text me later?"

"Always do." I sling my bag over my shoulder and head for the door, the Puerto Rico flyer burning a hole in my bag. The cold air hits me like a slap across the face when I step outside Brewed Beginnings. But I'm grateful for it because it shocks my system and clears the fog in my brain. I take a deep breath, letting the December air fill my lungs.

A week in Puerto Rico.

The thought lingers as I start walking to my car. A week away sounds great, especially because it means that my time at home will be shorter. Not that I have an issue with being home, but after being on my own at school, it's harder to adjust to being under my parents' roof again.

This trip would solve a lot of my problems.

I jump slightly when my phone buzzes in my pocket, and I nearly trip over my own two feet to grab it.

One new email.

From blaise.dalton@crestwood.edu.

My heart does this stupid little stutter that immediately annoys me. "Just open it, dumbass." I tap the notification.

To: willow.sanchez@crestwood.edu

Subject: Re: Interview Request - Senior Hockey Feature

Willow,

Thanks for reaching out. I'm available to meet you tomorrow between 2-4 P.M. We could meet at the library study rooms if so.

Let me know if that works.

Blaise

That's it. Short, direct, professional. Exactly what I asked for.

So why do I feel...disappointed?

"Get a grip, Willow," I whisper, shoving my phone back into my pocket without responding. I'll answer later, when I'm not standing in the freezing cold having an existential crisis over a four-line email.

I resume my walk to my car, my mind now split between Puerto Rico and tomorrow's interview. Two-to-four tomorrow. That gives me time to prepare and to remind myself that this is just another assignment.

Just another source.

Just another interview.

By the time I reach my car, my fingers are numb from the cold. I fumble with my keys, dropping them once before managing to unlock the door. Once inside, I crank the heat to maximum and sit there, waiting for warmth to return to my extremities.

The Puerto Rico flyer peeks out from my bag on the passenger seat. I pull it out and smooth the creases, reading the details more carefully this time.

"Cultural immersion activities...historical sites..." Before I can talk myself out of it, I pull out my phone again and call a number I'm very familiar with.

Mom picks up on the third ring. "Willow? Everything okay?"

"Yeah, Mom, everything's fine." I take a deep breath. "I wanted to ask you about something. There's this study abroad program over winter break to Puerto Rico, and they've opened up some last-minute spots."

There's a pause on the other end. "Puerto Rico?"

"Yeah. I know it's short notice, but it's only a week, and it counts for credit, and—"

"Slow down, sweetheart." I can hear the smile in her voice. "Tell me more about it."

I explain the program, the timing, and the cost. She listens without interruption, which is one of the things

I've always loved about my mom. She actually listens and hears me out before offering her thoughts.

"What about the holidays?" she asks when I finish. "Abue would miss you."

"I wouldn't leave until after the New Year," I assure her. "The program starts on the third."

Another pause. "And you really want to do this?"

Do I? The question hangs in the air between us before I respond. "I think..." I start, then pause for a moment before I continue. "I think I need this, Mom. A change of scenery. Something different."

She sighs, but it's not disapproving. "Well, you've always been independent. If this is something you truly want, we'll figure out the money part."

Relief floods through me because I didn't have any expectations. "Really?"

"Really. Send me the details, and I'll talk it through with your dad tonight. Apply just in case to see if you will get in."

"Thank you," I say, and I mean it. "I'll call you later."

After we hang up, I sit in my car for a few more minutes, the heater now blasting too-hot air into my face. My phone screen lights up with another notification. I sigh when it's a reminder about my deadline for this student housing article.

Reality crashes back in. I still have that article to finish and I need to respond to Blaise's email.

With a deep breath, I type out a quick reply:

To: blaise.dalton@crestwood.edu
Subject: Re: Interview Request - Senior Hockey Feature
Blaise,
Tomorrow at 3 P.M. works for me. Let's meet inside the library, near the entrance. Then we can see which room is open.
Thanks,
Willow

There, that's done. Now all I need to do is finish the student housing article tonight and apply for the Puerto Rico trip. It shouldn't be a long night, but busy enough that it will keep me distracted enough to not think about my interview with Blaise.

At least, that's what I hoped.

9

BLAISE

I show up to the library twenty minutes early.

That is mostly because I finished up a paper I was working on early and didn't have anything to do in the time I would have had free before I needed to be at the library. It is not because I am trying to impress her. What it does give me is time to get my head on straight about whatever questions she's going to ask during this interview.

I choose a seat that is near the entrance but just off to the side, giving me the perfect view of her when she arrives. Because I'm sitting in a slightly more secluded corner, it'll give me an opportunity to look at her, to figure out exactly how irritated she's going to be with me today because she has to interview me.

I've been overthinking this meeting since I got her email, and I wish I'd just shown up for the group interview. Yes, it would have taken some maneuvering because of the group project, but I could have made it work. After all, It would've been easier because the other guys were present to be the buffer between us. Instead, I'm here early, waiting for a one-on-one with the one person on campus who makes me feel like I'm losing my carefully constructed control every time I'm in the vicinity of her.

I flip open one of my political science books and pretend to read while actually watching the entrance. Three minutes until our scheduled time, and still no sign of her. My leg bounces under the table, a nervous habit I thought I'd kicked years ago.

The door swings open, and I straighten up before I can stop myself. It's just someone with an overloaded backpack. Not her. I exhale slowly and check my phone again. 2:58 P.M.

Maybe she's not coming. Maybe this is her way of getting back at me for missing the group interview. I wouldn't blame her, but Willow's always been professional, even when she's pissed off. Especially when she's pissed off.

Just as I'm considering emailing her, the door opens again, and there she is.

Willow Sanchez, walking into the library like she owns the place, her dark ponytail swinging with each step. She's wearing a coat that's unzipped and I get a glimpse of a burgundy sweater and black jeans. My eyes reach her boots before jumping back up to her face when I notice she's scanning the area, looking for me.

I raise my hand slightly, just enough to catch her attention. Our eyes lock, and for a split second, the fire that's usually in her eyes around me isn't there. It's in that moment I know I'm screwed.

Not because she looks good. *She does. Obviously.*

Not because I'm nervous. *I am. Completely.*

But because within what feels like a millisecond, the fire returns and her jaw tightens.

I watch her walk over to me, the confidence in her stride betraying nothing of what might be going through her mind. My own thoughts are an absolute mess, but I've always known how to hide them. I close my book harder than necessary, and out of the corner of my eye I see someone glancing over at me and I'm sure they are annoyed.

"Hey," she says when she reaches me, her voice clipped. No smile, no warmth. Just business.

"Hey," I return, standing up awkwardly before realizing I don't need to. I gesture to the chair across from me. "Thanks for coming."

She shrugs off her coat and drapes it over the back of the chair before sitting down. "I need quotes from you for the article. Should we find a study room?"

"Actually..." I look around. "It's pretty quiet here. Unless you'd prefer somewhere more private?"

Her green eyes narrow slightly. "This is fine."

She pulls out her notebook and phone, setting them on the table between us. "Do you mind if I record this?" she asks, already pressing a button on her phone.

"Go ahead."

She nods, all business. "Great. So, same questions I asked the others. What's been the most memorable moment for you this season?"

I lean back in my chair, trying to look relaxed even though my heart is hammering against my ribs. "Probably the game against Westlake. That overtime goal against them was amazing."

"You didn't score it," she points out.

"No," I admit. "But I set it up. Sometimes the plays that don't make the highlight reels matter more."

She writes something down, her handwriting quick and neat. "As a defenseman, you're often the unsung hero. Does that bother you?"

"No." The answer comes immediately. "I'm not in it for recognition."

"Then what are you in it for?"

Her question catches me off guard. It's not just the words, but the intensity behind them. For a split second, it feels less like an interview question and more like she's asking me something deeper.

"The game," I say finally. "The strategy. Finding order in chaos."

She doesn't write that down. Instead, she looks up, her

green eyes meeting mine directly. "And how does that translate off the ice? Finding order in chaos?"

There's something in her tone I can't quite place. It's not just professional curiosity. It's something else.

"It's how I approach most things," I say carefully. "Breaking complex situations down into manageable pieces."

"Including people?" The question comes out sharper than I think she intended for it to, or maybe she wasn't expecting to ask it at all. I pick up on it because she immediately glances down at her notebook as if she can't look me in the eye.

"People aren't puzzles to solve," I reply quietly. "They're more complicated than that."

The corner of her mouth twitches, and for a moment I think she might smile. She doesn't.

"The others talked about legacy," she continues, steering back to safer territory. "What do you hope the underclassmen take from your time here?"

I consider this, genuinely wanting to give her something useful for her article. "That there's value in doing the unglamorous work. Not every contribution is accounted for and that's okay. As long as it means the team is succeeding and winning games, that's what I prefer."

She nods, writing again. "And looking ahead, beyond graduation? What will you take from being a Red Wolf?"

"Perspective," I say. "Learning when to push forward

and when to hold the line. When to take risks and when to play it safe."

Her pen stills. "And which are you doing right now?"

I blink. "What?"

"Playing it safe," she clarifies, her voice neutral but her eyes challenging. "With this interview."

I tilt my head slightly. "I'm giving you honest answers."

"Are you?" She sets her pen down. "Because it sounds like you're giving me carefully constructed quotes that your coach would be very proud of."

I lean forward slightly. "What do you want me to say, Willow?"

"Something real would be nice."

We stare each other down for a moment and I end up breaking the connection. Much like I did the night we kissed after that party. This time, however, I don't leave her hanging. "Fine," I say, my voice dropping lower. "Real? I think about that Westlake game because it was the first time all season I felt like I was exactly where I was supposed to be. Not overthinking, not second-guessing. Just...present. I also didn't have a panic attack before I hit the ice so that was nice as well."

Her pen hovers above the page. The admission about my anxiety seems to have caught her off guard. For a moment, the professional mask slips, and I see something softer in her expression.

"You have panic attacks before games?" she asks quietly.

I look away, immediately regretting sharing that detail. "Sometimes. Not as much anymore."

"How do you manage them?" The question sounds genuinely curious rather than journalistic.

"Structure. Routine." I tap my finger against the table. "That's why I'm so methodical about everything. It keeps me grounded when my brain wants to spiral."

She writes something down, but she's not writing as fast. "Is that what the color-coded notebooks are about?"

I raise an eyebrow. "You noticed that?"

"Hard not to," she says with a slight shrug. "I noticed it years ago."

The fact that she's been paying attention to something so small about me makes my chest tighten in a way I'm not prepared for. "Yeah, well. Organization helps."

"And hockey?"

"Hockey helps too," I admit. "When I'm on the ice, everything narrows down to just the game. No room for overthinking, but sometimes getting onto the ice is a battle in itself."

She nods, but I can't read the expression on her face. For a moment, neither of us speaks. Part of me wonders if there is any more left to say. Did I answer all of her questions? Scare her off because I mentioned my panic attacks? It wouldn't be the first time in my life that someone has looked down on me because I have them.

"Does Knox know?" she asks finally, her voice soft enough that only I can hear it.

I hesitate. "Not really. Not the extent of it." My fingers drum lightly against the table. "Coach is probably the only person who really knows. It's not something I advertise."

"Yet you're telling me." It's not a question, but there's confusion in her tone.

"Yeah, well." I shrug. "You asked for something real."

She studies me for a long moment, and I resist the urge to look away. "I did. I just didn't expect you to actually give it to me."

"Will you put it in the article?" I ask. It hits me that I actually care about how she'll respond to this more than I realized.

She looks up and her green eyes search mine before she answers. "No," she says finally. "I'll keep that between us."

"Thanks." I feel my body relax slightly as she confirms this won't become a public spectacle.

"Don't thank me," she replies quickly. "It's not my story to tell." It's then that she glances down at her notebook before she clears her throat. "I think I have everything I need for the article."

"That's it?" The words escape before I can stop them.

Willow looks up, one eyebrow arched. "Did you want me to ask more questions?"

No. Yes. Maybe. I don't know what I want, except that I'm not ready for her to walk away again. "I just thought there would be more... hockey questions."

"I got what I needed," she says, but she doesn't move to

pack up her things. "Unless there's something else you think I should include?"

I hesitate because I'm trying to find a reason to keep her here and am having a hard time coming up with one. "Maybe about the team dynamics? The relationship between offense and defense?"

"Alright. Tell me about that."

"It's...complicated." I fumble for words, suddenly aware I've created an opening I don't know how to fill. "The forwards get a lot of the glory, but defense wins championships. There's this competitive edge that runs through all of us in numerous ways. What it all boils down to is that we have to trust each other completely and communicate. No matter what."

"Like you and Knox?" Her question is pointed, and I know she's not just talking about hockey anymore.

"Something like that." I meet her gaze. "I would say we trust each other wholeheartedly. Sometimes the people closest to you are the hardest to communicate with."

"I wouldn't know about that." She tucks a stray strand of hair behind her ear. "Communication has never been my issue."

It doesn't take a million guesses to figure out what she's referring to. "Maybe it's been mine," I admit quietly.

"That's...honest."

"You wanted real."

"I did." She fiddles with her pen. "I just didn't expect it to apply to...everything."

"It wasn't supposed to, but sometimes things just...spill over."

Her eyes flick up to mine, bright and intense. "Like that night?"

We both know exactly which night she means. "Yeah," I say, because there's no point in pretending otherwise. "Like that night."

"You never said anything. After."

"Neither did you."

"You pulled away," she reminds me, a hint of that familiar fire returning to her eyes. "Hard to say anything after that."

"I panicked. It wasn't my finest moment."

"That's putting it mildly." Her words have bite, but there's something else there too. Hurt, maybe. "You kissed me like...like that, and then just—nothing. For years."

"It wasn't nothing," I say without thinking. "Not to me."

She stares at me and I wish I knew what she was thinking about. For a moment, I think she might get up and leave. Instead, she closes her notebook slowly.

"Then what was it?"

The question feels like a trap, but I'm tired of dodging. "Complicated."

"That's not an answer."

"It's the truth." I run a hand through my hair, frustrated. "You're Knox's sister. My best friend's sibling. There are lines you shouldn't cross."

This time she rolls her eyes and I see the fire growing within them. "Sounds like a bullshit excuse to me."

"Is it?" I lean forward in my chair and allow my hands to hang between my legs. "You think Knox wouldn't have had something to say about it?"

"Knox doesn't control my life," she shoots back.

"No, but he's important to both of us." I move my hands and rub them against my jeans in an attempt to do something that would help me organize my thoughts. "And it wasn't just that. You were a freshman. I was a sophomore. The timing was—"

"Spare me the logistics, Dalton." She raises her voice slightly and I know it's only a matter of time before we begin to draw attention to ourselves in this quiet place. She must sense it too because she looks around before she returns her gaze to me. "If you weren't interested, you could have just said so instead of making me feel like I'd imagined the whole thing."

"That's not—"

My words die on my lips when her phone vibrates on the table. Willow breaks eye contact first, reaching for her device. She unlocks her phone and her expression shifts as she reads whatever's on the screen. A small smile appears on her face and for some reason, that has me concerned.

"Everything okay?" I ask, unable to help myself.

"Yeah," she says, still looking at her screen. "I got accepted into something."

The casual way she says it catches me off guard. Like she's both trying to share something important and pretend it doesn't matter all at once.

"Yeah? What is it?" I ask, curiosity getting the best of me.

"You don't need to worry about it." She slips her phone into her pocket, already gathering her notebook and her bag. I'm sure that is her way of nicely telling me to mind my business, which is valid. "Anyway, thanks for taking the time to meet up with me."

"It wasn't a problem. If you need anything else, you know how to reach me."

"That I do," she says as she puts her coat back on. She struggles for a hot second and the urge to help her is strong, but I hold back because I know it won't be welcomed.

She finally gets the coat on and I'm left to wonder what it is she got accepted to. It's clearly something that matters to her, based on that small smile. A job for the summer? Early graduate school program? A study abroad program for fall next year?

"Well," she says, adjusting her bag on her shoulder. "See you around."

She turns to leave and this time I let her because I can't find a reason that would get her to stay.

10

WILLOW

The email is still open on my screen. I've already read it three times, but I'm staring at it like the words might magically change. Each line is burned into my brain.

Congratulations. We're thrilled to welcome you to the Winter Abroad: Puerto Rico program. Attendance at orientation is mandatory. Please arrive on time.

I know what it says, front to back, side to side. But seeing it in writing makes it real, or more real than when I read it at the tail end of my interview with Blaise.

Blaise.

At least right now it makes sense why he's on my mind since I should be focused on finishing my Senior Night hockey article. The document sits open in another tab, a few paragraphs shy of completion. But instead, I'm fixating on his face when I casually dropped that bomb-shell about being accepted to "something."

I switch tabs and start adding more words to the Senior Night hockey article because I'm annoyed at myself for caring what Blaise Dalton thinks about anything I do. Knox's quote about loyalty stares back at me. I need to weave in Blaise's perspective, but every time I try to type his name, my fingers freeze.

"Focus, Willow," I mutter, reaching for my coffee mug only to find it empty.

I get up to refill it because the caffeine and the move-ment will clear my head. As my coffee maker starts doing its job, I pull out my phone and scroll to my messages with Ari.

> Me: I got in. Puerto Rico is happening.

She responds immediately.

> Ari: TOLD YOU SO!!!!!

> Ari: When do you leave?

> Me: January 5th. Right after the holidays. Orientation is tonight.

> Ari: Cool and perfect timing to escape the winter blues.

> Ari: Also, how'd the interview go? • •

I stare at her text. The coffee maker beeps behind me, signaling it's done, but I don't move right away.

> Me: It was fine. Professional. Got what I needed.

The lie sits heavy between my thumbs and the screen. Nothing about that interview was fine. Nothing about sitting across from Blaise Dalton was professional, especially when he stared me down and admitted to having panic attacks.

My phone buzzes again.

> Ari: That's Willow-speak for "something happened but I don't want to talk about it yet."

I roll my eyes.

> Me: Nothing happened.

> Me: Except he told me something personal.

> Me: And we almost talked about That Night.

> Me: But nothing happened.

I watch the typing bubbles appear and disappear three times before her response comes through.

> Ari: THAT'S NOT NOTHING.

I sigh, grabbing my coffee mug and walking back to my desk. My phone buzzes again. Ari isn't going to leave me alone.

> Ari: Are you going to tell me what he said or do I have to interrogate you?

I consider ignoring her, but that would only make things worse. She'd probably show up at my door and demand that I answer her.

> Me: He told me he has panic attacks. Including before games sometimes.

> Me: And it's one of the reasons why he's so methodical about everything.

I feel slightly bad for telling Ari about something Blaise suffers from, but who wouldn't tell their best friend if they knew she wouldn't spread it? I take a long sip of coffee, watching the bubbles appear and disappear again.

> Ari: Wow. That's...not what I expected.

> Ari: Did he say why he told YOU specifically?

I stare at my wall as I consider her question. Why HAD he told me? I'd pushed for something real, but I hadn't expected him to actually deliver.

Me: I asked him to say something real versus the corporate answers he was giving me.

Me: And then we kind of talked about the kiss.

Me: But my phone went off with the acceptance email about Puerto Rico.

Ari: WILLOW! You can't just drop that and not elaborate!

Ari: What did he say about the kiss??

With a heavy sigh, I run my hand across my face. He said it wasn't nothing. That there were lines you shouldn't cross. That it was complicated.

Me: Not much. Just excuses about why he pulled away.

Me: Knox. Timing. The usual bullshit.

Ari: And what did YOU say?

I groan. She knows me too well.

Me: I said they were bullshit excuses.

Ari: AND THEN??? I swear you're worse than a season finale of any drama in primetime.

Me: And then nothing. My phone went off, I told him I got accepted to "something," and I left.

Three dots appear, then disappear, then appear again. This is becoming a habit.

Ari: You're both impossible.

She's not wrong and I don't have a good response to that. I set my phone down and turn back to my laptop. The article stares back at me, still unfinished. Blaise's quote about defense winning championships sits in my notes, waiting to be incorporated into the document. I type his name, finally, and begin to place his perspective into the piece.

My phone buzzes again, but I ignore it. I need to finish this article before the orientation meeting about Puerto Rico. I type furiously, the words finally flowing. Brotherhood. Legacy. The unglamorous work behind the scenes. I pull it all together, crafting a narrative about what it means to be part of something bigger than yourself. By the time I've finished the conclusion, my coffee is cold and an hour has passed.

I read it over once, then again. It's good. Better than good, actually. It captures something I wasn't expecting about this team, something I'm proud to showcase in this piece: authenticity. I save the document and email it to my editor. Done. One less thing to worry about.

I glance at the time in the corner of my screen and realize I have about forty-five minutes before I need to head out for the orientation. Just enough time to unwind a bit.

After a good stretch, I close the article tab and open StreamTub. It's been my go-to for background noise when I need to decompress, and entertainment for years. The homepage loads with familiar thumbnails and auto-play clips, but it's the "Live Now: Co-Streams" section that makes my stomach jolt.

KingPin94 x CozyCraft4Eva — LIVE

Leo's username is bolded next to Cozy's, the thumbnail showing both their cams lit up in split-screen: him grinning like a smug idiot, her adjusting her headset while their avatars build some kind of pastel farmhouse in a blocky survival sim.

I shouldn't care.

I don't care.

But I click anyway.

"—and I'm telling you, Coz, this is gonna be the biggest build we've done together," Leo's voice fills my speakers, that familiar mix of confidence and excitement that used to make my stomach flip.

Once again, it's making me feel sick.

The smart thing to do was press the exit button and get on with the rest of my evening. However, I find myself watching for longer than I should.

"You always say that," Cozy laughs as her avatar placing down rainbow-colored blocks while Leo's character follows behind her. "Remember the underwater castle that crashed your server?"

"That was different," he protests. "I had, like, fifty mods running."

Cozy, whose real name is Lilly, and I chatted on occasion when I dated Leo, but I didn't realize they were still in touch. The thought bounces around my head as I watch as the chat scrolls by, filled with emotes and inside jokes I used to be part of. Leo leans closer to his camera, reading something, and then his face splits into that signature grin.

"Shoutout to CtrlAltDeceit69 for the tier three sub! Welcome to the Kingdom, my dude."

I should close the tab. Right now. And with a heavy sigh, I finally have enough willpower to commit to it.

I check the time again. Thirty minutes until orientation. I need to get moving, need to focus on something other than Leo and his content.

Puerto Rico. Focus on Puerto Rico and this orientation.

I grab my coat and bag, double-checking that I have my notebook and pens. The orientation packet mentioned bringing something to take notes with, and while I could use my laptop, I don't trust myself not to get distracted given how much my brain is racing even more than normal.

I quickly decide to drive across campus, considering how chilly it is out tonight. It also means I'm fifteen minutes early. If I would have realized that before I left my dorm, I would have stopped to get something quick. But at least I won't be drawing attention to myself because I'm rushing in at the last minute.

Given how no one is around right now, it's easy for me to find the room number from the email. I pause outside the threshold for a split second before walking through it.

Professor Wallace has her back to me as I walk into the room and pick an empty desk to sit at. I figure choosing a seat near the middle, not too close to the front but not hiding in the back either, is perfect. As I get settled, I glance up when I see someone else walk in out of the corner of my eye.

My heart stops.

Blaise Dalton walks in, his expression neutral until his eyes land on me. For a split second, I see surprise flash across his face and I'm convinced his mouth is about to drop open. However, he quickly catches himself and forces his expression to be neutral once more.

No. No way. This can't be happening.

But it is happening. Blaise gives a small wave to Professor Wallace. And then, because the universe apparently hates me, he's walking down my row.

"Is this seat taken?" he asks, gesturing to the empty chair beside me.

I want to say yes as a way to lie and claim I'm saving it for someone, but my mouth betrays me. "No."

He sits down and I do my best to ignore him. Here's to hoping he'll do the same and leave me the hell alone.

"Didn't expect to see you here," he says quietly as Professor Wallace distributes handouts to the front row to pass back.

"I could say the same about you," I mutter, keeping my eyes fixed on my notebook. "Don't you have practice or something?"

"Not tonight." He accepts the stack of papers from the person in front of us, takes one, and passes the rest to me. Our fingers brush, and I jerk my hand back. "Coach gave us the evening off."

I don't respond, focusing instead on the orientation packet now in front of me that I already printed out. The cover page has a colorful photo of what I assume is Old San Juan. Under different circumstances, I'd be excited.

"So," Blaise whispers, "this is what you got accepted to."

It's not a question, but I answer anyway. "Yes."

"Political history and culture of Puerto Rico," he reads from the packet. "Interesting choice for a journalism major."

I finally look at him, narrowing my eyes. "What's that supposed to mean?"

He shrugs, the motion fluid and annoyingly graceful. "Nothing. Just making an observation."

"Well don't."

The corner of his mouth twitches and I know he's fighting a smile. "Noted."

Professor Wallace clears her throat, drawing our attention to the front of the room. "Welcome, everyone, to the second session of the orientation for our Winter Abroad: Puerto Rico program. I'm Professor Wallace, and I'll be your primary faculty advisor for this trip."

But I barely hear anything that she's talking about because Blaise is going to be on this trip too.

That means a week of shared activities.

A week of group discussions.

A week of seeing him every. Single. Day.

"I opened up this session to those who attended the previous orientation in case you wanted to meet some of the new people that have recently signed up. Plus there is some more information that I would like to share with you and a few changes."

She clicks to the next slide: a detailed itinerary. I write down the schedule, adding little stars next to activities that sound particularly interesting. A walking tour of colonial architecture. A visit to El Morro fortress. A day trip to El Yunque rainforest. By the time Professor Wallace wraps up, I somehow managed to take some notes and my head is spinning.

"Any final questions?" she asks, looking around the room.

A hand goes up near the front. "Are the roommate assignments co-ed or single gender?"

"Single gender," Professor Wallace answers. "University policy."

A few more questions follow, but they don't take long for Professor Wallace to answer. When she's done, she says, "That's all for tonight. Remember to check your email for updates and complete your health forms by the deadline if you haven't already."

People start packing up, the room filling with the sounds of zipping bags and shuffling papers. I shove my notebook into my bag, eager to escape before Blaise can say anything else. This time the universe is on my side because he gets pulled into a conversation with someone else, allowing me to escape.

My phone buzzes in my pocket as soon as I reach my car. I know it's Ari, but I don't respond until I'm safely back in my room.

> Ari: How was orientation? Any cute study abroad prospects? • •

A bitter laugh escapes my lips as I reread her text. If only she knew.

> Me: You could say that. Blaise is in the program too.

I watch the typing bubbles appear almost instantly. Ari was on fire with her responses, apparently.

> Ari: WHAT?!

> Ari: ARE YOU SERIOUS?

Ari: This is either the best or worst thing
ever!

Ari: I can't decide.

Neither can I, is all I can think. Neither. Can. I.

11

BLAISE

No matter how prepared you are for early morning practices, it doesn't make getting up and getting on the ice any easier. I'm still performing well to keep Coach Johnson off my back, but I'm mostly going through the motions right now. I'm still reeling from seeing Willow last night at the orientation meeting, but I'm trying my best not to let it show.

I easily intercept a pass meant for Asher. In one fluid motion, I redirect the puck to Knox who's already streaking toward the opposite goal. My body knows what to do even when my mind is elsewhere.

"Nice read, Dalton!" Coach Johnson yells from the sideline. "That's what I'm talking about!"

I nod in acknowledgment, already positioning myself for the next play. The defensive drill continues, and I'm somehow executing every movement with precision despite the fact my thoughts keep drifting to the way Willow's eyes widened when she saw me walk into that orientation room.

Practice intensifies when Coach divides us into teams, red versus white. I'm paired with Harris, a sophomore defenseman with good instincts but still prone to rookie mistakes. When Levi breaks away with the puck, charging toward our goal, I call out positioning instructions to him while cutting off Levi's passing lane.

"Force him wide!" I shout, already anticipating Levi's next move.

Harris responds perfectly, angling his body to push Levi toward the boards. I swoop in at the exact moment Levi attempts to pass to Asher, stealing the puck and clearing it down the ice.

I'm on autopilot, my body executing plays while my mind keeps replaying fragments of last night. I'm excellent at compartmentalizing things in order to get through my day. It's not working today, but somehow I'm doing okay.

We do a couple more drills before Coach Johnson's whistle. "Time for a hydration break. You have five minutes!"

I skate toward the bench, tugging off my gloves and reaching for my water bottle. My throat's dry, but the burn in my legs feels good. Unlike everything else I'm trying to push down.

Knox plops down beside me and squirts water into his mouth. "That redirect you made? Filthy."

I nod, popping the top of my bottle. "He was telegraphing the pass."

"Still. You're locked in today." He bumps his shoulder into mine. He's in a better mood than I expected him to be in, but his usual grumpiness has become a thing of the past now that he's dating Selene.

"Yeah, well, I'm just reading his patterns which leads me to anticipating the play."

Knox gives me a sideways look. "You sound like a hockey textbook."

I shrug. "Just stating facts. Like I usually do."

"You good? You seem...I don't know. Off."

"I'm fine. Just focused and trying to end this semester on a good note." It's not a lie, but it's also not the full truth either. I'm focused on whether I should mention the fact that both Willow and I will be on this Puerto Rico trip together. Hell, I haven't even mentioned anything about this trip to the guys.

"You wanna grab breakfast after practice?" Knox asks, screwing the cap back on his water bottle. "Shit, we have, like, a minute until Coach calls us back on the ice."

"Yeah, I have time. Maybe we should invite the rest of the guys?"

Knox nods, already scanning the bench for the others. "I'll round them up after practice."

I take another swig of water, trying to focus on what Coach Johnson is going to throw at us next versus anything related to Willow and the Puerto Rico trip. It's gotten slightly easier, but the struggle is still there.

Coach's whistle pierces the air. "Back on the ice! Let's run the power play!"

We set our bottles down and slide our gloves back on. Knox gives me a quick fist bump before skating toward center ice. I follow, positioning myself at the blue line.

The rest of practice flies by. It includes more drills, more corrections, more praise and constructive criticism, which is Coach's style. By the time Coach dismisses us, I'm ready for a shower not only because I need to get this sweat off of me, but I need to ease my sore muscles. After going into the locker room and getting showered and dressed, I quickly realize I'm the first one ready to head out for food. I walk over to where the other guys are still packing their stuff up.

"I'm telling you," Wilder says as he stuffs his practice gear into his bag, "Professor Donovan's exam is going to destroy me. Who tests on the entire semester's material?"

"Every professor ever?" Levi replies, rolling his eyes. "That's literally what a final is."

"Yeah, but he's adding new material too! It's fucked up, bro."

"That's because you missed quite a few of his classes," Knox says, toweling his hair dry. "Can't blame Donovan for your poor attendance."

Wilder flips him off. "I had legitimate reasons."

"Sleeping through your alarm isn't legitimate," Asher chimes in, lacing up his shoes. "Neither is 'the vibe wasn't right today.'"

"You wouldn't understand my process," Wilder snaps as he zips his bag up.

I check my phone, scrolling through notifications while half listening to their conversation. Two emails from professors about final assignments, a reminder about a study group meeting tomorrow, and...an email from Professor Wallace with the subject line: "Puerto Rico Trip - Room Assignments."

I tap it open before I can think better of it.

"Earth to Blaise," Knox's voice cuts through my thoughts. "You still with us for breakfast?"

I lock my phone quickly, shoving it into my pocket. "Yeah, sorry. Just checking something."

"Important?" Knox tosses his bag over his shoulder.

"Just trip details," I say, keeping it vague on purpose.

Wilder raises an eyebrow. "Trip? What trip?"

Damnit. I didn't mean to let that slip. I hesitate as everyone's eyes are focused on me.

"It's a study abroad thing over winter break," I explain, trying to sound casual. "Political science department. Puerto Rico for a week."

"Puerto Rico?" Knox repeats. "The one Professor Wallace is running?"

"Yeah." I already know where this is going.

Knox stares at me for a long moment, and I can see the pieces clicking together in his head. "Willow mentioned she was going on a poli-sci trip to Puerto Rico."

The locker room suddenly feels ten degrees warmer. Levi and Asher exchange glances while Wilder's mouth forms a perfect 'O'.

"Did she?" I ask. "Small world."

"Yeah," Knox says slowly. "Small fucking world indeed."

Wilder, never one to read a room, claps his hands together. "Well, this just got interesting! Dalton and Little Sanchez, tropical island—"

"Shut up, Wilder," Levi cuts him off with a warning look.

"What?" Wilder holds up his hands defensively. "I'm just saying what everyone's thinking."

"When were you planning to mention this?" Knox asks, and I can hear the underlying tension in his tone.

I shrug, aiming for nonchalance. "It's just a school trip. And I literally found out last night when I walked into the orientation meeting."

"Wait," Asher interjects, "you just found out yesterday that Willow's going too?"

"Yeah." I run a hand through my still-damp hair. "Trust me, I was as surprised as anyone."

Knox studies me for a moment longer. "Alright. I believe you."

"Thanks..." My voice trails off because I'm not sure what to make of any of this.

"Can we please go eat now?" Wilder says and I would almost classify it as a whine. "I'm starving, and this drama is making me hungrier."

"It's not drama," I say firmly. "It's a school trip. That's it."

"Sure it is," Wilder says with an eye roll. "A school trip with the girl who looks at you like she wants to set you on fire. Totally normal."

"She doesn't—" I start, but Levi cuts me off.

"Let's just get food," he says, sliding between me and Knox. "Everything's better after pancakes."

He's not wrong. Food has solved many issues between the five of us, and I'm sure this will be no different. The tension in the locker room eases slightly as we file out, but I can feel Knox's eyes on me. He falls into step beside me as we head across campus.

"We good?" I ask Knox, keeping my voice low. The other guys are a few steps ahead being entertained by Wilder, who is talking about what food he is going to order.

"Yeah, we're good. Just caught me off guard."

"For what it's worth, I was surprised to see her there too because it's a trip mostly for political science majors."

"She's taking it as an elective," Knox says. "And to get away for a bit according to our mom."

"Get away from what?" I ask before I can stop myself. I don't want to seem as if I'm super interested in what Willow is up to, because it would raise every alarm bell in Knox's head.

Knox shrugs. "Hell if I know. That's just what my mom said when she texted me last night. Something about Willow needing a change of scenery."

"Makes sense. Winter in Virginia isn't exactly paradise."

Knox gives me a weird look before he speaks. "I mean, yeah, I don't blame her for going. I would go too if I didn't already have plans."

"So someone else is keeping secrets about what they are doing for winter break too?"

"It's not a secret if I haven't had a chance to tell you yet. Selene and her parents invited me to stay with them at a cabin they are renting in Vermont for a few days after Christmas."

"Wow. Spending time with the parents already? That's serious." I'm shocked and relieved we've moved away from the topic of Willow.

"It's not a big deal. But yes, we are serious."

"Spending a significant amount of time with the parents is definitely a big deal," I counter. "That's like...relationship level-up territory."

Knox shoves my shoulder. "Whatever. At least I'm not spending a week in Puerto Rico with someone who hates me."

And we're back to Willow. Great.

"She doesn't hate me," I say quickly, though I'm not entirely convinced of that myself.

"Could've fooled me," Knox mutters as we approach Brewed Beginnings. The scent of coffee hits us as soon as Wilder yanks open the door.

The place is decently packed with students who are grabbing coffee and food to fuel up before morning classes. I scan the room and thankfully, there is a table with four chairs in the corner.

As I follow the guys toward the corner table, I look over and see that Hailey's there, her brown hair pulled back in a messy bun, taking orders. Levi spots her immediately—no surprise there—and a dopey grin spreads across his face.

"I'm gonna go say hi," he says, already walking toward the counter.

"We'll grab the table," Asher calls after him, but Levi's already gone, making a beeline for his girlfriend.

Wilder rolls his eyes. "Whipped."

"Like you wouldn't act the same way if you were dating someone," Knox says, dropping into one of the chairs.

"Bold of you to assume I'd ever settle down," Wilder responds back, but there's something off in his tone. Before I can analyze it further, Asher grabs the seat next to Knox, leaving me to take the chair facing the counter and giving me a perfect view of Levi greeting Hailey.

"What's everyone getting?" Asher asks, pulling out his wallet.

"The biggest coffee they have and whatever has the most calories," Wilder says, slouching in his chair. "Practice destroyed me."

"You say that after every practice," I point out. I'm still watching as Levi leans across the counter and says something that makes Hailey's face soften for a millisecond before returning to her usual stoic expression.

"Because every practice destroys me. It's a consistent problem." Wilder yawns and then stretches his neck to look at the menu board. "I think I'm getting the breakfast burrito. I'm so glad they added that to their menu. No, wait. A blueberry muffin. No. I'm getting both."

Knox snorts. "Your metabolism is going to catch up with you someday."

"And when it does, I'll deal with it." Wilder runs a hand through his hair. "Live in the now, bro."

I'm about to respond when Levi returns to the table. "Hailey says they're swamped, but she'll try to come say hi when she gets a break."

"She looked thrilled to see you," I say, unable to keep the sarcasm from my voice.

Levi pulls a chair over and then plops down in it. "That was her happy face."

This turns into a back-and-forth between Wilder and Levi that I only half pay attention to. Instead, I pull out my phone to look over my schedule for today. Not that I didn't check it when I woke up this morning just before getting ready for practice. I only have a couple more weeks until the semester ends, then the holidays will come and go, and then I'll be on a plane to Puerto Rico.

Too bad I'm only prepared for two out of those three things.

12

WILLOW

I'm not fully sure why I didn't expect the crowd to be going wild at this game when I originally agreed to meet Isla Johnson here, but I quickly learned my lesson. After all, why would the crowd be quieter when it's the last hockey game of the semester?

The bleachers are packed. People are on their feet already and the puck hasn't even dropped yet. Students in face paint scream across the rink and I hear chants that sound like, "Let's Fucking Go, Red Wolves." I do a double take when I see someone waving a giant cardboard cutout of my brother's head.

What the actual fuck?

But you know what? Hell yeah.

Funny how I've avoided anything hockey related for years, and now I've been to two hockey games in less than a month.

"Willow!" I somehow hear Isla's voice and finally spot her waving from the media section. I make my way toward her and only have to dodge one guy whose beer sloshes dangerously close to me.

"This is insane," I say as I slide in beside her. She's got some of her camera gear spread out and I make sure not to disturb her process. "I thought Senior Night was ridiculous."

"This is nothing." Isla laughs, adjusting her camera lens. "Wait until playoffs. Dad told me it makes these regular season games look like a cakewalk." She checks her settings, then looks up at me. "Thanks for coming here to meet up."

"No problem," I say, though my body language probably screams otherwise. "I had nothing better to do anyway, and this will allow me to add a few finishing touches to the article."

That's a lie. I have plenty to do like packing for winter break, finishing two papers, avoiding thinking about Blaise. I will say that being this close to the action due to Isla's position is pretty neat though.

"I'll make sure to get you some great shots of the seniors for the article, and I can share their official head-shots," Isla says, lifting her camera to snap a test shot of the ice. "So, article's almost done then?"

"Yeah, just a few tweaks." I fiddle with my press badge, turning it over in my hands. "Got all the quotes I needed besides you and Coach Johnson."

"Dad's probably going to just end up emailing you his. But I can give you one. I'm honored you asked since I've only been the team photographer for the last couple of months."

Hearing that Coach Johnson would more than likely email me when I was told I would get a quote from him here is slightly annoying, but I understand how busy he is. At least this wouldn't be a complete waste. "I wanted a different perspective. Most wouldn't even think to interview the team photographer. Which is weird because I figure you'll probably know a whole bunch of things the guys don't realize you know. Not that you'll say anything negative."

Isla's smile grows. "Oh, I definitely see things they'd die if they knew I noticed. Including their little rituals and stuff, but I'll keep those quiet. For the article, though...I guess I will say it's fascinating to watch how they are very much different people, but move as a unit. Does that make sense?"

"I understand what you're saying, but can you please elaborate?"

Isla lowers her camera and looks at me. "They're so different in real life from one another. Knox is bad boy personified, Levi is the leader, Wilder is pure chaos, Asher is the backbone of the team, and Blaise is so precise that it hurts. But when they hit the ice, it's like they share one brain. They anticipate each other's movements before they happen."

I nod, scribbling her words in my notebook. This is exactly the kind of insight I was looking for.

"There was this moment last game," she continues, adjusting her lens again as the teams begin skating onto the ice. "Blaise didn't even look before making this ridiculous blind pass directly to Knox. Like he just knew exactly where Knox would be. That kind of connection is rare and I've photographed other sports games too."

My pen pauses at Blaise's name, but I keep my face neutral. "That's good. Really good, actually."

"Thanks," Isla says, lifting her camera as the crowd roars for the starting lineup introductions. "I've been thinking about doing a photo essay on team dynamics for my final project next semester."

The announcer's voice flows through the speakers as she introduces the visiting team first. I use the moment to jot down a few more notes, trying to focus on the article and not on the way my stomach tightens when the announcer calls Blaise's name and number.

"Got any other insights for the article?" I ask Isla, dragging my attention back to my notebook.

She's about to answer when her phone buzzes. "Sorry, it's Bailey. I need to check this."

While Isla checks her message, I scan the rink, watching the players as they prepare for the game. I do my best to look anywhere but at Blaise, and I have to admit I fail several times. Their warmups are entertaining to say the least, and I'm slightly irritated when Isla's voice directs my attention away from what is occurring in front of me.

"Shit," Isla mutters, looking up from her phone.

"What's wrong?"

"Bailey wants me to meet her near the media entrance after the game. Apparently there's someone she wants me to connect with about some content creators? I was hoping to just head back to my dorm and go to bed."

"Why content creators?"

"Bailey's on some mission to boost our social media presence," Isla says, sounding less than thrilled. "We've been doing more on social media with short form content. It's working, so they want to step it up a notch I guess."

"That makes sense," I say. Bailey is smart for pushing that angle. Sports content thrives on social media, especially hockey. "Is there anything I can help with?"

Isla shakes her head, already refocusing her camera as the players take their positions. "I'll handle it. Just another thing on my ever-growing to-do list."

The referee skates to center ice, puck in hand. Before I can stop myself, I'm leaning forward as the anticipation around what is about to go down increases. And just like that, the game begins.

I find myself tracking Knox and Blaise...the latter without meaning to. I pull out my phone to take a few pictures of Knox for my family. Mom and Abue would be proud that I showed up to a game without them trying to convince me to do so. Plus it forces me to only watch my older brother instead of following number thirty-three.

For someone who's supposedly been avoiding hockey, I'm weirdly invested in this game within minutes. The crowd's energy is infectious, and I find myself holding my breath when Knox takes a shot that pings off the crossbar.

"Damn it!" I mutter, surprising myself with how much I care.

Isla laughs without looking away from her viewfinder. "Don't worry, they'll get one soon. They always start a little slow."

She's right. Five minutes later, Levi threads a perfect pass to Asher who buries it in the net. The crowd erupts, and I'm on my feet before I realize what I'm doing. Isla's camera clicks rapidly beside me, capturing the celebration.

"Told you," she says with a grin.

The first period flies by, and I find myself actually enjoying the game. When Blaise absolutely levels an opposing player who was charging toward our goal, I catch myself nodding before remembering I'm supposed to be indifferent.

"That's going to make a great shot," Isla says, reviewing something on her camera. "Look at this."

She tilts the screen toward me, showing a perfectly timed photo of Blaise mid-hit, his expression intense and focused. Something twists in my stomach.

"Nice," I manage to say before looking away quickly. The last thing I want is for her to pick up on...anything.

The second period brings more intensity and stress for me. Knox scores on a breakaway that has the crowd losing their minds, and even I can't help but yell. My brother's celebration is pure joy, and I swear seeing him this happy almost brings tears to my eyes.

Not that I would ever admit that to him.

"Your brother's having a hell of a game," Isla says, snapping away.

"Yeah, he is."

During a break in play, Isla sets her camera down and stretches her arms above her head. "So, any other questions for the article while we've got a minute?"

I grab my pen and notebook again to take notes. "What's your favorite part of being the team photographer?" I ask. "Something that surprised you about the role?"

"I like capturing the quiet moments, actually. Everyone sees the goals, the big hits, the celebrations. But there's this...intimacy to the moments no one else notices. Like when a player's sitting alone, getting in the zone before a game."

I scribble this down, nodding. "That's perfect."

"Oh, and another thing—" Isla starts, but the buzzer sounds, ending the intermission. She quickly lifts her camera again as the players skate back onto the ice. "I'll tell you after."

The third period is pure chaos. The opposing team scores twice in quick succession, tying the game and sucking all the energy from the crowd. I find myself gripping the edge of my seat.

"Come on," I whisper as Knox narrowly misses a shot.

With two minutes left, Blaise intercepts a pass at our blue line and immediately fires it up the ice to Levi. The crowd rises to their feet as Levi fakes out a defenseman and slides the puck to Asher, who slams it into the net.

The arena explodes. I'm jumping up and down, screaming with everyone else. Isla captures it all, her camera clicking furiously as the guys pile onto Asher along the boards.

"HOLY SHIT, ASHER! That's game!" she shouts over the noise. It's easy to see how proud she is of her boyfriend, let alone the whole team. Her hands fly to her cheeks as her eyes dart from me to the ice and back again. "Unless they do something stupid in the next minute."

They don't. When the final buzzer sounds, I'm genuinely disappointed the game is over. I watch as the players congratulate each other, tapping helmets and gloves.

"I should go get some shots of them heading to the locker room," Isla says, gathering her equipment. "Want to come? We can try to grab those quotes from Dad after, but I make no promises. And then I have to meet with the content creators Bailey mentioned."

"Sure," I say, surprising myself with how quickly I agree. "Lead the way."

Both Isla and I pack our things and then I follow her through the crowd, down a set of stairs, and into a corridor I've never seen before. The hallway is narrow, lined with concrete walls painted red and white with bright fluorescent lights.

Isla flashes her media badge at a security guard who nods us through. "They'll be coming off the ice any minute."

We position ourselves along the wall where the hallway widens slightly. Isla lifts her camera, ready to capture the players as they file past. "Here they come," Isla whispers, and sure enough, I hear the distinctive sound of skate guards clicking against the floor.

Asher comes through first, his expression breaking into a wide grin when he spots Isla. He makes his way toward us and leans down to press a quick kiss on her cheek. "Hey, sunshine. Get any good shots?"

"Only about three hundred of you looking like a hero," she replies.

Asher notices me standing awkwardly beside her. "Willow? Didn't expect to see you down here."

"Just getting some final quotes for the article. That final shot was incredible," I explain, hoping he doesn't pick up on how nervous I actually am.

"It was nothing," Asher says with a self-deprecating

laugh. "That pass from Levi was ridiculous. I just had to not miss."

More players walk past us, some nodding when they see Isla with her camera at the ready. Knox emerges next, his hair plastered to his forehead with sweat. When he spots me, his eyebrows shoot up.

"Twice in one month? Who are you and what have you done with my sister?" he asks.

Touché. "Just doing my job," I reply, lifting my bag. "Great game, by the way."

"Thanks." He looks genuinely pleased at the compliment. "You sticking around after?"

"For a bit. Need to talk to Coach Johnson if I can."

Knox nods, then looks past me as more players emerge. "I'll be out in fifteen. Don't disappear." As he walks away, I turn to look at Isla, but she's busy chatting with Asher and taking more photos. It's then I feel like someone is watching me. I look slightly to my left and find Blaise standing there. Our eyes lock for a moment that stretches for far too long in my opinion. Much like Knox, his hair is damp with sweat and there's a fresh red mark along his jawline from what must have been a high stick that didn't get called. My throat goes dry.

Fuck. That's the last thing I should be thinking when it comes to my brother's best friend who rejected me years ago.

13

WILLOW

I manage to push those thoughts to the back of my mind and straighten my shoulders. I'm prepared for whatever he's going to throw at me.

"Sanchez," he says.

"Dalton," I reply.

"Here to complete your article or to write another one?"

"Same one. Sports isn't my beat." I resist the urge to fidget with my bag. "Congratulations on the win."

"Thanks," he says, but his blue eyes say a whole lot more. They stay locked on mine for another beat before he gestures to the mark on his jaw. "Worth it, though."

I find myself nodding before I can stop myself. "That hit you laid out in the second period was...impressive."

The corner of his mouth twitches slightly. "You actually watched the game?"

"Hard not to when I'm sitting in the media section."

"Right," he says, running his free hand through his damp hair. "Journalism duties."

The hallway feels smaller suddenly. I'm also very aware of how close we're standing and what this could look like if the wrong person walked up on us. Not to mention I'm supposed to hate him.

Supposed to? I do.

Blaise opens his mouth to say something else when a burst of laughter echoes down the hallway. We both turn to see Wilder making his way to the locker room.

"Anyway," I say quickly, desperate to end whatever moment was building between us. "I should let you go. You probably want to shower."

His eyes widen slightly at my comment, and I immediately want to crawl into a hole. "I mean—you know—after the game—" I stammer. *Calm the fuck down, Wills.*

"I know what you meant," he says, and there's that twitch at the corner of his mouth again. Not quite a smile, but something close to it.

"Dalton!" Coach Johnson's voice bounces off the walls but it's coming from further down the hallway. "Need you for a minute."

Blaise nods in acknowledgment, then turns back to me. "See you around."

"Yeah," I get out and I do everything in my power to stop myself from watching as he walks away.

What the hell was that? One minute I'm enjoying

hockey like a normal person, which is weird in itself. And the next I'm...what? Noticing the way sweat makes Blaise's hair curl slightly at the nape of his neck? Pathetic.

"Earth to Willow," Isla's voice cuts through my thoughts.

I jump because she's standing beside me, and I hadn't heard her approach.

"Fine," I say too quickly. "Perfectly fine."

"Uh...okay," Isla says. "Bailey should be here soon with whoever this content creator is. I'm hoping it won't take long."

I nod, grateful for the change of topic. I'm glad she doesn't know me as well as Ari does because she would have given me the third degree. "Maybe I can catch Coach Johnson before he gets too wrapped up in post-game stuff."

"Good luck with that." Isla laughs. "Dad's probably already deep in stats and game footage. But we can try."

We start walking toward the coaching offices when I hear a familiar voice that makes my blood run cold.

"...and the engagement numbers would be insane. Hockey content is blowing up right now."

I freeze mid-step. That voice. I'd recognize it anywhere.

Leo Kent. Why the fuck is he here again?

I turn slowly, hoping I'm wrong, but there he is, coming down the hallway with Bailey. Leo's frame fills the space, and if you didn't know different, you would think he was another player on the team. His signature smile plastered across his face as he gestures animatedly while talking. He hasn't seen me yet.

"Oh," Isla says beside me, her voice dropping. "That must be the content creator Bailey was talking about."

My stomach plummets. "Leo Kent?"

"You know him?" Isla asks, glancing between us.

Before I can answer, Bailey spots us and waves enthusiastically. "Isla! Perfect timing. This is Leo Kent. He's a gaming streamer with a huge following. Leo, this is Isla Johnson, our photographer."

Leo's eyes slide past Isla and land directly on me. His smile doesn't falter, but something cold flashes in his gaze. I think back to when he approached me at the Senior Night game and nausea fills my body again.

"Willow," Leo says. I hate the way he says my name. "What a surprise to see you here."

"Leo." I keep my voice flat, devoid of emotion. He will not get a rise out of me. He will not get a rise out of me. He will not—

Bailey looks between us, her eyebrows rising. "You two know each other?"

"We go way back," Leo says before I can respond. The implication in his tone makes my skin crawl.

I force myself to maintain eye contact. "Not that far back."

Isla shifts beside me, and I know she's curious about

what is going on. Guess I'm going to have to fill her in later.

"Leo's going to be collaborating with some of the players on content," Bailey explains, oblivious to the tension bouncing between us. "Gaming streams, behind-the-scenes stuff. We're hoping it'll boost our social media presence."

It's then that it clicks for me that this is the reason he was here during Senior Night. He was here on business. Interesting.

"Sounds great," I manage to say although the words taste bitter. "I should go find Coach Johnson for that quote."

"Actually," Leo says, taking a step closer, "I'd love your input on this, Willow. You always had such...creative ideas."

The way he emphasizes "creative" makes me want to scream. Or vomit. Or both.

"I'm sure Bailey has everything covered," I say, backing up slightly. "And I really need to finish this article."

Before anyone can respond, the locker room door swings open. Knox emerges, followed by Blaise. They both stop short when they see the group assembled in the hallway.

Knox's eyes narrow instantly when they land on Leo. The look in his eyes tells me he's about to go from zero to hundred in two point five seconds flat. "Kent. What are you doing here?"

Leo's smile doesn't falter. "Just talking business with Bailey," he says as he extends his hand toward Knox. "Congrats on the win tonight."

Knox ignores the offered hand, stepping closer to me instead. The protective big brother mode is in full effect. His jaw clenched tight enough that I can see a muscle twitching.

"Thanks," Knox says coldly, positioning himself subtly between Leo and me. "Bailey, what's this about?"

"The athletic department approved my proposal to boost our social media presence. Leo has an impressive following online, and we're discussing potential collaborations with the team," Bailey offers.

"With the team," Knox repeats. "As in us?"

"Several players, yes," Bailey continues. "Gaming streams, day-in-the-life content. His demographic overlaps perfectly with our target audience."

I catch the way Blaise's eyes flick between Leo and me as if he's trying to figure out what's going on. But he doesn't say a word.

"I should get going," I say, desperate to escape this situation. "Isla, I'll text you later about those photos. And I'll shoot Coach Johnson an email." The quicker I leave, the less likely Knox is to throw a punch.

"Thanks for stopping by, Willow. Isla, we have some details to work out, but that's basically the gist of what I was thinking," Bailey says before glancing at her phone.

"Leo and I need to nail down a schedule with some of the players. Knox, I'd love your input."

"I'll pass," Knox says flatly, not taking his eyes off Leo. "I need to talk to Coach about this."

"Come on, Sanchez. Let's keep it professional. This is a great opportunity for the team's exposure," Leo says with a smirk.

"I said I'll pass." Knox's warning is evident in his tone. "I'm going to talk to Coach about this first."

"Coach was okay with it as long as it didn't interfere with what you guys were doing on the ice or with your studies. This wouldn't start until next semester," Bailey adds.

I can see that she's trying to ease the tension, but it doesn't do a thing.

Out of the corner of my eye, I see Blaise shifts toward to Knox which means he closer to me now. It's as if he's preparing to intervene if needed. His movement is enough to get me to make my feet move. "Good night, everyone."

I break apart from the group and walk away. I'm several feet away when two people flank me on my left and right. With a quick glance, I confirm it's Knox and Blaise. Outside of what just happened, I kind of like having what looks like two bodyguards escorting me away from that shitshow.

"I can handle myself," I mutter just loud enough for the two men next to me to hear.

"Never said you couldn't," Knox replies. "But I'm not letting that asshole anywhere near you if I can help it."

"What's the deal with that guy?" Blaise finally asks.

Knox's jaw tightens further. "Ask Willow."

"It's nothing," I say quickly, picking up my pace. "Ancient history."

"Bullshit," Knox says. "That guy's a manipulative piece of—"

"I don't want to talk about it," I cut him off. "Not now. Not here."

We reach the end of the hallway, and I stop, turning to face them both. "I'm heading back to my dorm. You two can go back to...whatever."

Knox studies my face. "You sure you're okay?"

"I'm fine," I lie. "Just tired. It's been a long day."

"I'll walk you to your car," Knox offers, but I shake my head.

"Seriously, I'm good. Go celebrate your win. I'll text you tomorrow."

Knox hesitates, then pulls me into a quick, tight hug. I can't remember the last time we gave one another a hug. "Fine. But we're talking about this Leo thing later. I don't like him being this close to you or the team."

"Trust me, neither do I," I say against his shoulder before pulling away.

"I'll make sure Coach knows about this," Knox says, his voice taking on that determined edge I recognize all too well. "And Bailey. This collaboration or whatever isn't happening."

"Good luck with that," I say, adjusting my bag on my shoulder. "Bailey seemed pretty set on it and thinks it's a great idea."

Knox shrugs. "We'll see about that."

"Well," I say, turning so that my back is to the exit and then taking a step backward. "Congrats again on the win. I should go."

"Thanks. Text me when you get home," Knox responds.

I roll my eyes. "Yes, Dad. I will." Then I glance at Blaise before shifting my gaze to some random spot in the hallway. "I'll see you in Puerto Rico, I guess."

"Guess so," Blaise says quickly.

I wait a beat for him to say something else, but he doesn't.

I give a small nod and turn on my heel and leave the Red Wolves' arena. I replay the scene that happened just a few minutes ago three times on my walk to my car. Once I'm safely inside my vehicle, I lock the doors and rest my forehead on the steering wheel.

Ari isn't going to believe this shit.

14

WILLOW

The last few weeks have been...weird. Finals ended in a blur, and winter break has mostly been a mix of sleeping too much, feeling way too much, and pretending everything's totally fine. I've barely left the house and don't feel an ounce of guilt about it. My mom says it's normal burnout. I say it's what happens when your brain doesn't come with an off switch.

Now I'm at the airport, about to fly to Puerto Rico with a bunch of people I don't really know. The only thing that's making me nervous other than the trip itself is the fact that I'm going to be in close proximity to Blaise Dalton without my brother or any of his hockey teammates to be a buffer.

"Are you sure you didn't forget anything?"

While I'm grateful my mother's question brought my thoughts back to present day, I roll my eyes because I can't help it. It's the fifth time I've been asked this question and my answer still hasn't changed. "Mom, I triple-checked everything. And if I somehow forgot something, they have stores in Puerto Rico. Plus we're already at the airport. There isn't much I can do about it now."

She gives me a look. "I'm just making sure you're prepared, Wills."

"I know." I soften my tone. "But I've got this. Promise. You don't need to worry." I lean down to hug her and inhale her favorite perfume. For all my eye-rolling, I'm going to miss her. This is our prepping for what it's going to be like when I'm gone this summer due to my internship in New York City.

"Moms always worry, but I'm so proud of you for doing this."

"I'm proud of me too." And that wasn't a lie.

"Text me when you land," she says into my hair. "And every day after that."

"I will." I pull back and check the time on my phone. "I should go through security."

Dad steps forward then, having been silent during most of Mom's fussing over me. He wraps me in a quick, firm hug. "Have fun, kiddo. Learn something interesting."

"That's the plan." I smile up at him, grateful for his straightforward approach. If he became mushy over my departure, I knew it would be game over for me keeping any tears back.

With one last wave, I turn and head toward the TSA

line. The morning crowd isn't terrible, but there's still a decent number of people waiting to go through security. I take my place at the end of the line and pull out my phone to distract myself.

Two unread texts from Ari:

> Ari: Have the best time! Send pics of hot men!
>
> Ari: But not to your mom. She'll worry.

I smile and type back a quick response.

> Me: Just got to security. Will send pictures of buildings and food, not men.

I'm still smiling at my phone when I look around and spot Blaise. And he isn't alone.

He's standing with an older woman a ways away from security. If I had to guess, she is probably in her seventies and has her silver hair pulled into an elegant twist. I'm thoroughly impressed with her posture because it's impeccable. Not to mention she looks stunning in her navy-blue tailored wool coat.

Blaise continues to lean down, giving her his full and undivided attention. His entire demeanor has softened, the rigid control he normally maintains is nowhere to be found. He's gesturing with his hands as he explains something to the woman in front of him. My first thought is that she must be his grandmother, but I don't want to assume.

She reaches up and gently touches his cheek, her expression full of affection. Blaise's shoulders visibly relax under her touch and he smiles softly at her. This is a Blaise I've never seen. Not the guarded hockey player, not the focused student, not even the guy who'd kissed me senseless years ago and then acted like I was invisible. This is someone open and it's throwing me completely off balance and I'm sure it won't be for the last time on this trip.

The woman says something else before she gives his arm a final squeeze and then gestures toward the security line. He says one last thing before he gives her a big hug, then turns and starts walking my way.

My heart jumps into my throat and I quickly look down at my phone. It's easier to pretend to be engrossed in Ari's texts than to explain why I was staring him down. The line moves, and I move forward with my eyes still glued to my phone screen. I haven't read a single word, but he doesn't need to know that.

When I finally dare to glance up, he's just a few people behind me in the line and I notice that his expression is back to its usual neutral mask. But I saw how he reacted to that woman. I saw that other side of him, and now I can't unsee it.

Instead of the usual irritation I feel when he's around,

a different emotion flickers to life: curiosity. And I hate myself for thinking that.

Thankfully, I get through security without incident. I do my best to quickly gather my belongings and head toward the gate, deliberately not looking to see if Blaise is following even though I know we will meet up eventually.

I find our gate easily enough. It's less crowded than I expected, but then again, it's early. Several students wearing Crestwood hats and sweatshirts already sit near the windows. I recognize a few faces from the orientation, but no one I know well.

I spot Professor Wallace and someone I assume is another professor, standing near the gate agent's desk. She has some papers in her hand, and I guess she's trying to get us organized, which sounds like hell. She's wearing a button-down white shirt, jeans, a blazer, and sneakers. I wait until she walks back over to the group of students to greet her.

"Good morning, Professor."

Professor Wallace turns and a small, professional smile appears on her face when she sees me. "Willow, good morning. Glad you made it alright." She makes a note on the sheet of paper she has, and I assume it's to mark me as being present.

"Traffic wasn't too bad, thankfully," I reply, trying to sound more awake and upbeat than I feel.

"Excellent." She gestures with her head to the group of students. "Almost everyone's here, just waiting on a few stragglers. Find a seat, get comfortable. We should be boarding in about forty-five minutes."

"Thanks." I nod and immediately start scanning for somewhere, well anywhere, that isn't in the middle of the group. My social battery is already circling the drain and we haven't even boarded yet. There's a spot near a set of tables and chairs that allow you to hangout while charging your devices that looks inviting. It's not too close to everyone else, but close enough to hear if Professor Wallace decides to start yelling.

Looks perfect to me.

I sink into the seat, drop my backpack to the floor, and pull out my phone along with my EarPods. If I'd forgotten them, I knew I would have been on my knees begging Mom to overnight them to me because I need them like I need a security blanket. They help me shield myself from the general public because it's the universal signal that I want to be left alone.

I pop them in my ears and find myself scrolling through post after post on social media. I've come across a meme. An engagement announcement. An ad for skin-care I Googled once in 2022 and haven't stopped seeing since. But if I'm being honest with myself, I'm not reading or absorbing a thing. That's cause my brain's somewhere else entirely and it's circling around Blaise Dalton.

He was...different with her.

Gentle. Calm. And not that he isn't that way usually, but I could see that he treated her differently than everyone else. And it's not that I'm jealous of how and why he acted this way, it's just fascinating. Like whatever she said deserved his full attention, and he gave it without hesitation.

I look up and find the subject in question standing next to Professor Wallace. It looks like he also came through security unscathed. Good for him.

He's nodding at something Professor Wallace is saying and I can see that he's back to being "on". I quickly look away when his gaze starts to drift in my direction.

The last thing I need is for him to catch me staring.

I pull up my Spotify and hit play on a playlist I made specifically for this trip, but the music feels like background noise because my brain is so fucking loud. It's always like this. Many people think ADHD means I can't focus, but really it's that I'm focusing on *everything*. It's just not always on what I'm supposed to. Like I'll be listening to music, sure, but also thinking about how I forgot to reply to that email from three days ago, and whether I packed deodorant, and how I accidentally ghosted my therapist, and oh right, how Blaise looked soft for half a second and now my nervous system's acting like it's a national emergency.

It's exhausting.

Like trying to organize your thoughts while someone's throwing tennis balls at your head. Which are on fire.

I try a breathing exercise I saw on my feed a couple of days ago. In through the nose, hold, out through the—

Nope. Just made me more aware of how dry my mouth is.

I open my notes app and start to type something, hell anything, to get out of my head. Maybe a rough idea for an article I can write when we get back to Crestwood, but I only get as far as "remember to" before my fingers stop moving.

Because now Blaise is sitting down two rows across from me. Not next to me. Not near enough to talk. But enough that I can see him in my peripheral vision if I tilt my head slightly.

And of course, the second I think that, I *do* tilt my head. Slightly.

He's got his phone out and he's not paying me any mind. I try to read his expression, to get a glimpse of what he might be thinking, but I end up with nothing.

And because the universe clearly wants me to die of embarrassment, he glances up from his phone.

This time I don't look away fast enough.

15

BLAISE

You know that moment where you try to ignore something that has drawn you in to the point where everything else fades into the background? That's me right now because it's impossible for me not to notice her.

Willow is two rows away from me, and somehow she's the only person or thing I'm drawn to in this airport terminal. Everything else, including the announcements being made by the different airlines, a kid throwing a tantrum by the vending machines, even Professor Wallace calling out names to make sure that we're all here, all blurs into white noise.

Her dark hair is pulled back in a ponytail, and she keeps tucking loose strands behind her ear. A nervous habit I've noticed before. She's wearing headphones, probably to stop anyone from approaching her, but I can tell she's not really concentrating on what's playing through her speakers by the way her eyes keep darting around. She's always alert, always observing her surroundings.

This is dangerous territory. I shouldn't be memorizing the way she fidgets with her phone case or how she crosses and uncrosses her ankles. I definitely shouldn't remember that she smells like vanilla and coffee or wonder if that scent would intensify if I sat closer.

Knox would kill me if he knew how much mental real estate his sister occupies in my brain. The irony is, he's the one who put her there in the first place. He's the one who asked me over the holiday break to keep an eye on her while we were in Puerto Rico. Not like babysit her, per se, but just to make sure she's okay. I said of course I would. And now that request seems anything but simple.

I force myself to look down at my phone and click on a random email just to have something else to focus on. I quickly realize it's an old email from my political science professor confirming receipt of my final paper from last semester. I can try to review some old videos tapes that Coach asked me to look at, but it's pointless. I've already watched them multiple times. No matter how hard I try to concentrate on something else, my attention drifts back to her.

I shouldn't be studying the curve of her neck when she tilts her head or noticing how she chews her bottom lip when she's deep in thought. I definitely shouldn't be wondering what she's listening to, or if she's thinking about this trip, or if she's as aware of me as I am of her.

This isn't just inappropriate. It's a betrayal because Knox trusts me. He's my best friend, practically my brother. And here I am, unable to stop watching his sister like a stalker.

I've spent years building walls between us. Creating distance. Maintaining boundaries. All so I wouldn't have to confront whatever this pull is that keeps drawing me back to her. And now we're about to spend a week together in Puerto Rico, where those barriers are going to be tested every single day.

I run a hand through my hair, exhaling slowly. Get it together, Dalton. She's off-limits for a dozen different reasons if not more. The fact that she hates me should be reason enough. The fact that Knox would never forgive me is another. The fact that I pulled away from her that night and hurt her should be the final nail in the coffin.

But still, my gaze drifts back to her because I'm drawn to her like a moth to a flame. The fire that burns so bright within her is just the tip of the proverbial iceberg. I know there's more going on beneath that tough exterior she shows to the world. If things were different, I'd beg her to let me explore it and everything else with her, but alas, it can't be. It never will be.

This time when she looks up, our eyes meet.

She doesn't look away.

Neither do I.

It's only a few seconds, but it lands harder than I expect. There's no expression on her face, at least nothing obvious, anyway, but something passes between us. And I can't quite name what it is.

"Attention passengers for Flight 1372 to San Juan, we will begin boarding in approximately ten minutes."

The announcement cuts through all of my thoughts and brings me back to reality. I glance around and notice Professor Wallace gesturing for everyone to gather closer. I grab my things and make my way over to the group that's forming.

"Alright, everyone," she calls out. "Let's do one final headcount before we board. When I call your name, please raise your hand."

As Professor Wallace begins calling names, I deliberately position myself with my back to Willow. Out of sight, out of mind. Except that's never worked with her, has it?

"Blaise Dalton?"

I raise my hand. "Here."

Professor Wallace nods and continues down her list. I keep my eyes fixed on her clipboard, refusing to let my gaze wander again.

"Willow Sanchez?"

I hear a, "Here," from behind me. I resist the urge to look over my shoulder and give myself a small, mental pat on the back for my efforts. Once the roll call is complete, Professor Wallace gives us our boarding instructions.

We'll be boarding in groups, with her going first to make sure everything is set with the gate agents.

"Remember, you'll be sitting according to your assigned seats," she says. "If you have any issues, please see me before we board."

People begin to move back to their seats to gather their belongings. I take my time, making sure I won't accidentally bump into Willow in the process.

As I'm checking my carry-on, making sure I have everything I need for the flight, Professor Wallace approaches me.

"Blaise, do you have a moment?"

"Of course," I reply, straightening up.

"I wanted to check if you received the email about the room assignments?" she asks.

"Yes, I did. I'm rooming with Tyler Chesterfield, right?" I should probably introduce myself to him at some point.

She nods. "That's correct. I just wanted to make sure since a few students mentioned they hadn't received the information. You'll also be sitting next to him on the plane. Alphabetical order and all of that."

"Okay. All good on my end," I assure her.

"Excellent." She glances down at her clipboard. "Thank you for also offering to help if necessary."

"No problem," I tell her. "Just let me know if you need anything and I'll be happy to help."

As Professor Wallace walks away, the gate agent begins talking into the intercom once more. "Now boarding

Flight 1372 to San Juan. We'll begin with our premium passengers and those needing special assistance..."

My heart immediately kicks into overdrive. This is the last thing I needed to have happen before I got on this flight.

ID. I need my driver's license.

I check my back pocket and don't find my wallet there. Then, I unzip the front pocket of my carry-on, fingers fumbling with the zipper. It's there, right next to my wallet which is where I put it after I got through security. I touch it, feel its edges, then zip the pocket closed again. Check my phone to double check I have my ticket readily accessible. In case that fails, I printed out a copy that's in my folder with the trip's itinerary and other documents.

My chargers are in the side compartment. The medications I take are in the toiletry bag.

I unzip another pocket, check the contents, zip it back. Unzip, check, zip. The ritual usually grounds me, but today it's not working. My knee starts bouncing uncontrollably, but it's one way to get the nervous energy out of my body.

"Group A can now begin boarding."

My mouth goes dry. I'm in the next group. I should stand up, but my legs feel weighted. I run through the list again: Driver's license - front pocket; Chargers - side compartment; Medication - toiletry bag.

My hands are trembling now, making the simple act of

zipping my bag closed again nearly impossible. I take a deep breath in an effort to try to slow my racing heart, but it doesn't work.

Then I think about what Mom said when she dropped me off at the airport this morning. "You'll be fine," she'd whispered, and I'd nodded, pretending to believe her. Pretending I wasn't actually nervous about this trip.

"Group B, please have your boarding passes ready."

I stand and sling my bag over my shoulder. My body feels heavier than normal as I find a place to stand in the boarding line. Passport front pocket. Chargers side compartment. Medication toiletry bag. The mantra repeats, but my anxiety only intensifies. It feels as if I can't get enough air.

I unzip the front pocket again. Yes, my driver's license is still there. I zip it closed. Unzip. Check. Zip. My fingers won't stop trembling.

"Boarding pass, sir?"

I fumble with my phone, nearly dropping it as I pull up the QR code. The gate agent's smile feels like a spotlight on my failure to keep it together. She scans my pass and gestures me forward, but my feet have cinder blocks tied to them. Well, that's how it feels anyway.

"Have a nice flight."

I manage a tight nod and step into the jet bridge. My heart slams against my ribs, loud enough to me that I'm certain the people around me must hear it as well. Driver's license front pocket. Chargers side compartment. Medication toiletry bag. The ritual that normally anchors me feels useless now.

I reach the plane entrance. The flight attendant's practiced smile does nothing to calm me.

"Welcome aboard. 14C is on your left, about halfway down."

I nod and step into the cabin. It takes everything to force one foot in front of the other, and I can't stop double checking to make sure I didn't pass my seat until I reach it.

A guy, who I assume is Tyler Chesterfield, is already there, headphones on, staring out the window. He glances up, offers a quick nod, then returns to whatever he's listening to. I'll take that reaction because I have no desire to introduce myself right now. The middle seat is still open so I know I'll have to move so whoever is sitting there can get to their seat eventually.

I stow my bag in the overhead bin, and when I finally sink into my seat, I close my eyes and grip the armrests. Breathe. Just breathe.

People continue boarding, but I keep my eyes closed so that I can focus on my breathing and tune the movement around me out. In for four, hold for four, out for four. It's a technique my therapist taught me that rarely works when I'm this far gone.

"Excuse me? I need to get to that seat."

My eyes snap open. Willow stands in the aisle,

gesturing to the empty middle seat in our row. My brain short-circuits.

"Wait I thought...isn't seating assigned? In alphabetical order?" I manage to ask.

"It is." She shifts her weight as if she's nervous. Interesting. "But Professor Wallace said there was a mix up with my seat. Something about a family needing to sit together and since I was a late addition to the trip...."

"I...see," I say, though my brain is still processing what this means. I'm going to be sitting next to Willow Sanchez for the entire flight to Puerto Rico.

I stand up and put my hand out. "I can put your bag in the overhead bin."

She throws a look at me before she proceeds to lift her carry-on. "I can do it myself. Thanks."

"Fine." I step back, giving her space.

She struggles for a moment, but manages to get it in the overhead bin. I resist the urge to help anyway, knowing it would only irritate her more. When she finally slides into the middle seat, her arm brushes against mine, and I have to temper the warmth that flowed through me as a result.

"Thanks again," she mutters, though it sounds like she'd rather say anything else.

"No problem," I say quickly. I let out a long deep breath and close my eyes once more. The anxiety that was building in my body seems to have peaked and now is on a downward decline. The only thing I can think of is that Willow's presence is the cause.

And knowing that makes all the thoughts I've had about her so much worse.

Without a doubt, this is going to be a very long flight.

16

WILLOW

Sitting in the middle seat on a full flight is a unique kind of hell on Earth. but of course, since it's me, I end up right in the center of the inferno. Out of all the seats on this plane, of course I would be sitting next to him.

I'm going to be trapped between Tyler Chesterfield and Blaise Dalton for the next four hours. Many girls at Crestwood would die if they were in this predicament, yet I'm wondering if the same fate would take me out of my misery permanently. Tyler's already got his headphones on, blissfully unaware of my internal meltdown as he stares out the window. Blaise is pretending to read something on his phone, but I can feel the tension and awkwardness of this situation radiating off him.

This wasn't supposed to happen. My seat was supposed to be 28D, but when Professor Wallace pulled me aside at the gate, I had the feeling it would be due to something not going right.

"Ms. Sanchez, there's been a slight change to the seating arrangements," she'd said, adjusting her glasses. "A family with a young child needed to sit together, and since you were one of our last additions to the trip..."

I'd nodded, already dreading whatever was coming next.

"Your new seat is 14B, between Mr. Chesterfield and Mr. Dalton."

I'd almost laughed, because of course. Of course the universe would stick me next to my brother's best friend. And now I'm trying to wrap my brain around what I could have done to deserve this.

Now I'm hyperaware of every inch where my elbows might accidentally touch either of them. I've tucked myself in as tightly as possible, arms crossed, hoodie pulled down over my head. The middle seat has approximately six inches of personal space, and I'm determined to use every millimeter of it.

Tyler shifts in his seat, pressing his shoulder against the window and giving me an extra inch or two of space. Blaise, on the other hand, is grasping the armrest between us in a death grip. His knuckles are white, and I can't tell if it's from anxiety or from trying not to touch me.

Who am I kidding? It's the former.

When I shift my body slightly and let out a deep sigh, some of the tension shifts from my shoulders to my chest, particularly near my heart. To help combat it, I pull my phone out because I'm desperate for distraction. And with the way my luck is going, the flight attendant's voice crackles over the intercom.

"Please ensure all electronic devices are in airplane mode for takeoff."

Great. Even my digital escape route is blocked.

"You okay?" Blaise's voice is so quiet I almost think I imagined it.

"Fine," I mutter, not looking at him. "Just love being sandwiched between strangers for four hours."

"We're not exactly strangers," he points out.

"That makes it worse."

He doesn't respond to that, and I immediately regret what I said. It's not his fault Professor Wallace rearranged the seating. It's not his fault we're both here. It's not even his fault that my heart is racing from being this close to him.

The plane begins to taxi, and I swear my stomach is ready to leave my body. I hate takeoffs. Always have. I grip the edges of my seat as the engines roar louder.

"You can take the armrest," Blaise says suddenly.

I glance at him. "What?"

"The armrest. You can have it. Middle seat gets both armrests. It's the rule."

"There's a rule?" I ask, momentarily distracted from my takeoff anxiety.

"Unwritten airplane etiquette. Window gets the view,

aisle gets the legroom, middle gets both armrests. It's the only fair compensation."

Despite myself, I feel the corner of my mouth twitch. "Is that in the airline constitution somewhere?"

"Should be."

The plane accelerates down the runway, and I instinctively tense up. Without thinking, I grab the armrest and it's then that I quickly realize Blaise's hand is still there. His skin is warm against mine, and for a split second, neither of us moves a muscle.

Then I snatch my hand back like I've been burned.

"Sorry," I mumble, mortified because of what I've done.

"It's fine," he says, but he moves his hand away, giving me what I am owed.

The plane lifts off, and so does my stomach. I close my eyes, focusing on my breathing. In, out. In, out. Don't think about how you're in a metal tube hurtling through the sky. Don't think about the guy sitting next to you who's pretending this isn't awkward.

"Not a fan of flying?" Blaise asks after a moment.

"What gave it away?" I say through gritted teeth. "The fact that I'm barely breathing?"

"Yep."

I crack one eye open and find him watching me. One eyebrow is raised as if he's surprised by my reaction, but I'm disarmed by the fact that there is a certain amount of tenderness in his gaze. Something I haven't seen in years at this point.

"Takeoffs are the worst part," he offers. "Statistically speaking."

"Thanks for the reassurance," I say, but I'm not trying to be a complete asshole this time. "I'll be fine once we are in the sky."

Tyler moves again beside me, completely oblivious to our conversation as he continues to stare out the window. The plane finally reaches cruising altitude, and the seat-belt sign dings off. My death grip on the seat eases slightly.

"Better?" Blaise asks.

I nod, not trusting myself to speak. The fact that he noticed, that he cared enough to ask, is doing weird things to my insides that have nothing to do with turbulence.

"So," Blaise says after a moment, "did you get all your finals wrapped up okay?"

Small talk. He's making small talk. Which means either he's as uncomfortable as I am or he's taking pity on me. Neither option is particularly appealing.

"Yeah," I reply. "You?"

"More than okay," he says as he runs a hand through his blond hair. "Glad it's over, but also ready to jump back into things in a couple of weeks."

I nod as I reach for my EarPods, desperate for a wall between us. I pause when I realize how rude it is of me to put these in my ears while he's actively talking to me. The goal is now to complete the conversation so that I can have peace as quickly as possible.

"Same." I force myself to continue the conversation even though every cell in my body screams to escape it. "One more semester and then I'm done with my junior year."

"And then you have your internship in New York this summer."

The fact that he knows about it catches me off guard. "Knox told you?"

"He mentioned it." Blaise's eyes drop to his hands for a moment before returning to my face. "Sounds like a great opportunity."

"It is. A great learning opportunity that will hopefully lead to many more, including a job after graduation. Plus, it's a paid one so that's a relief."

"Paid internships are unicorns," Blaise says. "I spent last summer working for free at a political consulting firm. Great experience, terrible for my finances, but things are slowly getting better in terms of paying versus not paying interns."

"What about you?" I ask before I can stop myself. "Any post-graduation plans yet?"

"A few possibilities." He taps his fingers lightly against his thigh. "I'm hoping I get drafted, but I do have an interview with a think tank in D.C. when we get back. And Coach knows someone at the NHL Players' Association and there might be an opening there."

"Both sound very...you."

"What's that supposed to mean?"

"Structured. Strategic. Places where your color-coded notebooks would be appreciated."

This time he chuckles and it tickles my brain and other places. "You make me sound like a robot."

"Not a robot," I reply quickly. "Just...methodical."

Two flight attendants interrupt us because they're wheeling the beverage cart down the aisle. Tyler finally removes his headphones when one asks what he'd like to drink.

"Water, please," he says before immediately putting his headphones back on and returning to his window gazing.

"For you?" she asks me.

"Ginger ale, if you have it." My stomach's finally settled, but I'm not taking chances.

"Same," Blaise says when she turns to him.

The flight attendant hands us each our drinks, and I'm suddenly conscious of how I need to lower my tray table without accidentally elbowing Blaise in the process. I manage it with minimal awkwardness, though I feel him watching my movements carefully.

"Thanks again," I say as I give the flight attendant a small smile. Blaise does the same and then we sit in silence for a moment, both sipping our drinks. This is the perfect opportunity to put my EarPods in.

As I make a move to do so, Blaise speaks up. "How'd

the senior hockey spotlight article go? The one you interviewed me and the rest of the guys for?"

I hate that it takes me a few seconds to realize what
he's talking about, but this small talk with him is throwing
me for a loop. "It turned out well, actually. It got published
right before finals." I take a sip of my ginger ale. "My editor
said it was one of my strongest pieces."

"I'd like to read it sometime," he says. "When I have the
time, that is."

I tuck my hair behind my ear and shrug. "It's online.
Crestwood Chronicle website. Your quotes worked well
with the brotherhood angle I ended up going with."

He nods. "Brotherhood. That's...fitting."

I don't get a chance to ask him what he meant by that
because the plane hits a small pocket of turbulence. The
shift in tempo sends my ginger ale dangerously close to
the rim of the cup. I grip it tighter as I brace for another
bump that thankfully doesn't come.

"Sorry about that, folks," the captain's voice comes
through a couple of moments later. "Just a little turbulence. We should be through it shortly."

"Thank fuck for that," I whisper, but clearly it's not
low enough because Blaise chuckles and shakes his head.
As I'm about to plan what I should do next to entertain
myself, Tyler adjusts his position. His movement forces
me closer to Blaise, shrinking the already limited space
between us. Great. Now I'm practically wedged between
two human bookends with no room to breathe. I take

another sip of my ginger ale and try to focus on some-thing, anything, instead of how Blaise's arm is suddenly two inches closer to mine. Blaise doesn't say a word and neither do I.

The cabin lights dim slightly, and the flight attendants begin collecting trash. I hand over my empty cup and ignore the self-consciousness I feel as a result of having to pass my garbage over Blaise. Once that is out of the way, I finally grab my EarPods again and hope that music will drown out the static in my brain. I scroll through my playlists, unable to decide what would help most. Some-thing loud to block everything out? Something calm to settle my nerves? I can also start brainstorming new article ideas or stream a show if I so dare. My finger hovers indecisively over the screen as I wonder what to choose.

It's then I notice Tyler's head bobbing and realize he didn't try to give any trash to the flight attendants. I glance over to find his eyes closed, mouth slightly open. Great. He's asleep and he's slumped in a way that pushes me further into the middle, which means closer to Blaise.

I shift my body in an effort to reclaim my space without disturbing Tyler. I quickly find out that it's useless and it's only a matter of time before he'll be leaning on my shoulder.

"You can lean this way if you need to," Blaise says and I swear I almost jump out of my skin.

I look over at him briefly and say, "I'm fine," but I'm

not. I just don't want to have to deal with being even closer
to him on top of everything else.

I hit play on a random playlist and try to lose myself in
the music and ignore everything else around me. It
doesn't work. Instead of focusing on the lyrics, all I can
think about is how Blaise shifts in his seat every few
minutes and how his fingers occasionally drum against
his thigh as if he wants to get off this plane just as much as
I do. What I do appreciate is that he's not trying to crowd
me on this already space-constricting plane.

A memory flashes unbidden: Leo sitting next to me on
his couch, his arm slung possessively around my shoulders, fingers digging in just a little too tight. Always hovering, always controlling, always performing. Even when we
were alone.

Blaise shifts again beside me, and his elbow brushes
mine. He immediately pulls back, giving me space. The
contrast is so stark it makes my throat tight.

Leo never gave space. He took it.

No. I am not doing this. I am not comparing them. I'm
not thinking about either of them that way. However, my
thoughts return to Blaise when I watch him unbuckle his
seatbelt and rise to his feet.

I do my best to hide the fact that all my attention is on
him when I spot a sliver of skin peeking out from underneath his hoodie as he rifles through what I assume is his
bookbag in the overhead bin. It only takes him a minute
tops to pull a paperback out of his bag and settle back

down in his seat. When he starts reading, I find myself counting the seconds between each page turn. Seventeen. Twenty-two. Nineteen. Either he reads at an inconsistent pace, or I'm losing my mind.

Probably both.

I turn my attention back to my phone and try to find a podcast to listen to, but it irritates me more than anything. I return to music, something with a heavy bass that might help me drown out my thoughts. It doesn't work.

When I feel a tap on my left shoulder, I already know who it is. I take out one of my EarPods and say, "Yeah?"

"Are you always this restless?" Blaise asks quietly.

It takes me a second longer than it should to come up with a response. "Are you always this observant?" I toss back.

I can see a smile starting to form on his lips before he stops himself. "Occupational hazard. Defense means watching everything."

I don't know what to say to that, so I say nothing. I put my EarPod back in its rightful place and return to my phone, but my brain is still doing too much and not enough at the same time.

And we still have three more hours until Puerto Rico.

17

WILLOW

W hen my feet hit solid ground after being trapped on that plane from hours, I swear I could cry from the relief.

Not because I hate flying. I don't, besides having to deal with takeoff. However, being stuck in that middle seat for four hours and having to deal with Tyler's snoring and Blaise's existence? The latter I quickly left behind because I didn't want him to start up another conversation with me. I was starting to think this was a social experiment designed to test the last bit of my patience.

Not that I have any left. Especially now that twentyish students and two professors have to make their way to baggage claim in a completely different climate than we're used to in Virginia this time of year.

Yes, Puerto Rico isn't as warm this time of year as it is during other months, but it's warm enough for me to be thankful I stuck my winter coat in my checked luggage and decided a hoodie was all I needed until I got here. I take off said piece of clothing and tie it around my waist.

"Everyone!" Professor Wallace's voice is somehow louder than the airport announcements playing in both Spanish and English. "We'll proceed to baggage claim as a group, then board our shuttle to our hotel!"

I fall into step with the group, deliberately positioning myself near the back. The less social interaction required, the better. My brain feels like it's running on emergency power only. The faster I can get to my room, where it'll hopefully be just me and Madison Hollins for at least a couple hours so I can calm my nervous system down, the better. Of course, that's when someone laughs too loudly to my right. Another person is FaceTiming their parents already. Tyler is still half-asleep, and I watch as he almost stumbles into someone else who looks equally disoriented. I'm slightly jealous since I wasn't able to sleep at all on the plane and that would have helped tremendously.

"Hey, are you Willow?"

A girl with wavy blonde hair and warm brown eyes slides into step beside me as we follow the group toward baggage claim. She's wearing a Crestwood University sweatshirt and has an easy smile. Her vibe somehow doesn't irritate me on sight.

"Yeah, that's me." I give a small nod. "Apologies, but I don't know your name."

"Madison. Maddie for short." She extends her hand for

a quick shake. "I figured I should introduce myself before we're stuck sharing a hotel room for a week. Professor Wallace pointed you out."

I appreciate the directness. "Good call."

"I did want to let you know that I'm a morning person, but I promise not to be obnoxious about it," Madison says. "And as far as I know I don't snore, so there's that."

"Already better than Tyler on the plane," I mutter.

Madison laughs. "I heard him from three rows back with headphones on. I was impressed."

I find myself smirking at Madison's comment, which is a small miracle considering my current state. "Well, at least I know you'll be more tolerable than the guys I was sitting next to on the flight."

"First day of travel is always rough," Madison says, adjusting her backpack strap. "By tomorrow, you'll be living your best tropical life. Or at least that's what I keep telling myself."

We reach baggage claim and our group surrounds it. Professor Wallace and Professor Moore are still trying to maintain order, but it's clear everyone's exhaustion mixed with excitement is winning out.

"So what's your major?" Madison asks, staring down the empty carousel as if she has the ability to make our suitcases materialize.

"Journalism. You?"

"Mathematics." She tucks a strand of hair behind her ear.

That one word forces me to do a double take. It's as if someone threw a water balloon at my face. "I didn't know people actually majored in Math. That's not meant to be shady, but wow I'm blown away. That's amazing."

Madison laughs. "I get that reaction a lot. Math is cool when you really get into it."

"I'll take your word for it," I say, struggling to imagine anyone finding joy in the subject that gave me panic attacks throughout high school.

My attention is drawn to the baggage carousel because it starts turning. The first few suitcases start tumbling down the conveyor belt. When some of the students in our group move forward, Madison and I hang back slightly.

"So is this your first time in Puerto Rico?" Madison asks.

I nod as I watch the carousel for my suitcase. "I joined super last minute, but I'm so happy I did. At least I will be when we reach our hotel."

Her hand flies to her chest as her mouth drops open. "Same! I heard about the trip and applied the day the applications were due."

I spot a flash of familiar navy blue with a bright yellow luggage tag. "That's mine," I say, moving toward the carousel. I grab my suitcase, noticing immediately that there is a small tear on the handle. Hopefully it will keep itself together and won't be another thing I'll have to end up dealing with on this trip.

"Nice tag," Madison comments as I set my suitcase down. "Smart move. Everything looks the same otherwise."

"My mom's idea," I admit. "She's big on 'practical solutions to avoidable problems.'"

Madison points to a bright pink suitcase making its way around. "That one's mine. No tag needed when it looks like Barbie threw up on it."

I can't help but laugh as she retrieves her unmistakable luggage. She wasn't wrong.

"Everyone, once you have your bags, please gather by the exit doors!" Professor Wallace's voice cuts through the noise. "Our shuttle should be arriving momentarily!"

When we wrangle all of our things, our group steps outside and immediately gets hit with a wall of heat. It's not scorching by any means and I'm grateful that the humidity isn't that high here this time of year. I'm already regretting my choice of sweatpants for the flight and can't wait to change.

It takes a few minutes, but two white shuttles pull up to the curb and I assume these are our rides. Professor Moore gestures toward them with the enthusiasm of a tour guide on their first day.

"Group A in the first shuttle, Group B in the second, and Group C in the third! Your group assignments were in the email Professor Wallace and I sent yesterday!"

I pull out my phone to check which group I'm in while

trying to manage my suitcase without doing more damage to my handle.

"Group B," Madison says, peering over my shoulder at my phone. "Me too. Guess we're sticking together."

I nod, secretly relieved to have someone familiar beside me as we approach the second shuttle. It also means that if Blaise is on this shuttle, he won't be able to sit next to me. The driver, a middle-aged man with a friendly smile, hops out to help load our luggage.

"Bienvenidos!" he says, taking my suitcase. He doesn't take as much care with my handle as I would have, but I can't fault him for it when his job is to get us to our accommodations safely.

"Gracias," I say with a small smile.

Madison and I climb into the vehicle and find two seats in the middle of the bus. Madison slides in by the window, and I collapse next to her, my body finally registering just how exhausted I am. The air conditioning is blasting and I'm grateful for it.

"Look at that sky," Madison whispers, pointing out the window. "You don't get blue like that in Virginia."

She's right. Even through the tinted glass, the sky is a different kind of blue. The best way I can describe it is that it's deeper and more intense. It's absolutely stunning.

The shuttle fills up quickly. I spot Tyler coming aboard, looking much more awake than he did the last time I saw him. Still, he drops into a seat near the front, immediately leaning his head against the window. Poor guy.

Just as I'm thinking I might have escaped further awkwardness for the day, Blaise steps onto the shuttle. Because of course he does. Because the universe isn't done testing me yet.

He has a few choices about where he can sit, but he chooses the one directly across the aisle from me. Our eyes meet briefly before he looks away. I, in turn, force myself to stare out the window, pretending to be fascinated by the airport parking lot.

Someone at the front of the bus clears their throat and I look over to find Professor Wallace standing there. "Welcome, Group B! Our ride to the hotel should take about thirty minutes, depending on traffic. Once we arrive, you'll receive your room keys and have a couple of hours to freshen up before our welcome dinner at a local restaurant."

Two hours. One hundred and twenty minutes to shower, change, and try to become a functioning human being again. It doesn't seem like enough, but I guess it will have to do.

As the shuttle pulls away from the airport, I make sure to focus on the scenery outside of my window versus the man who decided to sit across from me. It feels like we've barely left the airport before I'm able to really pinpoint how much Puerto Rico differs from Virginia. The buildings aren't super tall, but they're bright and include many colors like peach, turquoise, and yellow. Some look freshly renovated, others are cracked and worn, but they still look very much a part of the same community. There's a bakery on one corner, a hardware store on the next, and a wall covered in a mural I only catch part of. It might have had waves and birds, but I blinked and it was gone.

"It's like a beautiful postcard, but better," Madison whispers beside me, her breath slightly fogging the window as she leans closer to get a better look at all of the sights.

"Exactly," I whisper before I'm hit with a thought. Why the hell am I not taking photos of what I'm seeing? I pull out my phone and start snapping photographs through the window. The colors, the buildings, the palm trees lining some of the streets. It all feels surreal after leaving the gray winter of Virginia behind just hours ago.

"You should put those on your socials," Madison suggests as she glances at my screen as I swipe through what I captured.

"I will and send them to my mom and Abue," I reply, snapping a few more.

The shuttle winds through the city, eventually turning onto a road that hugs the coastline. It takes another few minutes before the shuttle slows and turns onto a palm-lined driveway, and I quickly figure out we've arrived at the place we'll be staying for the week.

"This is really nice," Madison whispers as our driver parks the shuttle.

Professor Wallace stands and I know it's time for us to get more instructions. "We've arrived! Please collect your belongings and head to the reception area. Professor Moore will meet you there and will hand you your hotel keys."

Once we do what Professor Wallace says, I follow Madison toward the reception area, a breezy space with ceiling fans spinning lazily overhead and potted plants in every corner.

After a brief check-in process, I'm handed a key card with "Room 212" written on the paper sleeve.

"Looks like we're on the second floor," Madison says, flashing me her identical key. "Want to head up?"

I nod and start walking before I can say a word. We quickly find out that the hotel is arranged in a horseshoe shape around a central courtyard filled with plants and a small pool. Our room is on the second floor, accessible via an open-air walkway that overlooks the courtyard. When Madison unlocks the door, I'm happy at what we find.

The room is simple but beautiful. Two queen beds with crisp white linens, wooden furniture, and large windows that let in plenty of natural light. There's a small balcony with two chairs overlooking the ocean in the distance.

"Dibs on the bed by the window," Madison says, but I get the vibe that she'd switch with me if I asked.

"Take it," I reply, dropping my suitcase beside the other bed. "I prefer being closer to the bathroom anyway."

Speaking of which, the bathroom is small but clean, with a walk-in shower and toiletries lined up on a shelf. I'm already mentally preparing for how luxurious this shower is going to feel.

Madison flops onto her bed with a dramatic sigh. "I can't believe we're actually here."

"I know. It doesn't feel real yet," I say, unzipping my suitcase. It sticks for a moment before giving way. "I might unpack before I shower." And text Mom and Abue. Can't forget to do that.

"That's a good idea." Madison is already pulling clothes from her pink bag.

As I remove my folded clothes, I find myself categorizing: tops in one pile, bottoms in another, undergarments tucked away in the drawer. I'm doing my best to remain as organized as possible because I'm sharing a room with another person. If I wasn't? Clothes would be thrown all over the bed Madison has claimed as hers for the duration of this trip.

Madison tells me about her classes last semester, her family that lives out in Texas, how she's never been this far east before let alone to a Caribbean island. I make the appropriate noises at what seem like the right moments and that's enough to get Madison to think I'm fully invested.

"You're really organized," she comments, watching me arrange my toiletries on my side of the bathroom counter.

"I'm only doing it because we are sharing a room," I say, lining up my face wash, toner, and moisturizer. "My brain is full of chaos and my stuff usually is, but I don't want to be rude to you."

"That's really nice of you. Thanks," Madison says as she unzips a pink makeup bag covered in purple stars. "I have four older brothers, so I'm used to...things being messy for lack of a better word."

That draws my attention back to the conversation. "Four brothers? That explains the very pink/Barbiesque suitcase. Is that a part of your rebellion?"

Madison gives me the biggest belly laugh. "It is! Growing up, everything was sports equipment and stinky clothes, so I went full glitter princess just to claim some territory. Do you have siblings? Play any sports?"

"One brother. He's older than me and much more athletic." I don't elaborate that he's Knox Sanchez, hockey star. I'm not ready for the inevitable follow-up questions that always come with that revelation. Not that I'm ashamed of my brother in any way, shape, or form. While there's a chance she doesn't know who he is, if she does it's not a rabbit hole I want to go down right now.

She takes a break from unpacking and sits cross-legged on her bed. She picks up her phone and starts scrolling. "My oldest brother was the rodeo star of our family. Bull riding, calf roping, etc."

"Wait. Rodeo? Like actual bull riding?" I pause with a t-shirt half-folded in my hands.

"Oh yeah." Madison nods. "He was state champion three years running. Had all the local girls swooning over him in his Wranglers and boots."

"That's...not what I expected you to say." I sit on my bed because my clothes can wait. "Is he still competing?"

Madison lets out a laugh. "Oh hell no. He left our little town the day after graduation. Now he races in Formula 1. Lives in Monaco half the year."

I blink at her because there's no way I heard that right. "Hold up. Your brother went from rodeo to Formula 1? That's quite the career change."

"Machines with horsepower are machines with horse-power, I guess." She shrugs, like it's the most normal career trajectory in the world. "Mom nearly had a heart attack the first time she saw him going 200 miles per hour on TV. Dad just said he always knew my brother wouldn't stay put."

"That's honestly one of the coolest things I've ever heard," I admit. My brain immediately jumps to wanting to interview him about all of this and more, but I stomp that thought into the ground for now. "My brother just...plays hockey." Now it felt silly for me to be worried about her knowing what Knox did.

"What do you mean he just plays hockey?" Madison looks up from her phone and tilts her head as she studies me.

I shrug, trying to brush it off. "Nothing. He's great at it, but I meant hockey isn't as unexpected as going from bulls to racecars."

"Trust me, it wasn't exactly planned," Madison says with a laugh. "Tate—that's my brother—has always had this thing about speed. Used to modify his truck to go faster than anything else in the county. Nearly killed himself twice before he was seventeen."

"And your parents still let him drive?" I ask. Because she can't be serious.

"Let him?" Madison snorts. "They couldn't stop him. That's just Tate. When he sets his mind on something, it happens." She pulls out her phone, scrolls for a second, then hands it to me. "That's him."

I take the phone and stare at the photo. The man on the screen has Madison's same warm eyes, but his hair is much darker. He's leaning against a sleek red racecar, wearing a driving suit unzipped to reveal a plain white t-shirt. He looks like he belongs on a billboard.

"That's your brother?" I hand the phone back to her. "He's...wow."

"Yeah, that's what most people say." Madison laughs as she tosses her phone on her bed. "Anyway, do you want to shower first or should I?"

"You go ahead," I say. "I'll finish unpacking, and I need to text my mom." I'm proud of myself for reminding myself to do that. Again.

"You sure?" Madison asks, already grabbing her toiletry bag. "I have no problem waiting."

"Positive. Take your time."

As soon as the bathroom door clicks shut and the shower starts running, I exhale and roll my shoulders back. It helps to relieve the pressure that's been building in my body since we landed. Maybe since we took off. Maybe since I found out Blaise would be on this trip.

I finish unpacking and send my mom and abuela a text letting them know I was safely in Puerto Rico and hanging out at the hotel. By the time Madison emerges from the bathroom in a cloud of steam and coconut-scented body wash, I've managed to arrange my side of the room into something resembling order.

"All yours," she says as she takes her hair out of the clip she threw it up in. "The water pressure is amazing."

I grab my things for the shower and say, "Thanks. I'll be quick."

The second I close the bathroom door behind me, I lean against it and just breathe. The mirror is still fogged from Madison's shower, but I can make out my reflection. I look a bit rough, between being slightly frazzled and desperately in need of hot water to wash away the travel day. I strip off my travel clothes, toss my hair up into a messy bun, and step into the shower. Madison was right about the water pressure, and I close my eyes as the water hits my shoulders. For the first time since landing, I'm starting to really relax.

By the time I step out, the mirror is completely fogged again. I wipe a circle clear and stare at my reflection. My cheeks are flushed from the heat, but I look and feel more alive than I did twenty minutes ago.

I wrap myself in a towel and walk back into the bedroom, feeling slightly more human.

"Feel better?" Madison asks. She's now dressed in a bright yellow sundress that looks stunning against her complexion and hair.

"So much better. What time is the welcome dinner again?"

"Seven." Madison checks her phone. "We have about forty minutes."

I pull out a simple white sundress with delicate floral embroidery that my mom insisted I pack and hold it up. "Think this works?"

"Absolutely." Madison nods approvingly. "It'll look gorgeous on you."

I wrap up the rest of my routine, which includes getting dressed quickly, and while my hair is slightly damp, I assume it'll dry fast. Once I've added a touch of mascara, tinted moisturizer and lip balm to my face, I'm ready to go. I think I've done just enough to look put together without trying too hard.

"Ready?" Madison asks as she slips her feet into a pair of flip flops.

"As I'll ever be," I reply. I double check that I have

everything I need in my small cross-body bag I brought for occasions such as this.

The walk to the lobby is short but already feels more comfortable than when we arrived. When we get to the lobby, quite a few people from our group are already there. It's a relief that we aren't too early or too late.

That relief dissolves the second I glance over my right shoulder and catch Blaise looking at me. I didn't see him when we walked into the lobby, but now it's as if he's standing under a neon red sign with an arrow pointed down at him.

He's blatantly staring at me and it's obvious that he doesn't give a damn who knows it. He doesn't flinch. Doesn't pretend he isn't. He just keeps watching with a stern expression that makes me want to figure out what he's thinking.

And then his gaze drops slowly. I now have no doubt where his brain has wandered off to because I swear his eyes are tracking every inch of my body like he's committing it to memory. It's not a look you give someone by accident and it's definitely not the kind of look he should be giving me with the circumstances between us. I should be irritated. I should be *something*. But all I can do is stare back as if he's put me in a trance.

When he finally lifts his eyes to mine again, for a few beats, the world stops spinning on its axis.

But when Madison calls my name, I turn and look

away. Yet I'm still wondering what that was all about and how it will factor into the time we spend together on this island for the next week.

18

BLAISE

I tiptoe out of my hotel room and slowly close the door shut in an effort to not disturb my sleeping roommate. After all, it's nice that one of us gets to sleep in and I would be a complete asshole for disturbing his rest just because I haven't been able to get much.

Add another unfamiliar bed to the list of places I can't sleep. Sleeping in new places has always been difficult for me, which has always made away games rough. It's something I thought I would eventually get used to, but that hasn't been the case. Tyler's snoring, while not obnoxious, didn't help matters. Neither did the thoughts of Willow in that white sundress that kept circling my brain on an endless loop.

I check my watch as I head down the open-air hallway: 5:47 A.M. The sun's barely up, but my body clock doesn't care about vacation schedules. My body is ready to move and I need to honor it. The hotel is eerily quiet this early. The lobby is empty except for a sleepy-looking desk clerk who barely glances up from his computer when I walk by.

Outside, the morning air hits differently than Virginia. It's warmer and...saltier? It's a weird way to view air, but that's the best way I can describe it. I do some quick stretches as I look around the hotel property. There's a path that seems to lead toward the beach. Perfect.

I start with a slow jog to give my body time to wake up properly. I give myself grace as I pick up speed, and soon I'm running at a comfortable pace down a path near the beach. The waves crash rhythmically to my left, providing a soundtrack that makes me forget I left my headphones in my hotel room.

My mind drifts to last night's welcome dinner. I'd deliberately chosen a seat at the far end of the table, but somehow ended up with a perfect view of Willow anyway. That memory sends my thoughts spiraling and makes me even more grateful for deciding to go for this run. I need clarity and to clear my head, stat. Less than twenty-four hours in Puerto Rico and I'm already feeling like I'm off balance. I still need to get through a whole week in her presence and this is already starting off pretty rough if my behavior last night was any indication.

She'd caught me staring again, but I couldn't stop. I know it was wrong and completely agree with anyone if they say it wasn't my finest moment, but she'd truly taken my breath away and free will took over. Knox would have knocked some sense into me if he'd been there.

I push myself harder now, increasing my pace until my lungs burn. The physical discomfort is a welcome distraction from the mental spiral my brain has on a loop. The beach stretches ahead, in all of its beauty and is nearly empty except for a few early-morning walkers. I realize that this is the first time in a while I feel somewhat at peace. I'm not worried about my grades or hockey at the moment. What a relief that is, especially after almost having an anxiety attack on the plane down here.

As I continue running, flashes of what happened yesterday play in my mind like a movie I can't shut off. Having Willow sit next to me on the flight hadn't been on my bingo card. Part of me was thrilled, the other part wanted to switch seats because being next to her and not being able to actually enjoy spending time in her company felt unbearable. When our arms or hands would occasionally brush up against each other no matter how we tried to keep our distance, it took every inch of willpower to not react. I was forced to pretend to read the same page of my book for twenty minutes straight because I couldn't focus with her so close.

Then the shuttle ride from the airport, where I'd deliberately chosen the seat across from her because I wanted to be close to her again. What the hell was I thinking? Oh that's right. I wasn't thinking at all.

I slow down when I reach a long stretch of beach,

breathing hard, heart pounding against my ribs like it's trying to claw its way out of my chest. Sweat has made its way to the surface, and I do enjoy the burn, but it's not enough to stop the thoughts running through my head. Not even close.

I stop near some palm trees and lean forward with my hands on my knees. I force myself to focus on the rhythm of my breathing as I try to calm my racing heart.

In. Hold. Out.

Again.

I know I'm lying to myself by saying she's just another girl attending Crestwood University. Just my best friend's little sister. The second she sat down beside me on that flight, it was like my body forgot the rules I made with myself. Forgot the boundary I swore I'd never cross. Even now, I wish there was a way I could act on all the thoughts running through my head. Not all of them innocent and none I would dare say in front of Knox.

Not to mention, she fucking hates me. That I can't blame on her at all.

I stand up straight and stretch my arms over my head until my shoulders pop. I need to stop. Get my head on straight. I've been through harder things than this, but this feels like the most dangerous game I've ever played. Not that I want to play games with her...unless it has to do with videogames or fucking.

Dammit. Even the jokes in my head are betraying me now. And I can already feel Knox's fist trying to connect with my body as a result of the thoughts I'm having about her.

I turn to face the ocean, letting the salty air fill my lungs. The sun's climbing higher, lighting up the sky with a beautiful golden glow. While I have no issue with noticing the island's beauty, things would feel more peaceful if my mind wasn't such a battlefield. A war that I seem to be growing weaker in daily.

I never thought I would think this, but I need to get my shit together. For the team. For my own sanity. How will that happen, especially being in this close proximity with Willow? I have no idea.

After another quick stretch I start the run back to the hotel, hoping the endorphins will kick in and reset my brain. Or kick my ass enough that my brain will go quiet. I wish I had my gaming setup here because that would help a lot in terms of slowing down all the thoughts flying through my mind. But it looks like I'll have to rely on running and cold showers in order to make it through this trip.

The run back feels like it takes longer than it should. It could be because I've already exerted energy running here and was pushing my body harder than normal. While I do run to keep in shape, it's not exactly my forte. However, I know it's not just physical exhaustion weighing me down.

It's her. Always her. And that's something I'll have to live with.

I pick up my pace again, determined to punish myself

for my thoughts and finally slow to a walk as I reach the hotel grounds. I can't help but put hands on my hips as I'm trying to catch my breath. My shirt has grown damp and is slightly clinging to my skin. Instead of walking back up through the lobby, I pause once more and watch as the sun moves higher in the sky.

I want Willow Sanchez. Not just physically—though that is part of it—but all of her. The sharp comments, the fierce intelligence, the way she refuses to back down from anything. I want the girl who looked at me with fire in her eyes when I pulled away years ago. The woman who sat next to me on the plane yesterday, pretending I didn't exist while every cell in my body was aware of her.

It's not new. This feeling has been building since the night we kissed and even in moments where we wouldn't see each other for months. Pretending indifference hasn't helped either. The only thing that has changed is that I've gotten better at lying to myself about it.

I drag my hand across my face, feeling the stubble I haven't bothered to shave yet. "Fuck," I whisper to no one.

Knox would never forgive me. Our friendship would shatter. The team dynamic would fracture. And Willow? She'd probably laugh in my face.

I start walking back toward the hotel entrance. The desk clerk is now replaced by a cheerful woman who smiles as I pass through the lobby. I manage a nod but that's it because I don't feel like having a conversation with anyone right now. I manage to not run into anyone on the journey back to my room and enter it as quietly as I left it.

Tyler's still passed out under his blankets, with one arm dangling off the edge of the mattress. I take that as my sign to take my shower and get a move on with my day before he wakes up. I grab some clean clothes and head to the bathroom. I do what I can to not make too much noise because at least someone in this room should get some sleep. I strip off my sweaty clothes and step under the spray. I instantly feel less tense.

The water hits my shoulders and I close my eyes, letting it wash away the physical evidence of my morning exertion. If only it could cleanse my thoughts as easily.

By the time I rinse off and step out, the mirror is completely fogged. I towel off quickly and dress in a simple navy t-shirt and khaki shorts. As I'm brushing my teeth, I hear movement outside the door. Tyler must be awake.

When I exit the bathroom, Tyler is sitting up in bed, scrolling through his phone.

"Morning," I say, running a hand through my still-damp hair.

"Dude," Tyler mumbles, his voice thick with sleep. "What time is it?"

I wonder why he's asking me when he has his phone in hand. "Almost seven."

He groans and flops back against his pillows. "Why are you even up? We're on vacation."

"We're not on vacation technically, and I couldn't sleep," I reply, sitting on the edge of my bed to put on my socks. "I went for a run."

"A run? This early?" Tyler rubs his eyes, looking at me like I've grown a second head. "You're insane."

"Just habit." I finish with my socks and reach for my sneakers. "Besides, the beach was beautiful this early."

Tyler sits up again, this time fully alert. "What time do we have to be down at breakfast?"

"Eight," I tell him, checking my phone. "Professor Wallace is pretty punctual."

Tyler groans again, this time louder. "That's like...an hour from now."

"Which gives you plenty of time to shower and get ready," I point out as I finish lacing up my shoes.

"Or sleep for another thirty minutes," Tyler counters, already sliding back down under the covers.

I shake my head, unable to suppress a small smile. "Your call. But breakfast ends at nine, and today's itinerary starts right after."

"What's on the schedule again?" His voice is muffled by the pillow he's now hugging.

"We're doing some volunteer stuff in the morning. Free time in the afternoon, I think." I know exactly what we're doing, but for some reason adding 'I think' to the end of my sentence makes it sound better, at least to me.

"Wake me at eight." Tyler pulls the sheet over his head.

I'm about to respond when my phone vibrates in my hand. I pick it up and see a text notification from Knox.

Knox: How's paradise?

I stare at the notification for a moment, unsure how to respond. How's paradise? If only he knew what I was dealing with.

Me: It's fine. Just got back from a run. How's Vermont?

I set my phone down and glance at Tyler, who's already snoring again. I should just leave him be for now. There's still plenty of time before breakfast, and I'd rather not sit alone in the room with my thoughts.

My phone buzzes again.

Knox: Cold as balls, but Selene's family is cool. Her dad keeps trying to teach me ice fishing.

I smile at the image of Knox standing on a frozen lake, looking completely out of his element.

Me: Sounds rough. At least you're not stuck running in the heat.

Knox: Yeah that's the last thing I would be doing if I were there. How's Wills doing?

My heart rate spikes. Of course he'd ask about that. I hesitate, fingers hovering over the keyboard. What am I supposed to say? That I can't stop staring at her? That she looked incredible in that white dress last night? That I'm slowly losing my mind?

> Me: Fine. We got dinner with everyone last night. Today is the first real day and—

I delete the message and try again, carefully choosing my words.

> Me: She seems good. Haven't talked to her much.

I set my phone down on the bed and run a hand through my hair. It's not a complete lie. We haven't talked much, but not for lack of me thinking about it. About her.

The phone buzzes again.

> Knox: Cool. Just keep an eye out.

> Me: Will do. No worries.

I'm about to set my phone down again when another text comes through.

> Knox: Tell her to text mom. She's freaking out because Wills only sent one message since landing.

I laugh under my breath.

> Me: I'll pass that along if I see her at breakfast.

Knox: Thanks man. Gotta go. Talk later.

I toss my phone back onto the bed and exhale slowly. The thought of having to approach Willow with a message from Knox makes my stomach twist. She'll think I'm watching her to report back to her brother.

Which is exactly what I'm doing. Fucking great.

19

WILLOW

My eyes open to a stripe of sunlight slicing my face in half, and for one moment, I don't remember where I am. The bed is too firm and the air conditioner is on in January. This ceiling fan spins in slow, hypnotic circles above me. I'm in Puerto Rico. Right.

I groan and roll over, burying my face in the pillow. My brain is already firing in seventeen different directions, thoughts colliding and tangling like Christmas lights pulled from storage.

"Shit," I mutter, forcing myself to sit up. Madison's bed is empty and neatly made. Of course she's already up and functioning. Probably went for a jog on the beach or something equally horrifying for this hour.

I fight with my covers to get my phone and finally win. 7:42 A.M. Group breakfast starts at 8:00, which means I have exactly eighteen minutes to transform from swamp creature to presentable human.

The shower helps somewhat, and I make sure to avoid wetting my hair because the last thing I want to deal with right now is drenched hair. When I'm done, I throw on a sports bra, tank top, and athletic shorts. I figure that's practical for whatever volunteer activity Professor Wallace has planned. I throw my hair into a messy bun and grab my biggest pair of sunglasses from my bag. Last step: the oversized gray hoodie that's seen better days but it's my favorite so that's a win.

The door clicks open just as I'm shoving my feet into my sneakers.

"Oh good, you're up!" Madison chirps, looking infuriatingly fresh in a bright blue tank top and black shorts. Her hair is pulled back in a perfect ponytail, not a strand out of place. "I grabbed you a coffee from the lobby. Black, right?"

She holds out a paper cup like she's offering the Holy Grail. The smell hits me first, and for a second I consider getting down on the ground and kissing her feet.

"You're officially my favorite person on this trip," I say, accepting the cup with both hands. "Where have you been this morning?"

"Just exploring a bit. The sunrise was incredible!" She sets a small paper bag on the dresser. "Also snagged you a banana. Figured I would grab it just in case you missed breakfast."

My first instinct is to say something sarcastic about morning people, but I hold it back. "Thanks. That's...really thoughtful." It's weird cause we just met and I hate that my mind immediately goes to wondering if this is a ploy that will end up leading to me being backstabbed somewhere down the line. It wouldn't be the first time, and Madison's kindness is throwing me off. My brain can't process this much cheerfulness before coffee, so I just take a sip and let the bitter warmth shock my system.

She walks over to our curtains and opens them. The sunlight hits me like I just got smacked. "Professor Wallace said we're heading to some community garden today."

"Okay," I mumble, pulling my hoodie tighter around me. "I just need to get more coffee and food in me or I'm not going to be a pleasant person to be around."

"Not a morning person?" Madison asks. Her tone is somehow both sympathetic and amused.

"What gave it away?" I gesture at my entire existence. "The sunglasses indoors or the fact that I look like I just crawled out of a dumpster?"

She laughs, not offended by my morning personality. "My brother Cal is the same way. We used to have to throw ice water on him to get him up for school."

I take another long sip of coffee, feeling it slowly reboot my system. "Your family sounds...interesting. First Tate and now Cal."

"That's one word for it," Madison says, checking her phone. "We should probably head down. It's 7:52."

I nod, grabbing my phone, room key, and some other small essentials before tossing it into a small drawstring bag I planned on taking with me. The coffee is helping, but my brain still feels like there are some cobwebs that need to be cleared. Everything is too bright, too loud, too much. I swear I can hear the hallway lights buzzing overhead as we make our way to the elevator, and I wince behind my sunglasses. To make matters worse, I'm not even hung over.

"You okay?" Madison asks as we step inside the elevator.

"Yeah. Just..." I wave my hand vaguely. "My brain's loud today."

She nods like this makes perfect sense. "Let me know if you need anything."

The elevator announces that we've reached the lobby level, and I brace myself for what I'm about to hear. Sure enough, most of our group is already gathered near the breakfast area, their voices bouncing off the walls and ceiling. Professor Wallace stands at the front, clipboard in hand, looking far too energetic.

"Just need to grab actual food," I mutter to Madison. "Then find the quietest corner possible."

I make my way to the breakfast buffet, loading a plate with scrambled eggs, bacon, and toast. Maybe I'll do another round after I inhale this food. As I'm reaching for a napkin, a voice behind me says, "You look like you need more coffee."

I freeze. I know that voice without having to turn around. Of course. Of. Fucking. Course.

"I'm fine," I say, doing everything in my power to not look at Blaise as I grab my napkin with more force than necessary.

"Right." There's amusement in his voice that makes me want to dump my eggs on his shoes. "That's why you're wearing sunglasses inside."

I finally turn around and immediately regret it. He's standing too close, wearing a simple navy t-shirt that shows off his stupid perfect arms. His hair is still damp, probably from a shower, and he smells like soap and something else I can't place. Something clean and warm that makes my stupid brain short-circuit.

"Some of us didn't wake up at dawn to go jogging," I say, stepping around him toward the tables. I don't actually know if he did that, but knowing what I do know about him? Hell yeah.

"How did you—" He stops himself, following me. "Never mind."

And I was right, but instead of rubbing it in his face, I spot Madison sitting at a table near the windows and make a beeline for her. Of course Blaise trails behind me like a lost puppy. When I sit down across from Madison, he hovers for a moment before taking the seat next to her.

Not across from me, thankfully, but close enough that I can feel his presence.

"Morning," he says politely. "Blaise Dalton. Don't think we've officially met."

"Madison Hollins," she replies with a bright smile. "Nice to meet you."

"Hey, mind if I join?" Tyler appears beside our table. His plate is piled high with pastries, eggs, and fruit. He looks more awake than he did yesterday which is definitely a step up from how I'm presenting myself right now.

"Go ahead," Madison gestures to the empty chair next to me.

Tyler drops into the seat with a yawn and shoves half a croissant in his mouth. "Thanks."

I focus on my food, hoping if I don't make eye contact with anyone, they'll forget I exist. No such luck.

"By the way," Blaise says. "Knox texted me this morning."

I look up despite myself, but his words stop all movement including the fork that is halfway to my mouth. "And?"

"He said to tell you that you should text your mom. Apparently she's freaking out because you only sent one message since landing."

I roll my eyes behind my sunglasses. Great. Now I'm getting messages relayed through my brother's best friend like I'm not a whole-ass adult. "I texted her last night."

"Well, according to Knox, it wasn't enough."

Tyler glances between us, clearly sensing something but wisely choosing to stuff more food in his mouth instead of commenting.

"Fine," I say as I pull out my phone. "I'll text her again."

I type quickly, keeping it brief but detailed enough to satisfy my mom's worries.

> Me: Morning! Hotel is nice, roommate is cool, breakfast is good. Heading to volunteer at community garden today. Will send pics. Love you.

"Happy?" I ask Blaise after hitting send.

He shrugs. "I'm just the messenger."

"Right." I stab at my eggs with unnecessary force. "Thanks for the delivery service."

Madison clears her throat. "So, Tyler, what's your major?"

"Chemistry," he answers through a mouthful of food. "You?"

As they chat, I feel Blaise's eyes on me. I refuse to look up, focusing instead on methodically cutting my toast into increasingly smaller pieces.

"You should eat that instead of torturing it," Blaise says quietly.

"I wasn't aware I needed eating advice," I snap, but take a bite anyway because he's right and I'm hungry. Out of all of the seats in this dining area, why the hell did he decide to sit here?

Professor Wallace claps her hands together at the front of the room. "If I could have everyone's attention, please!"

Thank fuck. Maybe we can get this day started and I can stop pretending I don't feel Blaise's eyes on me.

"I have our volunteer assignments for today," she says. "We'll be working at a local farm that provides fresh produce to several community kitchens in the area."

I take another sip of orange juice and try to not squirm under Blaise's gaze. With a small sigh, I look down at my plate, refusing to meet his eyes. I don't want to give him the satisfaction of knowing he has any effect on me whatsoever.

I will not squirm. I will not squirm. I will not squirm.

"I've divided you into smaller teams to make the work more manageable," Professor Wallace explains. "Each team will have specific tasks assigned by the farm staff."

"Team One will handle irrigation work," Professor Wallace reads off of her phone. "Madison Hollins, Tyler Chesterfield, Emma Weiss..."

I close my eyes behind my sunglasses, willing her to put me in any group without—

"Team Two will be working in the herb garden. Willow Sanchez, Blaise Dalton..."

My stomach drops, then flips, then ties itself into a knot. And here I was thinking I could have a Blaise free day.

I don't move. Don't flinch. Don't even blink.

"...and David Miller," Professor Wallace finishes.

Three people. Just three of us in our little herb garden group. Nowhere to hide. Nowhere to run.

It doesn't matter, I tell myself. It's just a few hours of volunteer work. I can ignore him. I've been ignoring him for years. This is fine.

It's not fine. Nothing about this is fine.

Professor Wallace continues going through all of the teams, and when she's done, she asks, "Is everyone clear on their assignments? Our bus leaves in thirty minutes. Please be in the lobby by 8:45."

I nod at Professor Wallace's question. My face stays blank while my internal monologue goes nuclear. Great. Fantastic. Perfect. Just what this trip needed. Blaise Dalton and I playing gardeners and spending more together.

I drain my orange juice like it's a shot of tequila, all the while wishing it had the same numbing effect.

Madison touches my arm. "Herb garden, huh? That sounds nice and peaceful."

"Yeah. Peaceful. Super excited about...herbs."

I shift to the edge of my chair, angling my body away from the table and away from him. If I can just make it through breakfast without further interaction, maybe I can find a way to switch groups. Or fake an illness. Or knock myself out by hitting a glass bottle over my head.

"I'm going to get more coffee," I announce to no one in particular, pushing my chair back.

I take my time refilling my cup and from this position,

I can study the room while pretending to be deeply fascinated by the coffee condiments. From where I am, I can see Blaise still sitting at the table, now talking with Tyler about something. I want to know what they're talking about, but also I don't. I swear my life has become more about me being a walking contradiction than anything else. But at a certain point, I need to walk back to the table until it's time for us to leave.

I take a sip of my coffee and then begin my journey back. By the time I return to the table, Madison and Tyler are chatting about some mathematician I've never heard of, while Blaise is on his phone. I slide into my seat, keeping my eyes on my coffee.

"Almost time to go," Madison says, checking her phone. "Should we head to the lobby?"

"Yeah," I say as I stand up and grab the small bag I decided to take. "Let's get this over with."

I'm excited about volunteering, it's just *who* I'm doing it with that has me dreading every second. As I take another sip of my coffee all I can think is that at least I can say that none of this will be boring.

20

WILLOW

The shuttle drops us off at the entrance to the farm and I immediately regret every choice that led me to this point in my life. Because why are we doing this so early in the morning?

Professor Wallace claps her hands and launches into a speech about the farm's mission, using words like "community engagement" and "global citizenship" while the rest of us silently bargain with the universe for cloud cover.

Blaise stands two people to my left, perfectly stone-faced. He keeps his arms crossed and his eyes forward, like there's nothing else going on besides Professor Wallace talking. If I weren't so busy mentally trying to figure out if there's a way I can convince our shuttle bus driver to take me back to the hotel, I might actually appreciate the view. Instead, I focus on the way the sweat is already darkening his collar, which is both a comfort and a distraction.

"Willow! You're with Blaise and David in the herb garden," Professor Wallace announces, as if I didn't hear her make the announcement when we were back at the hotel.

My eyes land on David because there's no way I can look at Blaise. It's very obvious that he was class president in high school and thinks that translates to real-world charisma. He's got sandy hair, the kind of blue eyes you get called dreamy for, and a nice smile. I already hate him.

"Herb garden!" David says, like he's won a prize. He offers me a fist bump, which I ignore so completely he has to awkwardly drop it by his side. "Guess we're the dream team, huh?"

"If the dream is dehydration and insect bites, then sure," I deadpan, adjusting my bag higher on my shoulder.

"I'm Silas," a voice interrupts, saving me from having to respond further to David's enthusiasm. A man who looks to be in his mid-fifties approaches us as he's wiping his hands on a faded towel. "I'll be showing you the herb garden today."

He tells us to follow him with a quick gesture and turns to head down a dirt path. I fall into step behind him, conscious of Blaise and David flanking me like some bizarre honor guard.

"The herbs we grow here supply local restaurants

and community kitchens," Silas explains as we walk. "Many are traditional medicinal plants too and things my grandmother used to grow. Today we need to weed, trim back the overgrowth, and reorganize some sections." Silas points to a shed nearby. "Gloves, tools, everything you need is in there. I'll show you what needs doing."

He hands each of us a pair of gardening gloves that have seen better days. Mine are too big, the fingers extending a good inch past my own. David immediately offers to swap his for mine.

"I've got bigger hands anyway," he says with a wink that makes me want to throw the gloves at his face.

If he is alluding to what I think he is, throwing the gloves in his face is the nicest thing I can do right now. I'm so tempted to test his reflexes, but that might give him the wrong idea or worse, turn him on.

"I'm good," I say, already shoving my hands into them.

"Here," Silas says, handing each of us a small trowel and some clippers. "The basil needs trimming back and please be careful not to cut the new growth. The thyme needs weeding around it. The oregano and culantro are over there as well."

He demonstrates what he wants us to do, and I immediately get nervous. What if I mess this up? It's then I remember I didn't take my medication this morning, instead choosing to double dose myself with caffeine. This is going to be a hot mess. Literally and figuratively.

"Any questions?" Silas asks, looking between the three of us.

"I think we've got it," Blaise says, his voice cutting through my panic. He's pulling on his gloves.

"Great! I'll check on you in about an hour." He gives us a nod before heading toward the next group.

I stare at the herb garden before me. The plants are beautiful but jumbled together. I swear I can already feel sweat trickling down my back, and the sun isn't even at full strength yet.

"I'll take the oregano and sage," David volunteers, flashing that toothpaste-commercial smile.

"I'll handle the basil," Blaise says quietly. He doesn't look at me as he crouches down near a bushy section of plants.

Which leaves me with the thyme. Perfect. Weeding in this heat while my brain races in seventeen directions at once. I kneel down on the dirt and the moisture from the ground immediately makes me feel uncomfortable.

"Fuck," I whisper, shifting to find a drier spot. There isn't one.

I dig my trowel into the dirt around the thyme plants and pause as I try to distinguish between what should stay and what needs to go. The weeds look suspiciously similar to the actual herbs, and I immediately think I'm going to mess this up.

"You need to dig deeper," Blaise says from behind me. I nearly jump out of my skin.

"Jesus! Don't sneak up on people holding sharp objects."

"Sorry." He doesn't sound sorry. He sounds distracted. "The weeds have deeper roots. You're just getting the tops."

He's right behind me now, close enough that I can feel the heat radiating off him. Not looking. Not helping. Just...hovering.

"I've got it," I snap and push the trowel deeper.

I let go of the trowel as I try to adjust these ridiculous gloves for the fifth time in what feels like ninety seconds. They keep bunching at my wrists and the extra fabric makes it impossible to grip anything properly.

"Having trouble there?" David materializes beside me, his smile as bright as the sun beating down on us.

"I'm fine," I mutter, yanking at the loose strap dangling from my wrist.

"Here, let me." He doesn't wait for permission. Instead, he takes his own gloves off and reaches for my hand. "These old gloves have a trick to them."

I'm pretty sure the trick is that he just wants an excuse to touch me. And the desire to call him out on it is there.

"I've got this neat little hack," David says. "My grandfather taught me when we worked his garden back home."

I try to pull away, but he's already flipping the glove inside out at the wrist. "Really, I'm good. I can figure it out—"

"Just one second," he insists, folding the excess material back on itself and creating a sort of cuff. His thumb strokes across my palm as he works. "There. Perfect fit now."

I resist the urge to gag. "Thanks," I say flatly, pulling my hand away.

"My pleasure." David's smile widens. "You know, I've always had a thing for girls who aren't afraid to get their hands dirty."

"Is that right?" I turn back to my weeding, hoping he'll take the hint.

He doesn't. Instead, he crouches beside me, his shoulder brushing mine. "Absolutely. Shows character. Plus, you look cute when you're concentrating."

I'm about to tell him exactly where he can shove his observations when I hear Blaise clear his throat behind us. "She said she's good."

David glances up at Blaise, but his smile stays planted on his face. "Just helping her out, man."

We're outside, but the tension between us is now as thick as a heavy smoke. I can probably cut it with a pair of gardening shears. I look between them, confused by Blaise's tone and whatever else is going on here.

"I think the oregano needs your attention more than Willow's gloves do," Blaise says slowly as if he's making sure David understands every word.

David raises his hands as if he's surrendering, that infuriating grin still in place. "No problem. Just being friendly." He winks at me before returning to his section of the garden.

I stare at Blaise, who's already turning back to his basil plants. What the hell was that about? Since when does he care who flirts with me? Is he jealous?

The thought spins through my mind and I'm stuck wondering if this could mean...no, that can't be it. I watch him with disbelief, trying to reconcile his silence with his protectiveness. Seriously, what the fuck was that?

I know I should be annoyed, but instead, I'm something else. Something that feels like...hopeful and I hate that. Something I don't want to admit. I want to understand what he's doing, why he's doing it, anything that explains what just happened. Instead, I turn it over in my head again and again. Maybe I should chalk this situation up to being a glitch in the matrix or something.

"I can handle myself, you know," I say quietly, not wanting David to overhear.

Blaise doesn't look up. "Never said you couldn't."

"Then what was that?"

"Nothing," he says as he keeps his eyes fixed on the basil. "Just seemed like you weren't interested in his help. Nor did you want him touching you."

I'm suddenly at a loss for words. How did he—? Since when does he—? My mind races with questions I can't form, let alone ask. "Thanks," I finally say, my voice smaller than I intended. "I guess."

Blaise just nods once and while I'm pulling weeds, all I can think about now is that I have more questions than answers. As a journalist, none of that sits right with me.

And I'm determined to find out.

21

BLAISE

I'd hoped that all of the exercise I'd gotten today would have led to me being tired enough to pass out, but apparently that is not the case. I know this is absolutely ridiculous at this point, but here we are, and I need to do something about this fast.

With a heavy sigh, I reach for my phone on the night-stand, scrolling through my apps until I find the meditation one I downloaded months ago but never used. In the three seconds it takes the app to load, I hear Tyler snore, and I'm reminded that I should grab my headphones, so I don't disturb him. At least one of us can sleep.

I could watch some old content from some of my favorite streamers, but that would stimulate me versus making me tired. I plug in my earbuds and tap on "Sleep Sounds." The app offers me a menu of options: Gentle Rain, Ocean Waves, Forest Night, White Noise. I select

Ocean Waves and set the timer for thirty minutes, hoping that's long enough to shut my brain down.

The sound of water swaying softly back and forth fills my ears and I close my eyes in an effort to try to focus on the sound instead of the slideshow of today's events playing behind my eyelids. Willow kneeling in the dirt. David hovering too close to her. The flash of irritation I felt watching him touch her hand.

"Breathe deeply," a soothing female voice tells me. "In through your nose, out through your mouth."

I follow the instructions and feel slightly ridiculous. This isn't me. I don't do meditation apps. I solve problems through structure and planning, not breathing exercises.

But structure and planning aren't helping me now. Not with Willow.

The voice tells me to visualize a peaceful place. I immediately think of the beach from my morning run, except Willow is there, walking along the shoreline in that white dress from dinner.

"Focus on relaxing each part of your body," the voice continues. "Start with your toes."

I try. I really do. But by the time I'm supposed to be relaxing my shoulders, all I can think about is how tense they felt when David approached Willow, and how I couldn't stop myself from stepping in. He's lucky that's all I did to be honest. The thoughts that were flying through my mind in that moment would have landed all of us on a plane back home.

Knox would have done the same, I tell myself. I was just looking out for her like I promised.

But there was something else there. It was a surge of something possessive and irrational that almost made me act out of character.

I pull out one earbud and check the time. I've made it through twelve minutes of a thirty-minute session, and I'm no closer to sleep than when I started.

"Fuck this," I mutter as I yank out the other earbud.

I sit up in bed and run a hand through my hair. The room is dark except for the light coming from my phone. Tyler shifts in his sleep, mumbling something incoherent before settling again.

Maybe I need air. Maybe I need to clear my head. Maybe I just need to stop thinking about Willow Sanchez for five consecutive minutes.

I swing my legs over the side of the bed and grab a t-shirt, pulling it over my head. I throw on some gray sweatpants that I'd left folded on a chair near my bed. Maybe a walk will make me tired, doing what I couldn't manage to do with this mediation app. I slip on my shoes and grab my room key and phone, making sure I'm careful not to wake Tyler. I ease the door open and step into the hallway.

I think about heading to the beach again, but I end up slowing down when I hit the lobby. Maybe I'll find a chair in a corner and scroll through my phone until I'm too tired to keep my eyes open. I could have done it in my bed, but I'm hoping a change of scenery helps.

I take the stairs and when I reach the last step, I pause. Because that's when I see her.

Willow is sitting on one of the oversized couches in the far corner, her laptop balanced on her knees. She hasn't noticed me yet, probably because her hands are flying across the keyboard. Whatever she's typing must be intense because I'm not sure if she's given her hands a break in the time I've been staring at her.

She's wearing that oversized university hoodie again and I smirk at how it swallows her frame. Her hair is pulled back in a messy bun with strands escaping around her face, and she looks just as stunning as she did when I saw her at dinner last night.

Hell. I should leave. Turn around and go back to my room before she sees me. But I can't seem to make myself move. There's something about seeing her like this that stops me from doing the logical thing. Instead, I walk closer to her.

Her head snaps up suddenly and I swear her green eyes immediately lock on me. I should say something. Anything. But my voice gets caught somewhere between my brain and my mouth. We just stare at each other for what feels like minutes but is probably only seconds.

She breaks first. "What do you want?" Her tone is sharp and defensive. Her walls are up before I've even spoken a word.

I don't answer right away because I'm not sure how to respond. The lobby is silent except for the hum of the air conditioning, and it makes everything more awkward.

"Nothing," I finally say. "I couldn't sleep and saw you down here, so I walked over. What are you working on?" I ask and don't know how my answer and question are going to land with her.

The question seems to catch her off guard. Her eyes narrow slightly, and it's as if she's searching my face to see if I'm being sarcastic.

"Why do you care?" she asks, but I can tell she's not being as defensive as she was just seconds ago. That's a win in my book.

"I don't," I say automatically, then wince at how harsh it sounds. "I mean, I was just asking."

"I'm just...writing," she finally says. "Something about this trip."

"For the paper?" I take a step closer and am not sure if it's the right move. I don't want to crowd her but can't help but step forward because I need to be closer.

She shakes her head. "No. Maybe. I don't know yet." She closes her laptop slightly, not all the way, but enough that I can't see the screen. "It's personal. I'm still figuring it out."

"Mind if I sit?" I gesture to the other end of the couch.

She hesitates, then shrugs one shoulder. "It's a free country."

I sink down onto the cushion and I make sure to leave

plenty of space between us. "So," I venture, "personal writing?"

"Yeah." She tucks a strand of hair behind her ear. "I was thinking about how to capture what we're experiencing here. Not just the volunteer work but...I don't know. The impact. The culture. The way of life. Like how it's different from how we live in the US, but also the same."

She stops abruptly, like she's said too much. Her fingers tap nervously against her laptop.

"That sounds interesting," I say and mean it. "Different from your usual articles."

"That's kind of the point." Her voice has lost some of its edge. "I'm always chasing the next deadline, the next hot take. Sometimes I wonder if I'm just...creating noise."

I'm taken back by her confession, but I don't want to let her know I am because it might end this conversation. "I get that."

"Do you?" She looks at me skeptically.

"Yeah. It's like...everything has to be urgent all the time. Breaking news. A clickbait headline. And people need to be able to absorb it in ten seconds or less. But sometimes we need to switch things up."

She studies me for a moment. "That's...exactly it."

"But why are you up at—" she glances at her laptop screen, "—one in the morning?

I notice the subject change but don't call her out on it. "I don't sleep well in new places."

"Most people love that about travel," she says, not

judgmental, just observing. "Sleeping somewhere else. Having a break from routine."

"I'm not most people." I exhale slowly. "For me, routine isn't boring. It's...necessary."

She shifts slightly and I notice that she angles her body toward me. "Necessary? Why? Is it because of your anxiety?"

For a split second, I forgot I told her about that. And I'm surprised she remembered. "Yeah. Structure helps keep my mind from spiraling. Much like the color-coded notebooks."

That makes her laugh. "I actually think the color-coding is smart," she says. "Just don't tell anyone I said that. By the way. there's something I wanted to ask you."

It's the second time I'm taken by surprise in less than a minute. She actually wants to engage in a conversation with me? "What's that?"

"What was up with your behavior toward David today?"

Oh. I should have expected the question, but I'm still taken aback. I hesitate as I give myself time to think because I have to decide whether to tell her the whole truth or to phrase this delicately because of how awkward this could become.

"He was being pushy. You clearly didn't want his help and he wasn't taking the hint. So I stepped in." There. That should be good enough.

She studies me, her green eyes narrowing slightly. "That's it?"

"Should there be more?" I counter, meeting her gaze head on.

"No, I guess not. I just...it seemed...oddly personal."

"It wasn't." The lie tastes bitter. I clear my throat. "I'd have done it for anyone."

"Right." She doesn't sound convinced. "Now drop the bullshit and tell the truth."

Her direct challenge makes me freeze. I've spent so long constructing walls around my thoughts that having someone demand I tear them down is disorienting. But unleashing the feelings I have for her would cause more harm than good. I can't tell her that if given the opportunity, I would have had her bent over the damn garden and showed David what I thought of him touching her.

I can't say that. Not to her face. Not when we're finally having a real conversation.

"Knox asked me to keep an eye on you," I admit and I watch as her expression hardens immediately. "But that's not why I stepped in. David was being a dick, and you were uncomfortable. That's all."

"My brother asked you to babysit me?" I can see the hell she's about to unleash.

"He doesn't want me to babysit you. Just...look out for you."

"I'm not his responsibility. And I'm definitely not

yours." She shifts away from me, the small progress we'd made evaporating.

"I know that." It takes everything in me to not touch her. "Look, I would have said something even if Knox hadn't asked me to watch out for you. David was crossing a line."

She's quiet for a long moment, and I wonder if I've completely destroyed whatever fragile peace we'd established. "You're right," she finally says. "He was being pushy."

Well that went better than I expected.

"But," she continues, "I don't need you or Knox running interference for me. I've handled worse than David Miller."

I immediately think of Leo. I don't have the full story, but I know enough to understand that whatever happened wasn't good. "Fair enough," I concede but I stop just short of saying I'll back off. Because that would be one of the biggest lies I've ever told.

Silence stretches between us and I'm not sure how to label it. I don't think she's angry anymore, but I could be reading the tension between us wrong. What I do know is I need to speak up.

"I wasn't trying to rescue you," I say. "I just...couldn't not say something."

Willow turns her head and stares at me for several seconds before she asks, "Why?"

My throat tightens. "Because I saw your face. And I knew you were uncomfortable. That's it."

She doesn't speak right away again but adjusts herself so she's looking at her laptop. "I'm used to handling things alone," she says eventually. "Mostly because I don't tell Knox everything because I know he would freak. Plus, most guys don't care enough to notice."

I hate that that's true.

"I'm not most guys," I say before I can stop myself.

Her mouth twitches and a small smile forms. "Yeah. I'm starting to get that."

I can't let on how I'm affected by her comment. Instead I wait a few seconds and then clear my throat. "You want me to walk you back to your room?"

She glances at me, but this time it's not with anger or suspicion. She looks surprised by the offer. Then she nods. "Yeah. Sure."

And just like that, we stand without another word. I can confidently say that now we're not friends but also not enemies. Hopefully it's the start of something shifting into place. Whether I'm ready for anything that entails is another matter entirely.

22

WILLOW

"Is it weird that I'm actually excited about today?" I ask Madison as it becomes very obvious we're close to our destination. It feels silly to ask her that since we only just met on this trip, but I can't contain my excitement. Hiking is my jam and the thought of hiking through a rainforest is what dreams are made of.

Madison looks over at me with a grin. "Not weird at all. El Yunque is supposed to be incredible."

She's not wrong. I'm sure the photos I've seen won't do it justice. I'm already bouncing a little in my seat as I take in the scenery around me. There's greenery everywhere you turn to the point where if I didn't know I was actually in Puerto Rico, I would be questioning if this was reality.

"El Yunque is the only tropical rainforest in the U.S. National Forest System," Professor Wallace announces from the front of the shuttle as we pull into the parking area. "We'll be hiking one of the moderate trails today. Remember to stay hydrated and apply sunscreen before we start."

I shift in my seat because it's getting harder to keep still. This is the kind of adventure I live for and another reason I decided to join this trip at the last minute. When we come to a stop and the shuttle door slides open, I'm out of my seat before most people have registered we've arrived. When I step out of the vehicle, I immediately feel the difference in the air quality.

"Someone's eager." Madison laughs, following me down the steps of the shuttle.

"I've been dreaming about this since I saw the itinerary," I admit, adjusting my backpack straps. "I can't believe we are finally here."

"It's truly looks like something out of a movie," she says.

I can only nod in agreement.

"Alright everyone, gather around!" Professor Wallace waves us toward a small, covered area where a park ranger waits. "This is Angel, he'll be our guide today."

"Buenos días and good morning! Welcome to El Yunque. Before we begin, a few safety rules..." Angel says.

I'm doing my best to pay attention but it's hard. His voice fades into the background as I try to take in everything around me. My senses are overwhelmed, but I don't hate it. It must have something to do with me being here in this fresh air and being able to check something I've always wanted to do off my list.

"Willow." Madison nudges me. "You're supposed to sign the waiver."

"Right, sorry." I scribble my signature on the clipboard being passed around, barely reading the form. Death by rainforest would be a poetic way to go anyway.

Once everyone has signed the form, our guide leads us onto a trail and the rush of adrenaline that is already flowing through my body increases tenfold.

"This is incredible," I whisper, mostly to myself. My phone is already in my hand because I can't not take pictures. I continue walking in awe, not really talking to anyone because what is there to say when you're in this beautiful place?

"Watch your step here," our guide calls back as we reach a section where tree roots have broken through the path. "The ground can be slippery."

I carefully step over the roots and Madison walks beside me for a while. Eventually she walks faster so she can catch up to our guide and ask questions about the wildlife here. I don't mind. This is the kind of experience I prefer to absorb in my own bubble anyway. I keep moving, doing my best to take everything in as I go. Drops of rain start falling as we continue to move deeper into the forest. As a result, I end up throwing my hair up into a messy bun versus the low ponytail because I need to keep this hair off my neck.

The rain intensifies, quickly shifting from scattered drops to a gentle shower. I tilt my face upward and close my eyes, letting the water cool my skin.

"Glad I wore this," I murmur, glancing down at my black tank top and bikini top. At least I won't be dealing with a see-through shirt situation like poor Tyler, whose white tee is already plastered to his chest. The rain begins to pick up, and we pause to give everyone an opportunity to get their rain gear out. Water begins to stream down my face, but I can't be bothered to take out my rain poncho yet.

"This is amazing!" I call out to no one in particular, spreading my arms wide to embrace what looks to be turning into a downpour.

"You're getting soaked," a familiar voice says behind me.

I turn and find Blaise standing there, rain dripping from his blond hair. He's close enough that I can see water droplets clinging to his eyelashes. I hate that something about the way he's looking at me makes my stomach flip.

"So are you," I point out, wiping rain from my cheek. I watch as his gaze slips from my face to my chest, and I swear everything shifts. The playful moment comes to halt as his eyes lock onto where my soaked tank top clings to my skin and I assume it is revealing the outline of my bikini underneath. The thin black fabric might as well not exist with how clingy it's become in the rain and the way he's staring at me.

I should move. Should cross my arms. Should say something sarcastic to break whatever this is. But I don't. I just stand there, rain streaming down my body, watching him watch me.

His pupils dilate slightly and I watch as his eyes trace the curve where my bikini top dips under my shirt. When I move my hands to cover myself, it's then I realize my nipples are as hard as pebbles. It quickly dawns on me that that is also what caught his attention. My movement causes him to finally drag his gaze back to my face.

"You should..." he starts, stops, and then starts again. "You might want to put on your rain jacket."

My heart hammers in my chest, threatening to make a grand exit. "I like the rain."

"Willow," he says my name like he's issuing a warning.

I want to keep poking whatever 'this' is. Is it a wise thing to do? Nope, but am I going to do it anyway? Yep. "What? What do you want to say, Dalton?"

"That shirt is..." His eyes drop to my chest again, then snap back up. "Distracting."

I step closer because I feel more empowered due to his discomfort. I make sure that if we are being watched this looks completely innocent, but between the two of us, it's anything but. "Is it? I hadn't noticed." I tilt my head slightly. "You seem to be noticing enough for both of us."

His jaw tightens and I can see the muscle working beneath his skin. "We should catch up with the group."

"We should," I agree, but don't move. Instead, I run my

fingers through my wet hair, tucking some of the strands that fell out of the messy bun behind my ears. "But I'm curious now. What exactly is so distracting about my shirt, Blaise?"

I have no idea what has gotten into me, but apparently I'm out of fucks to give. I don't feel even a little bit guilty about what I'm doing. The embarrassment I felt when he turned me down years ago? Nowhere to be found.

The look he gives me could melt steel. "You know exactly what you're doing," he says.

"Do I?" I blink innocently. "Maybe I just like making you uncomfortable."

I'm playing with fire and know it. And it's also not going to stop me.

"Don't," he says quietly.

"Don't what? Ask questions you don't want to answer?"

"Don't ask questions you don't want to hear the answers to."

"But maybe I want to hear what you're going to say. Maybe I like it when you look at me that way. Hell, maybe I've been wondering what it would take to make you lose the control that you so carefully keep in place."

His eyes darken and I watch his throat work as he swallows. For a moment, I think he might actually reach for me, but instead, he clenches and unclenches his hands. "You have no idea what you're playing with," he says.

I can't tell if I shiver because of the way the tone of

his voice floats over me or if it's due to the rain. I step closer to him and say, "I know what I'm playing with." My gaze drifts to the swim trunks he's wearing before they meet his eyes again. "I also know what I *want* to play with."

I watch as Blaise has an internal battle with himself and it gives me a small bit of joy that it's because of me. Although he's not saying a word, the fact that he looks like he might pounce on me tells me all I need to know.

In an instant, Blaise's control snaps. His hand shoots out and his fingers curl around my wrist as he pulls me behind a massive tree trunk, away from the path and the rest of the group. He crowds me until my back meets the tree trunk and suddenly his body is caging mine. One of his hands ends up braced beside my head while the other is still gripping my wrist.

"Is this what you want?" His voice is low and his face is just inches from mine. "For me to lose control? Right here in the middle of a fucking rainforest with twenty people a few yards away?"

"Maybe," I whisper. "What are you going to do about it?"

His eyes drop to my lips, and for one heart-stopping moment, I think he's actually going to kiss me.

"Willow? Blaise? Where are you guys?" Madison's voice cuts through the moment like the water coming from the sky.

Blaise immediately steps back, putting distance

between us as if I've burned him. "Over here!" he calls back. "I'm just helping Willow get her rain gear out."

He reaches down to my backpack that I'd dropped without even realizing it, unzipping the front pocket where my rain poncho is stuffed. Madison appears around the bend in the trail with her pink raincoat that matches her bright pink suitcase.

"Everyone's waiting," she says, glancing between us. "The guide says we need to stick together because of the rain."

"Sorry," I say as I'm taking my poncho from Blaise. "I was having trouble with my bag."

Madison nods, but I can tell she thinks I'm full of shit. "Okay. Professor Wallace is about to do a headcount."

She waits for both of us to put our rain gear on, and soon all three of us are headed down the trail to join the rest of the class. Madison and I walk side by side while Blaise walks a few steps behind. I swear I can feel his eyes on my back, burning a hole into my soul. But since I can't leave a good thing alone, I turn and look over my shoulder at him briefly.

No words pass between us, but I know something has changed. Whatever this is, it's not what it was when we stepped into this rainforest.

And I'm not going to fight against it anymore.

23

WILLOW

I stare at my reflection in my mirror, smoothing my hands down the short black dress I've changed into and out of three times in the last twenty minutes. My hands shake slightly as I reach for my lip gloss, and I want to slap myself for being ridiculous. I hate that I'm this nervous. It's just dinner. It's not about Blaise. It's definitely not about what happened in the rainforest earlier.

Except it absolutely is. And it's all I can think about.

The memory of his body caging mine against that tree trunk keeps replaying on loop. The way his voice grew deeper when he asked if this was what I wanted. How his eyes dropped to my lips like he was fighting every instinct not to kiss me right there in the rain.

"You look amazing," Madison says from behind me, and I catch her reflection in the mirror. She's wearing a flowy coral dress that brings out her tan, looking effortlessly put-together while I'm over here having a full-scale wardrobe crisis.

"I feel ridiculous," I admit just before tugging at the hem of my dress. "This is too much, isn't it?"

"For dinner in San Juan? Not even close." She moves to stand beside me, fixing a strand of my hair. "Besides, you deserve to feel gorgeous."

I do feel beautiful, but that isn't the problem here. The problem is that I have to face Blaise again within this new dynamic and I feel completely unprepared. "It's not about feeling gorgeous," I say as my eyes meet hers in the mirror. "It's about—"

"About what happened on the hike today?" Madison raises an eyebrow. "Because whatever that was between you and Blaise, it definitely wasn't about getting rain gear out of your backpack."

I'm not surprised she knew, and it was a lame excuse at that. But also, fuck. "Was it that obvious?"

"To me? Yes. To everyone else? Probably not." She moves to sit on the edge of her bed. "So are you going to tell me what's going on, or do I have to guess?"

I turn away from the mirror because I suddenly need to move. "There's nothing going on. We were just...talking."

"Talking." I can see the air quotes without her having to make the hand gestures. "Is that what we're calling it when a guy looks at you like he wants to fuck you until you're screaming for mercy?"

"Madison! What the hell?"

"What? I'm just saying what I saw." She shrugs, completely unbothered by my mortification. "And trust me, that man was not thinking about rain gear."

I sink onto my bed, burying my face in my hands. "This is such a mess."

"Why is it a mess?" Madison's voice is gentle now. "He's gorgeous, you're gorgeous, there's obviously something there and we are in Puerto Rico..."

"Because he's my brother's best friend," I say through my fingers. "Because he rejected me once before. Because this trip is supposed to be about Puerto Rico, not whatever psychological warfare we've been engaging in."

"Psychological warfare?" Madison laughs. "Willow, that's not warfare. That's sexual tension so thick you could cut it with a chainsaw."

I peek at her through my fingers. "You think?"

"Honey, I thought the rainforest was going to sponta-neously combust because of you two." She stands up and moves to her suitcase. "The question is, what are you going to do about it?"

"Nothing," I say automatically. "Absolutely nothing."

"Uh-huh." Madison pulls out a small makeup bag. "Is that why you've changed outfits three times and keep checking yourself in the mirror?"

I hate that she's right and she hasn't known me for that long. I hate that I'm this transparent. I hate that despite every logical reason to stay away from Blaise

Dalton, I can't stop thinking about what changed today even if I can't name it.

"I don't know what I'm doing," I admit quietly.

"That's okay," Madison says, settling beside me on the bed. "You don't have to know. But maybe stop fighting it so hard and see what happens?"

"And if it all blows up in my face?"

"Then at least you'll know." She nudges my shoulder. "Besides, from where I'm sitting, it looks like he's fighting the same battle you are."

"You're not wrong—" My phone vibrates on the night-stand, and I reach for it. I could almost kiss whoever caused that notification to go off because I'm grateful for the distraction. I find a text from my mom to the group chat with my father, Abue, and Knox.

> Mom: How was your day, sweetie? Send pictures!

Right. I'd completely forgotten to update anyone since this morning. I quickly pull up my messages and start typing.

> Me: Day was amazing! Hiked through El Yunque rainforest and it was absolutely incredible. Heading to dinner in San Juan now. Here are some photos.

I scroll through my photos from today, selecting a few that capture the beauty of the rainforest and try my best not to let my mind drift to thoughts of what Blaise did to me there. But I fail. With a heavy sigh, I send them to the group chat and almost immediately get responses.

> Dad: Beautiful! Stay safe and have fun.
>
> Abue: You look so happy! The rainforest looks magical, and now I'm regretting not getting on the flight with you.

I can't help but laugh at Abue and the thought of her joining this trip with the rest of my class. She would definitely be the most popular person on the trip, and to be honest, it would be lovely to travel with her again.

> Knox: Damn, that place looks sick. You're hiking in those conditions? Be careful.

I roll my eyes at Knox's protective streak coming through even via text.

> Me: I'm fine, Knox. It was just a little rain.
>
> Knox: A little rain? That looks like a monsoon in the background of one of those pics.
>
> Me: It's a RAINFOREST. Rain is kind of the point.
>
> Mom: Are you eating enough? Make sure you're staying hydrated in that heat.

> Abue: And don't forget sunscreen! Your skin burns like mine.

> Dad: How's the group? Everyone getting along okay?

I hesitate at Dad's question and I'm not exactly sure why. That's a lie. I know it's because of *him*. I take a second to collect my thoughts before I send a response to the chat.

> Me: Group is good. Madison, my roommate, is awesome.

> Knox: What about everyone else? Blaise keeping an eye on things like I asked?

My stomach drops. Of course Knox would bring up Blaise right now. I glance at Madison, who is now sitting next to me and pretending not to read over my shoulder but definitely is.

> Me: Blaise is...fine. Everyone's fine. And I don't need a babysitter.

I want to yank out every follicle on Knox's head, but I refrain because it would only draw more attention to me.

> Knox: Good. You can trust him if you need anything.

Trust him. Right. If only Knox knew what he'd done to

me today. The thing Knox would trust is his fist meeting Blaise's cheek.

> Abue: Are you making friends? Meeting
> any nice boys?

I nearly choke on my own spit. Madison full-on snorts beside me.

> > Me: Abue, I'm here to learn about Puerto
> > Rican culture, not meet boys.

> Abue: You can do both. A little romance
> never hurt anyone.

> Mom: Your grandmother has a point. You
> work too hard. It's okay to have fun.

> Knox: Wait, what boys? What are we
> even talking about here?

> > Me: There are no boys. Abue is just
> > being Abue.

> Dad: Your brother's right to be
> concerned. Strange places, new
> people...

> Mom: Oh stop it, both of you. She's
> twenty years old and perfectly capable of
> taking care of herself.

> Abue: Exactly! When I was her age, I was
> already married to your grandfather. Let
> the girl live a little.

Knox: That's different, Abue, and a different time. You weren't surrounded by college guys on what is essentially spring break in January.

Me: This isn't spring break, Knox. It's an academic trip with professors and everything. And why am I explaining anything to you?

Knox: Because I'm your big brother and I worry. Sue me.

Madison leans over and whispers, "Your family is intense."

"It's usually not this bad," I mutter back, then type a response.

Me: I appreciate the concern, but I'm fine. Really.

Mom: Of course you are, sweetheart. We just miss you.

Abue: Send more pictures at dinner! I want to see the food and the handsome young men.

Knox: ABUE.

Abue: What? I have eyes and they want to see...things!

I'm laughing despite myself. They are doing the absolute most, but I do still love them.

> Me: You're all impossible. I'm going to
> dinner now. Love you.

I set my phone down after that, but it immediately buzzes again. It's Knox texting me privately.

> Knox: Have fun but not too much fun.
> And tell Blaise I said thanks.

I stare at the message, my stomach twisting. Tell Blaise he said thanks. Right. For looking out for me. Not for pinning me against a tree in the rainforest like he was ready to risk it all. But since he texted me without Mom, Dad and Abue, I can now tell him how I feel about him making Blaise my bodyguard.

> Me: Knox, I need you to stop asking
> Blaise to babysit me. I'm an adult.

> Knox: What do you mean babysit? I just
> asked him to keep an eye out. You know,
> make sure you're safe.

> Me: Same thing. And it's embarrassing. I
> don't need a chaperone.

> Knox: It's not about you needing one. It's
> about me feeling better knowing
> someone I trust is there.

I roll my eyes so hard they practically fall out of my head.

Me: Someone YOU trust. What about trusting ME?

Knox: I do trust you. It's everyone else I don't trust.

Me: Like who? Our professors? Madison? The guy who tried to help me with my gardening gloves?

Knox: Wait, what guy? What happened with gardening gloves?

Shit. I shouldn't have mentioned David. Now Knox is going to spiral.

Me: Nothing happened. Some guy was just being friendly and Blaise acted weird about it.

Knox: Weird how?

Me: Protective. Which was unnecessary because I can handle myself.

There's a longer pause before his next message.

Knox: Good. I'm glad he stepped in.

Me: KNOX.

Knox: What? If some random guy was making you uncomfortable, I'm glad Blaise was there.

Me: I never said he made me
uncomfortable.

Knox: Then why did Blaise step in?

I stare at the phone because I've just realized I've painted myself into a corner. Because the truth is David did make me uncomfortable but admitting that will only validate Knox's overprotective instincts.

Me: Can we please change the subject?

Knox: Fine. But I'm serious about having
fun. Just...smart fun.

Me: What does that even mean?

Knox: It means don't do anything that
would give me a heart attack if I found
out about it.

Madison lets out a belly laugh because she read the same text that I did. "Your brother would definitely have a heart attack if he knew what I witnessed today."

I elbow her in the ribs. I need at least one person in my corner.

Me: Your definition of heart attack
material and mine are probably very
different.

Knox: Probably. Love you, Wills. Be safe.

Me: Love you too. Stop worrying.

I set my phone aside and look at Madison, who's been watching this entire family drama unfold and she's barely holding her laughter in. I don't blame her and would be having the same issue if I wasn't the one at the center of said drama.

"Feel better?" she asks.

"Not really." I stand up and smooth my dress again. "Now I'm thinking about how Knox would react if he knew what actually happened today."

"What would he do?"

"Probably get on the next flight to Puerto Rico and drag me home by my hair." I grab my small purse from the dresser. "Or worse, he'd confront Blaise."

"And that would be bad because...?"

I pause and think about the question. Why would that be bad? Because it would embarrass me? Because it would force Blaise and me to confront whatever this is between us? Because it might ruin Knox and Blaise's friendship? And destroy their hockey team because Knox truly won't give a fuck?

All of the above.

"Because it would complicate everything," I finally say.

Madison stands and checks herself in the mirror one last time. "Maybe everything needs to be complicated. Maybe simple isn't working for you."

She has a good point. Whatever is building between us is going to snap at some point, much like Blaise's control earlier today. But the thought of anything else happening between us makes me want to toss caution to the wind or bury myself alive.

"We should go," I say abruptly. I have to stop this line of thinking before I spiral further. "Everyone's probably already downstairs."

"Ready to face the music?"

"As ready as I'll ever be." I slip my phone into my purse and head toward the door.

This dinner is either going to be amazing or a complete disaster. Based on how this day has gone, probably both.

24

WILLOW

The nightlife in San Juan is everything that I wanted and so much more. Not that I have so much experience with night life since I'm under twenty-one, but being able to walk into a bar or club here since the minimum age is eighteen is already a step up for me. But that's just the starting point.

This whole street feels like a celebration someone forgot to end. Every bar is pulsing with music, each one competing to be louder than the last. Normally this much sound and movement would have me overstimulated and looking for a way out, but tonight it feels like *freedom*. And I want to be part of all of it.

"This is amazing!" Madison yells.

She needs to raise her voice because of the reggaetón beat coming out of the nearest bar. She looks like she can't believe this is real either. I think we're both pinching ourselves mentally to confirm we are actually here and get to have this experience.

Blaise, Tyler, David, and a few other people from our group are walking behind us. I've been hyperaware of Blaise's presence behind me since we left the restaurant. Every time I laugh too loudly or lean into Madison while we walk, I can feel his eyes on me. It's like there's a spotlight following me around, and he's the one holding it. Or he's still very fixated on this whole bodyguard job that my brother promoted him to.

"Where do we even start?" I ask, but I'm already being pulled by the wrist toward a glowing purple-and-gold bar with an open front and a brass band layered over electronic beats. Curiosity wins. It always does.

The place is packed, and I quickly realize it is standing-room only near the bar. But for some reason, it doesn't feel claustrophobic. It feels electric.

"First round's on me," a voice says behind us, and I realize how close this person is to me because I can hear them clearly despite the music.

I turn to find Blaise standing close enough that I catch a hint of his cologne over the mingled scents of rum and salt air. I look over his shoulder and wonder if it's a coincidence that he's positioned himself between David and me.

"You don't have to do that," I say, but in order for him to hear me, I have to turn my head so that I can say it in his ear. It brings us even closer together.

"I want to." His gaze holds mine for a beat too long

before he turns toward the crowded bar. "What does everyone want?"

Madison immediately perks up. "Something tropical. Surprise me."

"Beer," Tyler calls out, already scanning the room, but for what, I have no idea.

David steps closer to me with that persistent smile still plastered on his face. "I'll take whatever the lady's having," he says, nodding toward me.

I resist the urge to roll my eyes. "I haven't ordered yet."

"Then I'll wait," he says, like this is somehow charming instead of mildly irritating.

Blaise stares him down before he turns to me. "What do you want, Willow?"

The way he says my name makes me want to melt into the ground or swoon. Or something equally as ridiculous. There's an edge to it and I like it more than I should.

"Hmmm...maybe a pina colada? OH in the pineapple!" I say, still looking at him. I'd seen a few vendors selling them on the way here and now seems like the perfect opportunity to order one.

"Perfect. Tyler, help me grab the drinks?" He turns to look at Tyler and when Tyler gives him the okay, they make their way through the crowd toward the bar.

Before I can process that he left, David slides into the space Blaise vacated. "So, pineapple drinks, huh? Very tropical of you."

"It's Puerto Rico," I say flatly. "Seemed appropriate."

"Touché, touché. You know," David continues, leaning closer so I can hear him over the music. "I was thinking we should explore more of the city tomorrow. Just the two of us."

Madison catches my eye and raises an eyebrow. I can practically see her biting back a laugh.

"That's sweet," I say, taking a step back to create some space between us, "but I think we have group activities planned."

"Not all day though, right?" David's smile never wavers. "Come on, don't you want to see the real San Juan? Not just the touristy stuff?"

"I'm pretty sure everything we're doing is the real San Juan," Madison interjects, and I could kiss her for it. "That's kind of the point of the trip."

David glances at her briefly before turning his attention back to me. "Sure, but wouldn't it be more fun with just...the two of us?"

The way he says it makes my skin crawl slightly. There's something about his persistence that reminds me too much of Leo. The way he'd never take no for an answer, always pushing until I gave in just to make it stop.

"I like the group dynamic," I say firmly. "More people means more perspectives. More opportunities to learn."

David's smile falters for just a second before he recovers. "Right, perspectives. But sometimes you need to step away from the group to really experience a place, you know?"

"I think I'm experiencing plenty," I say, gesturing around us.

Madison steps closer to me, creating a subtle barrier. "Besides, we're roommates. We've got plenty of girl time planned already when we have some free time on the schedule." She gives David a pointed look. "Right, Willow?"

"Absolutely," I say as I shoot Madison a look that I hope shows how grateful I am that she's doing this. "We've got so much planned."

Before David can respond, Blaise and Tyler return, and I don't think I've ever been happier to see Blaise in my life. He appears at my side, holding out a pineapple drink that looks exactly like what I'd imagined—complete with a little paper umbrella and everything.

"One pina colada in a pineapple," he says, extending it toward me.

When I reach for it, our fingers brush against each other as he transfers the drink to my hands. The contact sends a jolt up my arm that has nothing to do with the music or the energy of the bar. His fingers linger just a moment longer than necessary before he pulls away, but I don't mention it. Can't mention it.

"Thank you," I manage to say before taking a sip. The drink is sweet and cold and exactly what I needed to cool down the heat that's been building in my chest all evening.

Blaise nods, then hands Madison her drink. It's something pink and fruity with way too many garnishes. Tyler gets his beer, and David receives his pina colada with significantly less ceremony. Lowkey, I'm surprised Blaise brought him anything back.

"So," Madison says, raising her glass, "to Puerto Rico and new experiences!"

We all clink our drinks together, but I notice Blaise's eyes stay on me even as he touches his beer bottle to everyone else's. The drinks disappear faster than I expected. The pina colada is dangerously smooth, and the tropical sweetness masks whatever rum content is making my limbs feel loose and warm. Madison drains her pink concoction and immediately starts swaying to the reggaetón beat that's practically vibrating through the floor.

"I need to dance," she announces, grabbing Tyler's arm. "Come on, you're my partner."

Tyler panics. "I don't really—"

"Everyone can dance to this," Madison insists, already pulling him toward the crowded dance floor. "It's just moving to the beat!"

I watch them disappear into the mass of bodies, Madison's coral dress a bright splash of color as she spins Tyler around. He's laughing despite himself, and I can't help but smile at how she's managed to drag him out of his shell.

That's when David strikes.

"Perfect timing," he says, moving to stand directly in front of me. "Now we can have a dance."

I'm about to decline—politely but firmly—when I catch sight of Blaise over David's shoulder. He's gripping his beer bottle so tightly his knuckles have gone white. His jaw is clenched, and there's something dark and possessive in his eyes as he watches David lean closer to me.

The rational part of my brain knows I should say no. Should maintain the boundaries I've been trying to establish all day. But the irrational part, the part that's been wound tight since the rainforest, since that moment against the tree, wants to see what happens if I push.

"You know what?" I hear myself saying, my eyes still locked on Blaise. "Sure. Let's dance."

Blaise's expression shifts so quickly I almost miss it. The careful control he's maintained all evening cracks, just for a second, and what I see underneath makes my stomach nearly leave my body. Jealousy.

David's face lights up like he's won the lottery. "Really? Great!" He sets down his drink and extends his hand. "Come on, let's get out there."

I take his hand but keep watching Blaise. His beer bottle hits the bar with more force than necessary, and I see him take a step forward before stopping himself.

Perfect.

David leads me onto the dance floor and immediately pulls me closer than I'd prefer, his hands finding my waist as he tries to guide me into some approximation of salsa.

"You're a natural," he says, spinning me around clumsily.

I'm not really listening to him. Over his shoulder, I can see Blaise standing at the edge of the dance floor, his eyes tracking every move we make. When David dips me slightly, Blaise's jaw tightens. When David's hand slides lower on my back, I watch Blaise's control fracture a little more.

"This is fun," David continues, pulling me against him as the song shifts to something slower and more sensual. "I knew you'd be a good dancer."

His hand is definitely too low now, resting just above the curve of my ass. I should move it, should create distance, but I'm too focused on the way Blaise is staring at us. At me.

I turn away and look at my dance partner for a second. He gives me that award-winning smile just before I speak. "David," I start, finally ready to establish some boundaries.

But before I can finish the sentence, I hear, "Mind if I cut in?" Blaise's voice is calm, and I know it's bullshit. I look over at him immediately and know my plan worked. After all, Madison did say something about simple isn't working for us, right?

David looks up, clearly annoyed by the interruption. "Actually, we were just—"

"I wasn't asking you," Blaise says, his eyes never leaving mine. "I was being polite."

The threat in his tone is unmistakable. David's hands fall away from my waist immediately.

"Right. Sure. Of course." David steps back, hands raised in surrender. "All yours, man."

Blaise moves into the space David vacated, and suddenly the entire dance floor shrinks to just the two of us. His hands settle on my waist, firm and possessive, and I have to remind myself to breathe.

"That was rude," I say.

"Was it?" His thumbs trace small circles against my hip bones through the thin fabric of my dress. "Or was it necessary?"

The music shifts again, something slower and more intimate. Blaise pulls me closer, and I don't resist. Our bodies align perfectly, and I can feel the tension radiating off him in waves.

"You're jealous," I observe, my hands coming up to rest against his chest.

"Am I?"

"You are." I let my fingers trace the edge of his shirt collar. "You couldn't stand watching him touch me."

His grip on my waist tightens. "Willow."

"What? It's true, isn't it?" I tilt my head back to look at him fully. "You could've said something when he asked."

"I didn't think it was appropriate," he says.

I tilt my head. "But isn't the saying see something, say something? If you had, then I wouldn't have danced with him. And that would've made you a good boy."

I have no idea why those words came out of my mouth, but I don't regret them for a second. Because it's as if a light switch went off between us. Instead of answering, he spins me around so my back is pressed against his chest. His arms cage me in, hands splayed across my stomach as we move together to the rhythm. I can feel every line of his body against mine and there's no place I would rather be.

"I tried to be good, but you just had to tempt me. Now I want to show him exactly who you belong to," he murmurs against my ear.

I know for a fact that these words are making me dizzy. "I don't belong to anyone."

"Don't you?" His lips brush against my neck, just below my ear. "Then why are you letting me hold you like this? Why aren't you pulling away?"

Because I can't. Because every rational thought has fled my brain, replaced by wanting to be held by him. My brother be damned. Because the careful walls I've built around my feelings for him are crumbling with every touch.

"This is dangerous," I whisper.

"I know." His arms tighten around me. "I don't care anymore."

25

BLAISE

I take Willow's hand and lead her off the dance floor without another word.

She follows, and to be honest, I'm surprised she does. However, tonight it different. It's because neither of us want to pretend that this isn't a thing anymore.

We push through the crowd and I don't bother checking to see if David's watching or if Madison's noticed we've left. Text messages can confirm who we're with and we're we've gone. My focus is only on getting Willow alone.

The moment we're outside the bar, I turn us down a narrow alley between two buildings. It's slightly quieter here and is dimly lit by a single streetlamp, making it less likely we'll be spotted. Part of me is moving this fast because I don't want to give her time to realize she's supposed to be pissed at me for rejecting her years ago. Or to recall that we're not supposed to be doing this.

With every step I take, the more my control slips. Damn the consequences at least for tonight. I need this. I need her. I need us alone. I've been pushed to the edge and this is what it feels like to go over. I'm feeling slightly lightheaded already, and we've barely even started.

"Blaise—" she starts, but I cut her off.

"Do you have any idea what you've been doing to me? All day. Since we stepped foot in Puerto Rico?"

"What exactly have I been doing?" she asks, her voice breathless but defiant. She takes a step closer instead of backing away. "Tell me."

"You know damn well what. The way you looked at me in the rainforest. How you didn't bother trying to cover up once you saw me staring at your tits through your shirt. Dancing with that asshole just to make me lose my mind."

"Maybe I want you to lose your mind. Maybe I'm tired of you pretending you don't want this."

"Pretending?" The word comes out as a growl. "You think any of this has been easy for me? Watching you, wanting you, knowing I can't have you?"

"Says who? Knox? Some rule you made up in your head?"

"Knox would kill me."

She looks around as if she's trying to find something. "Knox isn't here." Her hand comes up to rest against my chest, right over my racing heart. "It's just us, Blaise."

The way she says my name is all it takes for the last thread of my restraint to snap in half. I move before I can think, before I can stop myself, before I can remember all the reasons this is a terrible idea. My hands frame her face, and I crash my mouth against hers like I'll die if I don't.

She tastes like pineapple and rum and something that's purely Willow. I've thought about what it would be like to kiss her again but never thought I would have the opportunity to do it again after I messed things up. She moans and her lips part, and I take full advantage, deepening the kiss without a second thought.

This isn't gentle. This isn't careful. This is years of want and denial and watching her from a distance when I had the chance finally exploding into something I can't control. I kiss her like I'll never get another opportunity, and hell, maybe I won't.

"Fuck," I breathe against her lips, pulling back just enough to see her face. Her eyes are dark, pupils wide from what I can see in this dark alleyway, and her lips swollen from my mouth. She's never looked more beautiful.

"Why did you stop?" she whispers, and I find myself wondering the same damn thing.

"I don't know," I admit. "I don't know why I stopped."

She pulls me back down to her and says, "Then don't do it again."

One thing's for certain, I don't need to be told twice.

My mouth crashes back against hers and this time there's no hesitation, no pulling back. My hands tangle in her hair as I press her against the brick wall behind us. She tastes like everything I've been denying myself, and I'm starving for it.

I can feel every curve of her body pressed against mine, and it's driving me insane. When she nips at my bottom lip, I nearly lose it completely.

"Willow," I growl against her mouth.

"I know," she breathes. "I know."

The chance of someone finding us is real, but I can't bring myself to care. Not when she's making me lose my mind with just her lips and I can't think straight. I've wanted this for so long that I'll take it on any terms and that includes us being reckless and getting caught. She's that addictive and I don't think I'll ever get enough.

That's a thought I can't focus on right now. My hands find the hem of her tight black dress and I groan as my fingers brush against her thighs. She gasps into my mouth, and the sound goes straight to my cock.

"Tell me to stop," I say against her lips, even as my hands slide higher. "Tell me this is crazy."

"It is crazy," she says. "And I don't want you to stop."

That's all the permission I need. My mouth moves to her neck, finding a spot just below her ear that makes her arch against me. I want to spend my time getting to know every inch of her body, but I tell myself that will come in due time even if that's not true. But what is true is I can't waste a single second.

"Someone could see us," Willow barely gets the words out. Her head falls back against the brick wall and it gives me better access.

"Let them," I growl against her throat. My hands grip her thighs, and before I can second-guess myself, I'm dropping to my knees in front of her.

Her eyes go wide. "Blaise, what are you—"

"I need to taste you, I need to know if you taste as good as I've imagined."

I can see the war that's waging within her playing out across her face. She wants me to do this, but she knows we're in an alley where anyone could find us.

"Here?" she whispers.

"Right here. Right now." I push her dress higher. "Unless you want me to stop."

I refuse to do anything she doesn't want me to do or that will make her uncomfortable. She stares down at me for a long moment, and I can see the exact second she makes her decision. Her hands tangle in my hair, and she says something, but I don't catch it.

"What did you say, sweetheart?"

This time she says it louder, "I want you to make me come."

"That I can and would love to do."

I push her dress up around her waist and groan when

I realize she's wearing a thong. I don't bother hooking my fingers in the waistband of her underwear in order to pull them down. There's no point and it feels like it would take up too much of our precious time. Instead, I push the fabric aside and as I touch her, I find her already wet for me. The discovery makes me groan against her inner thigh.

"Fuck, baby. Is this all for me?" I look up and catch her nodding her head, but I don't linger. I have a test that I need to complete in front of me and I fully plan on scoring an 'A'.

The first taste of her makes my head spin. She's everything I imagined she'd be and so much more. She's a mixture of sweet, intoxicating, and absolutely perfect for me. Her fingers tighten in my hair as I explore her with my mouth.

"Oh my—" she says and I barely hear her above the music that is coming from every direction. She might have said something else, but what I did hear as clear as day is her saying, "Blaise—"

It takes everything within me not to smirk when her words die on her lips, but I refrain. I'm focused on the task at hand, and I'm determined to lose myself in her completely. I use my tongue to trace slow, deliberate circles around her clit. Her fingers are anchored in my hair and her hips begin to move. I'm convinced it's only a matter of time before she starts humping my face.

And I'll enjoy every second of it.

I should stop.

Deep down I know I should.

We're in an alley. There are people everywhere, music in the air, the chance of someone turning the wrong corner and seeing exactly what I'm doing to her. She's Knox's little sister. She's off-limits. This isn't what good guys do.

But she tastes like sin, and I've never wanted anything more.

And right now, I don't give a damn about being good.

I move my head to take her clit between my lips, sucking gently while my fingers find her entrance. When I slide one finger inside her, she gasps and her hips buck against my mouth.

"You're so fucking tight," I say, but I'm not sure if she registered what I said. I move in and out of her slowly at first, letting her adjust to me while my mouth continues its work on her clit. Her body responds immediately, clenching around my finger as soft whimpers escape her lips.

"More," she breathes, and the desperation in her voice nearly undoes me.

I add a second finger, stretching her carefully as I curl them upward, searching for that spot that will make her see stars. When I find it, her entire body jerks against the wall.

"Right there," she gasps, her grip on my hair tightening to the point of pain, but I don't care. "Please, don't stop."

I wouldn't dream of it. I work my fingers deeper, establishing a rhythm that has her eyes rolling into the back of head. She's getting wetter with each stroke and it's then I know I was made to bring her body this pleasure.

"You feel incredible," I say because I can't help myself before returning my mouth to her clit. The combination of my tongue and fingers has her trembling, and I can tell she's fighting to stay quiet.

Her walls clench around my fingers as I curl them, hitting her G-spot again. "Blaise, I—" she starts, but the words shift into a moan when I increase the pressure of my tongue.

I love watching her lose control. The way her head falls back, exposing her throat that I can't wait to lick and suck given the next opportunity. How her fingers twist in my hair like she's trying to keep herself from falling to the ground. Not to mention the little sounds she makes when I change the angle or speed.

"That's it, baby," I encourage, pumping my fingers steadily while my mouth works her clit. "Let me hear you."

She's close. I can feel it in the way her muscles tense and how her breathing has become more erratic. I slide a third finger inside her, stretching her further, and she gasps at the sensation. "Too much?" I ask and regret that I made this silly move. I don't want to hurt her and might have just stalled her orgasm.

"No," she manages to get out but her voice is strained. "It's perfect. You're amazing."

The praise goes straight to my head, making me even more determined to make her fall apart. I pump my fingers faster, curling them on each stroke while my tongue flicks rapidly over her clit.

Her breathing becomes shallow, desperate. "I'm so close," she whispers.

Thank fuck I didn't ruin this. When her thighs start to shake, I know she's right on the edge.

"Come for me," I growl against her. "I want to feel you fall apart."

That's all it takes. Her orgasm slams through her body as she cries out my name. It's the sweetest sound. I don't stop, working her through tremors until she's pushing at my shoulders because her pussy is now oversensitive.

I slowly withdraw my fingers and press one last gentle kiss to each of her thighs before standing. She's leaning heavily against the wall, chest heaving, looking absolutely wrecked in the best possible way.

"Holy shit," she breathes, staring at me with wide eyes.

I can't help the satisfied smirk that crosses my face. "Good?"

She lets out a breathless laugh. "Blaise, that was—" She shakes her head, seemingly at a loss for words. "How did you—? There's no way you—"

I stare her dead in the eye as I stick each of the fingers that was inside her in my mouth one by one.

"You think I just *guessed* how to touch you like that?"

I wait a beat before I continue. "I've read articles and books, watched videos, took notes like I was prepping for an exam. Being a nerd has its perks. Especially when I'm using what I've learned to ruin you. Now let's get out of here."

26

WILLOW

Who knew I could easily follow instructions when it's required of me? Because he didn't have to tell me twice.

My legs feel like they're made of jelly as Blaise and I hurry through the streets of San Juan. When we get back to the hotel, I swear we are stumbling toward his room, but neither one of us is drunk. However, it feels like the only reason why I'm standing upright is because my hand is still clasped in Blaise's. I pray we don't come across anyone that we might know, including our professors, because having to explain this to anyone would literally make me want the Earth to open up and swallow me whole.

We reach his door and Blaise fumbles with his key card because his hands are shaking. Now whether he will admit that if I asked is an entirely different thing, but none of that matters. I completely understand how he feels. The adrenaline from what just happened is still coursing through both of us, and I can barely think straight. When the lock finally clicks open, he pulls me inside and immediately checks to make sure Tyler's bed is empty.

"He's still out," Blaise says, turning back to me. The relief in his voice is obvious and I feel the same way.

"Shouldn't you put a sock on the doorknob? To make sure he knows...what's going to be happening in here?"

The suggestion makes him pause, and for a second I think he might actually consider it. Then a small smile forms on his lips.

"I actually texted Tyler while we were walking back. I just wanted to make sure he actually didn't come back," he says, but he still turns the deadbolt. The click echoes in the quiet room, and suddenly we're truly alone.

I'm not even shocked. This is Blaise and he's always prepared. I watch as he puts his phone away and moves to sit on the edge of his bed. His eyes meet mine, and in that moment, the memory of our encounter in the alleyway rushes back, making me shiver.

"Come here," he says and holds out his hand for me to grab.

I walk toward him slowly because my nerves are shot. When I reach him, he doesn't pull me down immediately. Instead, his hands settle on my hips, thumbs tracing gentle circles through the fabric of my dress.

"We don't have to—" he starts, but I cut him off.

"I want to. I want this. I want you."

His eyes search mine, looking for any hint of uncertainty. "You're sure?"

I nod, not trusting my voice. He stands slowly, his hands sliding up to frame my face. When he kisses me this time, it's different from the alleyway. Softer. More careful. Like he's handling something fragile.

My hands find the hem of his shirt, and I tug upward. He breaks the kiss to let me pull it over his head, and I have to bite back a gasp. I've never seen him shirtless before, and I'm not sure what I was expecting, but it wasn't this. His chest is broader than I imagined, defined but not overly muscular, but his six pack is well defined. There's a thin scar above his left collarbone that I want to trace with my tongue. My fingers hover just inches from his skin, suddenly unsure.

"You can touch me," he says softly, reading my hesitation.

I place my palms flat against his chest and immediately feel the rapid beat of his heart beneath my hands. His skin is warm and smooth, and when I drag my fingers downward, I swear he stops breathing for a second.

"Your turn," he whispers, gesturing for me to turn around.

I do as he wants and he quickly reaches for the zipper on the back of my dress. He moves slowly, dragging it down inch by inch like he's unwrapping something sacred when I want him to act like he's unwrapping a birthday present. When the dress finally pools at my feet, I step out of it carefully and find myself standing in front of him in just my black bra and matching thong. Suddenly, my confidence wavers. This is Blaise. Knox's best friend. The guy who rejected me once before.

What if he changes his mind again?

"You're beautiful," he says as his fingertips trace along my collarbone. His touch is so light I barely feel it. "So fucking beautiful."

The compliment makes me smile, and suddenly the vulnerability I was feeling transforms into something bolder. Something that feels more like me. I step closer to him and I say, "Can I ask you something?"

"Anything."

I look up at him and move my hands, so my fingers trace the edge of his waistband. For a second I remember the way his entire body reacted to two simple words on the dance floor. "Did you like it when I called you a good boy earlier?"

The effect is immediate. His hands tighten on my waist like he's trying to pull me closer to him. I watch his throat move as he swallows hard.

"Why would you ask me that?" His voice comes out deeper than before.

"Because of the way you reacted." I let my fingers dip just beneath his waistband, not going far, just enough to make him tense. "Your whole body changed when I said it."

He's quiet for a moment, and I can see him wrestling with whether to answer honestly. Finally, he exhales slowly. "Yeah. I liked it."

The admission sends heat racing through my veins. "Why?"

"Because..." He pauses, his hands sliding down to grip my hips more firmly. "Because I guess I have a praise kink."

This powerful, always in control man who commands respect on the ice and in the classroom just admitted he has a praise kink. To me.

"A praise kink," I repeat, letting the words roll off my tongue as I watch his reaction. His jaw tightens, and I can see the flush creeping up his neck. "So when I tell you you're being good..."

"Willow." My name comes out as a warning, but his body betrays him because I feel his grip tighten on my hips.

"What happens when I tell you you're my good boy?" I ask, my voice dropping to barely above a whisper. "Does it make you want to please me even more?"

"Fuck yes."

The admission makes me want to be even more bold. I slide my hands up his chest and say, "I thought so. You were so good to me in that alley, Blaise. So thorough. So perfect."

A low groan leaves his lips, and suddenly his mouth is on mine again, hungrier this time. His hands roam my body with more urgency, and if his cock is any indication, my words are having the effect I want them to have on him.

"You have no idea what you do to me," he says in my ear, and I shiver as a result.

"Then show me," I challenge as my fingers play with his belt buckle. "Show me how fantastic you can be."

I undo his jeans and belt and both of them hit the floor with a soft thud. I immediately notice the tension in his body. There's something intoxicating about having this effect on someone who usually doesn't lose control.

"You're going to be the death of me," he says against my lips, but his hands are already working at the clasp of my bra.

"Good," I say back. "I want to wreck you the way you wrecked me."

The bra falls away, and suddenly his hands are everywhere. He's cupping and caressing my breasts and when his thumbs brush over my nipples, I arch into his touch, practically begging for more.

"I love how responsive and sensitive you are to my touch you are," he says it so low that I wonder if he's actually talking to me. "So perfect."

"That's very romantic," I toss out because this is getting serious very fast. "Very un-fuckboy of you."

He laughs softly. "I was never a fuckboy, Willow. Just a coward."

"Well, you're being very brave now." I let my hands slide down his chest again. "Almost heroically brave, one might say."

"Are you mocking my emotional vulnerability?" But he's smiling as he says it.

"Maybe a little." I grin up at him. "It's cute how you get all sincere when you're about to get laid."

"Cute?" He raises an eyebrow, and suddenly his hands are on my thighs, lifting me effortlessly. "There's nothing cute about me."

My legs wrap around his waist instinctively as he carries me the few steps to his bed. "Yes there is; you're very cute. Like a golden retriever who learned to sit."

He sets me down gently on the edge of the mattress. "You always do that."

"Do what?"

"Use sarcasm when things get too real." His fingers trace along my jaw. "You don't have to deflect with me."

The observation hits too close to home, making me want to retreat behind another joke. But the way he's looking at me stops the words before they form.

"This is terrifying," I admit quietly.

"I know." He brushes a strand of hair behind my ear. "It's terrifying for me too."

"Good," I whisper. "I'd hate to be the only one freaking out."

He moves back slightly, his eyes drinking me in like I'm something he's been waiting his whole life to see. His hands hover just above my skin, close enough that I can feel the heat radiating from his palms.

"I want to take my time with you. Is that okay?"

I nod because finding words is difficult. His fingers find the thin straps of my thong, but instead of pulling it down immediately, he traces the elastic along my hip bones.

"You're shaking," he observes softly.

"So are you," I point out, because his hands are trembling slightly against my skin.

He pauses, looking down at his own hands like he's surprised by their betrayal. "I am." He meets my eyes again. "I've thought about this moment for so long, and now that it's here..."

"Now that it's here?" I chime in.

"I want to remember everything." His thumbs continue their gentle exploration. "The way you look right now. How your skin feels. The sound you make when I touch you here." He presses a gentle kiss to the curve where my neck meets my shoulder. I make a soft gasp that makes him grin.

His fingers finally hook under the thin fabric at my hips. He pulls the thong down slowly, and I lift slightly to help him. When he's done, he tosses it aside without looking and I don't care where it landed.

"Wills, fuck," he starts to say as his gaze travels down my body. "You're..."

"Breathe, Blaise," I whisper, because his chest is rising and falling as if he's having a hard time catching his breath.

He lets out a shaky laugh. "Right. Breathing. That's...that's a good idea."

But instead of touching me, he just stares. His eyes trace every inch of my skin like he's committing it to memory. But I've had enough of this waiting game. It's time to put up or shut up.

I sit up to yank his boxers down. "Your turn."

He catches my wrists gently but firmly, stopping my movement. The sudden shift in his demeanor makes me pause, but not from fear. I feel as if the intensity has been kicked up a notch and where I normally would have tried to argue with him, I wait for his next instruction.

Happily.

"Not yet. Tell me what you want first."

"You know what I—" I start, but he cuts me off.

"No. I don't. And be specific." His grip on my wrists tightens slightly. "Tell me exactly what you want me to do to you."

The command in his voice sends a jolt straight to my pussy. "I want you to touch me," I manage to say.

"Where?" His eyes stare into mine. "Say it."

I can feel my cheeks reddening. "Blaise..."

"Say it, Willow. Tell me where you want my hands."

The words stick in my throat. I'm not used to this. I'm not the person who has to ask or voice what I want so explicitly in the bedroom. But the way he's looking at me, waiting for me to comply, pushes away any awkwardness I feel about it.

"I want you to touch my breasts," I whisper.

"Good girl." The praise makes me shiver. Looks like he's not the only one with a praise kink. "What else?"

"I want..." I swallow hard. "I want you inside me."

"How?" He leans closer. "With my fingers? My mouth? My cock?"

The crude words from his lips make me gasp. "All of it. Everything."

"That's not specific enough." His hands trail down my arms, leaving goosebumps in their wake. "Pick one. Tell me exactly what you want right now."

"Your fingers. I want your fingers inside me again."

"Where?" he presses, even though we both know the answer.

"In my..." I can't finish the sentence.

"Say it." His voice is firm but polite. "I need to hear you say it."

"In my pussy," I finally say. "I want your fingers in my pussy."

The satisfaction in his expression makes the butterflies in my stomach go into ultra drive. "There we go. That wasn't so hard, was it?"

Before I can respond, his hand is between my thighs,

and before I can blink, his fingers are sliding into my pussy. I arch into his touch as a soft moan escapes my lips.

"Still so wet for me," he murmurs approvingly. "Tell me how it feels."

"Good," I gasp as he circles my clit with his thumb. "So good."

"More specific," he demands, sliding one finger inside me. "Tell me exactly how good."

"I can't—" My words dissolve into a moan as he curls his finger.

"You can." He adds a second finger, stretching me. "Tell me, or I'll stop."

The threat makes panic flutter in my chest. "No, don't stop. Please."

"Then tell me."

"It feels incredible," I rush out. "Your fingers feel so good inside me. I love how you stretch me, how you know exactly where to touch me."

"Better." He rewards me by increasing his pace. "What else do you want?"

"I want to touch you too," I admit in between taking deep breaths. "I want to feel you."

"Feel me where?"

My face burns, but I force the words out. "I want to touch your cock. I want to know how hard you are for me."

He groans low in his throat. "Fuck, Willow. The things you do to me, but you know what would make this even better? I want you to beg for me."

27

WILLOW

The word "beg" hangs in the air between us like a challenge I'm not sure I want to accept. My pride rears its head, the same stubborn streak that's gotten me in trouble my entire life. I don't beg. I negotiate, I argue, I fight, but I don't beg. Especially not to Blaise Dalton, who's spent years acting like I'm nothing more than his best friend's annoying little sister whenever we were near each other.

But then his fingers slow to a crawl, barely moving inside me, and my body betrays every principle I've ever held.

"Please," I whisper.

"Please what?" His thumb circles my clit with the lightest possible touch, just enough to make me squirm. "Tell me exactly what you're begging for, kitten."

I want to tell him to go to hell. I want to flip him off

and storm out of this room with whatever dignity I have left. Instead, I hear myself saying, "Please don't stop. Please make me come again."

"Better." His fingers resume their rhythm, but still not fast enough. "But I want more than that. I want you to tell me how badly you need it."

"Blaise—"

"Say it, Willow. Say you need me."

The words feel impossible. Too big. Too real. Too close to admitting something I'm not ready to face. But his fingers are moving just enough to keep me on edge, not enough to push me over, and I'm rapidly losing the ability to think about anything except the orgasm I'm desperate to have.

As if I didn't just have one less than an hour ago.

"I need you," I gasp. "I need you so badly it's making me—-" I stop talking because I've lost the ability to describe this feeling.

The desperation in my voice breaks something in him. I see the exact moment his careful control crashes and burns. His eyes go dark, pupils blown wide, and suddenly his fingers are moving as if this is his only purpose.

"Fuck, when you sound like that..." He leans down to capture my mouth in a kiss. "I can't hold back anymore."

His free hand tangles in my hair, tilting my head back so he can trail his lips down my throat. Every touch feels electric and when his mouth finds my nipple, my eyes slam shut and I nearly launch off the bed.

"That's it, baby," he murmurs against my breast. "Let me hear you."

His fingers work faster now, hitting my G-spot and I swear I'm starting to see galaxies form behind my eyelids. I'm so close I can taste it.

"Look at me, kitten."

The nickname makes my eyes snap open to meet his gaze. There's something raw and vulnerable in his expression that takes my breath away. He's watching me like I'm the most beautiful thing he's ever seen, like he can't quite believe this is real.

"There you are," he whispers, his thumb pressing firmly against my clit. "I want to see your face when you fall apart for me."

The combination of his words, his touch, and the intensity in his eyes sends me falling over the edge. My orgasm crashes through me and I'm left wondering how it's stronger than the first time.

When I finally come back to myself, he's pressing soft kisses to my collarbone while his hand gently strokes my thigh.

"Holy shit." My voice is slightly hoarse. "What was that?"

He lifts his head to look at me, a satisfied smirk on his lips. "Good?"

"Stop fishing for compliments," I say, but I'm smiling as I pull him up for a kiss. "You know exactly how good that was."

He chuckles against my mouth. "Maybe I just like hearing you say it."

"Praise kink," I remind him, and he groans.

"You're never going to let me live that down, are you?"

"Not a chance. But I like it. A lot." I trace my fingers down his chest, following the line of hair that disappears beneath his boxers. "Now can I touch you? Please?"

"Wait. Before we...we should probably talk about a few things."

I pause, studying his face. The responsible side of Blaise is reasserting itself, and while part of me appreciates it, another part wants to tell that side to shut up and let us have this moment.

"Okay," I say carefully. "What kinds of things?"

He sits back slightly, running a hand through his hair. "The practical stuff. Are you...I mean, when was your last test?"

"My last—oh." Heat creeps up my neck. "I got tested three months ago. Clean bill of health. You?"

"Same. I get tested regularly, and it's been a while since..." he trails off, looking embarrassed.

"Since what?"

"Since I've been with anyone," he admits quietly. "Like, a long while."

This surprises me. "Really? But you're you."

"What's that supposed to mean?"

I cringe at what I said. "I didn't mean that. I shouldn't have said that. People don't have sex for all kinds of reasons. I mean you're hot and charming when you want to be. I just assumed..."

"That I was sleeping around?" He shakes his head. "I've been too focused on school and hockey. And honestly, after what happened between us before, I couldn't stop thinking about you. Made it hard to want anyone else."

The admission makes my heart skip, but before I can process it fully, he's leaning down to kiss me again. This time it's softer, more tender, and when he pulls back his eyes are searching mine.

I speak before he has a chance to. "I've been on the pill for years."

"Good. That's...that's good." His hand slides higher, cupping my breast. "But I'm still going to wear a condom."

The fact that he's being so responsible while his thumb is circling my nipple makes me want him even more. "Such a good boy," I whisper and watch his pupils dilate.

"Willow."

The warning in his voice is apparent, but I don't care. "What? You are. So careful, so thoughtful. And you're taking such good care of me."

"You're going to kill me with that mouth."

"Then let me kill you properly," I say, reaching for the waistband of his boxers again.

This time he doesn't stop me. I slowly pull the fabric down and free him completely. Holy shit. Maybe if I'd known he was this well-endowed before, I might have prepared myself mentally. He's thick and long, and the sight of him fully aroused makes my mouth go dry. I wrap my hand around him and when he groans at my touch, I swear it shoots straight to my pussy again.

"Fuck, kitten," he says, "Your hands..."

"Good?" I ask, using his own words against him as I continue stroking.

"So good," he confirms, his head falling back. "But if you keep doing that, this is going to be over before it starts."

I reluctantly let go, but not before pressing a kiss to his chest. "We can't have that."

He reaches over to the nightstand and quickly finds what he's looking for: a condom. For someone who hasn't had sex in a while, it's interesting that he has condoms ready to go, but once again, he's prepared.

"Let me," I say, taking the packet from him.

He stares at me as I tear it open and slowly roll it down his length. The simple act feels intimate in a way I wasn't expecting, and when I'm done, he cups my face in his hands.

"Are you sure about this?" he asks quietly. "Because once we do this, there's no going back."

I know what he means. This changes everything between us. Our history, our future, whatever fragile peace we've managed to maintain recently. But looking at him now, I realize I don't want to go back.

"I'm sure," I whisper. "Are you?"

Instead of answering with words, he kisses me deeply, pouring all his want and need into it. When he pulls back, his forehead rests against mine.

"I've wanted this for so long," he admits. "Wanted you for so long."

"Then have me," I say as if this is a normal, everyday decision.

He positions himself between my thighs and within seconds, I feel the head of his cock pressing against my entrance. We both hold our breath as he slowly pushes inside, inch by inch. The stretch is intense, bordering on overwhelming, but Blaise is taking his time.

"Okay?" he asks.

"More than okay," I manage. "You can move."

He starts slowly, letting me adjust to his size, which I'm so thankful for. He's bigger than I expected, stretching me in ways that make me make sounds I've never heard come out of my mouth. Every nerve ending feels like it's on fire, and I can't decide if I want him to go slower or faster.

"Just a little bit more, baby."

It takes me a few seconds to realize what he's referring to. He's not fully inside me yet. The realization makes my eyes widen because I already feel so full and there's more? My hands grip his shoulders as he continues his slow advance, every inch making me gasp.

"Breathe for me," he murmurs, pressing soft kisses to my jaw. "Just breathe, kitten."

I follow his instruction, forcing myself to breathe deeply as he finally ends up completely inside me. The fullness is overwhelming in the best possible way, and for a moment we both go still. Given how his arms are trembling, I can see that it is taking everything in him not to move yet.

He lets out a shaky breath and says, "You feel incredible. So tight, so perfect." His hands grip my hips again and then he says, "Give me a second or this is going to be embarrassing."

I love that I have this effect on him. I shift slightly beneath him and his grip tightens.

"Willow."

"What? I'm just getting comfortable." I shift again, deliberately this time, and watch his jaw clench.

"This is the way you want to do it? Fine."

Before I can process what he means, he pulls out almost completely and thrusts back in, hard. The sudden movement makes me cry out, my back arching off the bed.

"You want to tease me? Then I'm going to fuck you until you can't think straight."

His words send heat racing through my veins. This is a side of Blaise I've never seen before and I love it even though I'll probably never admit it out loud.

"Yes," I gasp as he leans forward, allowing me to wrap my legs around his waist. "Hell, yes."

"Look at you, taking my cock so perfectly," he growls

against my ear. "Like you were made for me. Such a good girl, letting me stretch this tight little pussy."

My toes literally curl at his words. I claw at his back and my nails dig in just enough to make him hiss against my neck. I wrap my legs tighter around him in an effort to bring him closer because of that perfect angle he just found.

"Fuck, baby," he groans, grinding deeper into me like he's trying to live inside my skin. "You keep doing that and I'm not gonna last."

"That sounds like a you problem," I pant, even as my voice wavers on the edge of another moan.

His laugh is dark and low, and it vibrates straight through me. "Then I guess I'll make it your problem too."

He shifts his weight slightly, changing the angle, and holy hell. There it is. Whatever spot he just found, it makes my whole body clench like a vice. My head tips back and a cry slips from my lips.

"Right there," I gasp. "If you stop, I'll never talk to you again."

"Never talk to me again?" He drives into that spot again. "That's a hell of a threat."

I can barely form words as he keeps hitting exactly where I need him. "I mean it."

"No you don't." His mouth finds my neck, teeth grazing my neck. "You'd miss this too much."

He's not wrong, but I'm not about to admit it. Not when he's being so smug about reducing me to a hot mess beneath him. Instead, I dig my nails deeper into his shoulders, earning another sharp intake of breath.

"Cocky bastard," I manage between gasps.

"You love it." He punctuates the words with another perfect thrust that has me seeing stars. "Love how I make you feel. Love how I know exactly what you need."

The worst part is he's absolutely right. Every movement, every touch, every filthy word from his mouth is exactly what I didn't know I was craving. Like he's been studying me, learning me, preparing for this moment.

"Blaise," I whisper his name like a prayer, and something in his expression shifts.

"I know, baby. I know." His pace becomes more urgent, less controlled. "You're so close, aren't you? I can feel it."

I am. The tension is building low in my belly, spreading outward like wildfire. My hands slide up to grab his hair. I pull him down for a kiss of pure desperation.

"Come for me," he says against my lips. "Let me feel you fall apart around my cock."

The combination of his words and one final, perfect thrust sends me tumbling over the edge. My orgasm crashes through me with an intensity that makes my vision blur, and I cry out his name as my body clenches around him.

"Fuck, Willow," he groans as his rhythm falters. "You're so...I can't—"

His release follows quickly after mine and is punctuated with the most animalistic groan I've ever heard. For a moment, we're both completely still besides how hard we are breathing.

When he finally lifts his head to look at me, there's something almost shy in his expression. Like he can't quite believe what just happened between us. I feel the same way.

"You okay?" he asks with a raspy voice.

"Yeah." I nod, still breathless. "Better than okay."

He slowly slides out of me and I laugh at the expression on his face.

"Sensitive?"

He nods just before he helps me shift onto the bed properly, tucking the sheet around me and brushing damp hair from my face with surprising tenderness. His fingers linger, stroking along my cheekbone like he can't quite believe I'm real.

"I'm going to toss this out and get a washcloth to clean you up and then we can go to sleep."

I rise up slightly so I'm leaning on my elbows. "Are you sure? What about Tyler?"

He shrugs. "I'll put a sock on the door or something."

I laugh, but he does reach over to grab his phone so I assume he's texting Tyler to let him know he might not want to come back tonight. When he walks into the bathroom, I lay down on my back again and sigh. I'm sure there's plenty we need to talk about but I'm ready to just enjoy this small little bubble we are in for a while longer.

Of course I was just lying to myself because I hear my

text message ringtone begin to play. I lean over and quickly find that at some point I put my purse on the nightstand so it takes me no time to get my phone. It's probably just Madison or Ari checking on me.

That is also a lie.

Knox: Hey, call me when you have a chance.

28

BLAISE

I wake before the sun rises even though I wouldn't mind getting a few more hours of sleep. Not that this isn't a natural occurrence even when I'm at home or at school, but something is very different about this morning.

My body knows something's going on before my mind catches up. There's warmth pressed against my side, soft breathing that isn't mine, the faint scent of a fruity shampoo ticking my nose.

Willow.

She's tangled around me like she belongs here. One of her arms is draped across my chest while her leg is hooked over mine. In the soft gray light filtering through the hotel curtains, she looks peaceful. The fierceness I usually see in her eyes and that she wears like an armor have melted away. It leaves behind something vulnerable and beautiful that makes my heart feel things it shouldn't.

I should move. Should put distance between us before she wakes up and realizes what we've done. Before the reality of last night crashes down on both of us. But I can't bring myself to disturb this moment. Instead, I let my eyes study her, watching the way her dark hair spills across the pillow and the soft rise and fall of her breathing.

What the hell am I doing?

The question hits me like cold water. This is Knox's sister. My best friend's little sister, who I've known since I was a freshmen and she was a senior in high school. But she's not that girl anymore. The woman sleeping beside me is fierce and brilliant and so goddamn beautiful it hurts to look at her sometimes. She's also stubborn and sarcastic and has a way of getting under my skin that no one else ever has.

And I think I'm falling for her. Hard.

The realization should terrify me more than it does. Should have me reaching for my phone to book the first flight back to Virginia. Instead, I find myself brushing a strand of hair away from her face and allowing my fingers to graze her cheek.

She stirs and a soft hum leaves her lips as she presses closer to me. The sound goes straight to my cock, which is already half hard from having her warm body pressed against mine.

"Mmm." Her eyes are still closed. "What time is it?"

"Early," I whisper. "Sun's not even fully up yet."

"What's wrong?" she asks with a sleepy smile.

Part of me wants to tell her how beautiful I find her in the morning, but I'm not sure if that's too weird. Instead I say, "Nothing. Why do you ask?"

"You look like you're having some kind of internal crisis." Her fingers trace lazy patterns on my chest. "Very dramatic because it's too early for this shit o'clock."

Her response makes me chuckle. "I'm not—" I start, but she cuts me off with a knowing look.

"Please. I can practically hear the gears turning in your head." She props herself up on one elbow, the sheet slipping down to reveal the curve of her breast. "Let me guess. You're spiraling about Knox, about what this means, about how we crossed some imaginary line."

The fact that she's read me so completely should be unsettling. Instead, it's oddly comforting. "Maybe."

She shifts so she's looking down at me fully and I wish I could make out every detail of her face. "Blaise, whatever this is between us...we don't have to figure it all out right now. We don't have to tell anyone anything yet."

I lean over and turn on one of the lamps because we can't have this conversation in the dark. "You want to keep this quiet?" I ask, studying her face for any hint of regret.

"For now, yeah. This is all very new. Hell, I hated you just a few weeks ago."

"Hated me?" I raise an eyebrow. "That's a strong word."

She rolls her eyes. "Fine. Strongly disliked. You made me want to scream into a pillow every time you spoke."

"I mean as long as I'm the reason you're screaming, that's a win."

A blush starts creeping up her cheeks. "You're such a dick."

"And yet, you love mine."

Her mouth falls open. "You did not just—"

I cut her off with a kiss, swallowing the rest of her sentence. When I pull back, she's glaring at me, but there's no anger in her stare.

"You're impossible."

"And you're beautiful, especially when you're trying to pretend you're not affected by me."

"I'm not pretending anything. I'm just saying we should be smart about this. Keep it between us until we figure out what it is."

"Agreed." I lean up to press a soft kiss to her collarbone. "Our secret."

"Our secret," she confirms, then smirks. She lays back down on her side. "Besides, I kind of like having something that's just ours."

"Just ours," I repeat as I wrap a strand of her hair around my finger.

"We should probably get ready for the day," she says, but even though the words fell out of her mouth, she's not moving away from me.

"Probably," I agree. "What time do we have to meet the group?"

"Not for another couple of hours. I do have to head back to my room though. I'm sure Madison is probably wondering what in the ever loving fuck happened to me."

My hand drifts down and finds her waist beneath the sheet. When I start dragging my finger up and down her skin, she shivers slightly as goosebumps form. Excellent. "That's plenty of time."

She tilts her head and looks at me. "Time for what?"

Instead of answering, I roll her onto her back and she quickly accommodates me so I can rest between her thighs. The sheet falls away, and I take a moment to drink in the sight of her in the lamplight. Last night feels like a fever dream, but here she is, real and warm and mine for whatever time we have left.

"Blaise." My name on her lips is half warning, half invitation.

"What? You said we have time." I press a kiss to her throat. "I want to make the most of it."

"You're insatiable."

"For you? Absolutely." I pause for a second before I say. "I really don't think one night is going to be enough. I'm thinking we have enough time to get some day action in as well."

That's really why I'm okay with going along with keeping this a secret. Not to mention it also gives me time to prepare for how to address this with Knox no matter how this situation goes.

"Oh really?"

I quickly nod and take my eyes off of her to look around the room before an idea forms in my head. "Have you ever watched yourself?"

Her eyes follow my gaze to the mirror across the room. "Watched myself what?"

"Orgasm."

"What? No."

"Shame. But I think we can rectify that right now." I slip out of the bed and walk over to where she's lying. I extend my hand for her to take. She stares at it for a moment, then at my face. "Trust me," I say quietly.

Her hand lands in mine and I help her to her feet. The sheet falls away completely, and I have to force myself to take my eyes off her or there's no way we are making it the few feet to the mirror.

With my hand on the small of her back, I guide her across the room until we're both staring at our reflections. At first we stare at each other in silence, taking in the image that we make together.

I lean down to whisper in her ear, "I want you to see what I see." My hands slide up to cup her breasts. "How fucking beautiful you are."

Her eyes meet mine in the reflection and I can see the surprise in them. I watch her face as my thumbs brush over her nipples and see the exact moment her lips part in a soft gasp.

"Blaise—"

One of my hands drifts lower while I keep the other on her breast, making sure to give it the attention it more than deserves. The other finds her pussy as I tell her, "Just watch."

She does as I say and the intensity in her stare is like she's afraid to blink and miss something. My fingers slide between her thighs, and I groan when I feel how wet she already is.

"Fuck, kitten," I mutter, loving the way my nickname for her sounds on my lips. "Look at you. Listen to all those pretty sounds you're making."

I'm proud of her for being able to keep her eyes on me. Every time her eyes start to drift closed, it's as if she remembers what she's supposed to do because they spring right back open, taking in everything that I'm doing to her.

I grin when her knees buckle slightly. It means I'm doing my job, and she doesn't react in a way that indicates she's completely nervous about falling, so I hope that means she trust me enough to know I will catch her.

My thumb brushes over her nipple and I watch in the mirror as her body responds immediately. Her nipple hardens under my touch, and her chest begins rising and falling faster.

"Look at yourself," I say as my other hand teases her pussy. "See how responsive you are? How perfect?"

Her breathing becomes more ragged as I alternate between her breasts, rolling one nipple between my fingers and giving each one my full undivided attention. She starts squirming in my arms and I have to adjust my stance to keep her steady.

"I can't—" she starts, but the words dissolve into a moan as I pinch gently.

"You can. Keep watching." My other finger slides deeper inside her. "I want you to see what you look like when you're about to fall apart."

"Blaise, please—"

"Please what? Tell me what you need."

"More. I need more."

I decide to throw caution to the wind and not focus on having her tell me verbatim what she wants me to do to her. Instead, I reward her honesty by adding another finger to her pussy, making her whole body shudder. Her hands reach back to grip my thighs and her nails slightly dig into me in order to anchor herself.

"That's it, baby. Let me hear those pretty sounds." My mouth finds the curve of her neck as my hands continue worshiping her body. "Your tits are so sensitive. I could play with them all morning."

She whimpers at my words and presses back against me. I can feel how wet she's getting just from this, and it takes everything in me not to spin her around and take her right here against the mirror.

"I can feel how close you are," I murmur, increasing my pace. "Your pussy is clenching around my fingers. You're so fucking wet for me."

"Oh God," she manages to say as her hips move in rhythm with my touch. "I'm going to—"

"Not yet." I slow my movements, keeping her right on the edge. "Tell me what you see."

Her eyes stay locked on our reflection as she struggles to find words. "I see...I see you touching me. And I'm barely hanging on."

"What else?"

"I see how my nipples are so hard they almost hurt. How I can't stop moving against your hand."

"Good girl." The praise makes her whimper. "Now watch yourself come for me."

I kick my pace up a notch and her reflection shows everything. The way her mouth falls open, how her eyes go wide and desperate as she watches herself unravel.

"That's it," I growl against her ear. "Look at how beautiful you are when you let go. I could watch you do this forever."

While she rides out every sensations of her orgasm on my fingers, I make sure I hold her as tightly as I can in my arms. The sight of her coming undone in the mirror and watching her face change because of the pleasure she's experiencing is the most erotic thing I've ever witnessed. When her breathing finally steadies, I turn her around to face me. Her legs are still shaky, and I keep her steady with my hands on her waist.

"Holy shit," she says, her forehead dropping against my chest. "That was..."

"Incredible," I finish for her, pressing a kiss to the top of her head. "You're incredible."

She looks up at me with those bright green eyes, and there's something different in them now. Something softer, more open than I've ever seen before. It's then I know I'll never forget this moment.

"Your turn," she says as her hands slide down my chest.

Before I can protest, she's dropping to her knees in front of me. The sight of her looking up at me from that position makes my brain short-circuit completely.

"Willow, you don't have to—"

"I want to." Her fingers wrap around my cock, and I have to brace one hand against the mirror behind her to keep from falling over. "I want to taste you."

Her tongue flicks out to taste the tip of my cock, and I swear my vision blurs. Every muscle in my body tenses as she takes me into her mouth, her eyes never leaving mine.

"Fuck," I say as I look up to see what we look like in the mirror. My free hand ends up tangled in her hair. "Kitten—"

She hums around me, the vibration sending shock-waves through my entire system. Willow takes me deeper and the sensation is overwhelming. I have to fight every instinct not to thrust into her mouth. Instead I let her set the pace, watching in fascination as she works me with her tongue and lips.

"You're so good at this," I manage to say because my voice is strained. "So fucking perfect."

She pulls back slightly, her tongue swirling around the head of my cock before taking me deep again. The contrast between the gentle suction and the firm pressure of her tongue is driving me closer and closer to the brink. My grip in her hair tightens, and she moans around me in response.

"Just like that, baby," I say as I watch her reflection in the mirror behind me. "That's how I fucking like it."

She continues working me to the point where I don't know which way is up or down. When she drags her tongue along the underside of my shaft before focusing on the sensitive spot just below the head, I know it's almost game over.

"Wait," I breathe, trying to pull back slightly. "I'm going to—"

But she doesn't let me retreat. One of her hands grips my thighs, holding me in place as she takes me deep again. The determination in her eyes tells me she knows exactly what she's doing, and she wants this as much as I do.

"Fuck, baby." My head falls back before I gather the strength to look down at her once more. "I can't hold back much longer."

She doesn't make a sound, but I know she heard me because her pace increases, alternating between deep, slow movements and quick, focused attention on the head of my cock. The combination is devastating.

I can feel the tension building low in my spine, spreading through every nerve ending. My orgasm builds and builds until I can't hold back anymore. My release hits me like a freight train, and I come hard into her mouth with a groan that echoes off the hotel room walls.

She doesn't pull away, taking everything I give her while maintaining eye contact that makes the whole experience even more intense. When the last waves finally subside, I'm left breathing hard and staring down at her in amazement.

"Open your mouth," I command as I drag my thumb across her lower lip. "And don't spill a drop."

She obeys, showing me my come in her mouth. The sight sends another jolt through me, even though I'm still coming down from my high.

"Good girl," I say as I help her stand up before kissing her. Tasting myself on her tongue makes something... primal stir within me. I can't quite explain it, but the urge to take her again is growing stronger by the second.

When our kiss naturally breaks apart, I notice that Willow has a smug expression on her face. I'm almost tempted to show her how quickly I can knock it off.

"Proud of yourself?" I ask, running my hands down her sides.

"Maybe a little." She stretches up on her toes to nip at my jaw. "You should see your face right now. Completely wrecked."

She's not wrong. I feel like she's taken me apart and put me back together in a completely different configuration. Everything feels raw and new and terrifying in the best possible way.

"Come here," I whisper, pulling her against me.

We stand there for a moment, both of us catching our breath. Through the window, I can see the sky beginning to lighten properly. It looks as if it's going to be another beautiful day in Puerto Rico.

"I should really go," she says quietly, but she doesn't move away from me.

"You should," I agree, even though every cell in my body is screaming at me to keep her here. To pull her back to bed and spend the entire morning mapping every inch of her skin with my mouth.

Instead, I force myself to step back and help her collect her clothes. Watching her get dressed is somehow just as erotic as watching her undress was. The way she slides that black dress back over her curves, how she runs her fingers through her tangled hair to tame it into something resembling respectability. I throw on a pair of sweats and a t-shirt too.

"Do I look like I spent the night getting thoroughly fucked?" she asks, turning to face me.

The question makes my cock twitch. "You look beautiful. But maybe run a brush through your hair before you see Madison."

She laughs. "Good point. She's probably going to interrogate me anyway."

"What are you going to tell her?"

"The truth." She shrugs, reaching for her purse. "And we'll probably giggle about it and she'll want details."

"She's going to love that answer."

"Madison's going to—" Willow stops mid-sentence as her phone buzzes from inside her purse. "Shit, I forgot to check my messages."

She pulls out her phone and I watch her face change as she scrolls through what looks like several missed texts. Her expression shifts from casual to concerned to something approaching panic.

"Fuck, fuck, fuck," she mutters, her thumb flying across the screen.

"What's wrong?"

"Knox has been texting. He sent three messages." She looks up at me with wide eyes. "He doesn't seem concerned, thank goodness, but yeah I should probably get back to him since he can see that I read the message."

My stomach drops. I grab my own phone from the nightstand, and sure enough, there are three missed texts from Knox. The most recent one makes my blood run cold.

> Knox: Hey man, big news. Leo's deal
> with the Red Wolves is officially off.
> Coach and Bailey called it this morning.
> Thought you'd want to know ASAP.
> Thanks for your help.

"Oh shit." It's all I can manage to say. "Leo's brand deal with the Red Wolves isn't happening."

"Wait, really?" Her voice is barely above a whisper, like she's afraid saying it too loud might make it untrue. "Leo's not going to be working with the Red Wolves?"

"That's what it says." I show Willow the message. "Knox says the deal's officially off."

The transformation in her expression is immediate. The tension I didn't even realize she'd been carrying in her shoulders melts away, and for the first time since I've known her, Willow looks genuinely, completely relieved.

"I can't believe it," she says as she sinks down onto the edge of the bed. "I was so worried about having to see him on campus."

"You don't have to worry about that anymore." I sit beside her, close enough that our thighs touch. "He's not going to be there."

She turns to look at me, and there are actual tears in her eyes. Happy tears, but tears, nonetheless. "This changes everything. I was dreading going back. Dreading the possibility of running into him on campus or hockey games." She stops, shaking her head. "Hell, I've been carrying this anxiety for weeks."

I reach over and take her hand, threading our fingers together. "You don't have to carry it anymore. And I didn't know you were thinking about going to more games."

"I was just starting to get back into the swing of going again, now there's whatever is going on with us," she admits quietly. "But I can use being there to see Knox to see both of you. I didn't realize how much I missed it until recently."

"Good," I say as I gently squeeze her hand. "I want you there. Both for Knox and..." I pause, meeting her eyes. "For me."

"Yeah?"

"Yeah. I've noticed that when you're around me in general, I'm calmer."

"You're calmer when I'm around?" she asks softly.

"Yeah. I know it doesn't make sense, given our history, but—"

"It does make sense." She shifts closer to me on the bed. "You make me feel grounded too. Like I can just...be myself without having to perform or prove anything."

The honesty in her voice makes me think things I shouldn't be thinking. This is dangerous territory we're entering and I'm not sure how to pivot.

"Willow—"

"I know." She stands up, smoothing down her dress. "I really do need to go."

"Yeah you do."

Willow grabs her bag, and I feel the loss as she lets go

of my hand. A second later, the distance is even wider between us.

Before I can say anything to pull her back, she takes another step toward the door. She doesn't look back as she moves, but I can see the shift in her shoulders. Moving away feels harder than staying here with me.

"Wills," I say and her hesitation tells me all I need to know. "Let me walk you back."

She pauses at my words with her hand already on the door handle. "That's sweet, but it's probably better if we're not seen together this early. Just in case."

"Right." I run a hand through my hair. "Smart thinking."

But neither of us moves. She's standing there with her back to me, and I'm sitting on the edge of the bed, both of us pretending this is just a casual goodbye when it feels like anything but.

"I'll see you at breakfast," she says without turning around.

"Yeah. Breakfast."

She finally turns the handle, opening the door just a crack, but then she stops. Her shoulders rise and fall with a deep breath before she turns back to face me.

"Fuck it," she whispers, and then she's crossing the room in three quick steps.

I stand just as she reaches me, and then her hands are in my hair and her mouth is on mine. When we finally take a breath she says, "I don't want to go."

"Then don't," I say, even though I know she has to.

"Madison will worry. And if I don't show up, she'll come looking."

"I know." I kiss her again, softer this time. "I know you have to go."

But my hands are on her waist, holding her close, and she's not pulling away. We both know what's on the other side of all this if she walks out of that door. Confusion about what this all means and where it leads are at the top of the list.

"Okay," she says, resting her forehead against mine. "Okay, I'm really going now."

"Okay."

She takes a step back, then another, but her eyes never leave mine. When she reaches the door again, she gives me one last look.

"See you soon," she says.

"See you soon."

She slips out, and the door clicks shut behind her. I stand there for a moment, staring at the closed door, feeling like something fundamental has shifted. Not just between us, but inside me. The careful control I've maintained for years feels like it's cracking, and I'm not sure if that terrifies me or thrills me more.

What the hell have I gotten myself into? However, I'm convinced there's no way this day could get any better.

29

WILLOW

I stare in awe as I take everything in because there's no way I'm in Old San Juan. Like we're actually walking on the cobblestone streets and are surrounded by the vibrant buildings that look like postcards have come to life. Professor Wallace is somewhere behind us giving historical context, but honestly, I'm too mesmerized to focus on the lecture portion of this experience. We're allowed to stay with our professors if we wish, but they've also given us free rein to explore a bit on our own as long as we're at the shuttle that will drive us back to our hotel by five o'clock.

Madison and I talked the morning after my rendezvous with Blaise and surprisingly, she didn't press me for details about Blaise. However the looks she kept throwing my way are more than enough.

I also got a call from Knox right after Madison and I

finished talking to follow up on his texts from the night before. He was just letting me know that Leo's deal with the Red Wolves had officially been pulled. What he doesn't know is that I already knew because I was with Blaise when he told him. At least I don't have to worry about Leo anymore.

I could also blame it on my ADHD and the fact that I'm becoming more overstimulated, but it has little to do with my surroundings and more to do with everything else that is going through my head and the man walking beside me.

I steal a glance at Blaise, who has his hands shoved deep in his pockets. He's wearing a simple white t-shirt and khaki shorts, looking effortlessly put-together while I'm over here trying not to think about how those same hands felt on my body just days ago. It sucked not being able to spend more time together, but it's risky seeing as how this is still a school trip at the end of the day. However, the memory of the night we spent together sends heat racing up my neck, and I force myself to focus on the uneven stones under my feet instead of my desire to jump his bones every waking second.

"Focus, Willow," I say under my breath, just as Madison appears at my side like she's materialized out of thin air.

"This place is unreal. The architecture is so just... perfection." She points toward a yellow building nearby. "Like that is stunning."

"Agreed. It's like someone painted the whole city in watercolors. Makes me want to take a million photos."

Madison, Tyler, Blaise, and I end up breaking apart from the group and finding ourselves walking along the El Paseo de la Princesa, a long, winding promenade that has been a part of Old San Juan since the eighteen hundreds. Trees sway overhead giving us some shade, but don't block our ability to take in the stunning views of San Juan Bay.

"Since you mentioned photos earlier, Maddie," Tyler's voice cuts through my thoughts. It's then I notice his hair is sticking up at odd angles, as if he'd been running his hands through it. "Madison, you've got to see this fountain. It's incredible."

Madison's entire face lights up. "Really? Lead the way, tour guide Tyler."

"Tour guide Tyler?" He laughs, falling into step beside her. "I like that. Very official sounding."

"You'd need a little flag on a stick to make it official," Madison teases, bumping his shoulder with hers. "And maybe a whistle."

"A whistle? What am I, a gym teacher?" The confusion is evident on his face.

"You know exactly what I mean." Madison grins as she pulls her digital camera out of her purse. "Come on, show me this fountain before the light changes."

I watch them walk ahead, Madison's animated

gestures and Tyler's eager responses creating their own little bubble of energy.

"They're cute together," I murmur to myself.

"Yeah, they are." Blaise's voice is closer than I expected, and I turn to find him studying me. "Tyler's been talking about her nonstop since we got here."

"Has he? That's sweet."

"Very sweet," Blaise agrees, but there's something in his tone that makes me think he's not just talking about Tyler and Madison.

We follow the cobblestone path until we reach Fuente Raíces, the fountain standing as a quiet testament to Old San Juan's layered history. It's more than just a pretty spot. It's a symbol of the island's roots, where the indigenous Taíno, African, and Spanish influences all converge.

"We should catch up with them," I say, but I don't move. Neither does Blaise.

The fountain creates a natural gathering spot, and I watch as Tyler animatedly explains something to Madison while she snaps photos. They're completely absorbed in what the other is saying. I haven't fully been able to pinpoint if there is something more than friendship blooming there yet because I've been too absorbed in my own shit.

"They don't have to hide," I observe quietly.

Blaise lets out a small sigh. "No. They don't."

The weight of our secret sits between us like a third person. Three days since that night in his room, and we've been playing this careful dance of making sure no one notices anything going on between us. It's exhausting and exhilarating at the same time. And how will we continue this when we get back to Virginia?

"Willow! Blaise!" Madison waves us over. "You have to see this up close."

We join them at the fountain's edge, where Tyler is pointing out details in the sculpture. "See how the three figures represent the cultural influences?"

I lean in to get a better look, genuinely interested despite my mind refusing to focus on any one thing. The figures seem to dance together, each distinct but unified in their shared space. It's beautiful and haunting given the history behind it.

I reach for my phone to take a photo, but my fingers fumble with the case and it slips from my hands. "Shit," I mutter, watching it bounce once on the cobblestones.

Blaise moves before I can even register what's happening, bending down to scoop it up. When he straightens and hands it back to me, our fingers brush. It's barely a touch. It looks like nothing to anyone watching, but to me, it's everything.

"Thanks," I manage to say, hoping my voice sounds normal.

"No problem." His eyes hold mine for just a beat too long before he steps back.

Madison, thankfully, is too busy adjusting her camera settings to notice our moment. Tyler is still examining the fountain like he's planning to write a thesis on it.

"The Taíno influence is fascinating," Tyler says, completely oblivious to the tension crackling between Blaise and me. "You can see it in the way—"

"Tyler, breathe." Madison laughs, lowering her camera. "You're about to hyperventilate over historical architecture."

"Sorry." He grins sheepishly. "I just find it interesting how all these different cultures created something beautiful together although that wasn't the goal."

None of us have to say what the actual end goal was because we all know. We stand at the fountain for a few more minutes, taking in the significance of it before we drift off and continue our self-guided tour of Old San Juan.

We drift from the fountain toward the heart of the marketplace, and suddenly we're hit with the scents of garlic, cilantro, and something sweet and fried that makes my mouth water instantly.

"Oh my God, do you smell that?" Madison stops dead in her tracks, nearly causing Tyler to crash into her back.

"Which smell?" Tyler asks, steadying himself with a hand on her shoulder.

"All of them," she says, spinning in a slow circle with her arms outstretched. "It's like someone bottled up every amazing smell in the world and dumped it here."

She's not wrong. The market stretches out before us in

a riot of color and sound that makes my senses go into overdrive. "I don't even know where to start," I admit, watching a woman flip what looks like plantains on a massive griddle.

"Start with these," Tyler says, already gravitating toward a stall selling small paper boats filled with golden-brown fritters. "Alcapurrias. My roommate at Crestwood is from Puerto Rico and he told me about these."

"What's in them?" Madison asks, peering over his shoulder.

"Taro root and meat, I think? They're fried." Tyler's already digging for his wallet. "Four, please," he tells the vendor in careful Spanish.

The elderly man behind the counter beams at Tyler's attempt at the language and hands over four steaming portions.

"Gracias," Tyler says proudly, then immediately turns to us after we thank him for buying us food. "Okay, who wants to taste it first or should we all do it together?"

"Together," Madison declares, holding up her fritter like she's making a toast. "On three. One, two—"

"Wait!" Tyler interrupts, nearly dropping his alca-purria as he fumbles for his phone. "We should document this occasion."

"Seriously?" I laugh, but I pose anyway, holding my fritter up to match Madison's.

"This is important," Tyler says as he snaps a photo. "My roommate will never forgive me if I don't have evidence."

"Your roommate's going to think you're a tourist," Blaise points out, but he's smiling as he says it.

"I am a tourist," Tyler shrugs. "Now, on three for real this time."

We bite into the fritters simultaneously, and the explosion of flavor makes my eyes widen. The crispy exterior gives way to something savory and rich, with hints of garlic and herbs I can't identify.

"Holy shit," Madison mumbles around her mouthful. "This is incredible."

"Language, Madison," Tyler teases, then immediately takes another huge bite.

"Says the guy who just inhaled half of his in one go," she tosses back.

I catch Blaise watching me as I eat, and when our eyes meet, he raises an eyebrow. "Good?"

"Amazing," I confirm, licking my fingers without thinking.

His gaze drops to my mouth and then my fingers. The heat rises to my cheeks as I realize what I've just done, but before I can feel too mortified, Tyler accidentally knocks over his water bottle while reaching for napkins.

"Shit!" he yelps as water cascades across the cobblestones. "Sorry, sorry—"

"Tyler, it's water." Madison laughs as she steps out of the splash zone. "Not acid."

"I know, but—" He scrambles to pick up the bottle. "I'm usually more coordinated than this."

"Usually?" Madison grins, bending down to help him retrieve the bottle. "So this is abnormal Tyler behavior?"

"Very abnormal," he confirms as he begins to blush. "I blame the alcapurrias. They've scrambled my brain with their deliciousness."

"That's the most ridiculous excuse I've ever heard." I laugh, watching him try to shake the remaining water off his hands.

"It's a perfectly valid excuse," Tyler replies. "Food-induced clumsiness is a real phenomenon."

"Is it now?" Blaise asks, his voice dry with amusement.

"Absolutely. It's right up there with vacation brain and —" Tyler gestures wildly while trying to think of something, but all he comes up with is air.

Madison dissolves into giggles, and the sound is so infectious that soon we're all laughing.

"Vacation brain?" Blaise repeats, raising an eyebrow as he steps closer to me to avoid a group of tourists pushing past us with oversized shopping bags.

His hand briefly touches the small of my back as he guides me out of their path, and the simple contact sends electricity down my spine. When the crowd passes, he doesn't immediately move away.

"You know," Tyler continues, "when you're somewhere new and your brain just...stops working properly."

"I think that's just you, Ty," Madison teases, but her attention is already shifting to another food stall. "Ooh, what are those?" She points to a vendor selling what looks like shaved ice topped with colorful syrups.

"Piraguas," Blaise says, his voice close to my ear. The warmth of his breath makes me shiver despite the temperature outside. "Want to try one?"

I turn to look at him. "Yeah," I whisper. "I'd like that."

Madison and Tyler are already heading toward the piragua vendor, but Blaise doesn't move toward them. Instead, he glances around, then nods toward a tree and I'm immediately transported back to the incident between us at El Yunque.

"Come here for a second," he says quietly.

I follow him to the shaded spot beneath the tree. "What—" I start, but he's already pulling out his phone.

"I want a picture," he says simply, holding it up. "Just us."

The request catches me off guard. We've been so careful, so deliberate about maintaining distance in public. "Blaise..."

"Not for anyone else," he clarifies quickly, his voice soft. "Just for me. For us."

It's then I realize this isn't about showing off or making some grand statement. It's about capturing this moment, this feeling, this thing we can't quite name yet.

"Okay," I whisper.

He steps closer and his free arm comes around my waist, pulling me against his side, and I let myself melt into him for just this moment.

"Smile," he says, but I'm already smiling because how could I not? The way he's looking at me, like I'm something precious he wants to remember forever, makes it impossible not to.

He snaps the shot, but neither of us moves apart immediately. Instead, we stay frozen in this bubble, his arm around me, my hand resting on his chest where I can feel his heartbeat racing.

"Let me see," I say softly.

He turns the phone so we can both look at the screen, and I'm somewhat surprised by what I see. We look...happy. Like any other couple you'd find walking down the street. My hair is slightly messy, and Blaise looks probably the most relaxed I've ever seen him. Our smiles look genuine and don't give away any of the secrets we've been keeping from the world.

"It's perfect," I say as I look up at him.

"Yeah," he agrees, but he's not looking at the photo anymore. He's looking at me.

For a moment, I think he might kiss me right here in broad daylight with Madison and Tyler just fifty feet away. The thought should terrify me, but instead, it makes me lean closer.

"Willow! Blaise!" Madison's voice brings this moment to a quick halt. "You have to try this coconut one!"

"Coming!" I call back to Madison.

Blaise pockets his phone, and for a second his fingers brush against mine. "We should—"

"Yeah," I interrupt, not trusting myself to hear whatever he was about to say.

As we start to make our way toward Madison and Tyler, Blaise says something that almost stops me in my tracks. "When we get back to campus, what happens to us? We only have two more days before we head back to Virginia."

I've been so careful to not think about it although it's been sitting there like the elephant in the room. Two more days. Then we're back to being Knox's sister and Knox's best friend, back to pretending whatever this is doesn't exist.

"I don't know," I admit, but keeping my voice low just in case Madison and Tyler can hear us. Not that it matters so much since they both know what we did a few nights ago, but this still feels like it should be a conversation for Blaise and me. "I keep trying not to think about it."

"But you have been thinking about it." It's not a question. He knows me well enough now and I hate it and like it at the same damn time.

"Haven't you?" I counter, stealing a glance at his profile.

His jaw tightens slightly. "Every fucking day since we got here let alone after we spent the night together."

"What do you want to happen?" I ask, then immediately want to take the question back. Too late for that now.

Blaise is quiet for so long I start to think he's not going to answer. When he finally speaks, it's as if he's flipped my world on its axis. "I want to keep seeing you. I want to figure out what this is without having to sneak around like teenagers."

"But Knox—"

"Knox is my best friend, but he doesn't get to dictate my life. Or yours. I'm tired of letting fear make decisions for me."

The determination in his words should be reassuring, but instead it makes my stomach twist into one big knot. Because while he's talking about not letting fear control him, I'm drowning in it. Fear of Knox's reaction, of changing the dynamic between all of us, of what happens if this thing between Blaise and me crashes and burns.

"It's complicated," I say and immediately feel lame for pointing it out.

"Everything worthwhile is complicated."

I want to argue with him, to point out all the ways this could go wrong, but Madison's laughter reminds me we're not alone.

"We should catch up," I say, nodding toward where Madison and Tyler are now trying different flavored syrups on their piraguas.

"Willow." Blaise catches my wrist gently, stopping me. "We don't have to figure it all out right now. But I need you to know I don't want this to end when we get on that plane."

"I don't want it to end either," I whisper.

Relief floods his features. "Good. That's...good."

"But I'm scared," I add, because honesty seems to be the theme of this conversation.

"Of what?"

Of everything, I want to say. Of my brother's reaction, of what this could do to the team dynamics, of the way you make me feel. Of what happens if you decide I'm not worth the complications.

Instead, I just say, "Of it not working out. Of making everything weird."

"Things are already weird," he points out with a small smile. "Good weird, but weird."

Before I can respond, Tyler appears beside us with two piraguas in hand. "Okay, you two have to settle a debate. Madison thinks the coconut is better, but I'm team mango. Here, try both."

He thrusts the shaved ice treats toward us, and I'm thankful for the interruption. Blaise and I each take a spoonful of each flavor, our fingers brushing as we pass the cups between us.

"Definitely coconut," I declare after tasting both.

"Mango," Blaise says at the same time.

Tyler throws his hands up in victory. "See? I told you mango was superior."

"You told me no such thing," Madison protests, appearing with her own coconut piragua. "You said, and I quote, 'I think maybe mango might be good.'"

"That's basically the same thing."

"That's not even close to the same thing."

I smirk as I watch them bicker, but part of my mind is still stuck on Blaise's words. *I don't want this to end when we get on that plane.* The problem is, I don't know how to want something this big without also being terrified of it.

After Blaise buys our piraguas and we start walking again, he falls into step beside me. His hand brushes against mine as we navigate through a crowd, and for just a moment, his fingers catch mine and squeeze. It's a small gesture that is more than likely not noticeable to anyone else, but it feels like a promise. Or maybe a question.

Either way, I squeeze back.

30

BLAISE

I can't believe this is our last night in Puerto Rico. The thought loops in my head as I nurse the same drink I've had for the past hour. It's the only drink I've had since I sat down at the hotel bar and dining area to celebrate the end of our trip. Tyler's telling some wild story about nearly capsizing the kayak he was in when we were exploring Laguna Grande, a bioluminescent bay, this afternoon and people are laughing at his antics.

I even throw in a grin here and there, just to stay part of the action. But every time I glance across the bar, my smile dies on arrival.

Willow has barely touched her drink. Not to mention she's doing that thing where she looks at everything but me. I watch her fingers trace the rim of her glass and it reminds me of the way she traced patterns on my chest the morning after she spent the night in my hotel room. It drags everything about that morning back to the forefront of my mind.

Well that's a lie because it never left.

My gaze drifts to her mouth, and I'm right back to the time we spent fucking in the mirror. The sounds she made. The way she dropped to her knees and—

"Blaise, you listening?" Tyler's voice cuts through my thoughts.

"Yeah, man. Kayak. Nearly died. Hilarious." I take a long pull of my beer, hoping it'll cool me down, but of course it doesn't.

But my eyes find her again. She's wearing an orangish sundress and it's doing an excellent job of making her skin look golden in the bar lighting. The dress also brings out the gold aspects of her green eyes and I know this even though she's not looking my way. Instead, she's focused on Madison, nodding along to whatever she's telling her.

Then something shifts, but I'm not exactly sure what. Madison leans closer to Willow and whispers something in her ear. Willow's eyes finally find mine across the room, and there's something different in her expression, but I can't name it.

Then, they both stand.

My heart rate kicks up a notch as they make their way toward our table. Tyler's still talking, but his voice fades to background noise as Willow approaches. The orange dress moves with her body, and I have to grip my beer bottle to keep myself from reaching out when she's standing in front of us.

Madison slides into the chair next to Tyler while Willow takes the empty seat across from me.

"So," Madison starts. "We could hear Tyler talking about the kayak trip from all the way across the room."

"Could you really?" Tyler asks, looking genuinely surprised. "I wasn't being that loud, was I?"

"You were being exactly that loud," Madison confirms with a grin. "But don't worry, it was entertaining. Something about almost becoming fish food?"

"Okay, that's a slight exaggeration," Tyler says while laughing. "The water was only like four feet deep where we were."

"Four feet of bioluminescent water that you nearly drowned in," Willow adds, and I'm relieved to hear her voice. She's been so quiet tonight.

"I didn't nearly drown," Tyler says defensively. "I just... almost got temporarily acquainted with the water."

Madison snorts. "Is that what we're calling it?"

"Yeah, because that's what it was." Tyler throws his hands up as if he's given up trying to explain himself.

"Whatever happened to Tyler in the water," Madison pauses dramatically before she continues, "we should probably call it a night soon. Early flight tomorrow and all that."

I glance at my phone. It's barely ten-thirty. "Early? Our flight's not until—"

"Actually," Madison interrupts, standing abruptly and stretching her arms above her head, "I'm exhausted. Tyler, want to walk me back to my room? I promised to show you the souvenirs I'm taking back home."

Tyler's face lights up. "Really? Yeah, absolutely." He's already pushing back from the table.

"Perfect." Madison grins, then turns to Willow. "You don't mind if I steal Tyler for a bit, do you? We can catch up tonight."

"Of course not," Willow says, but her voice sounds strange. "You two have fun."

"Great!" Madison practically bounces on her toes. "Tyler, come on. And Blaise?" She fixes me with a pointed stare. "Make sure Willow gets back to our room safely, okay? It's late."

Before I can respond, she's already linking her arm through Tyler's and steering him toward the elevator. Tyler throws a confused wave over his shoulder as they disappear.

And then it's just us.

"That was subtle," I say after about a minute of silence.

A small smile tugs at the corner of her mouth. "Yeah, subtly doesn't know Madison apparently."

"Was she trying to be your wing woman?"

Willow's eyes finally meet mine and she says, "Maybe."

I lean forward, lowering my voice so no one nearby can hear us. "What did she say to you?"

"She asked me if I was going to spend our last night in

Puerto Rico pretending I don't want to be alone with you."
Willow's cheeks turn slightly pink. "And then she told me
she was going to fix it."

"And what did you tell her?"

Willow takes a shaky breath. "I told her I was scared."

"Of what?"

"Of wanting this too much." Her voice drops to barely
above a whisper. "Of what happens when we leave here."

I reach across the table and cover her hand with mine.
I know I'm taking a risk by doing this in public, but right
now, I don't care.

"We don't have to figure out tomorrow right this
second," I say. "But we do have tonight."

She stares down at our joined hands for a long
moment before she speaks. "Your room, right?" she asks
quietly.

My heart starts racing. "Definitely. Tyler won't be back
for a while."

She nods, then finishes the rest of her drink in one
gulp. "Okay."

I throw money on the table and stand, offering her my
hand. She takes it without hesitation, and I help her to her
feet.

We walk to the elevator in silence. Once the doors
close and we're alone in the small space, Willow turns to
face me.

"I've been thinking about the other night," she says
softly.

"Yeah?" My voice comes out rougher than intended.

"Yeah." She steps closer. "I've been thinking about a lot of things."

The elevator dings at my floor, and the doors slide open. I lead her down the hallway with my hand on the small of her back. When we reach my room, I get the door open on the first try and give myself a mental pat on the back. The door closes behind us with a soft click, and suddenly the careful distance we've been maintaining since we were both last here crumbles.

"Come here, kitten," I say firmly, and she doesn't make me ask twice.

Willow crosses the space between us in two steps, her hands finding my chest as I pull her against me. When our mouths meet, there's a feeling of desperation surrounding us because we know our time is running out. Tomorrow we'll be back to reality, back to how complicated all of this is and the boundaries we need to keep in place. But tonight is ours.

"I want you," she whispers against my lips. The words shoot straight from her mouth and into my soul.

"You have me," I tell her, meaning it in ways that go far beyond just tonight. "You've had me for a while now."

Her confession breaks something open inside me. I frame her face with my hands, studying every detail like I'm trying to memorize her for when this all becomes a memory even though I hope it doesn't.

"Say it again," I whisper.

"I want you, Blaise. I want this."

That's all the permission I need. My mouth crashes against hers. My hands find the zipper of her dress, sliding it down slowly while she works at the buttons of my shirt.

When her dress pools at her feet, I have to step back to look at her. The sight of her in her strapless white bra and matching panties makes my mouth go dry.

"Fuck, you're perfect," I mutter mostly to myself.

She reaches for me, but I catch her wrists gently. "Wait. I want to try something different tonight."

Her eyes widen before she raises an eyebrow at me. "Different how? The mirror play again?"

Instead of answering, I move to the bathroom and grab a couple of towels, spreading them on the floor near the foot of the bed. When I turn back to her, she's watching me with a mixture of confusion and anticipation.

"Trust me? And if there's anything you don't like or don't want, let me know and I'll stop immediately."

She nods without hesitation, and that hits me harder than anything else could. I guide her down onto the soft towels, following her movements as she settles on her back. I take a moment to just appreciate how beautiful she looks spread out beneath me.

"What are you thinking about?" she asks softly.

"About how I want to worship every inch of you," I admit as I press small kisses along her collarbone. "About how I want to make you feel things you've never felt before."

My mouth travels lower and I take my time to undo her bra and play her breasts before continuing down her stomach. When I reach the edge of her panties, I look up to meet her eyes.

I hook my fingers in the waistband of her panties and slowly drag them down her legs before I toss them aside. The sight of her naked under me makes my cock throb in my jeans.

I adjust myself before I say, "So beautiful. So fucking perfect."

I start slowly, pressing soft kisses to her inner thighs before finally giving her what we both want. The first taste of her makes me groan against her skin. She's already wet, and when I begin my feast, her hips buck up toward my mouth.

"Blaise," she gasps, her fingers making their way into my hair.

While my tongue has its fun with her pussy, I slide one finger and then a second inside her. The sound she makes sends heat straight to my cock. Her grip in my hair tightens as I establish a rhythm that has her breathing becoming more erratic.

"That feels so good," she whimpers.

I curl my fingers, searching for her G-Spot because I know that will drive her wild. When I find it, her whole body jerks and she cries out my name.

"Right there," she gasps. "Don't stop."

I wouldn't dream of it. I focus all my attention on that spot while my tongue continues its relentless pace against her clit. Her breathing becomes more shallow, and I can feel her muscles starting to tense.

"I'm so close," she pants as her thighs begin to tremble around my head.

I increase the intensity, adding a third finger and stretching her carefully while maintaining that perfect angle. Her back arches off the towel, and I know she's right on the edge.

"Let go for me, kitten," I murmur against her. "I've got you."

That's all it takes. Her orgasm crashes over her with an intensity that takes us both by surprise. Her body shakes beneath my mouth as she cries out and I move back to watch her. Then something different happens. A rush of warmth hits my fingers and the towel beneath her as her body releases in a way I can tell is completely new to her.

"Oh my God," she gasps, her eyes flying open wide with shock and embarrassment. "I'm sorry, I didn't—I've never—"

"Hey, hey." I move up her body immediately, gathering her in my arms. "Don't apologize. That was incredible. You're incredible."

Her face is flushed, and I know it's a mix of post-orgasmic bliss and mortification. "That's never happened before. Not with anyone."

"Good," I say, before pressing a kiss to her forehead. "I'm glad I got to be your first for that."

She looks up at me and I can see that she is still slightly dazed. "Really? You're not grossed out?"

"Are you kidding me?" I stroke her hair to wipe it away from her face. "That was the sexiest thing I've ever experienced. The fact that I made you feel that good..." I trail off, shaking my head. "You have no idea what that does to me."

A small smile tugs at her lips. "I can feel what it does to you," she says as her hand makes its way to my jeans.

I groan at the contact. "We should get cleaned up first."

She nods, but I can see that she is still a little overwhelmed by what just happened. I help her sit up, making sure she's steady before I stand and extend my hand to her.

"Come on," I say gently. "Let's get you in the shower."

She takes my hand and lets me pull her to her feet. Her legs are still slightly shaky, and I keep my arm around her waist as we walk toward the bathroom.

"The towels," she says as she spares a glance back at the evidence of what we just did.

"I'll take care of them later," I assure her. "Right now, I just want to take care of you."

Deep down, I know that's one of the top two things that I would want to do in life: take care of her and play hockey, in that order. As we make our way to the bathroom, I can't think of a better way I could have spent my last day in paradise.

31

WILLOW

By the time I make it back to my dorm, I feel like my bones have been replaced with boulders. My arms barely work as I swipe my card and push it open. The hallway and common area are empty and everything would be quiet if it wasn't for the muffled thud of someone's music playing from their room.

I somehow make it to my room and let the door slam shut behind me with more force than necessary. My backpack hits the floor as I shrug it off my shoulders and I'm only slightly grateful that I left my laptop here, so it didn't suffer any injuries when my bag hit the ground.

My temples are pounding, and I know it's from the exhaustion that is settling into my body. I press my fingertips against them, trying to massage away the tension that's been building all day. Between this being the first week back at Crestwood and figuring out my new classes, the things I need to do for Crestwood Chronicle, and pretending everything is normal when nothing feels normal anymore, I'm completely drained.

I collapse backward onto my bed without bothering to take off my shoes. Honestly, they're the only thing keeping me from passing out right here and now. Moments like this, I'm glad that I don't have a roommate because no one can judge me for how I look right now.

I only get about a minute before my ringtone begins to play. Part of me wonders why my phone couldn't break when my bag hit the floor, but the other part of me knows I would be upset and Mom would be pissed if that happened, so here we are.

I somehow make it off my bed and manage to get to my bag without my entire body dropping to the floor. I pull my phone out and see that it's Ari.

And if there is one person who will not accept "Sorry, fell asleep!" as a valid excuse for avoiding her calls, it's her. Well, sometimes.

It takes a second for my guilt to beat out exhaustion. "Hey," I answer as I flop back down on my bed.

"Willow? Girl, what's up?" Ari's voice is all bright, which instantly makes me want to crawl under the bed and die. "You alive? You sound like you got hit by a bus."

It's too much. All of it, all at once. I almost say as much. "It was only a small one," I mumble. "I'll recover in a semester or two."

She snorts and it almost makes me want to laugh. "You

know I take time out of my busy schedule to check in and this is the thanks I get. You should feel so lucky I don't call your mother and file a missing person's report."

"I think she'd up the reward if you told her I was already dead."

"You're such a drama queen," she says, and I almost laugh for real because look who's talking. "You want me to bring you a funeral casserole, or do you want to actually tell me what's up?"

I close my eyes and picture her: stretched out across her own twin bed, laptop open to six tabs, a legal pad of to-do lists on her knees, her phone always tucked between chin and shoulder. It almost makes me feel better knowing that somewhere on campus her room is just as full of chaos as mine. Except hers is much neater chaos.

"I'm fine. Really," I say, trying to sell this version of events to her even though I know it won't work.

"You're a lousy liar," she says. "I've known you for too long, Wills. If you're going to lie, at least make it believable. Or sell the rights to your fictional tale to Hollywood."

There's nothing I can say that will stop her, so I just roll my eyes and sigh. "Fine. Everything's fine. Classes are fine. Campus is fine."

"Put all that in writing and I might believe you," she says. "Have you seen Blaise on campus yet?"

I refuse to let her know this question actually makes my heartbeat speed up. "It's the first week, Ari, I've barely seen anyone. Except for professors and the people that work in the dining hall. Oh Madison and I grabbed coffee at Brewed Beginnings yesterday."

"Liar," she says again, stretching the word until I can feel her suspicion reaching through the phone. "I've seen you track down people for interviews like you worked for the FBI, but you haven't seen Blaise."

I pinch my nose, try to keep my voice even. "Maybe a couple times. He's around."

Ari goes silent for a bit. I can hear her flipping a page. "You haven't talked?"

I pause for a second before I respond. "Yes. We've been texting a lot actually. But we're both trying to keep it low-key." There. I said it.

Ari knows more than anyone how much I edit myself because sometimes I just don't want to get into the details of the topic at hand. Which is funny given what I'm studying and what I plan to do after graduation. Based on the fact that she's still silent, I'm sure she's glaring at her phone because she's on high alert after that answer. "And how's that going? Is he being normal?"

"He writes essays for texts every so often, but I have no idea if that's normal for him. Let's be real, he's probably using me as a warmup for his poli sci mid-terms."

She makes a fake gagging sound. "Hot. There's nothing sexier than a bibliography."

"Or a thesis statement," I say with a straight face and immediately regret giving her a joke to run with.

That makes her laugh. "Do you two even sext or do

you just cite sources and argue about Oxford commas the entire time?"

"We don't argue about Oxford commas," I say, fighting a yawn. "We agree. The Oxford comma is essential and anyone who thinks otherwise is a monster."

Ari isn't amused with me. "You are a lost cause. I bet your couples' safe word is Chicago Manual."

That does it. I snort, which sets off a round of coughing, which in turn makes my brain feel like it's been shaken inside a snow globe. "Okay, so maybe we text like nerds. It's not the worst thing."

"Yeah, okay, but the lack of gossip is offensive. Has he said anything about seeing you again? Going on dates? Hellooooooo."

"Honestly, nothing major to report," I say, fighting the urge to prop my phone on my face and close my eyes. "We're both busy and don't want to anyone to run and tell Knox. That's the deal."

"That's smart," Ari says, though I can hear the disappointment in her voice. She loves drama that doesn't include her almost as much as she loves solving other people's problems. "But seriously, after Puerto Rico and everything that happened between you two, I'm surprised you're managing to keep things so...casual."

Puerto Rico. Just thinking about it makes me wish I was back there. I haven't told Ari everything yet, but she knows enough. She knows everything changed there and now we're just in this limbo of our own making.

"It's not casual," I say quietly. "It's just...careful."

"Careful can be good," she agrees. "But don't be so careful you miss out on something real."

I want to tell her that it already feels real. That the texts we send aren't just intellectual foreplay, but actual conversations that mean something to me. That I find myself checking my phone constantly, not for assignments or deadlines, but for his name on my screen. But that's exactly the kind of thing I can't say out loud. Not yet.

"Speaking of real," Ari continues, "we need to catch up properly. I feel like I haven't seen your face in forever. Want to grab lunch tomorrow?"

"Tomorrow sounds perfect," I say, already feeling a little lighter at the thought of seeing her. "I could use some normal human interaction that doesn't involve pretending I'm fine when I'm not."

"Good. I'll text you. We can grab sandwiches, and you can tell me all the things you're not telling me right now."

"Deal. But I'm warning you, it might be boring."

"Honey, your life has never been boring. Complicated as hell, yes. Boring, never."

After we hang up, I let my phone drop onto my bed and stare at the ceiling. I should probably get up, take a shower, do something productive with what's left of the evening. Instead, I just lie here, too tired to move but too wired to actually fall asleep. My fingers reach for my phone again before I can stop myself. I know I should leave it alone and try to get some actual rest, but I'm already scrolling through my messages to find Blaise's name.

Our text thread is longer than it should be for two people who are supposedly keeping things casual. The timestamps show we've been messaging daily since we got back from Puerto Rico, sometimes late into the night when we should both be sleeping.

I scroll up to yesterday's conversation and feel my stomach tighten as I reread the exchange.

Blaise: How was your day? You seemed stressed in your last message.

Me: Just the usual first-week chaos. Nothing I can't handle.

Blaise: You know you don't have to handle everything alone, right?

Me: Says the guy who probably color-codes his stress levels.

Blaise: Only on Tuesdays.

Me: Such a smartass.

Blaise: You like it when I'm a smartass.

Me: Maybe. Depends on the context.

Blaise: What context are you thinking about right now?

That's where the conversation had shifted. Where the playful banter took on a different turn that made my pulse quicken even now, reading it again.

> Me: Wouldn't you like to know.

Blaise: I would. Very much.

> Me: Then you'll have to use your imagination.

Blaise: My imagination has been working overtime since Puerto Rico. It's becoming a problem.

> Me: What kind of problem?

Blaise: The kind that makes it hard to concentrate in practice. The kind that makes me think about your hands when I should be thinking about defensive strategies.

I remember staring at that message for a full minute before responding.

> Me: Just my hands?

Blaise: Among other things.

> Me: Elaborate.

Blaise: Not over text. Some things require a...face-to-face conversation.

I scroll down to this morning's messages, and the tension is even more obvious.

Blaise: Good morning. Sleep well?

Me: Define well.

Blaise: More than three hours, no
nightmares, woke up in your own bed.

Me: Two out of three. You?

Blaise: Same. What's keeping you up?

And there it was. The opening for honesty that I'd completely dodged.

Me: Just the usual insomnia that I tell
everyone is actually me being a night
owl. You know how it is.

Blaise: I know how it is when you're
avoiding something.

Me: I'm not avoiding anything.

Blaise: Aren't you?

Me: Are you psychoanalyzing me via
text now?

Blaise: Would you prefer I do it in
person?

Me: That's probably not a good idea.

Blaise: Why not?

Me: You know why.

Blaise: I know what you keep telling
yourself. That's different.

Me: Blaise...

Blaise: What are we doing here, Willow?

Me: I don't know what you mean.

Blaise: Yes, you do.

And that's where the conversation had died hours
ago. No response from either of us because what was
there to say? He was right, and we both knew it. I did
know what he meant, and I was avoiding it wholeheartedly.

Instead of dealing with that, I toss my phone down on
my bed and walk over to my laptop. Maybe I can get some
work done for the Chronicle or at least pretend to be
productive while my brain processes everything that's
happened today.

The desktop appears and I automatically check my
email first and the only thing I find are our campus newsletter and some spam. Then I click over to Discord
because why not? I haven't checked on it in a couple of
days and I do have friends that I still game with online.

There's a notification. One new message request.

My cursor hovers over the notification icon. One
message request from someone named *CozyCraft4Eva*.
The username is familiar, but I can't place it. It's not
uncommon for people to try to message because they find

me through mutual gaming contacts all the time. But something about seeing this request feels different.

I click.

CozyCraft4Eva (Lilly): Hey. I know this is random. But I heard you used to date Leo. Something happened and I don't know who else to talk to.

The words hit me like ice water. My hands freeze over the keyboard, cursor blinking in the empty reply box. Leo. Of course it's about Leo. No matter what I do recently, it seems like I can't get away from hearing about the fucker.

I stare at the message until the letters start to blur. My relationship with Leo was a big deal years ago and a lot of people knew about us. Yet this message makes my stomach want to flee my body. This girl knows something and now I know that something happened. Why else would she reach out when I haven't been in Leo's life in years?

I should close my laptop. Delete the message. Pretend I never saw it.

But my finger hovers over the keyboard, and despite every instinct screaming at me to run, I can't look away. Because this girl, there's something about the simple message that is ringing every alarm bell in my head.

WillsNet56: Who is this? How did you find me?

The response comes back faster than I expect, like she was sitting there waiting for me to reply.

CozyCraft4Eva (Lilly): I'm sorry. I know this is weird. My name is Lilly. I'm a sophomore at Thornfield College.

Leo and I have been...we've been seeing each other for a few months.

My blood turns to ice. The familiar nausea that comes up whenever I think about him rises in my throat as memories I've spent years burying claw their way to the surface.

WillsNet56: What happened?

CozyCraft4Eva (Lilly): I don't really know how to say this. But I think he's been lying to me about a lot of things. And when I asked around about his exes, your name came up. People said you two dated for a while in high school.

WillsNet56: We did.

Two simple words that don't even begin to cover the disaster that was Leo and me. Dated makes it sound normal, healthy, like something you'd smile about years later. Not like the slow-burning nightmare it actually was.

CozyCraft4Eva (Lilly): Can I ask what he was like? As a boyfriend, I mean. I'm starting to think I don't really know him at all. Not to mention there have been other things...

This girl has no idea what she's asking me to relive. But there's something in her messages that reminds me of myself at seventeen, confused and isolated and starting to realize that the person I loved was slowly destroying me. With that thought, I quickly make a decision on how to handle this.

WillsNet56: Please share your story and I'll share mine.

32

BLAISE

As I take in the scene in front of me, I can't help but ask myself the same old question: Why am I here? I sink deeper into the corner of the couch and debate whether that's the right move when Knox jumps up and waves his controller around like he might launch it at our television.

"Are you fucking kidding me?" Knox shouts at the screen. "That was clearly interference!"

"Dude, you literally skated into him." Levi laughs, not looking up from his own controller. "That's not interference, that's you completely missing the plot there."

"I fucking saw it, the ref is—"

"The ref is a computer program," Asher points out dryly. "It doesn't have bias against your terrible gameplay."

"My gameplay isn't terrible," Knox says, but his voice

cracks slightly on the last word as his player gets checked into the boards again.

I watch them argue, but soon their voices blend into background noise because I really don't give a damn. It doesn't matter who wins or loses because my mind is somewhere else entirely. Has been since I walked through the door twenty minutes ago and realized I was waiting for someone who might not even show up.

I pull out my phone and check the time. Seven-thirty. No new messages.

"Blaise!" Wilder's voice makes me stop staring at my phone. "Back me up here. Tell these idiots that the Titans' power play is garbage this season."

"Sure." I shrug, not really listening. My eyes drift to the front door, then back to my phone screen.

Wilder tosses a throw pillow at me when I don't explain my reasoning. "That's it? That's your analysis?"

"Deep stuff," Asher adds, smirking. "Really insightful commentary there, Dalton."

I catch the pillow and set it aside, forcing myself to pay attention to the conversation going on around me. Knox has moved on from complaining about the refs to arguing with Levi about defensive positioning, while Asher and Wilder debate whether the current Titans roster could beat last year's team.

"You're all wrong," I say, just to contribute something. "The problem isn't the power play or the defense. It's—"

The front door opens.

My words die in my throat as voices carry from the entryway. I see our guests for the evening file in one by one.

Selene walks in first, laughing at something over her shoulder. Isla, Hailey, and Jade follow behind her, chatting about who knows what.

And then my jaw almost drops when I see the woman I'm obsessed with: Willow.

She steps through the doorway like she owns the place, scanning the room with those sharp green eyes. When her gaze finds mine, there's the briefest flicker of acknowledgement before she looks away.

"Ladies!" Wilder calls out and he hops out of his seat. "Perfect timing. We were just proving that Levi has no idea how hockey actually works."

"I heard that," Levi mutters, but he's grinning.

I watch Willow shrug out of her coat. She's wearing dark jeans and a cream sweater that makes her skin look even brighter under our shitty lighting. She hangs her coat on the back of a chair before finding a seat on the other side of the room.

Away from me.

My stomach drops like I've just taken a hit to the boards. I wasn't expecting her, not really. Knox mentioned the girls might stop by, but he didn't say Willow would be with them. She usually avoids coming over here like the plague, so it was the last thing I expected. I hope I'm keeping up the mask I've been wearing every time I'm near Knox or else I'm screwed.

Willow looks completely unaffected. Like Puerto Rico was just another vacation, another week that came and went without leaving any marks. The way she sits down on one of our couches while laughing at something Jade whispers to her makes me wonder if she's as affected as I am and she's just doing a better job of hiding it. Out of the corner of my eye, I see Wilder move and spare a look his way. He glances up mid-conversation and I watch as his gaze lands on Jade for just a second too long before he looks away like it never happened. Huh. Makes me wonder what he was saying or thinking about his best friend.

I don't give myself an opportunity to explore it. Instead, I turn my attention back to the videogame, but I'm not really watching. Every few seconds, my eyes drift her way. Her hair falls over one shoulder, and I find myself remembering how it felt between my fingers.

"Blaise, you're up," Knox says, holding out a controller.

"What?" I blink, realizing the game has ended and they've been talking to me.

"Winner plays next," Knox repeats, eyeing me strangely. "You okay, man? You seem distracted."

"Just tired," I lie, taking the controller. "You know how it is."

I settle back into my spot and start a new game with Asher, but my focus is shot. Willow laughs again, and the sound cuts through all of the noise in my head like it's meant only for me. I glance over without thinking, and for a split second, our eyes lock. Her smile falters slightly, lips parting just enough that I remember exactly how they felt under mine. For that moment, it's like we're the only two people in the room.

Then Selene says something that makes Willow turn away, breaking whatever moment that was. My hands tighten on the controller as I force myself to look back at the screen.

"Dude, you just scored on your own goal." Asher laughs. "What the hell was that?"

"Shit." I shake my head, trying to refocus. "Sorry. Brain's somewhere else."

The rest of the game passes and things don't get any better. In fact, the best way I can describe it is that it was a blur of missed shots and terrible plays. Thank fuck this isn't a real game or else I'm convinced Coach would bench me. I can't concentrate with Willow in my peripheral vision, the way she tucks her legs under herself on the couch, how she absently plays with a strand of hair while listening to the other girls.

"I'm getting another beer," I announce, standing up abruptly. "Anyone want anything?"

A chorus of requests follows me to the kitchen. As I'm pulling bottles from the fridge, I hear footsteps behind me.

"Mind if I grab some water?" I'm both surprised and not that it's Willow standing behind me.

I don't turn around immediately. Can't because all hell would break loose within me. "Course not."

Willow slides past me and it's close enough that my arm tingles where her sweater grazes my bicep. I keep my eyes on the fridge, staring at a random shelf instead of her face, but the urge to pull her close is strong.

She fills her glass in silence, then glances sideways at me. "You look like you're about to interrogate that six-pack," she says, voice just above a whisper.

She's not wrong, but I don't give her the satisfaction of a smile. "Trying to decide if it deserves to live," I say, grabbing a random bottle and popping the cap.

She leans against the counter and looks at me with her eyebrows raised. "You going to ask what I'm doing here, or just keep pretending you weren't surprised?"

I risk a look and I don't regret it. She's so fucking beautiful. "You're allowed to hang out here. Your brother lives here after all."

She snorts. "I avoid this house like it gives me hives. You know that."

"So is this some kind of punishment? Are you putting up with my presence as some sort of penance?" I toss out without taking a beat to think about it.

Instead of answering right away, Willow takes a sip of her water before her eyes land on me. "Or maybe Selene guilt-tripped me into it. Jury's still out."

"I'm shocked Selene got you to do anything," I admit. "Isn't she on your list of mortal enemies?"

"You're thinking of Hailey. Selene's just...exhausting, not an enemy. We can file Ari under that as well."

There's a moment where neither of us says anything and then we both start laughing. When we sober up, Willow clears her throat and says, "I really came back here to talk to you about something. It's a pretty big deal to me."

That makes me pause for a second because I don't know where this could be going. I turn to her to give her my full and undivided attention. "What's up?"

"You ever get a message from someone you thought you'd erased from your head forever?"

"Yeah," I say. "Not my favorite experience."

"Me neither. Except this wasn't Leo." She sets her glass down with more force than necessary. "It was someone he's dating. Or was. Or...I don't know, maybe in his head he's dating her and she's just another girl he's screwing over."

"What did she want?"

"Answers, I guess? She found me through some mutuals, and to be honest I'm not sure how. She asked for the tea on Leo. Kept it low-key at first, like she was looking for tips on how to manage his bullshit." Willow looks up at the ceiling before she looked back at me. "But then she said he'd started doing stuff. Scary stuff. She wanted to know if...if it was something to worry about. Which I quickly told her yes that's scary as hell."

"What did she say?" I feel my anger starting to grow and I know my reaction depends on what she shares next.

"She said it started out normal," Willow begins but I notice the shift when she sighs, "but then he got weird. Like, sending messages all hours, pushing her to send stuff she wasn't comfortable with. The texts got more explicit." Her fingers drum against the countertop, rest-less. "Kept asking if she was talking to other guys, even though they weren't actually dating. He'd say really nice shit in public, but then he'd turn around and pick her apart in private. Make her apologize for things that were literally not her fault. He's refined the technique since high school, I guess."

Something in me snaps because I realize I can't let her continue this story without me at least holding her. I don't care if anyone walks in on us at this point. Let 'em. I appreciate that she is trusting me with this and in this moment, I know she needs me more than any explanation I would give about what's happening between us.

"I'm sorry," I say as I set the beer down and close the gap between us. I pull her into my arms and she doesn't move away. Her eyes dart to the side, then back to me, as if she's trying to forecast the outcome a thousand possible ways before picking one.

"Yeah." She shakes her head. "The thing that got me was how much her messages sounded like mine. Like, the same phrases. The same—" She bites the inside of her cheek. "He's got a playbook. He just tweaks it for whoever he's with." She swallows, and for a second I see every wall she's ever built trembling.

"So what did you do?" I ask, forcing my anger to stay flat and steady. All that matters is her. Not the urge to hunt Leo down and break his fucking face.

Willow's foot bounces, barely making a sound against the tile. The only reason I know she's doing it is because I feel her body shake against mine. "I told her to get out. Run, block his number, whatever it takes because that was me. I see what I went through in her. Questioning whether this was bad or not because other guys did way worst things. Leo just made me cry every couple days and gaslit me into thinking it was normal. Or would threaten to leak everything he knew about me online."

"You know it wasn't your fault, right? You know that, Wills."

"I know. Intellectually." She shrugs. "Emotional reality is trickier. What I also know is that he can't keep getting away with this. He gets to act like a shitty person in private but the world's golden boy in public and it's not right."

"You're right. He shouldn't get to keep his reputation while he's destroying people behind closed doors." I run my thumb along her shoulder, hoping to relieve the tension there. "What if you went to his management team? His sponsors? I'm sure they wouldn't want someone like him representing them."

Her head tilts up to look at me. "What do you mean?"

"Think about it. Leo's whole brand is built on being this wholesome gaming influencer, right? Family-friendly content, positive role model bullshit. If his management knew he was harassing women, sending explicit messages, threatening to leak personal information..." I pause, watching her process this. "That's not just morally fucked up, it's a liability. Sponsors don't want to be associated with that kind of scandal."

Willow's eyes widen slightly. "You think they'd actually care?"

"Money talks. And right now, Leo makes them money because people think he's a good guy. But if that image gets shattered publicly, he becomes a risk they can't afford." I shift so I can see her face better. "The woman who contacted you, if she's willing to speak up, and you're willing to back her up with your own experience..."

"That could actually work," she says slowly, and I can see the wheels turning. "I mean, I documented everything back then. Screenshots, emails. I kept it all because I thought I was going crazy and needed proof that it really happened."

"You were protecting yourself. That was smart."

She lets out a shaky breath. "I never thought I'd use any of it. I just wanted to forget he existed."

"But now you have a chance to make sure he can't do this to anyone else. He shouldn't have the privilege of having his platform. Because, above all else, it is a fucking privilege."

For a moment, neither of us speaks. I can hear Knox's voice carrying from the living room and assume any second someone will be in here wondering what the hell we're doing because it's taken us so long to come back.

"It's scary," Willow admits quietly. "Going up against someone with that kind of platform. What if they don't believe us? What if it backfires?"

"Then at least you tried. And you won't be alone in this." The words come out before I can stop them, and I realize how much I mean them. "I'll help however I can."

She looks up at me and I can see the shock on her face. "You would do that?"

"Of course I would. This matters to you, which means it matters to me."

She thinks about it for a minute before she finally says something. "I need to think about it. It's a big decision. Going after someone with Leo's reach...there could be consequences I haven't considered."

"Take all the time you need," I tell her, meaning it. "But whatever you decide, you don't have to face it alone."

She nods. "We should probably get back," she says, glancing toward the living room where Knox's voice has gotten louder. "Before someone comes looking."

"Yeah." I reluctantly step back, immediately missing the warmth of her body against mine. "Can't have people thinking we're actually capable of having a civil conversation."

That earns me a small smile. "Heaven forbid."

I grab the beers I'd originally come for, while Willow picks up her water glass. As we head toward the doorway, she pauses.

"Blaise?"

"Yeah?"

"Thank you. For listening. For not making me feel crazy about all this."

"You're not crazy. And you never were."

She gives me one more look before we walk back into the chaos that is currently my living room, but the weight of what she just said and how brave she has been, is the only thing on my mind.

33

WILLOW

I tap my fingertips on my desk as I wait for the clock to strike three in the afternoon. I've been sitting here for ten minutes, waiting for this call to start while my heart slams through my body like it's trying to escape. To calm myself down, I snatch a peach ring that's sitting in a bag on my desk and put it in my mouth.

When I glance at my screen again, I see Lilly staring at her phone. We've been sitting here in silence with our microphones muted because we didn't want the representative for Edgehaus Management to hear us talking about anything. Since she has her camera on, I can see that she looks as tense as I feel. Her blonde hair is pulled back in a ponytail, and she keeps playing with it as well as adjusting her position like she can't get comfortable either.

We haven't met in person yet, but we've spent hours on Discord trading stories, breakdowns and helping each other name the things we used to excuse. It's strange how close you can get to someone so quickly when you've both survived the same kind of manipulation.

It's still hard for me to believe that we decided to do this. Part of me still can't believe Leo's management company agreed to hear us out. Maybe they'll actually do something or maybe they're just covering their bases. I guess I won't know until after this call is done.

I check the time again. Three minutes past our scheduled start. Interesting, but nothing too alarming yet.

My phone vibrates on my desk and I see it's a text from Blaise.

Blaise: How are you feeling?

I don't answer because if I start typing to him, I might lose whatever composure I've managed to scrape together for this moment.

I nearly jump out of my skin when a soft chime indicates someone else has joined the meeting. This is it.

"Good afternoon, everyone. Thank you for joining today's call." The voice is polished, professional, but there's no face to match it. Just a black screen with the name "Dorian" in white text. How fucking rude is that? Especially when we are talking about a serious matter? And that's red flag number one for me.

Another chime sounds.

A second name appears: "Talia Quinn."

Her video turns on, but her camera is aimed just slightly off-center, like she didn't expect to be on. She adjusts quickly, offering a small, polite smile that actually feels... human.

"Sorry I'm late," she says gently. "Talia Quinn, Talent Relations at Edgehaus. I'll mostly be listening in, but I'm happy to clarify anything along the way."

There's a pause. Not awkward, but just long enough for me to register the difference between how they just appeared on the call.

I glance at Lilly's camera feed and see her tilt her head slightly. I wonder if she's picked up on the same thing I noticed.

"I'm Dorian from Edgehaus Management," the voice continues. There's something about the way he's speaking that feels rehearsed. "I have Ms. Willow Sanchez and Ms. Lilly Voss on the call today to discuss some concerns that have been brought to our attention."

The way he says our names sounds like he's reading them off a script for the first time and makes my stomach drop to the floor. There's no warmth, no acknowledgment that we're real people who reached out because we needed help. I'm getting the vibe that we're just names on a document somewhere.

Talia doesn't jump in, but I notice her expression shift slightly, but I don't know her well enough to read it or her.

I unmute my microphone and say, "Thank you for

taking the time to meet with us. We appreciate you hearing us out."

"Of course." Another scripted response. "Before we begin, I want to assure you that we take all concerns seriously and handle them with the utmost discretion. Now, I understand you both have some feedback regarding one of our talent's conduct."

Feedback. Like we're complaining about customer service at a restaurant instead of reporting sexual harassment and emotional manipulation.

"I think feedback is putting it lightly," Lilly speaks up. "We're talking about a pattern of inappropriate behavior that has affected multiple women. I've found out since I reached out to Willow that she and I aren't the only ones."

"Yes, of course. I misspoke." But his tone doesn't change at all. Still that same professional detachment. "Please, go ahead and share your experiences. I'm here to listen."

Talia shifts slightly on camera. She still doesn't speak, but for some reason it's reassuring.

I take a breath and launch into my prepared talking points. I explain the timeline of my relationship with Leo, the way his behavior escalated from charming to controlling. The messages that started sweet and became demanding. The way he made me question my own judgment, my own reality. "For example, when I was with him, he'd use personal details I'd told him in private to embarrass me in front of other people—friends, even viewers. He'd turn it into a joke, so I couldn't call it out without looking like I was overreacting. It made me question my own reactions all the time. He created this power imbalance and then made me feel like it was my fault for noticing."

When I finish, there's a pause that stretches too long, but maybe that's just me. "I see. That sounds very concerning," Dorian says, but his tone hasn't shifted at all. "Ms. Voss, would you like to share your experience as well?"

Talia clears her throat. "If I may interrupt, Willow, thank you for telling your story. I know it's not easy. Apologies Lilly. Please continue."

It's only a few words, and she keeps her expression carefully neutral, but something in her tone softens how tense I feel.

Lilly nods and begins her story. She talks about the late-night messages that became increasingly explicit, how Leo would alternate between love-bombing her with compliments and then tearing her down minutes later. The way he'd demand photos and then make her feel guilty for hesitating. As she speaks, I watch her hands shake slightly, and I want to reach through the screen to hug her.

"He made me feel like I was crazy for being uncomfortable with some of the things he said and wanted," Lilly says. "Like I should be grateful for his attention. And when I tried to set boundaries, he'd twist it around and make me apologize."

Talia looks down at something, before he looks back at the camera. "I'm really sorry you went through this."

There's a pause before Dorian speaks. "Thank you both for sharing. I can imagine this was difficult. We appreciate your bravery in coming forward."

The phrase sounds like it came straight from a PR handbook. I wait for him to ask follow-up questions, to request evidence of what happened, to show any sign that he's actually processing what we've told him.

Instead, he says, "We take these things very seriously, and we will review this information internally."

My instincts from journalism and how I like to do thorough research kick in. "What does that review process look like?" I ask, leaning forward. "Who will be involved? What kind of timeline are we looking at?"

"I can't get into the specifics of our internal procedures," he deflects smoothly. "But I can assure you that all reports are thoroughly investigated."

Red flag number two. He's giving us nothing concrete, no indication that our reports will lead to any actual action.

"Will Leo be informed that we've told you these things?" Lilly asks.

"That's part of our confidential process," he says. "We handle all matters with appropriate discretion."

"That's not really an answer," I press. "Are you saying he will be told, or he won't be told? Because if he finds out we reported him, there could be retaliation."

"I understand your concern, but I can't discuss the specifics of how we handle these situations. What I can tell you is that we follow all proper protocols."

"Willow's point is valid. Transparency around outcomes does help prevent further harm. Even if names can't be shared, patterns can be addressed," Talia chimes in.

Dorian stops, but he doesn't acknowledge what she said. Lilly and I exchange a look. This is going nowhere fast and I feel like we are getting stonewalled in real time.

"Can you at least tell us what kind of consequences he might face if you determine our reports are valid?" Lilly asks.

"I can't speculate on potential outcomes. Each situation is handled on a case-by-case basis. We will review this thoroughly, I can promise you that."

There it is again. "We will review this." Like we're filing a complaint about a defective product instead of reporting predatory behavior.

"What does thoroughly mean?" I push. "Days? Weeks? Months? And will we be updated on the progress?"

"The timeline varies depending on the complexity of the situation. As for updates..." He pauses. "Yes, we'll be back in touch to let you know how this turns out."

I press the mute button and lean back in my chair, fighting the urge to roll my eyes. While it was slightly better than the rest of the bullshit he's been saying, the "We'll be back in touch" sounds like corporate speak for "we'll call you, don't call us." This guy could teach a masterclass in saying nothing while sounding official.

"Let me be more direct," I continue after unmuting my microphone. "Are you planning to take any immediate action to prevent Leo from potentially harming other women while you conduct this review?"

"That's...that's a complex question that would depend on the findings of our review process."

"So the answer is no," Lilly says flatly. "You're not going to do anything to protect other women while you take your time deciding whether or not we're telling the truth."

Another pause before Talia speaks up. "In some cases, we've recommended temporary suspensions or removed talent from brand-facing opportunities during active reviews," she says carefully. "That's not a guarantee, but... it *has* happened before."

Dorian doesn't respond immediately. I can't tell if he's annoyed or caught off guard. Maybe both.

"That context is helpful," I say. Because it is. It's the first real thing anyone on this call has said that sounds remotely like accountability. And it didn't come from him.

Talia glances sideways on her camera like she's bracing for Dorian to shut her down. When he doesn't, she sits back, but I can tell she's not as comfortable as she was when she got on the call.

"That's slightly misleading—"

I interrupt whatever Dorian is about to say. "How is it misleading? Because from where I'm sitting, that sounds like a move in the right direction to prevent business as usual for creators like Leo who clearly have no issue harming women."

There's a longer pause this time while he mutes his mic. It makes me wonder if he's consulting his notes or getting advice from someone else. When he unmutes his microphone, I do my best to keep my expression neutral, but what he says makes me want to throw something across the room. "I want to assure you both that we take these things very seriously."

The repetition of that sentence makes my skin crawl. I try to keep a professional tone to my voice, but the struggle is real. "You keep saying you're taking this seriously, but you haven't asked for any evidence. You haven't asked for dates, names of witnesses, screenshots or like anything that would actually help you investigate."

"Well, we appreciate you sharing your experiences with us today," he says, completely sidestepping my point. "This information will be very helpful as we move forward."

"Helpful how?" Lilly jumps in. "You haven't told us anything about what moving forward actually means."

"As I mentioned, we will review this thoroughly through our internal channels—"

"Stop," I cut him off. "Just stop with the corporate speak for a minute. We're talking about a man who has used his platform to manipulate and harass women. Are you going to do anything concrete about it, or are you just going to shuffle this into a file somewhere and hope we go away? Because there are other avenues we can take, including going the legal route."

There's a pause, and when he speaks again, there's a slight shift in his tone. Less polished, more careful. "I'd like to keep lawyers out of this if possible. We prefer to handle these matters internally when we can."

The threat is subtle, but unmistakable. He's essentially warning us not to escalate this legally while giving us nothing in return. "You prefer to handle things internally," I repeat slowly, but then something clicks, and I decide to push on it. "And how has that worked out for the other women who've reported him?"

Talia sighs but she doesn't look away. She also doesn't back Dorian up so he continues talking.

"I can't discuss other cases—"

"So there are other cases." Lilly's voice is sharp. "You just admitted there are other women who've come forward about Leo."

"I didn't say that. I simply can't discuss confidential matters involving other individuals or clients."

"Okay, so where does that leave us?" I ask although I already know the answer deep down in my soul.

"As I said, we will be in touch once we've had a chance to review everything discussed today. Thank you both for your time, and we appreciate your bravery in bringing these concerns to our attention."

Talia opens her mouth like she might speak, but Dorian disconnects from the call. Just like that.

She stares at us for a couple of seconds. Then she looks directly at the camera.

"Thank you both again," she says softly. "I'll make sure that you get the justice you deserve."

She hesitates just long enough for me to wonder if she means it. Then she nods once, and she's gone too.

I stare at my screen in amazement because there's no way that just happened. My hands are still positioned over the keyboard like I'm about to type something, but there's nothing left to say. The call is over.

Lilly's face is mirroring exactly what I'm feeling. Confused. Frustrated. Empty.

"Well," she says after a long moment. "That was..."

"Useless," I finish.

"I was going to say disappointing, but useless works too."

I lean back in my chair, replaying the entire conversation in my head. On paper, it looked like everything it should have been. Professional, scheduled meeting time, opportunity to share our experiences. But underneath all the polite language and corporate protocols, it felt like we'd just been managed rather than heard.

"He never asked for specifics," Lilly continues. "No request for screenshots, no follow-up questions about dates or incidents. Nothing that would actually help build a case."

My fingers drum against my desk. "And the way he kept repeating the same phrases. 'We take this seriously,' 'internal review process,' 'appropriate discretion.' Like he was reading from a script."

"Because he probably was." Lilly's voice is bitter. "God, I feel so stupid for thinking they'd actually care."

"You're not stupid. We both hoped for better." But even as I say it, something sits wrong in my stomach. The whole thing felt choreographed, like we were being walked through motions rather than participating in a genuine discussion.

Lilly sighs on screen. "So what now? Do we just wait for them to call us back in six months with some bullshit about 'insufficient evidence'?"

I don't have an answer for her. Dorian's parting words echo in my head: We will be in touch. But I doubted he actually would.

However, Talia's words still lingered. "I'll make sure that you get the justice you deserve." She seemed as if she meant it and that we could trust her. That was and the fact that we did the right thing was the only thing I could hold on to.

"I need to think," I say finally. "Process all of this."

"Yeah. Me too." Lilly's image flickers as she adjusts her camera. "Thanks for doing this with me, Willow. Even if it didn't go how we hoped."

"Of course. We'll figure out what comes next."

After she logs off, I'm left alone with my laptop screen and the growing certainty that we've just been politely dismissed. I close the browser window and stare at my desktop wallpaper as I run through the call again. Nothing he said was outright wrong. He listened, he acknowledged our concerns, he promised to review everything. But there was no urgency, no indication that our reports would lead to anything. It was just the smooth, practiced language of someone whose job is to make problems disappear quietly.

My phone buzzes. Blaise again.

Blaise: How is it going?

I stare at the message, trying to figure out how to explain how disappointed and frustrated I am. How do you describe the feeling of being handled?

Me: Are you around? The call with Leo's management is over and I don't trust them.

His response comes immediately.

Blaise: Yes. Where do you want to meet?

I quickly type out the location where we should meet and grab my coat, phone, and purse. Before I head out the door I walk over to my closet and start digging through it quickly. It's then that I find something I forgot I had until this very moment.

One of Blaise's jerseys. I quickly toss it on the bed along with my other stuff just before I start removing the shirt I already have on.

Maybe there's a chance I can salvage this day after all.

34

WILLOW

Two weeks, four days, a get together at the hockey house, and loads of cryptic text messages since we left Puerto Rico, and I find myself driving to the same Crestwood overlook where bored upperclassmen come to drink, fuck, or think about if there are other life forms outside of our universe. It's the middle of winter, and the trees give off a creepy vibe against the sky that is slowly turning to night. The lake is frozen solid, the parking lot a patchwork of black ice and snow. Nobody is out here.

And that's the whole point.

I keep my engine running while I check my phone. No new messages. The silence between us lately is its own kind of communication. When I see headlights in my rearview mirror, coming up the hill behind me, my pulse flips. I already know it's Blaise, but I stare the vehicle down to confirm.

His car pulls up a few spaces away and I watch as his headlights that were cutting through the evening light go dark. My heart hammers against my ribs as I watch his silhouette through the windshield. Even from this distance, I can see the tension in his shoulders, the way his hands grip the steering wheel like he's fighting the same internal war I am.

The cold air seeps through my car windows, but my body runs hot because I know what's coming. The memories of what he did to me in Puerto Rico have haunted me ever since, and I can't wait for another round. It's been too long. Way too long.

I undo my seatbelt and grab my phone with shaky fingers. I somehow manage to quickly send him a message.

> Me: Hi.

The response is immediate. I watch his door open before my phone even shows the message as delivered. He steps out into the frigid air, his breath forming clouds as he walks toward my passenger side.

When he reaches my car, I unlock the doors. He slides into the passenger seat, and for a moment, we just sit there in silence. This is the first time we've been alone since we hopped back on the plane taking us to Virginia, and it's as if we don't know what to say or do. Blaise pulls off his beanie, and I can't help but think that his blond hair is about to get even more messy if I have my way.

"Hey," he says quietly, his voice sounds rougher than usual.

"Hey yourself." I do my best to turn in my seat to face him properly, but having a steering wheel in front of me makes that difficult. "Just got done with the call with Leo's management company."

"Doesn't sound like it went that well."

"Well, it went okay on the surface," I say. "His manager was polite. Said all the right things. Promised to escalate it internally." I pause. "But it was all bullshit. No follow-up questions. No sense of urgency. It felt like he was just there so he didn't get fired. He did promise to reach back out to us with any findings so at least there's that. But I'm not sure how much I believe him."

I hesitate for a second, then add, "There was another person on the call named Talia from the company as well. She didn't say much, but I'm not going to lie it felt good to have her there because it seemed like she got it."

Blaise is quiet for a few seconds, then runs a hand through his hair like he's trying to find the right words to say. "That's good and hopefully the next thing you'll hear is that he's getting the boot. I hate that you even had to make that call," he adds, glancing over at me. "You shouldn't have to be the one chasing accountability."

I study him for a moment and can sense the irritation

and anger radiating off of him in waves. He's angry for me. But there's nothing I can do about the situation right now and I don't want this to completely ruin this precious time we have together.

"Anyway," I say, nudging his knee with mine. "How was practice?"

"Rough. Coach is pushing us hard for the next series coming up." He shifts, his knee bumping against the center console, but doesn't comment on my changing the subject. "Knox mentioned you."

My stomach tightens cause I'm not sure where this is going. "What did he say?"

"Thanked me for looking out for you while in Puerto Rico, which is odd that he just brought it up. Too bad he doesn't know how well I look after you, huh?"

This is the last thing I expected Blaise to say and I can't deny that it takes my horniness up another level. I can already see where this is going, which is what I expected, but we should get the small talk out of the way.

"How's the team handling the workload?" I ask, trying to steer us into safer territory, Thankfully, it works.

"Fine. Good. Same as always." His answers come quickly, as if he's distracted. He's staring out the windshield at the frozen lake now, but I can feel him watching me from the corner of his eye.

"You're not going to tell me why you picked this spot?" he asks, still avoiding looking at me.

I shrug, then pick imaginary lint from my coat sleeve

to give myself something to do. "I like the view. Also the chance of anyone else being up here was pretty small."

"Ah, so you just didn't want anyone to see us," Blaise says. He says it flat, quiet, and it could almost be a joke, but there's nothing funny about the shape of his mouth.

"Well, it's not like we're subtle when we're around each other," I say. "Somebody would notice eventually." I keep my eyes on the trees, finger tapping the steering wheel.

That's what makes Blaise look at me. "That makes sense since I'm sure whenever we're in the same space, my eyes will always find you. I haven't stopped thinking about you," he says. "I thought it would fade after we got back, that once we were back to our routines it would be... easier."

"Has it been?" I ask, trying to keep my voice neutral when it feels like I'm handling dynamite.

He shakes his head. "No. Not for one second."

I suck in a breath and watch it fog up the driver's side window. "Not for me either," I admit. There. I finally said it out loud. "If anything, it's worse. Every time I walk past my mirror, I think about you because I remember..."

"Your mirror, huh?" he murmurs, and I can feel the heat in his words.

"Yeah." I rest my forehead on the steering wheel for a second. "This is so fucking stupid, Blaise."

"It is, but what other option do we have right now? You want to face your brother? I have no issue with that, but I know how you feel about it unless you've changed your mind."

I haven't changed my mind about Knox, but sitting here talking about it feels like we're wasting precious time. My hand moves before I can think better of it, reaching across the center console to rest on his knee.

The moment my palm makes contact with his jeans, his entire body goes rigid. I glance down and notice his hands are clenched into fists on his thighs.

"You're gripping your legs like you're about to launch into orbit," I observe, letting my thumb trace a small circle against his knee. "What's that about?"

He lets out a ragged breath as if he has the whole world on his shoulders. "Willow..."

Thank fuck he let me change the conversation topic. "What? I'm just asking a question." I slide my hand higher, just slightly, watching the way his breathing changes. "You're sitting there all tense like you're afraid to move."

"I'm not afraid."

"No? Then what *are* you doing?" I lean closer, close enough that I can smell his shampoo. "Because from where I'm sitting, it looks like you're trying really hard not to touch me."

His eyes finally meet mine and there's something dark and hungry in them, which is the best way I can describe it. "Maybe I am."

"Why? Are you going to keep pretending this is just a

casual conversation, or are you actually going to do something about the fact that we're finally alone?"

Something snaps in his expression. The careful control he's been maintaining since he got in my car fractures, and suddenly his hand is covering mine, pressing it firmly against his thigh.

"You want to know what I'm doing?" His voice is low and rough. "I'm trying not to drag you into the backseat and fuck you until you're screaming my name loud enough for the whole county to hear."

The crude words send heat straight to my pussy. "And what's stopping you?"

"The fact that it's fifteen degrees outside and your car windows will fog up so fast anyone driving by will know exactly what we're doing."

I laugh, surprised by how turned on I am by his restraint rather than frustrated. "And that's why I picked this place. You've been thinking about this a lot, huh?"

"I've thought about nothing else for over two weeks." His thumb strokes across my knuckles. "Every night, every morning, every goddamn time I close my eyes."

The confession makes my confidence surge. I shift in my seat, angling my body toward him more fully. I lean across the center console and brush my lips against his ear. "Then maybe you should stop thinking and start acting."

Before he can respond, I'm already moving. The confined space of my car makes it awkward, but I manage to climb over the console and settle into his lap. Thankfully, we are in my car because there's no way I would have been able to make it work if he was in the driver's seat. The look of shock and desire on his face makes every uncomfortable angle worth it.

"Willow—" he starts, his hands automatically reaching for my hips.

"Nope." I catch his wrists, pressing them back against the seat. "Hands stay right there. On the seat or on your thighs. Don't move them."

His eyes widen slightly. "What?"

"You heard me." I settle more fully into his lap, and his hard cock pressed against my core through our clothes makes us both inhale sharply. "I want to see how long you can behave yourself."

"This is already fucking torture," he says, but his hands stay exactly where I put them.

"Good." I roll my hips slowly, deliberately, watching his face as I grind against him through his jeans and my leggings. "I like seeing you like this. All wound up and desperate for me."

His knuckles go white as his grip on the seat tightens. "Fuck, kitten."

The pet name makes me move faster, finding a rhythm that has both of us breathing hard within seconds. The friction is perfect, even through our clothes, and I can feel how hard he is beneath me.

"You like this, don't you?" I whisper in his ear before I

run my tongue along the edge of his jaw. "Being told what to do?"

"At times, yes," he admits. "Fuck, yes."

"That's what I like to hear." I lean back slightly so I can look at him properly. I brace my hands on his shoulders for balance and to not embarrass myself if I fall over. "You're being such a good boy, keeping your hands exactly where I told you to."

His jaw clenches at the praise, and I feel his cock twitch beneath me. The reaction makes me grin wickedly.

"Tell me what you want," I command, slowing my movements to an agonizing pace that leaves us both struggling to maintain our positions.

"I want—" He stops, swallowing hard as I circle my hips in a way that makes his eyes nearly roll back. "I want you to keep doing exactly what you're doing."

"Just this?" I grind down harder, watching the way his mouth falls open. "Nothing else?"

"Fuck." The word comes out strangled. "I want these clothes gone. I want to be inside you. I want to make you come so hard that you forget your own name."

"Mmm, that sounds tempting." I trace my fingers along the collar of his shirt. "But I think I like having you at my mercy like this."

"You're going to kill me," he gasps as I find a particularly good angle that makes us both moan.

"What a way to go though," I tease, picking up the pace

just enough to make his hands move toward me before he catches himself.

"Willow, please—"

"Please what? Use your words and tell me what you want." I'm so glad I can finally throw that back at him.

His head falls back against the headrest. "Please let me touch you. I need to feel you."

I consider his request as I'm watching the way he's fighting every instinct to grab me. The control he's showing, the way he's letting me lead, makes me want to reward him.

"Not yet," I decide, earning a frustrated groan. "You haven't been good long enough."

But even as I say it, I can feel my own control slipping. Getting properly fucked after a long, stressful day is just what any doctor would order, or that's my belief. However, this isn't just about getting off in the front seat of my car. This is about something deeper, something I've been craving without even realizing it. Control. The ability to call the shots, to have someone as composed and careful as Blaise completely at my mercy.

"You're shaking," I say, taking on the role of Captain Obvious.

"You're making it impossible to think straight," he manages to get out.

I lean forward until my mouth is right against his ear. "Good. I don't want you thinking. This should be nothing but pure instinct at this point. Fuck," I whisper as I start to feel my own release coming closer. I didn't think I'd even get close just from doing this.

"Let me touch you," he pleads again. "Please, kitten. I need to feel you."

The desperation in his voice nearly breaks my willpower. Or maybe I'm just getting too close to the edge to care about power games anymore.

"Wait. I have something to show you," I say. I sit back just enough to unzip my coat.

It only takes him a second to realize what I have on. "My jersey? Wait what—"

"The night you kissed me for the first time. It was also the night you stayed up and made sure that I didn't get sick after drinking too much. Even though I was upset because you rejected me, I still wanted to keep something from that night, so I chose this."

He swallows hard, but doesn't say a word. It's as if he doesn't know whether to kiss me or apologize. Maybe it's both.

"I can't believe you kept it all this time," he whispers.

I nod. "Even when I hated you, I never stopped wanting this."

"It still looks better on you than it ever will on me," he says with a small, broken smile.

I lean in and kiss him and it's as if we're speaking a language only meant for us. He kisses me back like he's sorry for all of it. Like he'd take every bad decision back if it meant this moment could've happened sooner.

When we finally break for air, he says, "I need to fuck you with my jersey on."

And that's all it takes for me to get this show on the road. "Okay," I say against his lips. "Now you can touch me."

His hands are on me before I finish speaking, one gripping my hip while the other tangles in my hair. The kiss he pulls me into is everything but soft and sweet and I wouldn't have it any other way.

"You drive me fucking crazy," he growls against my mouth as his hands guide my movements, helping me find another rhythm all together.

"Good," I gasp, my head falling back as the sensation becomes overwhelming. "I want to drive you crazy. I want to be the thing you can't stop thinking about."

"You already are," he confesses. "You have been since Puerto Rico. Since before Puerto Rico, if I'm being honest."

The admission sends me spiraling toward the edge faster than I could have ever imagined. It's then that I'm willing to admit to myself that this isn't just physical and it never was.

"Blaise," I whisper, and he knows exactly what I need.

His hand slides between us, finding the spot I want him most even through my leggings and he applies just the right pressure to send me flying over the edge.

I come with his name on my lips and while I'm still processing what happened, I say, "I want you inside me. Right now."

"Yes, let me grab a condom and then—"

"I already told you I'm on birth control. I want to feel what it's like to have you, just you, inside me."

"Willow." My name comes out like he's not sure if he heard me correctly. "Are you sure?"

I'm still trembling from my orgasm, still riding that high, but I've never been more certain of anything in my life. This isn't some impulsive decision made in the heat of the moment. This is me choosing him, choosing us, choosing to stop hiding behind fear and logistics and all the reasons this shouldn't be happening.

"I'm sure." I shift in his lap, feeling how hard he still is beneath me. "I want all of you, Blaise. No barriers, no holding back."

His hands tighten on my hips, thumbs tracing circles through the fabric of my leggings. "You know what you're asking for?"

"I know exactly what I'm asking for." I lean down to brush my lips against his. "I'm asking you to stop treating me like I'm going to break. I'm asking you to give me everything you've been holding back. Because I know you have been."

The last thread of his control snaps. Something in my voice must convince him because suddenly his mouth is on mine, kissing me with everything in him. His hands move toward my leggings and I think he's going to grab my waistband, but he goes straight for the seam in between my thighs.

The fabric doesn't stand a chance and gives way with a very loud rip. I gasp at the sudden sensation of cold air hitting my skin and because I can't believe he. Just. Did. That.

"Fuck," he breathes, his fingers immediately finding the wet heat between my legs. "You're so ready for me."

I am. I've been ready since the moment he got into this car, maybe since the moment we left Puerto Rico. His touch is exactly what I need especially when he slips two fingers inside me easily.

"No more waiting," I say, fumbling with his belt buckle. My hands are shaking, whether from the cold or anticipation, I can't tell. "I need you now."

He helps me, lifting his hips so I can push his jeans and boxers down enough to free him. The sight of his cock, hard and ready, makes my mouth water.

"Come here," he growls, positioning himself beneath me.

I rise up on my knees, using his shoulders for balance as he guides himself to my entrance. The first touch of him against me, skin to skin with nothing between us, makes us both freeze.

"Last chance to change your mind," he says.

Instead of answering, I sink down onto him slowly, taking him inch by inch until he's buried completely inside me. The stretch is overwhelming in the best possible way. He's bigger without the condom, or maybe it just feels that way because I can feel everything, but I'm still shocked that we're actually doing this. "Fuck, I...don't know what to say." My sentence ends with a moan.

"I know." His forehead is pressed against mine as we both struggle to adjust. "So tight. So perfect. Just...give me a second."

But I don't want to give him a second. I want to move and feel everything he's been holding back. I do wait for a moment out of respect for him, but when I shift slightly, the movement sends shockwaves through both of us.

"Kitten..."

His sentence dies on his lips when our eyes meet. Here's another line we've crossed and there's no coming back from it. And for some weird reason, I'm perfectly okay with that thought.

With that in mind, I begin to move. The cramped space forces us closer together. Every move we make is more intense because we can't get the leverage we want. I'm practically pinned against the roof of my car, but I don't care. The awkward angles, including the way my knee keeps hitting the door handle and the fact that we're both still half-dressed doesn't matter to me one bit. All because I'm satisfying a craving I've had for what feels like forever.

I swear our bodies are coming together as one shakes the whole car. I grip the fabric of his hoodie for balance as I set the pace, taking as much of him as my body will allow. I feel everything, hot and slick and impossibly deep, and the way his fingers dig into my thighs tells me he's barely hanging on.

"Slow down," he somehow manages to say. "Or this isn't going to last long."

The warning shoots electricity through me. "Is that supposed to be a problem?" I ask, grinding down harder and rolling my hips just to watch his eyelids flutter shut.

"You're evil," he groans. His grip alternates between gentle and bruising, like he's torn between worshipping me and pinning me in place. At this point, I don't care if he does either one or both.

I want him to lose it. I want him to snap so completely that he can't remember anything but me. "I think we both like me when I'm this way."

"You're right. I love you like this. Confident, in control, taking what you want."

The words hit me harder than they should. Not the love part because I know he's talking about us in just the heat of the moment but the way he sees me.

"Then let me have what I want," I whisper, picking up the pace despite his earlier warning.

"Fuck it," he growls against my mouth. "I can't hold back anymore."

His hips surge up to meet mine, and suddenly every thrust hits deeper than before and the angle has me seeing my life flash before my eyes.

"Yes. Just like that," is all I can say, and I'm impressed that I managed to do that.

One of his hands makes his way up my body until it comes to a stop near the base of my throat. "Is this okay?" he asks.

I nod and say in between taking quick breaths, "I want a necklace only you can give me."

His fingers wrap around my throat with perfect pressure. It's firm enough that it makes me wetter, yet gentle enough that I know he'd never hurt me. The combination of his hand around my throat and the way he's filling me completely pushes me right to the edge again. My vision blurs as I recognize what is coming next. Me.

"Come for me," he commands. "I want to feel you fall apart around my cock."

His words, combined with the pressure of his fingers and one final thrust, send me crashing over the edge. My orgasm rips through me with an intensity that makes my whole body shake. I cry out his name as I clench around him, riding him as every wave hits me.

"Fuck, Willow," he groans. "You're so—I can't—"

His release follows immediately after mine. A tired smile forms on my face due to his moan that's so loud, it sounds like it bounces off of every surface in the car. His hand falls away from my throat to grab my hip as he empties himself inside me completely.

We stay frozen like that for several long moments, both of us breathing hard and trying to process what just happened. I can feel him inside me, and I'm in no hurry to move.

"Well," I say finally as I'm still trying to catch my breath, "this is going to be interesting to clean up."

Blaise lets out a low chuckle. "I have some napkins in my glove compartment. I'll just have to run out and get them. And you..." He points at my torn leggings. "You're going to need a new pair of those."

"These were my favorite leggings," I say, though I'm grinning as I do.

"I'll buy you ten new pairs." His eyes are soft as he looks at me. "Twenty if you want."

"Such a gentleman, offering to replace the clothes you destroyed." I shift slightly and we both inhale sharply at the sensation. "Though I have to say, that was worth a pair of leggings."

"Just one pair?" He raises an eyebrow. "I'm insulted."

I laugh, pressing a quick kiss to his lips. "Fine, it was worth my entire wardrobe."

We fall into comfortable silence again, and I let myself enjoy this moment of peace before reality creeps back in. It's then I realize I've come to a decision. "Blaise," I say quietly as I play with the strings of his hoodie. "We don't have to talk about this now, but I think I'm ready to talk about us and how we should approach Knox."

He does a double-take. "Wait, are you serious?"

"Well, yeah." I meet his eyes but my confidence takes a small dive. "I mean, we can't keep sneaking around forever. And this...what we just did...it feels like more than just fooling around, doesn't it?"

"It is. For me, at least." He pauses, studying my face. "Are you saying what I think you're saying? That this is more than physical and that we are in a relationship?"

"I mean...isn't it? Unless you're hooking up with other—"

"Don't even fucking say it," he says firmly. "There's been no one else since you and it was a while before that."

I remember him saying that and it calms me down. "Good. I'm glad we're on the same page, but before we talk about Knox, we need to get cleaned up. I refuse to talk about my brother with your cock inside me."

That makes Blaise chuckle. "Deal."

35

WILLOW

It's almost eleven P.M. and my dorm room looks like a complete and unmitigated disaster. Clothes are everywhere, including my bed, my desk chair, and the floor where I threw them after changing outfits three times this morning. Textbooks are scattered across my desk like I actually had the motivation to study tonight, which is a complete lie.

I can't focus on anything. Can't sit still. Can't stop replaying the conversation with Lilly and Leo's manager from several days ago. My mind won't stop. I try reading, then doomscrolling, then rearranging the chaos into some other formation of chaos, but nothing sticks for more than a minute. I'm so deep into the next round of self-loathing that I don't hear my phone vibrate until it does it twice in rapid fire. I freeze. I count to three. I flip the phone.

Ari: Hey. You up?

Ari: I know you are.

I don't answer. I don't even open the notification. Instead, I try to guess what she's going to say before the next text arrives.

Ari: Just watch this. Sorry.

My phone buzzes again and this time it's a link. Now I know Ari wouldn't send me a link that would lead to some bad shit, but I don't want to click it.

My gut is screaming at me to open it while my heart is telling me to delete it and pretend Ari never sent it. That way I can crawl under my covers and disappear until morning. Because there's a good chance that wherever this link leads me to, I won't be getting a wink of sleep tonight.

In situations like this, I've learned that I need to listen to my gut because she will never lead me wrong. I tap the link.

The video loads instantly. Leo's face fills my screen, that same cocky grin I remember from when we were together. He's in his usual streaming setup: gaming chair, neon lights, energy drink strategically placed for sponsorship visibility. His chat is moving too fast to read, but I can see the hearts and fire emoji flooding the sidebar.

"—I mean, look," he's saying, gesturing broadly at his camera, "some people will literally do anything for attention these days. Anything." He shakes his head. "It's honestly kind of sad when you think about it. Like, imagine being so desperate to stay relevant that you have to..." he trails off with a knowing smirk, letting his audience fill in the blanks.

My stomach drops through the floor because I know exactly what he's talking about. He doesn't say my name. He doesn't have to. That's Leo's specialty. Say just enough and then let his fanbase connect the dots. That way, they can draw their own conclusions while he maintains plausible deniability. But we both know exactly who he's talking about. The timing isn't coincidental. Nothing with Leo ever is.

And that's when it hits me: he fucking knows. Not just generally, not through gossip. He knows because someone told him. Dorian said the review would be confidential. Talia looked me in the eye and said she'd make sure we got the justice we deserved. But here he is, mocking us live to thousands of people.

Somehow, it's her betrayal that stings more. Because I thought she saw us. Because for a second, I believed she meant it.

It's clear they both lied straight to our faces and now Leo is getting rewarded because of it. New sponsors. More engagement. Because the only thing that matters is protecting their golden goose and burying anything that could force the money train to stop.

"But hey," he continues, taking a sip from his energy drink, label pointed toward the camera so we can all read it clearly, "I'm not here to throw shade at anyone. I'm just saying, some people need to learn when to let go, you know? Like, move on already." He laughs, and the sound makes my skin crawl. "Anyway, enough about that drama. Let's get back to the game."

The video ends. I stare at my phone screen until it goes black, then stare at my own reflection in the dark glass.

My hands are shaking.

This is retaliation and a betrayal rolled into one. And now he's doing what Leo does best: weaponizing his platform against anyone who threatens him.

I set my phone down on my nightstand like it might explode. Then I pick it up again. Put it down. Pick it up.

Ari's follow-up text appears before I can decide what to do with my hands or my phone.

> Ari: I'm so sorry. Someone shared it on socials and after you told me about how the call went...I thought you should know.

> Ari: Want me to come over? We can talk shit and figure out what to do about this. I've been ready to kick his ass ever since you told me about him.

I don't respond to Ari. Instead, I open every social media platform I can think of, searching for Leo's name and any mention of what just happened.

The posts start appearing immediately.

A Twitter (I refuse to call it X) thread with fifteen retweets: "Anyone else catch Leo's stream tonight? Sounds like someone's still pressed that he's doing fine without them. * * "

An Instagram story screenshot from his stream, reposted with the caption: "Tea 🍵 When your ex can't let you level up in peace."

A Reddit post in r/streamerdrama: "Leo Kent calls out desperate exes on stream. Alludes to this being connected to the Red Wolves deal drama."

My thumb keeps scrolling. The comments get worse.

"They're just mad he's successful without them."

"Imagine being so thirsty over your ex moving on that you try to sabotage his career."

"Some girls really can't handle rejection lmaooo."

Each comment hits me like I'm being jumped in a fight, but I can't stop scrolling. Can't close the app. Can't put the phone down.

"Probably just wants attention."

"Classic crazy ex behavior."

"Leo deserves better than dealing with psycho exes."

The room starts spinning. I'm hyperventilating now, gasping for air that won't come. My vision tunnels until all I can see is the screen, comment after comment tearing me apart while strangers who don't know my name decide who I am.

And I know it's only a matter of time before my name leaks.

My phone buzzes again. A notification from an account I don't recognize. It's then I realize I spoke too soon.

"You ruined a good man's career because you couldn't handle being dumped. Pathetic."

Then another.

"Stay in your lane and leave Leo alone."

And another.

"Nobody wants to hear from bitter exes. Take the L and move on."

They're finding me. Somehow, without Leo ever saying my name, they're connecting the dots and coming for me directly. My hands shake so violently I nearly drop my phone, but I can't stop reading. Can't look away from the digital mob forming in real time.

Then it clicks in my mind that I'm probably not the only one experiencing this. Lilly is probably getting hit even worse than I am. She is a streamer and has a public platform herself. If they found me this quickly, they've definitely found her.

I slam my phone face down on my bed and lunge for my laptop, nearly tripping over the pile of clothes I discarded earlier. My fingers fumble with the power button, then drum impatiently against my thighs while it boots up. The seconds feel like hours.

Discord loads and immediately I see the little notification bubble next to Lilly's name. Three unread messages, all timestamped within the last hour.

CozyCraft4Eva (Lilly): Willow are you seeing this?

CozyCraft4Eva (Lilly): They're in my DMs. Like actually in my fucking DMs saying the most vile things.

CozyCraft4Eva (Lilly): I can't breathe right now.

My heart shatters. I type back as fast as my shaking fingers will allow.

WillsNet56: I'm here. I just saw the stream. Are you okay?

The response is immediate.

CozyCraft4Eva (Lilly): No I'm not fucking okay. They're calling me a lying whore who's jealous of his success. Someone found my Instagram and they're commenting on photos from when I was 16.

CozyCraft4Eva (Lilly): How did this happen so fast? Him and his management team are assholes.

WillsNet56: I don't know. I wouldn't be surprised if they leaked our names on their end to keep Leo's name clean. We came forward when so many women won't have for various reasons.

I guess I knew why many women don't come forward in these types of situations, but it didn't completely click for me about why until just now. I hate that it took me having to experience it before I realized the gravity of what just happened.

I stare at my cursor blinking after those words, and something cold settles in my chest. We did everything right. We went through proper channels. We documented everything. We trusted the system that was supposed to protect us, and instead it fed us directly to the wolves.

The betrayal cuts deeper than Leo's retaliation. Dorian and Talia who we assumed would maintain confidentiality, told him everything. Our names, our statements, probably every detail we shared on that call where we thought we were safe. That's worse than not doing the investigation. What makes it worse is I'm sure he's not the only one who okayed Leo being told. Whoever sat back silent or gave final approval is just as guilty.

CozyCraft4Eva (Lilly): This is so fucked up. What are we supposed to do now?

I don't have an answer. For the first time in my life, I'm completely out of moves. Every strategy I might have used feels useless against this machine Leo's built around himself.

WillsNet56: I don't know. I'm so sorry, Lilly. This is my fault. I convinced you to come forward with me.

CozyCraft4Eva (Lilly): Stop. This isn't your fault. This is exactly what they want. They want us to blame ourselves instead of them.

She's right but knowing that doesn't make the guilt any lighter. I convinced her we were doing the right thing.

I told her the system would protect us. I was so fucking wrong.

My phone buzzes again and I assume it's more notifications. More strangers dissecting my life, my choices, my worth as a human being. Instead I focus on the message Lilly just sent.

CozyCraft4Eva (Lilly): I think I need to step away from the internet for a while. This is too much.

WillsNet56: I understand. Take care of yourself. I'll figure something out.

But I won't figure anything out. As soon as I send that message, the weight of my own lie hits me hard. I close the laptop and sit in the silence of my destroyed room, surrounded by the evidence of my inability to function like a normal human being. Then again, what is normal anyway?

I walk over to my bed, and I see my phone screen lighting up with another notification. Then another. The harassment is accelerating, spreading like wildfire across platforms I didn't even know existed. Each time my phone vibrates it makes me flinch. I do my best to quickly deactivate my social media accounts for the time being and then flip over to my text messages.

There are seventeen unread messages from various people, but my eyes go straight to Blaise's name. Nothing from him, but I assume it's because he's asleep.

I stare at his messages with my thumb over the keyboard, I start typing.

> Me: Can we talk?

I read it back and immediately delete it. Too needy.
Too desperate. He'll ask questions I don't have answers to,
he'll want to fix things I can't let him fix.

I try again.

> Me: Hey, rough night. Could use some
> company.

Delete. That sounds like I'm using him as a distraction, which maybe I am, but I don't want him to know
that.

> Me: Hey, what are you doing? Just
> wanted to let you know I'm okay, just
> dealing with some stuff.

Delete. He'll see right through that lie. Blaise knows
me too well now, can read the spaces between my words.

I set the phone down and press the heels of my palms
against my eyes until I see flashing lights behind my lids.
The truth is, I want him here. I want his arms around me,
want him to tell me everything will be okay even if we
both know it won't be. I want to bury my face in his chest
and pretend the outside world doesn't exist.

But I can't let him see me like this. Can't let him
witness how completely I'm falling apart. This raw,
exposed version of myself feels too vulnerable, too
broken. What if he looks at me and sees what Leo's

followers see? What if the girl who can barely hold herself together isn't the same one who confidently took control in the front seat of her car?

Instead of listening to my gut this time, I turn my phone off, crawl into bed and pray for sleep that never comes.

36

WILLOW

By the time Ari parks her car in the parking lot of Crestwood Arena, I've convinced myself I'm fine. Not good, not stable, but fine. It's a lie I've been telling myself, but here we are.

Even though I deactivated my social media accounts days ago, I decided that deleting the apps themselves would also be wise. It wasn't out of strength, but pure exhaustion, and I've told myself multiple times that I'm allowed to feel this way.

But that doesn't matter right now.

What matters is I'm about to surprise the guy I've been ducking for the last couple of days due to this situation. He doesn't deserve the way I've been acting and frankly, neither do I. Shutting him out hasn't been the best move, and I know I need to apologize for it, but with being overwhelmed with everything, I didn't know what to do. So here I am, even though I'm still a hot mess. I pull my baseball hat down lower over my face and let Ari lead the way into the arena.

The event isn't even technically open yet, but the Crestwood Red Wolves' fan event already has a ton of volunteers and early bird superfans walking about. All the tables are draped in red-and-white tablecloths with Red Wolves decor everywhere. There's a separate, smaller line off to the side that I assume is the table where the team will be signing their autographs for who knows how long. No sign of Blaise or Knox yet. I scan the area twice just to be sure.

Ari glances back at me and I know she knows I'm freaking out. She's wearing a sick pair of mirrored sunglasses, even though it's cloudy and we're inside. "You wanna check out the merch table first?"

"Nah, let's just walk around," I say, keeping my voice low. My heart isn't up for merch or small talk. I want to keep moving, keep breathing, keep the momentum before I can start making up reasons to bail and go back to my dorm room.

We roam around the perimeter of the arena floor, past the concession stands and photo booths, until I catch sight of something that makes my blood freeze.

A microphone. Professional lighting. A camera setup that's too polished for a simple fan event.

And then I see him.

Leo.

He's positioned near the tunnel entrance, angled perfectly to capture both himself and the Red Wolves branding in the background. His usual streaming setup, but mobile. Portable. Strategic. He's talking animatedly to his camera, that practiced grin plastered across his face like he belongs here. Like he's still getting that brand deal.

My shoulders lock. The pulse in my ears drowns out everything else. I can't hear Ari's voice, the crowd noise, the music playing over the arena speakers anymore. Everything narrows to this single, brutal realization: He's here to film content so he can go viral.

Not to apologize. Not to make amends. He's weaponizing this event, using the Red Wolves' platform to rehabilitate his image. To spin himself as the victim who's been wrongfully excluded from something that was "rightfully" his. And he's doing it at my college, the place where I have to see many of these people day in and day out.

That's when I'm finally able to admit to myself that I'm done letting him control the narrative. I don't think about what I'm going to do. I don't plan what I'm going to say. I just move.

I walk across the arena floor like I own this place. I'm not rushing or charging. I head toward him like I have every right to be here because I do. This is my school. My space. And he doesn't get to poison it with his performance.

The closer I get, the clearer his voice becomes. He's

mid-sentence, gesturing toward his camera with the same fake-ass charisma that used to make me think he actually cared about something other than himself.

"I think it's cool when teams do stuff like this. It gives fans a chance to actually meet the players and give back to the community. I'm glad I was able to come here today even after everything that has gone on the last few days."

It's then I realize not only is he trying to go viral, he's trying to get on the Red Wolves' good side to have them extend him another opportunity to do content with them. And that's when I step into the frame.

Not beside him. Not behind him. Directly in front of his camera, cutting off his perfectly curated shot.

"Hi, Leo."

My voice is calm. Even. The kind of tone I use when I'm explaining something to Abue because she's not as tech savvy as the rest of us.

He freezes mid-gesture, his practiced smile faltering for just a second before snapping back into place. "Willow. Hey." He tries to angle the camera away from me, but I move with him. "I'm actually in the middle of—"

"I know exactly what you're in the middle of." I don't raise my voice. Don't need to. "You're in the middle of lying to your audience about why you're really here."

His laugh sounds forced. "Come on, don't be dramatic. I'm just here supporting the team—"

"You're here because your deal got canceled." The words come out clean and sharp. "You're here because you need content to spin the narrative after your management leaked Lilly's name and mine to you, and you decided to weaponize your platform against us."

I watch his face change. The mask slips just enough for me to see the panic underneath.

"Look, I don't know what you think happened—"

"I know exactly what happened." I take a step closer, and he actually backs up. "You found out we came forward about what you did to us, and instead of taking accountability, you decided to paint us as bitter exes who can't move on. You sent your followers after us without ever saying our names directly, but you let your management do it for you. Very smart. Very calculated."

His camera is still rolling. I can see the red light in my peripheral vision, but I don't look at it. Don't acknowledge the hundreds or thousands of people probably watching this live. My focus stays locked on him.

"That's not—you're twisting things—"

"Am I?" I tilt my head slightly. "Because from where I'm standing, it looks like you're exactly where you've always been. Using your platform to tear down women who threaten your image. The only difference is now you're doing it in my space."

"Your space? This is a public event, Willow. You don't own—"

"I go to school here. This is my campus. These are my people. You lost your deal with this team because of your own actions. Not because of anything Lilly or I did. We didn't ruin your career, Leo. You did."

"You're overreacting—"

"I'm overreacting?" I laugh because I can't help it. My tone is sharp enough to draw blood without laying a finger on him. A few heads turn our way because of the commotion this is causing, but I don't care.

Let them watch.

Let them hear.

"You want to know what's actually pathetic?" I continue, my voice still perfectly level. "It's being so threatened by women telling their truth that you have to send an army of strangers to attack them online. It's standing here right now, trying to manipulate this situation into content for your brand."

This is my opportunity to do what I should have done a long time ago. When he adds nothing to the conversation, I keep going. "I watched you twist the truth, spin it on stream, and call it healing. You're not a victim. You're just an asshole with Wi-Fi who will do anything to protect his brand. Including ignoring what's right."

He reaches for me and I shove his hand away, hard. I don't give him a chance to respond before I continue. "You didn't break me. You broke the version of me that believed you could be better. Stream that."

The crowd that has gathered around us has gone completely silent. I can feel dozens of eyes on us, phones probably recording from multiple angles, but all I see is

Leo's face cycling through emotions, and I'm able to pinpoint anger, panic, calculation.

That's when I notice movement out of the corner of my eye. Blaise appears at the edge of the crowd, but he doesn't rush forward. Doesn't push through to get between us. He just stands there, steady and still. I appreciate that he isn't running in to save the day.

Leo's eyes flick to him, which I find interesting, and then back to me. "Look, this is getting out of hand—"

"No," I cut him off. "What got out of hand was you thinking you could come to my campus and turn your consequences into content." I take another step forward, and this time he doesn't back away. "But you miscalculated something."

"What's that?"

"You thought I'd stay quiet. You thought I'd disappear like a good little victim and let you rewrite history." I feel something shift inside me, like a door I've kept locked finally swinging open. "But I'm done being quiet about who you really are."

That's when I hear Ari's voice from somewhere behind me. "Got it."

I turn slightly and see her lowering her phone, a satisfied expression on her face. She's been recording this entire exchange. So not only is this being streamed live, but if he tries to spin it, we have backup.

Perfection.

Leo's face goes white. "You can't—"

"Actually, we can." Blaise speaks for the first time. "Public space, public event. No expectation of privacy when you're literally streaming to thousands of people."

Blaise pulls out his phone and looks at Ari. "Send me that clip and I'll post this after the event. Between my followers and the rest of the team's social media reach, it's guaranteed to go viral."

The color drains completely from Leo's face. He knows what that means. Blaise has thirty thousand followers just on Instagram alone, and that's before you factor in Knox, Levi, Wilder, Asher, and the rest of the Red Wolves' roster. When they share something, it spreads through the sports community like wildfire.

"You can't be serious," Leo says.

I can see the fear in his eyes. I refuse to fight the grin that shouldn't be on my face since I'm still trying to be professional. I'm failing horribly though.

"Dead serious." Blaise's tone doesn't change. "The truth always has a way of making its way out of the darkness and into the light, doesn't it?"

I can see that Leo is trying to find the words to say, but they won't come out. His camera is still recording, capturing every second of his public humiliation. The irony isn't lost on me. He came here to control the narrative, and instead he's about to become the story.

"This isn't over," he finally manages to say. The barely controlled rage that is boiling to the surface can be heard in every word.

"You're right," I say. "It's not over. Because now everyone gets to see exactly who you are when you can't hide behind carefully edited content and paid moderators."

I turn to face his camera directly, speaking to his audience for the first time. "Hi, Leo's viewers. I'm Willow Sanchez. I'm one of the women he's been calling desperate and attention-seeking on his streams. I want you to know that everything you just witnessed? This is the real Leo that he's tried to hide from you under the curated branding I'm sure an extensive team pulled together. The things you've heard by now about him are all true and that's only the tip of the iceberg."

Leo fumbles for his phone, probably trying to end the stream, but it's too late. The damage is done, and we all know it.

Blaise steps closer, not to me, but positioning himself where Leo can see him clearly. "You've got about thirty seconds to pack up your equipment and leave before security gets involved."

"Security?" Leo's voice cracks slightly. "You can't just—"

"Actually, we can." The voice comes from behind us.

Knox emerges from the crowd, in his Red Wolves sweats gear, flanked by Levi, Asher, and Wilder. The expression on his face is the same one I saw just before his fist ended up in Leo's face after he found out about some of the things he did to me in high school.

"This is a team event, and you're not welcome here."

My heart stops. Knox heard everything. He saw everything. And he's standing with Blaise, not questioning why
his best friend just threatened to amplify a video of his
sister confronting her ex.

Leo looks between the hockey players surrounding
him, then at me, then at his still-recording camera. He's
outnumbered and outmaneuvered, and he knows it.

"This is harassment," he tries weakly.

"No," I say, my voice steady as steel. "Harassment is
what you did to Lilly and me. This? This is accountability."

Knox takes another step forward. "Pack it up. Now."

Leo's hands shake as he fumbles with his equipment,
mumbling under his breath about lawyers and defama-
tion while the crowd disperses. I stand there for about
thirty seconds, watching him move when I feel a gentle
touch on my elbow. It's Blaise.

"Can we talk? Privately?"

I nod, suddenly aware of how many people are still
watching us. He guides me toward a quieter corner near
the concession stands, away from the crowd and the team.
My legs feel unsteady now that the confrontation is over,
like all the fight has drained out of me. But damn did it
feel good to do what I did.

"Ari sent me the clip and I did post it, but that's not
what I want to discuss. What I want to talk about is how
you've been avoiding me," he says once we're alone. It's not
an accusation, just a statement of fact.

"I know." I can't meet his eyes. "I'm sorry. I didn't know how to—"

"How to what?" He steps closer to me. "How to let me help you? How to trust that I'd want to be there for you?"

The words hit harder than they should. "It's not that simple."

"Isn't it?" His hand finds my chin, tilting my face up until I have no choice but to look at him. "Willow, I've been going crazy these past few days. Watching you shut down, shut me out. Do you have any idea what that's been doing to me?"

"I was protecting you—"

"From what? From caring about you? From wanting to be with you through the hard stuff?" His voice drops to barely above a whisper. "Because it's too late for that. I'm already in too deep."

"Blaise..."

"I love you. I love your fire, your stubbornness, the way you just took down that asshole without breaking a sweat. I love how you make me want to be better, braver. I love you, Willow, and I'm tired of pretending that's not terrifying and perfect at the same time."

Everything that just happened to me fades into the background because nothing else matters but us in this moment. All I can see is his face, hear his words and study the way he's looking at me like I'm something precious he's afraid to lose.

"I love you too," I whisper, the admission falling from

my lips before I can stop it. "That's why I was so scared. I couldn't bear the thought of dragging you into this mess, of having you see me fall apart."

"Then you don't understand what love means." His thumb traces my cheekbone. "It means I want to be there for the falling apart. It means you don't get to decide what I can handle."

"I know. I'm sorry. I'm so—"

He cuts me off with a kiss, so soft but full of everything we've been holding back. When we break apart, I rest my forehead against his.

"We're really doing this?" I ask. "In public? No more hiding?"

"No more hiding," he confirms. "I want everyone to know you're mine. Starting with—"

"Starting with me?"

We both freeze. Knox's voice cuts through our bubble like ice water. He's standing about ten feet away, with his arms crossed. How long has he been there? How much did he hear?

My stomach drops to my shoes as I realize our secret is no longer secret.

37

BLAISE

It's amazing what you can hear when the rest of the world comes to a stop. Or that's what it feels like after Knox found Willow and me kissing just seconds ago. The words echo in my ears like they're coming from underwater. Knox's voice. Three simple words that shatter everything we've been building in secret.

My hand is still cupped against Willow's cheek. Her breath is warm against my mouth. The taste of her kiss lingers on my lips, but now Knox is here, watching us, and I can feel the careful walls we've built around this thing between us crumbling in real time.

I don't pull away from her. Not yet. But when I do, I don't go far. I know it's time to defend this relationship.

"Knox," I say as I turn to face him. "We need to talk."

"Yeah." His eyes move between us, taking in how we're standing. "We really fucking do."

I've been preparing for this moment since Puerto Rico, maybe since the first time I realized what Willow meant to me years ago. The knowledge that I might lose my best friend has been sitting in my gut for what feels like weeks, but standing here now, with her still close enough that I can smell her shampoo, I know exactly where my priorities lie.

I'd rather lose Knox than lose her. The thought should terrify me more than it does.

"Knox." I keep my voice steady, meeting his eyes directly. "I'm not going to apologize for this."

His jaw tightens. "For what, exactly? For going behind my back?"

"For falling in love with your sister."

I watch Knox's face change, cycling through surprise, anger, and potentially hurt. But I don't take back a single word I said. Nor will I ever.

"In love?" Knox's voice is flat. "You're in love with her?"

"Yes." I don't hesitate. "I'm in love with Willow, and she's in love with me. This isn't some casual thing, Knox. This isn't me messing around with your sister."

Willow steps closer to me, her hand finding mine. The gesture is small but deliberate and effective. She's choosing to stand with me, even knowing what it might cost us.

"Knox," she says quietly, "we didn't plan this. It just happened."

"When?" His eyes dart between us again. "How long has this been going on?"

I could lie. Could minimize it, make it sound newer than it is. But I'm done with half-truths and careful omissions. "Since Puerto Rico. We made it official a few days ago."

"Puerto Rico." Knox runs a hand through his hair. "Fuckin' A Blaise. You've been lying to my face for weeks."

"I haven't been lying—"

"Bullshit." His voice rises slightly. "You've been the best of friends and talking to me about all types of shit and yet you couldn't tell me that you're fucking my sister."

Willow flinches at the crude words, and something protective flares in my chest. "Don't talk about her like that."

"Like what? Like she's my sister? Because she is." Knox takes a step closer. "She's my sister, and you're supposed to be my best friend."

"I am your best friend. That hasn't changed."

"Everything's changed." Knox shakes his head. "You think I don't know what this means? You think I'm stupid? This is going to fuck everything up."

I know he's right that everything has changed, but it doesn't change anything. If anything, it crystallizes what I already know. I'm not backing down. Not from this. Not from her.

"Maybe it will fuck things up," I say. "But I'd rather have that than pretend this doesn't matter."

Knox stares at me like I've grown a second head. "Are you serious right now?"

"Dead serious." I squeeze Willow's hand tighter. "I know what I'm risking here, Knox. I know what this could cost me. But I'm not walking away from her. I can't."

"You can't?" He stares me down with his mouth slightly open as if he's seeing me for the first time. "Holy hell, you are serious."

Willow steps forward then, placing herself between Knox and me. I watch her shoulders straighten, see her chin lift the same way she did when she faced Leo. When she didn't realize I was standing there on the sidelines watching her taking on that asshole.

"Knox, stop. Just...stop."

Knox's attention shifts to her completely. "Willow—"

"No, let me talk." She takes another step toward her brother, closing the distance between them. "You want to know why we didn't tell you? You want to know why we kept this secret?"

"Yeah, I do."

"Because I was scared." The words come out in a rush, like she's been holding them back for weeks. "I was terrified, Knox. Everything in my life was already falling apart. The Leo situation, the harassment, feeling like I couldn't trust anyone. And then there was this thing with Blaise that felt...real. Important. And I didn't know how to tell you."

Knox's expression softens slightly, but his jaw is still tight. "You could have—"

"Could have what? Come to you and said, 'Hey Knox, I'm falling for your best friend while my ex is trying to destroy my life online'?" She laughs, but there's no humor in it. "You would have lost your mind."

"Maybe I would have," Knox admits. "But that's not your call to make."

"Isn't it?" Willow's voice rises slightly. "It's my life, Knox. My relationship. My choice about when and how to tell the people I care about."

I watch this exchange and quickly realize I'm torn between pride at how she's standing up for herself and concern about where this is heading.

"Does that include not telling me about what was going on with Leo?" Knox asks.

"To be fair, she didn't tell me the full story either and —" But I stop talking when Knox glares at me.

"You want to know about Leo?" Willow sighs before she continues. "Fine. I didn't tell you because I was already drowning, Knox. The harassment, the threats, watching Lilly get torn apart online...it was all too much. I was barely keeping my head above water. And then there was this." She gestures between herself and me. "This beautiful, terrifying thing that made me feel like maybe I wasn't completely broken."

Knox's expression shifts into something that doesn't resemble anger, but I'm not sure what to call it.

"I was scared," she continues. "Scared that if I told you about Blaise, you'd make me choose. Scared that you'd hate him for caring about me. Scared that I'd lose both of you in different ways. I didn't know how to tell the person I love most in the world and the brother I'm terrified of disappointing that I'd found something good in the middle of all that chaos."

"You think you could disappoint me?" Knox looks as confused as I feel. "How?"

"Knox." Willow's laugh is shaky. "I've been disappointing you for years. The Leo thing in high school, dropping out of pre-med, changing my major three times—"

"That's not—" Knox starts, but she cuts him off.

"It is. And I couldn't handle the thought of adding this to the list. Of watching you look at me like I'd made another mistake." Her voice drops to barely above a whisper. "Especially when this doesn't feel like a mistake. This feels like the first thing I've gotten right in my love life in years."

Knox looks at me then, really looks at me, and I see the exact moment something clicks for him. "You really love her," he says. It's not a question.

"More than I've ever loved anyone," I answer without hesitation.

"And you?" Knox turns back to Willow. "You love him?"

"Yes. I love him, Knox. I love how he makes me feel strong and safe at the same time. I love that he sees me and doesn't try to fix me or change me. I love him enough that I'd rather have you hate me than give him up."

Knox runs both hands through his hair, looking between us like he's solving some impossible equation. Finally, he lets out a long breath. "Fuck."

"Knox—" Willow starts.

"No, just...fuck." He shakes his head. "You should have told me."

"I know," she says quietly.

"But I get it." Knox's eyes meet mine. "I get why you didn't. And I get why you'd risk our friendship for her."

The admission surprises me. "Knox..."

"She's worth it," he says. "She's always been worth it. I just wish you'd trusted me enough to tell me."

"I know. And I'm sorry." She looks back at me before returning her attention to her brother. "We both are."

Knox looks down at his sister with a small smile on his face. It would be funny to point out how easily she was able to get past his bad boy persona and hit his heart, but now isn't the time. "You're happy?" he asks her.

"Yeah," she says. "I'm really happy."

Knox nods slowly, then turns to me. "You hurt her, and best friend or not, I'll end you."

"I know," I say. "But I won't."

"Good." Knox extends his hand. "Then I guess we're okay."

I step toward him and shake his hand. "We're okay?" I ask again to be doubly sure.

"We're okay." Knox grins suddenly. "But next time you want to date my sister, maybe give me a heads up? This whole dramatic revelation thing is exhausting."

Willow laughs and the sound is bright, free, and music to my ears. "There won't be a next time, because there won't be anyone after Blaise."

"Damn right there won't be," I murmur, pulling her closer.

Knox makes a gagging sound. "Okay, that's enough. I may be okay with this, but I don't need to watch you two be gross about it. Also, if I had to choose who I'd want to date my sister out of the fuckers behind me, it would be you."

"Thanks?" I'm not sure if that's a compliment, but I decide to take it as such.

Before Knox can offer a rebuttal, there's a loud crash from somewhere behind us. We all turn to see Wilder standing over near a concession stand, but thankfully there doesn't seem to be any injuries nor does anything look out of place. What's strange is that Wilder doesn't have his usual smile on his face and he's not trying to rile anyone up with his jokes. He looks like he's about two seconds away from doing something incredibly stupid.

Following his gaze, I spot Jade, Levi, and Hailey near the team merchandise table, laughing at something a tall guy in a Crestwood basketball hoodie is saying. The guy seems to have his attention mostly on Jade, and it doesn't take an astrophysicist to determine what's going on here.

"Oh shit," Willow mutters under her breath.

"What's wrong with Wilder?" Knox asks, but even as he says it, his eyes track to where Wilder is looking. "Oh. Oh no."

I watch as Wilder takes a step forward, then stops himself. His whole body is tense, like he's fighting something deep within himself. The guy with Jade says something that makes her throw her head back and laugh, and Wilder's face darkens even more.

"He looks like he's about to commit a felony," Willow says.

"Probably because he is," Knox says. "Someone should do something."

But that something seems to have happened without any of us having to do a thing. The guy in the basketball hoodie gives Jade a small wave and he leaves the group. Jade's eyes drift around the room until they land on Wilder. The biggest grin appears on her face and she runs up to him and gives him a big hug.

"What is going on there?"

Willow's question makes both Knox and me look at her, but I answer first. "Wilder's in love with her."

"And Jade?" Willow asks, watching as Jade practically bounces on her toes while talking to Wilder, who still looks like he's been hit by a truck.

"Has absolutely no clue," Knox finishes. "It's painful to watch."

I study the interaction across the arena. Jade is talking about something that has her extremely excited while Wilder nods along with the expression of someone trying very hard to act normal when their entire world just shifted. The contrast between her obvious excitement and his barely controlled tension is almost comical.

"How long has this been going on?" Willow asks.

"Since sophomore year," I say. "Maybe longer. Wilder's never said anything directly, but it's pretty obvious if you know what to look for."

"And she really doesn't know?"

Knox shakes his head. "Jade thinks they're just friends. Best friends, and he's dated other girls while they've been friends, so I don't blame her."

"That's..." Willow pauses, watching as Jade grabs Wilder's arm to pull him toward the photo booth. "Actually kind of heartbreaking."

"Yeah, well, welcome to Wilder's life," Knox says. "Guy's got it bad, but he's convinced she's out of his league."

"I mean she is technically...as most women are. Present company included." That earns me a swat on the chest from Willow.

Surprisingly, Knox agrees with me. "You're not wrong. Speaking of, where's my woman?"

He walks away from both of us before we can respond

to him, and all I can do is chuckle. I can't say I'm not happy to be alone with Willow again.

"So," she says, turning to face me fully. "That went better than expected."

"Did it?" I raise an eyebrow. "Because for a minute there I thought your brother was going to punch me in the face."

"He still might, if you're not careful." But she's smiling as she says it. "I can't believe we just did that."

"Which part? You taking down Leo or us finally telling Knox the truth?"

"Both. All of it." She runs a hand through her hair and lets out a deep breath. "I feel like I've been holding my breath for weeks."

I reach for her hand and her fingers thread through mine. I bring our joined hands up to my lips. "So we're doing this?" I ask quietly, my mouth still close to her skin.

Her eyes meet mine. "We're doing this."

"Good," I say, lowering our hands but not letting go. "Because I'm not letting go ever. I love you."

"I love you too."

I'll never get tired of hearing those words come from her lips.

EPILOGUE
WILLOW

Six Years Later

The view is the same, but everything else has changed. I open my eyes to sunlight streaming through floor-to-ceiling windows. For a moment, I'm disoriented. While the room I had when I first traveled to Puerto Rico six years ago was nice, it was nothing compared to this.

Six years. It's hard to believe that it's been six years since we first came to Puerto Rico on a winter abroad trip. Now we're back, but everything has changed. We've changed.

I turn my head and there he is. Blaise is still asleep and I'm surprised since he still doesn't sleep well in beds that aren't ours. Although I will say that he seems to have no issue with sleeping when I'm with him. I resist the urge to trace the stubble along his jawline with my fingertip. Although he's usually clean shaven, I love when he lets his facial grow.

I quietly and carefully leave the bed in hopes of not waking Blaise up. His season ended three weeks ago when he and his teammates won the Stanley Cup. The whirlwind of everything that comes with being champions was the wildest time of both of our lives, and while we're both happy that it happened, we are also happy to get back to the place where everything really began for us.

As I walk into the kitchen area of our suite, my phone vibrates on the kitchen counter and I almost trip as I try to get it. The notification that appears on my phone makes my heart skip a beat: the Pacific Post wants to run my investigative piece on harassment in college athletics. Six months of research, dozens of interviews, and now one of the most respected publications in the country wants to feature it.

I set the phone down and cover my mouth with both my hands to keep from yelling in excitement. Holy shit. This is real life. We made it. Both of us. Not just to some arbitrary finish line, but to a place where success feels sustainable rather than frantic. I lean against the counter and let myself really absorb this moment. Blaise's Stanley Cup championship still feels surreal and that's after watching him lift that trophy. His mom and I cried tears of joy and it was absolutely magical seeing years of dedication finally pay off in the most spectacular way possible. And now this. My article getting picked up by one of the most prestigious publications in journalism.

We've built something neither of us saw coming back then. Success that isn't fleeting, along with careers we're both proud of. Not to mention we've grown and nurtured a love that's weathered public scrutiny, career pressures, and the general chaos of two people figuring out how to grow together instead of apart.

The best part isn't the accolades or recognition, though. It's about our happiness and how it's grown over the years. It's about some of the mundane things we do like how we choose each other daily in different ways or argue about whether we're watching hockey highlights or true crime documentaries before bed.

I quickly make and pour myself coffee from the fancy machine I barely know how to use. Once I've checked that task off my agenda, I step out onto the balcony. We waited way too long to come back here, but I'm so happy we finally made it happen.

The sliding door opens behind me. I don't need to turn around to know it's Blaise because if it wasn't that means someone has broken into our suite to murder me. And, well, I knew it was only a matter of time before he woke up because I wasn't in bed anymore.

"Morning," he says with a deeper voice than normal due to him still waking up. His arms circle my waist from behind, pulling me back against his chest.

"Good morning." I melt into him with both hands on my coffee cup to keep it steady. "Sleep okay?"

"Better than I have in weeks." He presses a kiss to my temple. "What's got you up so early? And why do you look like you're trying not to lose your shit?"

I turn in his arms, unable to keep the grin off my face any longer. "Remember that investigative piece I've been working on? The one about harassment in college athletics?"

His eyes sharpen immediately. "The one you've been obsessing over for months? What about it?"

"They want it." The words tumble out in a rush. "The Pacific Post wants to run it. Front page of their Sunday edition."

The way his expression changes after the words fell out of my mouth is comical. "Willow." He sets his hands on my shoulders. "Are you serious?"

"Dead serious." I can't stop smiling. "Six months of work, and they called it 'essential journalism that will spark necessary conversations.' Essential, Blaise."

He lifts me off my feet, spinning me around on the balcony until I'm laughing and coffee is threatening to spill everywhere. When he sets me down, his hands frame my face.

"I'm so fucking proud of you," he says. "This is huge, Willow. This is everything you've been working toward."

"I know," I lean up to kiss him and when I pull back I say, "It feels surreal. Like I'm living someone else's life."

"No. This is your life. The one you built by refusing to stay quiet, by chasing the truth even when it was hard."

We stand there for a moment, holding each other on the balcony, before he takes my hand and leads me toward the railing. "I love our life," I tell him, the words simple but weighted with everything we've been through.

"I love our life too. Think we'll still be coming back here in another six years?"

"I hope so," I say, imagining us older, but still choosing each other against whatever life throws our way.

"Though maybe we'll be married and have some company by then."

I can't help but grin. "Married?" The word slips out before I can stop it. "And I assume you mean children."

Blaise just shrugs. "It's not like we haven't talked about it, kitten."

We have talked about it numerous times. There have been many late-night conversations about the future, about what we want our life to look like in five years, ten years. But hearing him say it here, in this place where we first really found each other, makes it feel different.

"We have," I agree. "Though I didn't expect you to bring it up before I've even had my second cup of coffee."

"Sorry." He grins, not looking sorry at all. "But being back here...it makes me think about how far we've come. How much I want to keep building this with you. How much I love you."

"And I love you too," I say back, meaning every word.

After I take another sip of my coffee, Blaise takes my cup out of my hands and puts it down on the small table that was conveniently placed out here. He pulls me back into his arms and gives me a kiss that tells me how bright our future is with him by my side.

It's then that I realize one thing: this wasn't supposed to be a love story. But it became one anyway.

IF YOU WOULD LIKE to read a bonus scene featuring Willow and Blaise, you can grab it here.

Jade and Wilder's story will be the next book in this series.

ACKNOWLEDGMENTS

Whew. When I tell you this book was a journey, I truly mean it. Writing what I know took on a whole different meaning when it came to putting this book together. It also made me realize that the original harm I endured was nothing compared to how it felt to be betrayed on multiple fronts throughout this saga.

What I do hope is that, if you've been through something like this, this story provides some closure and healing for you. If it helps just one person, I'll be thrilled.

I would like to thank the real "LillyV" for giving me her blessing to tell this story. Without you, this story would be vastly different, and I thank you for stepping forward even when you were met with adversity.

Thank you to those who walked with me behind the scenes. Your love runs deep and you've helped me more than anyone will ever know.

Andra, you're so amazing at capturing my vision. Thank you for creating this.

Ellie, thank you for helping me promote my most personal book yet. I can't wait to work on the next release with you.

Jane, thank you so much for keeping my author life in tip-top shape. Without you, I would be a complete wreck.

Chrisandra and Elizabeth, I can't thank you both enough for jumping on this project and being so patient with me, as usual. On to the next one!

Kim, thank you so much for your thoughtful comments about this book—including watching me write the last chapter. Your feedback was amazing and funny, and I can't wait to work with you on my next book and other projects.

And of course, I can't forget to thank every single reader for picking up this book. The fact that you took time out of your day to read my words means the world to me.

Thank you so much.

ABOUT THE AUTHOR

Emery Paige is a dreamer, a word crafter, and a wine lover. She has been a writer and reader for as long as she can remember. Being able to call herself a romance author is a dream come true.

When she's not pouring her soul into her next romance, Emery can be found indulging in her love for music or watching YouTube, where she enjoys everything from travel vlogs to fashion and cooking.

If you would like to keep in contact with her, please visit her website (www.emerypaigebooks.com) or sign up for her newsletter to receive the latest information about her and her books.

She's also on Instagram and TikTok.

ALSO BY EMERY PAIGE

Sidelined Love

Penalized Love

Caputured Love

Guarded Love

TBA

.

www.ingramcontent.com/pod-product-compliance
Lightning Source LLC
Chambersburg PA
CBHW052344110726
47901CB00005B/1350